Val got that creepy feeling, a prickling certainty someone was crouched behind her, waiting. She looked at the rearview mirror. For a sickening moment she actually saw the luminescent orb of his eye staring back at her. Panic clutched her throat. She glanced in the backseat. Nothing there but trash. I'm alone, she thought. Then she heard his voice call, "Help me," as clearly as if he'd been back there with the diet cola cans, old gym shoes and the faded, rolled-up script. "Help me, please," cried the man who wasn't there . . .

PAT WINTER

DRIVER

PINNACLE BOOKS   NEW YORK

DRIVER

An original Pinnacle Books edition, published for the first time anywhere.

First printing, February 1982

ISBN: 0-523-41278-9

Cover illustration by Paul Stinson

Printed in the United States of America

PINNACLE BOOKS, INC.
1430 Broadway
New York, New York 10018

Thanks
Francine Brandt, Curt DeGraw, Joelle Dobrow,
Robert Hoskins, Jill Roberts and, especially,
mother editor Gaye Tardy

For **Misha,** *whoever he is*

DRIVER

8-3
9 - 4:30

Ryan
fri 4 - 9
sat 8 - 3
sun 9 - 4:30

PROLOGUE

The dark 450 SL took the slick Mulholland switchback like a snake. It was a beautiful car, designed with the slightly bowed lines of the Parthenon so that one always seemed to be looking at it from below, as an object of veneration.

The car was in prime condition. The driver pushed it just past forty with the toe of a worn running shoe.

"Slow down—" demanded the dark girl beside him.

"It's a precision machine," the driver replied as he savored the rising smell of her fear. Her sweat heated the perfume he had impulsively bought for her—Pheremone—Fairy Mound she innocently called it, at $200 an ounce.

"Please."

"It's built for this." He squeezed the muscles of his ass against the vibrating seat. For a moment the car was full of the sounds of tires sucking pavement and the parallel conversation of the windshield wipers clapping with a song on the radio.

"You're really scaring me." The rain almost drowned out her voice.

Temporary street maintenance signs flashed yellow warning lights at a flooded curb. The car fishtailed but the driver kept control. "See?" he demanded, as if he had proved his point because the car was still on the road. "Why spend forty-five thou on a car if it can't—"

CHAPTER 1

Val came awake in the darkness with the image of the car going off the road in the rain.

The feeling that she was going with it pulled her bolt upright, gasping for breath. The image was already fading from the inside of her sore eyelids. The dream, she groaned.

Three nights now, three nights with the same damn dream.

Darkness came up from the inside as she fell back onto her pillow and into numb sleep.

The dream stayed with her all the next day just on the irritated fringes of her mind. She had a million small things to do, places to go. Not enough sleep, the dull nibble of a headache threatening but never quite breaking through. Lots of driving in heavy traffic. The mechanic just confirmed the Citroen, her good gray friend, needed a transmission overhaul and a new clutch. It was an oldie; parts were getting scarce.

"Least three fifty, four hundred dollars," he said sympathetically under his honest grime, then smiled good-bye when she said she'd think about it. "Don't wait too long, miss," he cautioned.

The mechanic's awful estimate rattled in her ears as she walked across the garage lot, unlocked the driver's door of the gray Citroen and climbed inside as she had done hundreds, maybe even thousands of times before.

Immediately she got that creepy feeling, a prickling certainty that there was someone crouching down in the backseat waiting to reach out and grab her. She'd never had the feeling in broad daylight before.

Val looked in the rearview mirror. For a heart-pounding second she expected to see some sinister face come floating up into view. Nobody's here, dummy, she scolded herself. She rubbed the short hair on the back of her neck under ginger-colored braids she sometimes played with unconsciously.

I'm just on edge.

Still, she would've sworn . . .

She started the car and would have backed out, but she had to satisfy her nerves. The feeling of a presence was too insistent. She twisted around to look over the driver's seat, her clothes rustling unnaturally in the old car. There was nobody there, of course. Nothing in the backseat but a couple of scripts, an empty soft drink can, an old pair of gym shoes.

She laughed softly at her silliness as she unset the emergency brake and headed for the health club. She really needed the yoga class today. In anticipation she hummed the soothing mantra "Ommmmm," matching the pitch of the engine vibration as the car rolled along.

Val couldn't believe her luck when she saw an old lady in rhinestone shades pulling a Caddy out of a spot right in front of the gym. Such parking luck on Ventura Boulevard at this time of day was not to be believed. The Caddy inched out. Val watched with penetrating hazel eyes made mysterious by flecks of blue. She had a piquant mouth and wide, almost Indian, cheekbones. All in all, a watchable face in the opinion of an increasing number of casting directors, a beautiful face that also registered genuineness of emotion. Even frowning, as she was at the moment, Val's face was appealing.

She was frowning because some guy in a Rolls was backing up, no doubt aiming for her parking place when the rhinestone grandma vacated it.

"Oh, no you don't," Val muttered, very gently easing the shaking Citroen into first. She rode the clutch with a doubtful prayer and waited to take what was rightfully hers.

Grandma was cautious. She was tentatively nosing her gunboat out when she killed the engine.

4

By now several drivers behind Val were taking the slowdown personally. The trucker in back of her car glued his fist to the horn and had the nerve to nudge her I BRAKE FOR ANIMALS bumper sticker. Figuring to lay a mean glare on him, Val looked into the rearview mirror.

The insistent feeling she was not alone slithered up her neck, and by some trick of reflection she saw dark rain and the headlights of a car moving too fast on a winding mountain road. . . .

The road. The car. The dream again. The driver teasing the girl in the passenger seat. The windshield wipers oddly in time with a rock song on the radio.

Yellow lights flashed in the rain beyond the roiling windshield. The car fishtailed. "See—" the driver said, proud of his machine, "why spend forty-five thou on a car if it can't—"

The girl's scream cut him off. She saw the mudslide before he did. He avoided it by pulling the car into a parabola six feet wider than the roadbed.

Headlights cut the night. The car arched out, no longer a ground machine, but a flying thing true to its design. It just hung there in the slanted streaks of rain, like the cartoon cat that doesn't fall until it looks down.

A freeze frame. Val remembered they had used that special effect in a series of cereal commercials she had been in last year . . .

". . . commercials *I* was in last year," Val forced herself to say out loud, hearing her own voice above the rain, still not seeing her car and the daylight traffic around her. "This is not happening . . . this is not happening . . ." she said, clinging to the reality of her own voice in the middle of the dream or illusion or whatever it was. She willed her mind to focus on what was actually around her—the old car on Ventura Boulevard on a hot afternoon. Not a rainy hillside where she appeared to be watching the imminent end of two people and a pretty machine.

"This is just a dream," Val reminded herself, "just like the other dream I had the past three nights."

Except this was broad daylight. She was not at home in bed with Frank's warm, comforting body beside her.

"Just a dream," she said, feeling sunlight on her arm. She could smell car exhaust: It had never smelled so good as she felt herself being pulled, pulled ever so gently back to the real world. She was about to open her eyes when she distinctly heard the voice of the man in the doomed Mercedes as though he were in the back seat of her Citroen.

"Help . . ."

Val opened her eyes. She was staring into the rearview mirror, alone in her car. There was nobody in the backseat. The truck that had been impatiently honking behind her was gone. The Rolls was maneuvering into her parking place. It was obvious that Val had lost several seconds while she was having the vision.

The Rolls's driver glanced back at her with a smirk on his face.

But she must have had some parking luck left because the car ahead of him was pulling into traffic. Val whipped into it and set the brake. Only then did she let herself think about what she had experienced back there, the vision of the cruel sexy man and the scared girl in the flying car.

She was so shaken she didn't immediately shut off the engine. She breathed deeply, the way she had learned to relax in yoga class. She tightened and loosened the muscles in her hands. It was working; she began to breathe more evenly.

"Ommmmm," she chanted the soothing sound and was already feeling more relaxed.

She lay her forehead on her knuckles that were still gripping the steering wheel. Her eyes stung from lack of sleep and smog.

"Help . . ." she heard his voice say as near as her

6

elbow. She peeked one eye open and looked to the right under her flexed arm, but she was alone.

"Who are you and what do you want?" she asked the voice, expecting no answer. The dream image was completely gone, but there remained fragments of the fear, pain and anger of the man in it.

"Help . . ." It was definitely the man's voice. In it was a peculiar quality of familiarity; Val felt she had heard this voice somewhere before. The other times in the dream, nobody had spoken directly to her. Now she was hearing him clearly; she clapped her hands over her ears.

"Help me," the voice repeated. She was hearing it from a spot behind her eyes, inside her own head. "I'm so cold."

"Who are you?"

"I am me . . . mee . . . meesh . . ." He was fading.

"Who are you?"

"I'm Val."

"Help me, Val." It was the cry of a small hurt child, of a lover or a brother or a friend. It tore into Val's empathetic heart like the cry of any beautiful wounded creature she might have the power to save. Her maternal instincts were always aroused by the suffering of any bedraggled beast, especially if it were furry, frightened or just about finished.

The man's voice held all those qualities plus an erotic undercurrent Val found irresistible.

But another less vulnerable part of Val's mind recalled the yoga suggestion to be cautious tending wounded tigers.

Val's knuckles were white around the steering wheel. She looked up, a little dazed. Something about the dream or vision—what was it?—whatever, something about it threatened Val personally.

Maybe Frank was right. He had several theories about these dreams. Suddenly she needed to hear his familiar voice, even if he did insist she was nuts or had been working too hard, or had suffered too much rejection in her struggle to make it as an actress. She had to make contact with someone who cared. As her live-in partner for two years, Frank qualified. She saw a telephone at the curb.

Val reached down and shut off the engine, gut-aware but not yet conscious that she had joined the crucial territorial battle of her life.

Even though she was on the phone, Maxine Wise couldn't help but be intrigued by the little drama playing itself out beyond her new office window. Maxine couldn't figure why the lovely young woman in the rattletrap foreign car let the bully in the Rolls take that parking place—especially after the girl stood up for it and looked ready to fight for it if he pushed her. She seemed to have blacked out or something, although Maxine did not have an unobstructed view.

Maxine half heard her mother's phone voice say something about the fact that her new office was not in Beverly Hills.

"It isn't supposed to be Beverly Hills, sweetheart," Maxine said patiently. She was listening just enough to respond now and then, but she was still watching the girl who was now getting out of her car.

"The traffic over there is terrible, though it's bad enough here in Encino, not to mention the rent," Maxine continued.

She was sitting on the edge of the new desk in the old building—a remodeled bungalow in a prime location, even if the plumbing was ready for the Museum of Science and Industry.

"The best thing is that it's practically next door to the gym." She didn't mention to Mum that the bathroom sink leaked.

During all this Maxine had not taken her eyes from the girl beyond the plate-glass window where two sign painters were charging her a hundred a day to talk politics with each other. The younger of the two was scraping off an old real estate sign on one window while his elder partner lettered in a new one that would

8

read FINDERS, INC., M.S. WISE, PRIVATE INVESTIGA-
TIONS.

Just from the way the girl moved to the telephone
booth, she had to be a dancer, Maxine thought, never
quite losing the sense of her mother's conversation, but
not fully listening either.

The girl clutched a gym bag and purse as though
clinging to reality itself. She moved with grace and bal-
ance as she stepped into the booth, even though she was
awkwardly digging into her purse, obviously for a coin.
The girl looked familiar. Probably a member of the
gym, Maxine decided. She was petite, maybe twenty-six,
graceful and vulnerable at the same time like a long-
legged doe. She was wearing her golden brown hair in
little-girl braids, which she toyed with like a child. That
put a bittersweet pang into Maxine; the unconscious
gesture reminded her of Melodie.

With one ear still to Mum's voice, Maxine picked up
one of three photos on her desk, a plastic heart-shaped
frame around the face of a girl of about seven in
braids, with a front tooth missing from a glorious
smile.

The girl in the phone booth looks like Melodie,
Maxine thought. Like Melodie would have looked if
she had lived to her middle twenties. Maxine prided
herself that she had developed a mature perspective
over the ancient, tiny death; she had gotten over it. But
here was this stranger who brought the grammar
school portrait of her only daughter to life sixteen
years later with a stab to the heart of Maxine Sarah
Wise.

Her mother was saying something about how it was
a good thing Maxine's office was so close to home, so
she could work on what Mum called Maxine's "domestic problem."

"Honestly, Mum, you do have a way with euphemism," Maxine said. "Hugh can't get it up and you
make it sound like we need a new roof or something."

* * *

9

The moment she heard the tone of Frank's voice, Val knew it had been a mistake to call him.

There would be no comfort from the man. He hated his job as a commercial film editor, which he held only to make money while he was trying to break in as a TV director. He was very good—had directed several award-winning documentaries, but was miserable with frustration that surfaced whenever he had a bad day on the job he considered beneath his talents.

"What do you want?" he snarled without knowing who was on the telephone line.

"Frank," Val blurted out, then tried to calm her voice. "It happened again." She sounded to her own ears more hysterical than it was good to sound. "I had one of those crazy dreams about the flying car on the way to the gym."

"While you were driving?" There was true alarm in his voice. Frank loved more than anything to worry, especially about Val, who was someday going to be his star and his wife. All that hinged on his getting a show to direct. "My God, three nights without sleep and now you're having visions while you're driving—"

"Well, while I was parking." She nervously bit one of her braids.

"Whatever—"

"I'm okay. I just needed to hear your voice."

"What you need is a couple of hours with Phil."

"I told you I'm not going to see a shrink, especially Phil. Frank, I think somebody's calling, like telepathy."

"There's no such thing as telepathy, woman. You're overwrought and having nightmares."

"This is different."

"How?" The patronization in his voice was unmistakable.

"They're feelings. Fear, pain . . . you know . . ." She felt inarticulate when she tried to explain what made these visions seem almost like telephone signals: There was another personality on the other end sending. Val was receiving. "You have to experience it," she finally said in frustration. "They're messages, cries

10

for help." She stopped just short of describing the man's voice.

"From inside your own head."

The church across the street started broadcasting a chimed hymn before ringing the hour. The old song sounded a bit thin above the worldly, materialistic shuffle of Ventura Boulevard. Val glanced up at the steeple cross.

"Maybe I'm possessed," she joked lamely, thinking about the rite of exorcism and how ridiculous the whole thing sounded.

"Huh?" Frank almost snarled.

"Nothing—never mind," she answered, the weight of being alone now oppressing her more than it had before she called him. "I needed to hear a loving voice, is all."

"What you need is a couple of hours with Phil," Frank was saying, "to get rid of these dreams of yours."

Val's mouth was set resolutely as she listened to his lecture. She idly twisted the braid she'd been chewing around a finger, brushing the tip against her cheek. She was barely hearing his words as she remembered again the image of the dream. The dream wasn't hers; no use explaining to Frank. The dream belonged to the man in it. She wondered who he was.

CHAPTER 2

When Tanna saw his heavy-lidded eyes moving rapidly with a dream, she knew her private duty patient would be coming around soon.

When dreams linger, reality can't be far behind, Tanna recalled from an old rock song. It was true. If he could dream, then he could waken.

She had just come on duty to find this new assignment had been given to her without even asking—they were taking her for granted here. Still, she thought as she looked him over, this patient's bound to be interesting.

He had one of those eternal faces. When this man is ninety, she thought with frank appreciation, he'll still be sexy. Appraised separately, his features were nothing special, even awkward. The nose, crooked even before the accident, was still bluish, though the swelling had gone down. Too odd to be handsome, that nose, but it went so well with the rest of his face, she was sure something had been surgically reconstructed. Pronounced cheekbones, deep-set eyes. Probably dark brown, with his coloring.

Tanna sniffed diffidently. Probably another smart-ass Jewish boy. She removed the dressing from his forehead. The incision made to relieve the concussion was healing nicely. It would leave only a small scar.

She lifted one of his hands, his most graceful feature—at least that she could see at the moment. His palm was not callused, but his fingers had guitar indurations—"bones" they used to be called by jazzmen. He had a long thick lifeline with many tributaries. That fit his profession. Tanna knew from the corridor gossip he was a TV actor.

Rich, spoiled boy-man, Tanna thought. Had it given to you all the way. Never had to face a disappointment, but now you will. None of your money will help this time. Her grandfather had been one of the first Southern black judges, so Tanna Henderson had never been poor. Her harsh judgment of her new patient was from what she'd read of him and what she regarded as the mark of indulgence on him. She suspected that this made him weak.

She reached behind herself and slid open a nylon curtain to let in more light from the louvered window. Yes, she almost said out loud, the kind of man who attracts women even when he's unconscious or near death.

"But you'll make it," she whispered, unable to resist him and instinctively wanting to help him. She looked around, knowing she was alone but suddenly self-conscious. The man on the bed stirred. His other hand twitched.

Tanna wondered what he was dreaming.

Probably reliving the accident that put him here, she thought. So many of them do, replaying it over and over while they adjust to their injuries.

Sometimes they dreamed of their childhood, a time before their accidents, a time when they were innocent and loved and protected from injury.

Tanna hadn't looked up his chart yet, but from what she could see this one must've been in a terrible wreck. He was still unconscious, though the accident had happened over two weeks ago. She had heard one of the other nurses talking about how they brought him in from UCLA Emergency on Saturday.

He was to be turned every two hours. She'd wait to do that with the help of the orderly who was on duty in the next few minutes. After tonight she'd be with this man almost all the time; he would be her only patient until his release, or until his family found another private duty nurse they liked better than Tanna. She decided to give them no reason: She was going to do everything in her power to keep this case.

He was due a maintenance dose of Librium, and so she deftly prepared the injection from the medication tray she had brought into Room 20 a moment ago.

She didn't have to inject him, but simply inserted the needle into the Y section of the IV tube. His eyes rolled a moment longer, then slowed as the drug took him into a deeper inner space than the dream.

Tanna lay the syringe on the tray and stood watching him breathe. Very gently she reached out and touched his face. The skin was cool.

An unchecked beard gave him a wild look, like a wicked prince, even though he was completely passive. Tanna licked her ample lips, the only movement in the room except for the monitoring equipment that regis-

13

tered his vital signs and the subtle drip of the IV solution. Outside there was a world of light and sound. Traffic noise floated up two stories from the boulevard below.

In here, it was quiet, arrested.

Tanna smiled. She knew a good way to waken the sleeping prince. She lifted the sheet.

"Henderson!" The nursing supervisor's voice made Tanna jump. She was in the corridor and getting nearer. Tanna quickly dropped the sheet without checking the bandages, grabbed the medication tray and left the room without making a sound. Hers and the nursing supervisor's voices faded down the hall.

Moisture collected at the corner of the patient's left eye and spilled down his cheek, a remote, emotionless tear.

Everything was white, clean as a hospital sheet. It was part memory and part dream.

The little boy had been lost in the snow a long, long time. He cried at first but the freezing tears stung his face, so he stopped. He still cried inside, though, lonely, lost and cold, wishing his Rosa would hurry up and find him. He was getting sleepy and wanted to lie down. Aunt Rosa called it a blanket of snow. If only he could just lift up a satin edge of it and curl up to go to sleep, he'd wake in the morning and everything would be okay.

He heard Aunt Rosa's voice.

"Misha . . ." she called in the crisp air. Pale dawn was rising behind the pines. "Where is that little boy of mine?"

"Help," his small voice answered. He heard the crunch of her boots coming to find him.

"Who is this little boy?" she asked, pulling at a freezing-wet, fuzzy bedroom slipper and the cold little foot inside it.

It was an old teasing game between them. She'd ask "who" questions because this child had loved to play

14

hide-and-seek and make-believe since before he could talk.

"Who is this?" she repeated, secretly terrified that the child was frozen. She hugged him into her fur coat like a great mama bear.

"I am Misha," he said from the muffled warmth.

He was alive.

"You were sleepwalking again, my Misha," Aunt Rosa said, lifting him up. Misha felt such love for her when she lifted him up against her bosom, he nearly passed out in four-year-old ecstasy.

"Did you think I would leave my son out in the cold to die? To become a Popsicle?" She hugged him, emphatically no.

He lay his cheek against the fur of her collar and patted her on the back as she walked through the crusted snow to the huge rock farmhouse. She talked soothingly as she stepped, stepped, stepped. "Do not be afraid of death, little one." He could hear her as much through the contact of his body against hers as he could through his ears.

"Someday death will come to you, but don't fear. Death will give you another body, an astral body, to live in."

Misha didn't understand what Rosa meant, but her words sounded warm and good. He hummed happily against her fine coat, listening to her words. "But that is a long time from now, let us go inside to warm up this little body."

Misha was so happy to be safe in the arms of his lovely Aunt Rosa, he did a thing that totally shocked her. He took her plump young matron's face in his baby hands and planted a kiss right on her cupid-bow lips, his little goldfish of a tongue slipping into her mouth, his little teeth hard and clicking and wet with the honey of his spit.

Aunt Rosa nearly dropped the beautiful, impudent child she had mothered beyond decency since her sister and brother-in-law had died in a plane crash two years

15

before. Already the mother of four big healthy boys, Rosa doted on her last one, her adopted baby, Misha.

She never told anyone that the precocious baby had French-kissed her out on the Vermont farm road that day. She kept it to herself. She didn't even tell her husband Lazlo. He suspected as much already.

Michael Christopher Stefano was going to be a terror.

"Val? *Val?*" Frank's voice sounded as though he were going to crawl through the telephone receiver in Val's trembling hand.

"I'm okay," she said.

Actually she wasn't. She had closed her eyes in a blink while Frank lectured her and had experienced another vision, a snow field and the terror of a small boy—what was his name? Mitch? No, it sounded more like Misha, a child, lost, cold, afraid. Then the image was gone, just as quickly as it had flashed into her mind. "Nothing, Frank."

Val had to lean against the phone booth to keep from collapsing. Her knees felt like wax in the blistering sun.

"You're acting crazy."

"Don't call me that." She wished she had never given in to the weakness of calling him.

"I want you to make an appointment with the shrink."

"No!" Her voice was shrill.

"Why not?" he shot back.

"Because!" she nearly screamed, then by great effort of will lowered her voice because she didn't want to give him any more ammunition. "Because," she pronounced each word overprecisely, "I am not crazy, Frank."

Maxine glanced up again to see the girl at the phone booth, but the elder painter's handiwork caught her eye. She carried Mum's conversation with her to the open front door.

"Hold on a minute," she said into the receiver, then muffled it against her breast. "Hey," she called to the painter. "The tail on the *s*—"

The painter nodded, obviously proud of his work.

"This is Ventura Boulevard, not lower Santa Monica; what we're striving for here is discretion. No curlicues on the *s*'s."

Across the street the church chimes were grinding out an old slow song. Maxine shut the door against the incessant noise. On the other side of the window the painter wiped off the offending letter.

Maxine lifted the receiver to continue talking with Mum when she heard another voice on the line, far away and thin, the way voices interrupt your pauses when you call the East Coast. She instinctively looked up at the girl in the phone booth, who was gesturing emphatically as the telephone voice said. ". . . am not crazy, Frank."

Then the voice was gone, lost in the wires.

"Hello?" Maxine said and Mum answered. "I thought they disconnected us," Maxine said, still watching the girl, but no longer able to hear what Maxine was sure had been the same girl's voice in the phone multiplex phenomenon. She wandered back over to the desk while Mum picked up the thread of her advice about what Maxine should do to solve her domestic problem. Maxine saw that her telephone cord had stretched to knock over the heart-shaped picture frame.

"So that's how you'd solve my domestic problem, huh?" She bent to pick up the frame and was sorry to see it was cracked.

"I can't believe I'm hearing my own mother advise me to go out and procure for my husband." But Maxine was never really surprised at anything Mum said. "What do you mean, biblical precedent?"

Maxine caught movement at the phone booth. The girl was hanging up in obvious fury, then gathering up her gym bag and purse with her left hand. But she

17

seemed hesitant as she looked around. The conversation had upset her.

Across the street the electronic church chimes began tolling four o'clock.

The girl glanced at the steeple, and seemed to be poised on the brink of something more than a curb.

"Sarah and Abraham—Mum, you haven't darkened the synagogue door since . . ." Maxine was saying. The girl glanced over her shoulder, assessing traffic as she stepped into the crosswalk.

"Oh," Maxine said, intently watching where the girl might go—she'd bet the church. "I know just the kind of girl who'd catch Hugh's eye. But he'd never go for it. He loves me too much."

The girl ignored the whistles from a city maintenance crew working at a manhole: The recent rainstorm had wrecked the sewers.

"Look, darling, I have a pile of work to do and I still want to get to the gym sometime this afternoon," Maxine said as she put the broken picture in her purse. "Love you too—bye."

She set the phone aside, watching the beautiful girl walk over to a gardener on a ladder propped against a tree.

Maxine stood there at the window, tapping a perfect fingernail against a perfect tooth, considering the possibilities.

CHAPTER 3

"Come down, you devil," the gardener was saying to the stubborn nest of mistletoe. He was the nearest of several workers picking up debris from the storm two weeks ago. Branches littered the lawn and rose garden of the church.

Val had to smile at the intensity with which the old man attacked the weed. She stood below the tree, watching him before he saw her.

Her first acting teacher taught her that the essence of her art could be found in the behavior of people going about their lives. She collected little bits of *schtick*—the peculiar ways of bus drivers dealing with heavy traffic, bag ladies and their layered shopping carts, children doing almost anything when they think they're not being watched, and tough survivors like this lean, wrinkled old gardener shaking the captured mistletoe with a rusty rake.

He seemed surprised to find he had an audience.

"Mistletoe sucka tree dry and kill it," he said in answer to the bemused curiosity on Val's face. She couldn't place his accent: Maybe it was Russian.

"I thought it was good luck," she said, shielding her eyes from the brilliant sun.

"Not for tree."

Val looked around as she said, "I guess the storm did a lot of damage—is the chapel closed?" She could see wooden barriers blocking the main and side entrances.

"You got a problem, young lady?" the old man asked, stepping off the ladder, wiping his face with a bandana that once was red.

"I'd like to talk to a priest."

"None in chapel. Carpets all ruined. You got a problem, honey?" The old man's eyes narrowed at what he thought might be her problem; and he would have reached out and touched her golden arm, except that Val instinctively moved back out of his reach.

"You go around there," he said, pointing to a back door beyond the carpet trucks and piles of sodden rolls of rugs that littered the sidewalk.

Val was already moving. The old gardener shook his head after her, thinking she was burdened with the timeless, simple woman's complication.

The heavy oak door groaned as Val entered the cool gloom. She was momentarily blinded. She had never

19

been in this part of the church before, so she moved tentatively down a hallway toward sounds of the carpet-laying team to the right in the chapel and the *trit* of electric typing to the left. She followed the typing.

At the first doorway she peeked inside to find a young, modern-habited nun pecking away at an IBM. The little silver ball was fairly flying, but when the nun saw Val she promptly clicked off the machine, favored Val with a cordial smile and said, "May I help you?" as if she really meant it.

"A priest?" Val was suddenly choked up and had to clear her throat. She really dreaded explaining the dreams to a stranger.

"I—eh, have a personal problem."

The nun stepped closer with a concerned look on her face. "Problem pregnancy? We have an excellent class for—"

"Not that personal."

The nun took her elbow. "You Catholic, dear?"

"Of course." Val had been to this church three times in eighteen months on holy days. But she considered herself a good Christian if a bad Catholic. She had the right to be here.

"I have to ask, you know," the nun was saying as she steered Val out into the hallway toward another small office. "You'd never believe all the crazy sad people who come in here asking weird things—non-Catholics wanting to taste the Eucharist, last rites before suicide, crazy things like that." The nun looked at Val as she paused outside a closed door.

"Only last week some poor woman ran in here after a fight with her husband, screaming that she was possessed." She shook her head sadly and reached for the door handle, so she didn't catch Val's reaction to the possession comment.

"They all want exorcism, you know," the nun continued, opening the door on a cramped, windowless room dominated by a huge overstuffed couch. "Ever since that awful movie."

She indicated Val should give herself up to the

20

couch, assured her that Father would be with her in just a moment and took her cordial smile away.

Val was still wearing her reaction to the possession comment. Something heavy was settling on her: She knew it was futile to seek help here. She peered around the door. The hallway was empty except for the hammering of the carpet layers. Val ducked out of the office, glad to leave that hulking piece of furniture sagging under God only knows how many years of priestly bottoms and lonely spilled-out burdens.

She felt only a little guilty for running out. She just couldn't tell the holy man straight out that she thought she might be getting telepathic messages and just wanted to know if there was anything to this possession stuff.

She crossed the street, glancing back at the steeple and its hollow cross.

"Nobody will ever believe me," Val said, stepping onto the curb. "I'm going to have to handle this all by myself."

A painter just over there was finishing a sign about a private investigator: M.S. WISE. Maybe he could help her, find out if there had been an accident like the one she was sure she was seeing played over and over in the dreams.

Of course, private detectives were expensive. Well, there was always her credit card. Val had been careful and still had $300 to her limit.

If she could prove there really was an accident like the one in the dreams, maybe Frank would stop saying she was crazy. The nerve of him making an appointment for her with old Freudian Phil, who would just smile lewdly if she were to confess she had a dream about a flying car. What would he say now that she was not only hearing a voice from the dreams, but was conversing with the man she dreamed about?

"Finders, Incorporated?" Val said to get the painter's attention.

"Open for business tomorrow," he snapped.

21

"Do you know how much they charge to find someone?"

"Come back tomorrow, sugar."

Val backed off, shouldering her gym bag, thinking how splendid it was going to be to go inside her gym where there were no rude sign painters, no mothering boyfriends, no predatory hardhats—no men of any stripe—and work her body for her own pleasure until she dropped.

Maybe Frank was right and it was all therapy, exercise and vitamins. L–Glutamine, he insisted she take this month. Last month, he was excited about vitamin E. Hormonal imbalances, etc. All you are is an overactive pituitary gland, he told her once. She had thought that sounded so scientific then, but now it made her seethe—him and his whole-wheat shrink, always trying to keep her dependent.

Val knew with fair certainty she was not losing her marbles.

She walked faster to the gym door, anticipating the exhilarating workout the yoga class always gave her, and the steam afterward.

The parking lot was full; that meant the gym was crowded. Lukewarm-to-cold showers. Oh well, she sighed. It hadn't been her day.

"What did that girl want?" Maxine asked the elder painter. She'd been trying to get a plate over an electrical outlet, but the screw wouldn't fit, and the outlet seemed for some reason to be sticking out foo far. She'd given up in exasperation, thinking that Hugh would fix it for her if she remembered to ask him.

Maxine had been standing when out of the corner of her eye she caught the girl walking away from the painter as though she had been talking to him.

"I told her you wasn't open for business until tomorrow."

"What did she want?"

"Wanted to know how much you charge to find someone," he answered, not looking into Maxine's eyes as he officiously cleaned a small brush handle. He was steamed at her over the curlicue on the *s*. Well, to hell with him, turning away her business.

Maxine Wise put no credence in karma, destiny or weird culty things like that, but she wondered why she and this girl were so suddenly thrown into each other's path. Maxine didn't like coincidences; they made her uncomfortable. She could always, however, sense when someone was in the kind of trouble that brought her business. Mum called it second sight for practical purposes. Maxine just called it lucky.

She darted inside the office, grabbed her own gym bag and keys and closed the door behind her. "The phone company will be here before you leave," she said to the painter, as she locked the door. "They know what I want—will you please let them in and leave the keys on the desk." She handed him the keys and walked away.

She figured she didn't owe him anything more. She hurried to the gym. That's what she needed, to get the kinks out. She wanted to be her best tomorrow.

She was throwing an office warming on Friday, at home, because the office was so small. But Wednesday was her first official day of business. She allowed herself this one concession to luck—that she would be completely ready for that business on the first day. So many little things had gone wrong, like the plumbing, the phones, the sign.

But now for a little while she could relax and enjoy the luxury of exercise, a hot shower and a sauna before going home. She hadn't been home for supper last night, and it was a family time she liked to share with Hugh and the boys no matter what else happened during the day. It was a tradition she had been able to maintain all during her working years at least fairly well, and she wasn't about to let them all start drifting apart and not eating right just because she was opening her own office.

"*Ms.* Wise," the painter spat when Maxine was far

23

enough away not to hear. In one quick motion he painted an elaborate tail on the *s* in FINDERS, INC. His partner glanced over, clucked a couple of times and shrugged. Wha'd he know, anyway? He was just an apprentice.

Maxine saw the gym was crowded, but she didn't expect anything else this time of day with all the office people coming over the pass from Century City and UCLA, dropping by the gym to get ready to have a good evening.

It hadn't been long since Maxine had been part of that daily two-way drive at rush hours. She was glad to be out of the freeway rat race, glad to be her own boss, glad to be able to concentrate on the specialty that best fit her natural curiosity and inclination. She loved finding missing persons, and though it was often sad work, she wouldn't rather be doing anything else.

She idly thought over her situation as she entered the reception area of the gym. The girl she was following was signing in after several women who were chatting their way through the door marked MEMBERS ONLY.

The girl followed them through while Maxine signed in on the roster. She'd done it so many times it was an automatic gesture. She noticed the neat signature above her own: *Leslie Valentine.*

"Hi, Maxine—caught any bad guys lately?" the receptionist asked brightly. It was mildly annoying to be asked questions like that, but Maxine tried not to take offense. She supposed she'd do anything to break the boredom if she were behind that desk all day long. "Has Kathy got a massage hour open?"

"Six-thirty."

"No, I want to be home tonight," Maxine said and grabbed a towel from a neat stack.

"My astrology book says this week is great for new beginnings, so looks like you have good luck with your office."

"Thanks. I don't believe in anything occult, myself."

"Maybe it works anyway."

"I can use all the help I can get," Maxine replied, opening the door to the MEMBERS ONLY sanctuary.

Conversations brewed everywhere in the crowded locker room. A couple of Maxine's personal gym favorites were rapidly speaking in their native Hungarian. The animated, rapid-fire dialog was punctuated here and there with American phrases, and like American cheese in a blintz, it had an unexpected effect. The Americanese was mostly for consumer goods. She caught the phrase "sliding glass door" sandwiched between exotic words.

Maxine moved through the congregation of female bodies in all states of health, age, body type, color and undress.

Then Maxine saw the girl from the phone booth. As she passed in front of the Hungarians, the elder woman nudged her friend and chattered something in her native tongue that ended in the phrase "TV commercial." So that's why she looked familiar.

The girl, now in leotard, footless tights and leg warmers, trotted up the stairs to the dance studio. The class was fifteen minutes started, but Maxine decided to take it anyway. She tossed her things into the nearest available locker and hurriedly changed.

No floor space was available in the huge second-story classroom. It was exceptionally cool here, and the blinds had been drawn so light was subdued. Eastern music—soft, rapt, serene—wafted from the record player.

The class, led by the soft-voiced instructor, was into the Salutation to the Sun, a long series of muscle stretches. The girl—Leslie—was already into the routine, and Maxine could see with some envy that she was good. Because there was no room on the floor, the girl had taken a position in an alcove just off the main classroom. There was space for one more body there, so Maxine took it. She picked up the slow beat of the

25

instructor in the middle of the posture and heard her bones mildly pop as she started stretching.

It felt delicious. During the twenty years Maxine had been with the L.A. County Sheriff's Department, she had religiously attended the gym. But since her retirement six months ago and the first boring months of what was supposed to be fun, she hadn't gone as often as she should have. Then when she had the idea to open her own missing persons bureau, there was suddenly no time for anything except preparations for opening the office.

As she lengthened her arm muscles, she wondered what the girl's problem might be. It must be interesting, especially if that had been her on the phone earlier with someone—a husband? a boyfriend?—who thought she was having a breakdown.

Not what Maxine had expected for her first official client. But part of the reason she got a private detective license was because she loved the excitement and unexpectedness of missing persons work. Those years in the missing persons bureau had left her a junkie: Maxine was hooked on finding the story behind each person. She could read other people the way some housewives consumed romantic novels.

Mum called Maxine a *yenta*. In her grandmother's Russia, Mum often told her daughter, Maxine would have been the village matchmaker and general agent for whatever somebody wanted from somebody else. Maxine was good at such work because she was possessed of a natural curiosity about the inner workings of her fellow human beings. She wasn't satisfied merely to know people; she had to find out what made them tick. She operated on the principle that everyone was in conflict with something or someone. Find that conflict and you found the core of the personality.

As green felt is to a gambler, so was thinly veiled conflict to Maxine. The girl working so hard at the yoga exercise next to her was broadcasting conflict.

Soon Maxine was part of the generally synchronous movement of the class.

But still Maxine wondered. What was the conflict that she had sensed in the girl earlier, even before she knew this Leslie Valentine would seek her professional services?

Maxine could hardly wait to find out.

CHAPTER 4

"Dr. Raymond may have made you private duty on this Stefano case," nursing supervisor Carson lectured, "but you should know I opposed it. I'll be watching you every minute. This case is sensitive because of who Mr. Stefano is. Very special treatment."

"I give all my patients very special treatment, Mrs. Carson," Tanna replied, cleaning the medication tray so that she did not have to make eye contact with her supervisor.

"I'll bet you do." Carson eyed her sideways. "You don't fool me, hot mama. I've suspected you fool around with comatose patients." Carson's fierce personality had submitted to only one opponent—age. She had once been a pretty if not beautiful black woman, and now she was old. She never found a replacement for her looks, and it made her bitter.

"If I ever catch you messing around with that man, adding a celebrity to your trophies, I'll—" The unspoken was intended to intimidate Tanna with dire possibilities.

"Appeal to the life force, Mrs. Carson," Tanna said with excessive mildness.

"The life force—ha! Don't give me that godless propaganda about life force, you hear. Sex therapy, all that." She pointed a menacing finger at the younger woman.

"You listen to me and you listen good. You may be

a favorite with the powers-that-be around here, but you don't show me nothing, you hear? I told Raymond not to put you on this case, and if I catch you getting cute with that poor man, I'll have your cap. I swear I will. Understand?"

Tanna controlled her fury.

"Is that clear?"

"Yes, ma'am." Tanna didn't look up.

Carson strode off, leaving footprints on the wet linoleum the maid was swabbing down. A staff nurse, Meg Geller, ambled up to the nurses' station after shooting a glance at the supervisor's departing back.

"She's after you."

Tanna busied herself with paperwork on the injections.

"Why?" Meg persisted. She and Tanna had been friends since nursing school; in fact, she got this job through her friend Meg. She was an inch from leaving because of Carson but was waiting to find something else first. The trouble was, this place was her source of private duty patients.

"Mmmmmmm," Tanna answered, notating the Stefano injection with a meticulousness that channeled her fury away from Carson.

"I've never been so close to a TV star before," the white girl said. Tanna loved her friend Meg, but sometimes she was just too gushy. Who cared that he was a celebrity? That didn't make this patient more important than any other. Tanna looked away because she didn't want to display her judgment of her friend. Meg meant well.

Meg picked up his file. "Michael Stefano," she muttered, flipping through it. "Thirty years old. Traffic accident two weeks ago. Transferred Saturday night from UCLA Emergency. Hmmmmmmm. No phone calls. All visitors must be cleared through Dr. Raymond."

Tanna listened but showed no unusual interest. It might appear she didn't care or was preoccupied. Actually she was glad Meg had saved her looking up the file.

28

"Concussion relieved immediately," Meg continued, "but there's no indication why he's been unconscious so long. Unusually high medication." She sighed and looked toward Room 20.

"Poor guy. He doesn't know—yet."

"I suspect he'll be waking up soon," Tanna answered, replacing the injection schedule. "He was dreaming a minute ago."

"They've really got him juiced," Meg said. Tanna winced; she hated such informality about their work. But she didn't express her feelings to Meg who was re-reading the file.

"Well, this explains why Raymond is so nervous. Not only is he our first genuine celebrity, but his uncle is Lazlo Stefano." She looked up at Tanna.

"So?"

"You don't know who Stefano is?"

"No."

"Big TV producer who just happens to own this place."

"What?"

"Tax write-off," Meg said confidently, having gleaned that information from the *National Enquirer*. Tanna had seen her reading the tabloid several times and had been surprised to see her trying to hide it.

Tanna watched the maid washing the floor near Room 20's closed entrance. She was getting more interested all the time in her new private duty case. Most of the people in this plastic palace were the cast-off parents and grandparents of sons and daughters in the entertainment industry who could afford to forget about them. The work, while it paid better than most convalescent hospitals, was about as exciting as the patients' breakfast—oatmeal. Sunnyrest was a fairly new building in Encino that had started out as an intensive care hospital. But it went bankrupt almost immediately. It was bought by the present owner and converted into a convalescent home, so most of the ultramodern lifesaving equipment was rarely used. Rarely did she have any but the most mundane geriatric cases, so the promise of someone different and interesting within these modern but somehow dismal walls excited Tanna.

The maid moved closer to the nurses' station with her mop and pail.

"You recognize him?" Meg asked, breaking the small silence filled only by the swishing sound of the mop.

"I saw him in a couple of movies."

"His TV show is on reruns every day," Meg said, thinking out loud as she looked at the swinging doors of the recreation room where a TV set was on sixteen hours a day. She could hear it now.

"I never cared much for Westerns," Tanna said. She was checking the chart to see who else was scheduled for an injection this afternoon. Goldman was slated for a vitamin B shot at seven.

Because of her private duty assignment, after today she would be responsible for none of this paperwork except his. But today she was doubling with her old duties.

"Well," Meg said, setting aside his chart. "He sure is pretty." Tanna secretly smiled in agreement; she picked up his file and began reading the notes on his surgery. She stepped aside so that the maid, Phyllis, could mop the floor behind the station. Meg moved over, too, saying, "Too bad he'll never play cowboys and Indians again."

Inside Room 20 it was very quiet.

He was dreaming again, reliving the nightmare.

The 450 SL seemed to be taking forever to fall. It began tumbling just before it hit nose-first on the rain-soaked hillside. There was no fire, just a grinding crunch as the car tried to screw itself into the ground. Bedrock stopped it on a steep angle.

In the darkness the prevalent sound was running water, a flood of it all around, tugging at everything in its path—rocks, bushes, hands and feet.

The next sound came from above. A machine of

30

some sort, and lights, but in fragile beams that illuminated only small patches of the darkness.

Someone shouted and he felt immensely pleased and satisfied. They had found him. Everything was going to be okay.

"You hear, Jan?" he called out to his passenger.

The runoff threatened to choke him, so he shut up, straining to hold his head above water.

He was pinned, that was for sure, but he felt no pain. He could move his toes, but oddly, not his legs. He could feel he'd lost one shoe; cold, rushing water ran with enough force to separate his toes.

"Shit," he muttered, trying to hold his torso off the ground, away from the water. It had taken weeks to break in those running shoes. They were nearly perfect. Now he'd have to start all over with another pair.

The beam of light struck him like a physical blow. He closed his eyes and called, "Over here," feeling proud that he was remaining calm, not getting hysterical.

"Jan," he called again, but couldn't hear if she answered or not.

Someone was rappeling down the cliff, spinning away, then slamming closer.

Someone else up on the road called down, barely audible in the rain, saying something about a two-way radio.

The rescuer brought himself closer to the upside-down car. "Bring the light to the left just a tad—"

The victim pinned beneath the window edge said, "I think the car's a goner." He was trying to see over his shoulder, but the incline and rushing water kept him from succeeding.

"Yeah," replied the paramedic.

He could barely see his face in the light from above; young, blond, frowning as he surveyed the damage and what he must do to extricate the victim. "You just take it easy."

"Awful way to treat a Mercedes. Jan was pissed at me—she's over there someplace."

Another paramedic in a yellow rain slicker joined the first, handling the two-way radio while the first man cut off the jeans. He slammed the needle into the guy's ass with the muddy water washing over him while his buddy held the guy's face out of the water with one hand and the two-way with the other. "Go ahead and do it, then," said a voice on the crackling radio.

The paramedic was talking to someone in a much drier, warmer place a few miles away, and they used a few clipped Latin-sounding words; something about disarticulation. The drug just injected was not enough against the adrenaline pumping through the victim's body. He was lucid several times, insisting he could feel his toes.

He demanded to see the producer because he did not like these special effects. He told that to the extras, the actors playing the paramedics. "I want you to call the effects people," he demanded as they lifted him from under the mangled car. It had taken less than ten minutes to cut him out. Once, the wreckage shifted, undermined by water. The tricky part was getting the stretcher up the steep hillside while the flood took rocks and bushes out by the roots around him.

"Call S.A.G.," he was loudly insisting as they put him into the ambulance.

"What's he talking about?"

"Dunno. They say funny things sometimes."

They were near the end of the intricately changing Salutation to the Sun. Every muscle in Maxine's body was screaming for release, but she was determined to finish the sequence. She glanced at the girl, Leslie, beside her.

Suddenly Leslie stopped the routine.

She stood with her weight on one foot, staring into her own reflection in the mirror. Her hand went to her temple, and what was surely a frown of pain shot between her eyebrows.

"Are you all right?" Maxine asked, full of the momentum of the exercise.

"I'm, uh . . ."

"You look a little faint." The girl looked more than that. She was chalky white. "Come on," Maxine urged, guiding her by the elbow to a bench along a wall of the alcove, out of sight of the rest of the class.

"Thank you," the girl whispered as she dropped to the bench.

"You need a drink of water?"

"No, no. I'm okay. Really," she said, looking a little rosier.

"Did you black out?" Maxine sat beside her.

"Kind of—I haven't been getting enough sleep lately." Maxine thought there was something guarded about her as she wiped a sheen of sweat from her forehead.

"It's Leslie, isn't it?"

"How did—?" The girl looked up with a faint surprised smile. This close she didn't really look like Melodie at all, Maxine was relieved to discover. Just the braids and that reminder in the smile.

"You spoke to the painter outside my office."

The girl nodded, breathing more normally now.

"I saw he'd been rude to you. I couldn't ignore you—you looked so worried."

The girl might have nodded, but it was a small movement.

"I was coming to the gym anyway. This seemed like a good time. My name's Maxine Wise."

The girl definitely looked surprised at this, then smiled again. "I thought you'd be a man. I'm sorry."

"Culture warps us all. Don't worry about it, Leslie."

"I'm Val. I don't use my first name."

"You look like you need someone to talk to, Val."

She looked directly at Maxine with unblinking hazel eyes. It was a frank, appraising stare, a search of Maxine's own gaze for any sign that Val could trust her.

"I don't think I'm going to be able to finish this class," Val said finally. Behind them, the sitar music swelled as thirty-five ladies of many shapes and sizes strained for serenity.

"I have to admit," Maxine concurred, "I was pooped and glad for an excuse to stop."

Val nodded as if speaking was too much effort. When she stood she acted dizzy again.

"Okay?"

"Yeah."

Val let Maxine lead the way through the swinging door and down the stairs. She moved slowly.

"You're still shaky. You on a diet or something?"

Val paused at the landing. "I haven't had much appetite lately."

She looked at Maxine again. How much would this woman be able to believe? How much should she be told? All I want to know, Val considered, is if there was an accident like the one in the dream. She was sure it happened in the last storm; surely there would be some kind of record of the accident, records that this woman knew how to research.

I certainly don't have to explain to her how I saw it, Val thought with relief.

"I guess my conscience is bothering me," she said tentatively, watching the older woman's reaction.

She was cool; there wasn't any. She stood two steps below, waiting patiently for Val to continue when she felt like it.

Just on a whim, because Val wasn't into astrology at all, but just to see the way this person leaned, Val said, "I'm a double Pisces and I guess I'm just sensitive."

Maxine's eyebrow went up almost imperceptibly.

"I guess you don't believe in that stuff," Val said.

"Not in the least."

Val smiled faintly. She stepped further down the stair while holding onto the banister. If M. S. Wise discredited astrology, she wouldn't even consider telepathy.

"Why is your conscience bothering you?"

They moved together into the hallway between the stairwell and the locker room still teeming with patrons. This was a relatively private spot in the otherwise public building.

Val took a deep breath. "I saw an accident about two weeks ago—I don't remember the date—but one of the last nights of the storm. I, uh, had some marijuana on me and didn't want to get involved with the police. I just didn't stop. I want to find out what happened to the people in the car." Val was surprised how easy it was. Not exactly a lie, because she'd never been good at direct lies, though she could act a part without any trouble. But out and out untruths were not her game. Selected facts she could manage. Frank would laugh at the marijuana bit. It was he who smoked the stuff, and not Val.

"I'm just Catholic enough to believe I can make up for not reporting it if I light a candle. You know, pray for them. It would help if I knew their names."

"Maybe they're okay."

"Nobody in that car could possibly be in good shape today."

Maxine looked as if she expected to hear more.

"That's all there is," Val said as someone moved past them into the locker room.

"You can describe the car and location?" Maxine said later in the steam room, the next time they had a moment of privacy.

"A red or wine-colored Mercedes. In a canyon—I was lost in the rain, but it was in the Hollywood Hills. There were two people inside—a man driving. A woman was in the passenger seat."

"How do you know that if it was dark?"

"They passed me at a light," Val said, thinking fast.

"What made you finally want to check it out?" Maxine asked, oddly veiled by the steam so that Val couldn't see her features clearly. Like a woman confessor, Val thought, secretly smiling at the idea. The incident at the church seemed like a joke now.

"For three nights now I've had a recurring dream about it," Val said, trembling involuntarily with a flash recall of the latest dream that had stopped her exercise so suddenly a moment ago. She couldn't honestly call them dreams anymore, because they were happening in

35

daylight. Each dream was like a puzzle piece; when it all fit together there would be a coherent pattern that would show what was really happening.

In this last one the flying car had finally dropped and the vision continued from the point of view of someone inside the wreckage. She knew without knowing why she knew that this was the point of view of the man who had been driving, the man who had been called Misha in the vision of the child in the snow field. This was the same man who called out to her, though she couldn't put all of it together in sequence yet, she knew one was there. She was sure he was calling after the accident. Misha. She hugged herself in the steam, but could find no comfort from the cold, wet image of the last vision. Now Val was sure the driver of the car—Misha—was alive, but his passenger—he had called her Jan—was not. The man had called from the depth of some terrible misery, called so that only Val could hear.

"A terrible nightmare," Val added and realized she had not spoken for a long time. Maxine was watching her patiently.

"Can you help me?"

"Yes."

A swirl of steam boiled in the dim, tiled room as another woman entered.

"Can you come to my office tomorrow, say ten-thirty?"

"Yes."

There was much more to say, both Val and Maxine thought separately, but it would have to wait for a more private place.

CHAPTER 5

Phyllis was mopping the floor as fast as she could because her feet were killing her. She muttered to herself below the range of hearing of the two young nurses up the hall.

She had muttered her way across the hall of Sunnyrest Convalescent Hospital, and now approached the intensive care room where the girls said there was some TV celebrity or somebody like that. Phyllis was curious so she mopped more quickly.

Her mop entered Room 20 first, a swishing, almost animate thing that left behind a wet trail like a sea creature. Its sound was rhythmical, subtle above the traffic murmur outside and the polite *whir-plink* of the vital signs monitor near the bed.

Phyllis regarded the ashen young-old face of the sleeper. She'd never seen him before. "He ain't so much," she muttered. He'd never been on "Fantasy Island" or "Merv." She'd never seen his face startled by *National Enquirer* cameras.

He couldn't be such a big deal.

His injuries provoked her curiosity but she didn't dare break the rules by going any nearer to him or, God forbid, touching the covers.

She went back to mopping. Phyllis was quick but she wasn't thorough. She shot a single swipe of the mop under the TV fellow's bed and let it go at that. "He won't care," she sniffed. "Will ya?"

She bumped the metal rails and he opened his eyes.

"Cold," he said softly.

It totally startled the old woman, so that she almost lost her mop.

"It's okay, it's okay," she said, backing toward the

37

door, her mop still nosing the floor. "Go back to sleep."

He lifted his head but couldn't maintain it. His eyelids drooped and he appeared to be taking Phyllis's advice as he fell back to the dented pillow.

"My feet are so fucking cold."

At first he closed his eyes and his breathing deepened. But something stirred in him and he blinked awake again, suddenly lucid and possessed of energy that had been dammed in him during two weeks of unconsciousness. Phyllis didn't take her eyes off him.

He grabbed the cold metal rail that had been raised to keep him from falling out of bed and pulled with trembling arms. On one elbow he had to stop and rest with his sweat-dappled forehead against the metal bar.

Phyllis saw that he wasn't going to give up, so she hobbled through the door in her version of a run to tell the nurses the patient in Room 20 was coming around.

Tanna was filling Meg in on the patients she'd be taking care of now that Tanna was on private duty. From Room 20 they heard the prolonged scream "Noooo" and then heard glass breaking.

Tanna nearly knocked Phyllis down as the old woman came out of the room with a surprised look on her face. The scream from behind her had frozen her. "He's woke up," she said but Tanna was already through the doorway.

Her patient had smashed the IV bottle against the side bed. He was hacking at his wrist as she ran to him, already screaming with him. She grabbed his hand, but he lashed out at her with the jagged bottom of the bottle. Blood spurted out of his wrist with each heartbeat. It splattered his face and the sheets and Tanna when she got in its path.

Meg ran behind him and caught his hand before he could inflict more damage. By now Tanna was streaked with blood. Some got into her eye and underfoot; she slipped against the bed while Phyllis stood in the doorway whimpering.

From another area an orderly, Bunch, came running.

In the still damp hallway he met Dr. Raymond, chief physician and administrator of Sunnyrest. Normally the doctor would have left by four in the afternoon, but he had stayed to clear up some paperwork on the hospital's few Medicare patients.

Bunch swung around the nurses' station and grabbed a crash cart almost without stopping.

Dr. Raymond, his gray hair flapping in a forelock over his eyes, unlocked the drug room and quickly found the medication set aside to subdue hysterics. A few doors away Michael was still screaming; Raymond could hear a woman's voice yelling with him. Together the old doctor and the big quiet orderly headed for Room 20 where the V.I.P. patient was screaming, "I won't live like this—"

Tanna still held his arm, restricting the artery. Raymond was aiming on the run, liquid squirting from the syringe in his hands.

"This patient was just medicated, Doctor," she said, struggling to hold on to her patient. Raymond seemed to wave aside her remark as he let the patient have it in the nearest visible spot on his inner arm. It was amazing that he hit a vein, under the circumstances. He tossed aside the syringe and took from Bunch's offering hands a strip of tourniquet material. Only when he had applied it and the blood no longer spurted did Tanna let go of Michael's sticky arm. Meg was pouring alcohol from the emergency cart onto Raymond's hands.

Then he quickly stitched the jagged wound.

Later he washed his hands at the adjoining bathroom with Tanna. Meg was guiding the maid out of the way and closing the door.

"Stabilize a new IV setup," Raymond said to Bunch, who was removing the stained linens from around the gently snoring patient.

"You want I should get the vest?" Bunch drawled slowly. Nothing ever seemed to upset Bunch, Tanna realized as she watched him awaiting the doctor's orders.

The man was always calm. She hadn't figured out if he were just dumb or if he possessed true serenity.

Raymond gloomily regarded his new patient, whom he was already sure was going to disrupt his staff. "No, not the Posey vest. Just restraints for his hands will do, thank you, Bunch." He favored the orderly with a smile, a rare act for the old man.

Bunch went off with the linen to get the restraints. Tanna accepted a towel from Raymond. He looked very old and a little palsied now that the crisis was over. It was the first surgical emergency he had had to deal with in the several years he'd been head of this place.

Tanna was impressed that he had done such a masterful job, but she felt sorry for him now as he shook his head.

"The family insists on special treatment, on all this secrecy."

Tanna wiped blood from her face.

"The uncle isn't in the country," Raymond continued, stepping closer to the bed. "He's in China making a movie—in the meantime I've got to keep this boy on ice . . ." Tanna was touched by the sadness in her boss's voice, but she was chilled by the implications of his words.

"So that's why he's so heavily sedated," she said, knowing already she was stepping out of bounds, but not really caring.

Raymond regarded her as she moved beside him.

"It's not good for him," she said softly.

"With all his uncle's money, he couldn't be getting better care."

"He needs to wake up."

"I can't believe what I'm hearing," said another voice entering the room behind them. It was Carson. "Since when does a junior nurse instruct a physician about medication?"

Raymond and Tanna turned together to include Carson, who was tightly hugging herself as she approached.

"It's obvious this patient is overmedicated."

"How dare you—" Carson started.

"It's all right," Raymond interrupted. "I encouraged her. Let her speak, Carson."

"It's my recommendation," Tanna continued, refusing to return Carson's icy stare, "that this patient needs to regain consciousness and begin therapy—"

"Well, I never—"

"Henderson," Raymond said to stop Carson, "Mr. Stefano has ordered that his nephew be kept quiet until he can return and personally supervise his therapy and recovery."

"Since when do we let family members direct the care of our patients?"

Raymond regarded Tanna somberly. "Maybe you aren't aware that Mr. Stefano owns this hospital."

"And pays your salary," Carson cut in.

"I'm working for just one person," Tanna said, looking down at her patient. "He's my only concern."

Carson snorted a laugh. "She's concerned, all right. Go on, ask her. Ask her what she was doing earlier—that may be the reason he woke up so hysterical. *She* woke him up—go on, ask her now."

Tanna flared at Carson, but Raymond stepped between them. "Please, this isn't the time or place for charges."

"She has no charges—no proof. Just accusations."

"Well?" Raymond asked his nursing supervisor. "Do you want to file charges against her?"

Carson wavered, clutched herself more tightly and marched from the room. Raymond sighed and started to follow.

"Stay with him," he said at the door. "He may say some crazy things—according to the uncle's secretary they haven't spoken to each other for six months. He may accuse the old man of anything." He looked intently at Tanna. "The moment I saw this young man, I knew you were the private duty to care for him, Henderson."

Tanna was touched that he was taking up for her.

41

"I'll reduce his medication now that you'll be with him all the time. I believe Carson is wrong about you, Tanna. But," he warned, "you take great care."

She nodded and smiled, and he left, closing the door.

Tanna moistened the towel and used it to bathe the patient's face.

His eyes were no longer rolling beneath the lids. He was really out, would sleep twenty-four hours on what they had given him in two injections. She wiped a trickle of blood from under the gauze on his wrist.

Poor baby, she thought. Don't blame you for being mad. I'd be mad, too. She touched his odd, handsome face again, letting her hands move down his chest and stomach to the sheet that covered his lower body.

She lifted the covers.

Everything looked snug and in place with the bandages on the stumps of his legs. The amputations had been exactly at the knee—not conventional, but from the information on file it had been field surgery under extreme circumstances. He was lucky to be alive.

The hospital gown was stained from his self-attack, so Tanna slipped it off him.

His chest was agreeably hairy and his stomach flat. Tanna touched the soft inner thigh on either side of his sex. Despite the catheter, his cock stirred.

"Well, I'll be damned," Tanna said to herself. "I thought I was going to have a nice knish, but I have something else entirely." Something rare these days.

She was delighted her patient was uncircumcised.

CHAPTER 6

"Open sesame."

Maxine watched the two-car garage door swing up under the influence of the opener she was activating in her hand. All our gadgets, she mused, things that would've been considered magic a hundred years ago are now commonplace.

Hugh wasn't home yet. His silver Datsun wasn't inside the garage. This week he was testifying in a big strangler case in superior court. Probably having a drink with the prosecutor, an old college buddy.

She pulled her Rambler station wagon into the garage and switched off the engine. She had a briefcase, gym bag and purse to carry in, so it took a minute to get it all together and struggle out of the car. She could hear the TV set on in the house.

Maxine directed the door to close and walked into her kitchen on the side of the huge ranch-style one-story home she and Hugh had nearly paid off.

She saw Tim's dune buggy at the curb as she opened the window over the sink to let some air in the stuffy room that still smelled of burned eggs from breakfast.

The blare of the TV on down the hall in the den greeted Maxine like another smell. It was turned to a fast-food commercial that echoed off the walls and gave Maxine an odd feeling of being a stranger in her own home.

She wasn't given to internal soliloquies and shook off the bizarre reverie. She dropped her gear on the floor.

"Hi," she called. No sound from the boys interrupted the TV audio. The program had switched to the logo of a rerun the boys were infatuated with. They'd watch anything, but their current favorites were

43

"Emergency," "Star Trek" on the third rerun and this noisy Western. Judging from the blare of theme music, the awful thing was just starting. Lots of firearms, lots of yelling, fighting, riding. Cut to the chase, Maxine thought, reminded of her only contact with the film industry, a neighbor on their Sherman Oaks street who had been second unit director on something like Clint Eastwood movies. At a couple of block parties she'd not liked him; he was always saying, "Cut to the chase," when he was bored, and his boredom threshold was about that of a six-year-old "Sesame Street" addict.

Maxine added her gym clothes to the load already in the washer and switched it on the longest cycle.

The machine's whir helped to cover the offensive noise coming from the den.

Maxine stood with the refrigerator door open for nearly a minute, going over every item in the larder. Leftovers, mysterious Tupperware dishes; stinking gifts of aluminum foil and baggies, with water and vivid colors condensing inside. Six gallons of milk in plastic cartons with spouts—delivered by a milkman who loved this run full of healthy baby-boom teenagers. Lots of eggs in their individual plastic sockets. An assortment of sticky L'Chaim preserves, condiment jars, canned beer and a tray of limp vegetables. But nothing for supper.

She couldn't face the market tonight.

She was just about to suggest that Tim drive over to the Colonel's when she heard another of the pushy ads for take-out food—hamburgers this time—and decided none of that tonight, just because she found the commercials so generally offensive.

She opened the freezer door and took out a three-pound roll of ground beef. She reopened the vegetable tray and found some not-quite-gone mushrooms and a sprouted onion.

As she closed the door Tim entered the kitchen. He started rummaging through a cabinet after a small growl of greetings. "Hi, Mama."

44

"Put the crackers away," Maxine ordered pleasantly as she rinsed the mushrooms. "Get the big skillet out for me, will you."

Tim found it and turned on the flame. "You want this hamburger meat in it?"

She nodded, picking out the best mushrooms. Mum said never get them wet, but how did she get the grit *all* off if she didn't get them wet?

"Get the buggy fixed?"

"No," Tim answered as he dropped the frozen log of meat into the pan. "Ralph is asking too much for a brake job. I'll do it myself." He tossed aside the plastic wrapping without looking, and deftly extracted a handful of crackers.

"Don't drive that thing until you can stop it."

"How'm I supposed to get it fixed if I don't have wheels to get the parts?"

"The R.T.D.—"

"I hate the bus. It's torture—pure torture."

He put the cracker box under his arm and started to leave the kitchen.

"Put them back," Maxine said without looking at him.

"We're hungry."

"Why didn't you come in here and start supper? Would that have killed you?" Now she pinned him with a stare.

"I just got home," he shrugged.

"How did Ben's little league game go?" It was an important one, she remembered as she took a package of spaghetti from the cupboard.

"They lost. He's pukey. I thought some crackers would cheer him up."

"I'll bet you did," she said, grinning. He returned the good humor. Long, blond Timmy standing beside the cabinet, one ear bent on hearing the show that he had just started in the other room, crackers falling out of his fist—Maxine saw a flash of Hugh in her eldest boy-man. "Here," she said, handing him a saucer for the crackers.

45

He reached for the refrigerator door.

"No milk—you won't be hungry."

"I'll gag if I have to eat this stuff without something to drink."

"A small glass, then. And take some to Ben."

"That little drip thinks he's too much already."

"Be nice, Tim." She urged him with a smile and touched his long-fingered hand that was so skilled at basketball.

Just then she heard with relief Hugh's Datsun pull up with a squeak outside. A last ray of sunlight speared through the eucalyptus trees and caught her husband getting out. She watched him through the window above the sink.

Hugh, six four, graying now, but with a head of bushy hair he'd never lose. Tall, graceful, a great dancer. How I love that man, Maxine thought. It had never diminished over the years.

He slammed the car door and inspected a minuscule spot on his auto's surface. Then, satisfied as he scraped off the dirt, he turned and headed for the house, squinting in the sun. He waved and smiled when he saw his wife watching him.

"Hey, old girl," he said as he entered the back door, already squirming out of his tie, dropping his jacket and briefcase next to Maxine's. "How was it?"

"Well, I'm just about ready—would you mind stopping by on your way in tomorrow?"

They met in a quick hug, then she went back to the sizzling meat.

"What's the problem?" He tossed his tie onto his jacket.

"I broke the screw for that big electrical outlet plate—it looks awful. Would you mind fixing it for me?"

"I don't have to be in until two in the afternoon."

"How'd it go in court?"

"Well, Judge Whitefield never admits more than half my testimony—a nitpicker, you know. Like always, he threw out most of what I said. But I think we convinced the jury this guy shouldn't be back on the street." As a police psychologist, Hugh felt each and every miscreant was his personal responsibility.

He opened the refrigerator door and found a beer.

"You see Nelson?"

"We went to Phillipe's—remember that place?"

When they first met as USC students, Maxine and Hugh would hang out at the delicatessen in Chinatown. Over the years thousands of students had scratched their names into the soft brick walls. It brought back memories of those happy days just to think about the two-story building with its backless stools, sawdust on the floor, hot-mustard pots, venerable waitresses serving up pink eggs and hideous pickled pigs feet, Dos Equis beer, macaroni salad and the best French-dip sandwiches in L.A.

"So, you're not hungry."

"I didn't eat. Just chewed the fat with Nelson." As he filled her in on news from their old school chum, Maxine thought about her husband and his incongruous mixture of Manhattan and Georgia. Hugh was born and raised in Atlanta, where his daddy still ran and owned a department store at Route 73. Hugh never did have a Southern accent, but he often used Southern expressions that never failed to endear him to his wife.

"So, what's for supper?"

"Spaghetti."

"Sounds great," Hugh replied, sucking at the beer.

After a few minutes of busywork at the stove, she said, "The sign painters are terrible." She turned down the flame. "But I got my first official client this afternoon. I don't count the religious cult case the department referred to me."

"So, who's the first client?"

"She's a beautiful TV actress."

"This is beginning to sound like some detective story—Sleuth in trenchcoat in an office with a sign painted on the door. Enter the beautiful, mysterious girl with money as no object, begging the sleuth to find her missing husband.

"I sure wish you'd let me buy you a trenchcoat, Maxi—" Hugh caught himself. "I'm sorry, sweetheart. Don't know what made me say that."

She hadn't let anyone call her Maxi since her father died a dozen years ago. She'd been a daddy's girl in a family of brothers, so he had called her Maxi as a special tribute.

The word shortened a family name from her mother's side of the family; her father used Maxi to designate the Latin meaning of the maximum, the greatest. Growing up, Maxi loved it, though her mother refused to call her anything except Maxine. Daddy's Maxi was a wonderful connotation for the only girl in a houseful of boys, but after the old man died it had a melancholy sound to her. Hugh was great about her wishes; he immediately switched to Maxine as she asked him to do at her father's funeral, and only slipped now and then. Because her husband changed to Maxine, everyone else eventually did, too, until now nobody but Hugh ever thought of her as Maxi, and he hadn't done so out loud in years.

"Well, the girl *was* mysterious," Maxine was saying after she forgave him the slip. "She may be a nut, for all I know." She took out her big green spaghetti pot and filled it from the faucet. "Wants me to find out the names of some people in an accident she ran away from—"

"God, not hit-and-run."

"No, she just didn't report seeing it. I think she's straight about not being directly involved. But she is kinda spacey—smokes grass, an actress. She's done a lot of commercials."

She turned, wiping her hands on a dish towel.

"Anyway, she's my first official client."

Hugh raised his beer can in a *salud*. "Congratulations, Madame Private Eye." He reached out and pulled her to him, kissing her on the forehead.

48

Maxine snuggled her hips up to his. "Huh?" she asked provocatively.

"Hmmmmm," he answered, finishing off the beer in one swig. "The meat's burning—" He reached past her for the spatula and stirred the crackling but certainly not burning ground round.

A burst of gunfire flared from the den.

"Down, boys," Hugh bellowed and ambled off down the hall. The sound dropped from 9 to about 8.7 on a scale of 10. After the moment it took Hugh to reach the den, the volume dropped to 5.

Maxine watched him until he stepped from her sight. She was trying not to worry. There had been a time, and not so long ago, when she would have had to convince Hugh they couldn't drop everything and make love right on the kitchen floor. Now he didn't respond at all. Just a phase, Maxine told herself, thinking of all the books she'd been reading on midlife crisis. Not to worry. When she took the garlic from the freezer she saw only two bags of ice, so she emptied all the trays and bagged the cubes for the party. She returned to the stove, stirring dinner, trying not to worry.

Tanna was looking for Mr. Goldman. It was past seven and time for his injection. The old diabetic often slipped away—hated shots. He wasn't on the roof, where he and several of the other ambulatories liked to spend their afternoons. The gym roof a couple of doors away and one story lower blossomed like a meadow on sunny afternoons with nubile ladies taking in the sun. But it was too late for that entertainment now.

She found him in the recreation room, where a couple of the others were watching TV, talking over the boring parts. Goldman had gone to sleep in his wheelchair.

She walked up to the group quietly, seeing that they were absorbed in a loud political discussion over the beginning credits of a show called "Pard'ners."

The name Michael Stefano flashed on the old black-and-white screen, in front of that face, the face

49

now serene under a massive chemical blanket back down the hall. The face on the screen was made up to look like the Hollywood version of an American Indian. How well the sharp Balkan features contributed to the stereotype—the dark hair, hawk nose, olive complexion. Everything except the eyes. Tanna had expected them to be brown, but when he raged a couple of inches from her eyes earlier she'd seen that they were a deep sea green. Well, maybe the producers of "Pard'ners" rationalized away those incongruous European eyes as the legacy of the character's white mother. He was playing a half-breed, that much Tanna knew from having seen the show in a bar or somewhere else when her attention had been divided. TV was her least-favorite entertainment.

She stood behind Goldman's chair, watching the series's logo for the first time. Michael Stefano was an athletic, lithe man whose grace made him seem larger than his frame looked on the hospital bed down the hall. His technique was not so much acting as a bountiful energy transferred to whatever character he was playing. Whomever he was supposed to be portraying, like so many TV actors, he was always just a charming version of himself. The little screen couldn't lie like the stage or the big screen. It was too intimate, too close to the pores and lashes of the real person behind the role. Tanna knew all this instinctively as she watched him on the flickering little screen.

With the beard and his present condition he was hardly recognizable as the actor on the screen. He was highly attractive jumping around with his "Pard'ner," a burly good-ole-boy type of Western marshal played by an older actor named Robbie Dobbs, according to the name flashing on the screen at that moment. The raucous music continued under a montage of the two "Pard'ners" romping, riding, fighting the inevitable bad guys, kissing the women, and generally acting the parts of a U.S. marshal and his Indian sidekick in a back-lot rendition of the Oklahoma Territory.

"Well, Miss Henderson, how you like our celebrity?"

50

one of the old men called to her when he saw her so absorbed in the inane bit of television action. Just then, on screen, the Indian whipped a long knife from a hidden shoulder scabbard and flung it expertly. It was a startling, swift action, finely practiced for the TV stunt. His face was part of the body English of delivery. The knife *thunked* into a tree trunk, pinning a bad guy by the collar just centimeters from fatal injury to the jugular vein and carotid artery.

Even though she was sure it was just calculated movie magic, the animal grace of the man executing the throw gave her a visceral thrill. Not a man who would take easily to handicapped life, she thought to herself.

"Just another patient, and I love you all," Tanna said brightly. She touched Goldman's bony shoulder, waking him from his doze.

"Huh?"

"Time for your shot, Mr. Goldman," she said, taking the handles of his wheelchair.

"No, no," he protested, trying to slow down the chair by grabbing the wheel grips. "Let me watch my program first."

"You weren't watching that show."

"Not that drivel," Goldman said disdainfully, waving a hand at the TV set. "It's seven and I want to watch the news."

"Right after our injection." She glanced back at the TV set for another look at Michael, but by now a fast-food commercial had replaced him.

"It's not our injection, goddammit. It's mine. I have to take it all by myself."

Behind them someone switched the channel and called, "Don't worry, Reg—the news will be waiting for you."

Tanna wheeled the grumbling old guy away, chuckling to herself. Goldman wielded a lot of power with the other male patients. Not only because of seniority—he'd lived here two years. He also owned the only

51

set of binoculars with which they perused the sunbathing nubiles over on the gym roof.

"Mum says I should find you a girl," Maxine said later, on her side of their bed. Hugh was propped up so that a puddle of light fell on the news magazine he was reading.

"You know, like Sarah and Abraham."

"If I remember correctly," Hugh said without taking his eyes from the page, "Sarah should have been more patient."

"Well, Mum doesn't suggest you actually take another woman—she just thinks a girl would . . ." It was suddenly sticky, and Maxine realized with chagrin that she didn't want to say exactly what a girl would do.

Hugh put aside the magazine and pulled Maxine up on his lap. "Silly girl, you are a silly girl." He played with her dark hair, running his fingers thought it. "I don't want anyone but you."

"I'm glad," Maxine muttered into the covers, trying to get closer to him, to find, under his pajamas, some patch of bare skin she could fondle. She felt him draw back involuntarily.

"I'm sorry," he said. "Maybe I should find *you* a lover."

"Hugh!"

"Well, why not?"

"I love you—I don't want anyone else."

"We do have a problem, don't we, old girl?" He turned off his bedside lamp and settled a little into the covers.

"I think," he finally said, close to her in the dark, yet far away, "I'll go see Samuelson."

She didn't respond.

"Well? What do you think?"

Maxine stirred negatively. "You haven't had any pain, have you?"

"They say there isn't any pain at first."

She was racked by his heavy masculine sigh. She

found his furry arm and held on to it. "You haven't been keeping anything from me, have you, Hugh?"

"No," he answered with sweet emphasis, rubbing her neck and shoulders with his strong hands. She'd never known this man to lie.

"Never felt better. It just might be smart to check out the physical possibilities, that's all."

Maxine felt sick, elevator-stomach sick, the way she felt last year when she had that lump in her breast; it turned out just to be a cyst, but she had been terrified and disconsolate until it went away.

"Corona, that Bunco captain. Remember him?"

"Yes." She rolled over, staring at the black ceiling.

"He had it. Prostate—"

"Don't tell me."

"He's okay. Eight months ago, they operated and now he's fine. Says he's better than before. Well, that's probably an exaggeration. You know Corona."

"He's much older than you."

"Fifty-two."

"Oh." Hugh was forty-nine.

He maneuvered farther down into a sleeping position. She felt his hand groping for hers and met it in the dark middle of their bed. "It's going to be all right."

"I know."

"Look, I'm okay. Just to make sure."

"You're right."

"What we both really need is a vacation, just the two of us. Go to Mexico, maybe." His work kept some new vital case in the forefront of their lives. There hadn't been time to take a vacation alone in nearly ten years. Right after Maxine retired they took a two-week camping trip with the boys, but that was all.

"I'm committed now through the summer," she said.

"Six months. Then you and I get away together. Promise."

"Promise."

"No matter what you're working on. No matter what I'm working on, right?"

53

"Right."

"G'night, love."

"I love you."

Tight hand squeeze already relaxing. The darkness of their bedroom was velvety. Her loins ached. She wished she could masturbate, but it always seemed like such a piddling substitute. How long had it been for Maxine and Hugh? She was sad that she couldn't even remember the last time they had made love.

For more than five minutes Maxine lay staring into the dark. She knew she wasn't going to get right to sleep.

Prostate cancer.

The dreadful words repeated themselves in her mind, no matter what else she tried to think of. No, God, not cancer. Not my virile, handsome Hugh. She remembered bittersweetly how she used to call him Huge in bed and just between themselves when they were first married.

"Tell me again you haven't had any pain, Hugh."

He was sound asleep. Nobody with a terminal illness could sleep such blissful sleep, Maxine thought, barely able to make out his features in the dark. She reached out to touch his face, but she let her hand fall short on the pillow. She didn't want to wake him. No use their both lying awake, worrying.

You don't have cancer, my darling. What you have is far worse than cancer and far more difficult to cure. What you have is age.

Mum's right. A girl is just the medicine for mid-life blues. I can do this for this man, she thought triumphantly; I love him that much. That girl will turn him on and I'll be waiting in the wings, the happy wife ready to take over from there. She tried to remember the details of the biblical story of Sarah and Abraham. Hugh was right; Sarah should have waited. But she wanted an heir. All Maxine wanted was a horny husband. Val wouldn't even know she was playing the part of the other woman. What was her name in the Old Testament? Hagar. Whatever happened to Hagar?

Maxine couldn't remember in her growing sleepiness. Didn't she end up in the wilderness?

Just a story. Just a myth, Maxine thought cozily, ready to relax now that she'd made up her mind to get Hugh and Val together under an innocent pretext and let nature take its course.

She felt so encouraged by the prospects, she decided not to bill the girl. Two, three hours' work at the most at the county building.

She was reasonably sure she'd have the names of the accident victims by noon. She can be praying by one, Maxine thought. Praying. Sure.

She sure did wish she knew what the girl was really after.

CHAPTER 7

Tanna was off at eleven but she stayed fifteen minutes late Tuesday night to tend to some small duties connected with her former schedule and to help Bunch turn Michael. This would be her last eight-hour shift for a long time.

She said good-bye to everyone and stepped into the warm Southern California evening.

She took off the sweater she always wore at work, as she walked along the sidewalk of the street that crossed Ventura. She had chosen her small, attractive apartment within five minutes of the hospital. That was another reason she hadn't earnestly looked for another job. Often she would change into street clothes at work and not even go home, but would head for her VW and a party bar in Westwood, or more often, a dive down near NBC in Burbank.

But tonight her mind was full of thoughts about the new patient. Some of these troubling thoughts were about the primary do's and don'ts of the profession. The major don't she was wrestling with was the hardest: You cannot help them if you fall in love with them.

Everything she had learned in school and every experienced nurse she'd met confirmed that one no-no. I can help him only if I don't need him, she thought as she walked soundlessly in her crepe-soled white shoes.

Desire can so easily replace compassion. The only good nurse was one who put her patients' needs above her own. Trouble was, she always loved some patients more than others. She figured that was okay, so long as she didn't fall *in* love with any one of them. She had never worried about the gray area between the two ideas. Now she was forced to.

She reached her apartment but couldn't settle down to a TV movie or a book. She had dog-eared a page in a thrilling Stephen King novel that morning before going to work. Now any fiction seemed pale in comparison to the turn her real life had suddenly taken with this new patient.

She shouldn't feel this way about a case, one of the hundreds and no more or less important than any case in her career. It shouldn't mean so much, occupy so much of her thoughts, especially so early on in the case.

She couldn't stand it. She had to gain a perspective.

She hurriedly dressed in tight jeans, a slinky 1940 batwing blouse and spike-heel shoes. She drove the VW on the nearly deserted Ventura Freeway to the Riverside off-ramp, heading straight for the little bar where the NBC crew sometimes drank themselves silly. She'd had her eye on one of them, a sweet tall lanky boy, for several nights now.

She played some backgammon and drank a beer, waiting for the news crew to get off work and enter their watering hole. The bartender knew her; so did many of the regulars. It should have been an easy, relaxed time in a familiar place.

But Tanna was tense. She felt stirrings she thought

had been laid to rest long ago. By the time the network crew arrived, she was keyed up, and her favorite among the men mistook her anxiety for sexual heat. They left together before he finished his first beer.

He didn't even get his van started. She was unzipping his fly, down on him before he got the key in the ignition.

He was used to getting it under all kinds of circumstances and didn't protest, nor did she when he slipped his big, rough engineer's hands into the batwings to fondle her breasts.

The van rocked a couple of times and it was over.

"Um-mm, mama," the guy drawled in a Southern accent she'd missed before. He wanted to return the favor now that she'd finished him off, but she wiped her mouth and pulled away before he could get her Levi's down.

"I got what I wanted, honey," she said. By then they were behind the front seats, on a foam rubber mattress and sheepskins. She fastened the blouse with its single huge button while he stroked her crotch with a practiced thumb.

"You sure?" he insisted.

"Sure, I'm sure." That black-mama routine was handy for all kinds of circumstances. You're just here to give me a perspective, she thought.

"You'd like what I can do for your"—he was nuzzling, entering her ear with his tongue—"joy button."

"There ain't a thing you can do for me," she said flatly, looking for her purse. She didn't often refer to her secret because it challenged them; they always thought they knew what she was talking about. She had enjoyed taking this man, playing with his big clumsy puppy-dog body, but for some reason it hadn't accomplished what she'd intended to accomplish.

"Let me show you," he said, loosening her zipper.

She impulsively decided to *show* him. Let him discover my secret for himself, she thought, anticipating his surprise. Some of these TV people thought they'd seen everything.

He licked his lips as he slid the snug designer jeans down around her firm ass and parted the lace of hair.

No labia, no clit, just a rosy spoon of flesh. On his haunches on the mattress, naked, with her on her knees in front of him, he leaned back. He was speechless. He looked questioningly at her.

"Awh . . ." he said, genuine sadness in his voice. She was sure he'd never seen such uncluttered womanhood before. "Where is it?"

She brought her jeans up and secured them.

"Don't be sad for me, sweet man," she said, touching his chin.

"I was just a little baby." She was actually enjoying the telling of it, she realized poignantly. She might even cry, though she had never cried over this before. How could she miss something she never had?

"You mean . . ." he stammered, "Somebody did that"—the thought seemed too awful to articulate—"on purpose?" He'd been around. He had heard about the Arabs and what they do to little girls to keep them in line when they grow up. He could only remember the first part of the word for the operation, but he had never seen its results before.

"No, no," she corrected him mildly. "Not mutilation. I was born with an infection. When I was a few hours old they performed a clitoridectomy to save my life."

He looked relieved.

"There are compensations . . ." She bent over to kiss him, bringing his tongue into her wonderful mouth with gentle suction to show him why he shouldn't feel sorry for her.

"So, *Deep Throat* is real," he said, probably astounded for the first time since he developed his cultivated TV cynicism.

"Everything is real to somebody," Tanna replied. She slipped out through the side door and shut it gently. There was no way he was coming after her, at least for the few seconds it would take him to get his pants on.

Tanna hurried to her car and zipped home via freeway. She felt she might be able to sleep now, but she was still troubled. She took a mild Valium, reminding herself she had to be on duty at 10:00 A.M. She set the alarm and lay down.

But she couldn't get Michael out of her mind.

Being with that other man had not made a dent in the hard shell of her feelings. She couldn't sleep. By 2:00 A.M. she was dozing, but only fitfully. During one lucid period she got up and stared out of a window at the streetlight and shadows below. The night was luminous.

When she returned to the cold sheets she made her decision out loud: "If at any moment I feel I can't handle it, I resign this case." She slipped a sleep mask over her deep lovely eyes, but the darkness didn't fool her for a moment.

She lay there with her thoughts.

There had never been any pain connected with not having a clitoris. She did not feel that she, as a baby, had lost something in the same sense that Michael, as an adult, had lost something.

For Tanna it had simply never been there. There was nothing to mourn as Michael would mourn the loss of his legs.

She hadn't even known about it until her early teens when her down-to-earth mama explained it all in precise terms. She even supplied the textbooks, and they had ripened Tanna's budding interest in nursing.

"You won't miss it for a second," she could still hear her mother saying. Mama had been the victim of painful menstruation, painful sex and several painful childbirths.

"Besides, it'll keep you from making mistakes. You'll eventually find a good man and love him for the right reasons. I envy you."

Tanna was normal in every other way. Her mother assured her she would someday be a healthy mama herself with healthy children.

Tanna had immediately read about Moslem customs, and learned the medical details of her own infant clitoridectomy. With her mother's help she did not develop morbidity about her one flaw. She was kind of proud of the smooth symmetry the surgeon had left her. There was nothing repugnant about her. She was in a way innocent, unobstructed, like the smooth hollow of a pearly shell.

Very soon she had discovered the compensation—her incredibly sensitive nipples, lips and tongue. She matured thinking Mama was right about her; there was nothing lost.

Now, tired and unable to sleep with tension building in her, Tanna wasn't so sure. Until now, she had felt complete, beautiful and fully responsive as a woman. But here in the damp wrinkled bedclothes, she felt something was missing.

She thought of Michael.

I can help him, she reminded herself, only if I don't start to need him. And she repeated her vow until the mumble of her words took her down into fitful sleep.

CHAPTER 8

"Val...?"

She sat upright with the sound of the man's voice in her ear.

She didn't answer, but he kept calling her name. Frank was snoring beside her. By the digital clock it was 3:33 A.M.

"Val?"

She listened. Definitely she heard it, didn't dream it. The voice could be coming from just over there in the shadows, in those clothes she knew she threw across a chair.

"Please, help me. They've tied me down . . ."

Quietly, with exaggerated slowness, Val pushed back

the covers and got out of bed. Frank's snoring changed, and she froze, breathless, as he stirred and turned over, all the time with the man's voice in her ear calling, "Val . . . Val?"

But Frank slept like a rock.

She stepped out into the chilly darkness, needing to pee. Something had wakened her, she remembered fuzzily. As if on cue, she heard the voice call, "Val . . . are you there?"

It was unmistakably the voice of the man in the dream.

She stumbled to the toilet and sat down. The instant paralyzing cold informed her that Frank had again forgotten to put the seat down. Her butt chilled on the porcelain and she urinated with the water lapping against her backside.

"Stupid . . ." she mumbled at Frank. Suddenly that forgotten toilet seat symbolized all the problems she'd ever had with Frank. She was still half-asleep, so she just went on and peed.

Something moved there in the shadows. She caught her breath.

"Who?" she managed to gasp.

"I am Misha."

She strained to see in the darkness. What had looked like the shadow of a man crouched in a corner now looked more like Frank's bathrobe thrown on a towel rack. Faint reflected lights from a passing car gave the illusion of movement.

But, damn, she could hear him breathing. When he spoke again it was as though he were sitting on the fuzzy bathroom carpet at her feet, the voice was so near. "I'm lost. Can you help me?"

"I'm Val. I don't know if I can help you. Where are you?" she asked as she stood, shivering, feeling filthy. She closed the bathroom door lest her strange conversation waken Frank.

"I am . . . here," Misha finally answered.

Val twisted on the shower faucets. Hot. Cold. Blend hot and cold: there. That's it. She stepped inside.

61

"I was driving in the rain," Misha said as the stinging water hit Val's skin. In the dark the sensation was stronger.

She felt the pressure of a man's hand on her hip, the warmth of him standing behind her. She didn't look around; she didn't want to break the fantasy, and she knew he wasn't really here.

She could feel him all along her back, her shoulders, buttocks and down the backs of her legs. The water cascading against her helped to preserve the illusion that she was bathing with a lover.

"Can feel water on my back. I think I'm dreaming water on my back," he said in a dazed way. Then: "On my legs. Isn't that funny, that I'd feel water on my legs?" Val felt hot stinging water on her thighs. She parted her pubic hair and felt the man tasting her.

Then abruptly he was gone. She felt singularly rejected, but didn't try to reach out for him. She abandoned the water for a towel, dried off hurriedly and stumbled back to bed. Frank was snoring as though the world were in the same place that it had been a day ago, a week ago, before there was a Misha, before the world had narrowed down to Misha.

She dreamed sex dreams and in the morning there was compensation.

For the first time since the dreams started, she and Frank made love.

Frank was not as powerful a lover as Val might have desired, but this morning wasn't half bad, she couldn't help but analyze as she lay on their rumpled sheets, her belly still tingling against the wet spot their fuck had left on the bed. Frank was singing in the shower. Steam rolled out of the bathroom through the open door.

Val felt lazy, indolent, like a full tigress on a tree limb.

The sheets felt good against her skin; silky. They smelled like a nest with the sweat of lovemaking. Val snuggled, still horny, though she had been satisfied earlier. She had to admit, she always felt like that after making love with Frank. It never quite scratched the itch.

She rolled over.

The air cooled the dampness on her skin. Her nipples rippled. She slid her palm across her abdomen. Goosebumps rose beneath her hand and she knew she could come again. It needed only the pad of a finger to bring it off before Frank finished his shower. She played, luxuriating in the sensation of a blossoming flower speeded up in stop-frame animation, lulled by the sound of Frank's baritone singing a misremembered medley of Beatle lyrics.

She had the distinct, pleasant sensation that she was not alone. She knew who was near even though he didn't speak.

"Misha. . . ?"

She had not felt his presence (not counting that fuzzy dream last night) since late yesterday in the yoga class when she had had the flash memory of him pinned beneath the wreckage in the pouring rain and had heard his voice demanding that the ambulance driver call the Screen Actors Guild. He had faded away after that, and last night she did not have the recurring dream of the flying car. But Misha was with her here now.

He didn't call out as he had before. He seemed to be hovering nearby, just out of touch. He wasn't sending thought pictures. He was just there.

The thought that he was with her while she brought herself to climax thrilled and fascinated Val. Misha was here right now, watching—no—he was experiencing her pleasure.

She purposefully held back her climax to see if she could use the sexual linkage to make a closer verbal connection with him like they had yesterday. That would make the sex even better, she thought. Maybe they could use the telepathy. The possibility gave Val an added surge of will; climax was very close.

Telepathy, she said to herself, telepathy. This was

63

the first time she consciously regarded what they were experiencing as telepathy. A rational corner of her mind knew she would have to find out more, go to a library to learn what to expect from the phenomenon she had never taken seriously before.

"Misha . . . it's me. Val." She felt him draw closer. The idea of lamination came to her. She felt that his personality was laminated over hers; his transparency was red and hers was blue; the product of their superimposition was a vibrant purple, the color of blood and vital organs. Strange to have four kidneys, she mused with no revulsion; two hearts, two lacy networks of nerves and veins and vessels. Two tongues; four nipples; the palms of four hands, like the Hindu God Shiva, with the sensitive tips of twenty touching fingers. Four thighs embraced and embracing around the beating dark red flesh of her clitoris plus his penis.

She'd be able to hold off only a moment longer. She thought, telepathy: This was how it was for a man. She was surprised and delighted to find that it was pretty much the same as it was for a woman. There were differences in intensity here and there, but all the parts corresponded in the heat of lamination.

"Misha . . ." She could restrain her climax no longer. She felt the strong mental thrust from him—as close to the real thing as it needed to be. Her body was earthquake country, trembling with aftershocks. Just before the bodyquakes began she felt him pull out, with the impression that there was some kind of pain connected with his penis. But she was too far into delicious release to think about anything. The warm lapping waves started in the zone between her navel and pubes, widening in circles until the whole room seemed to vibrate with her pleasure.

It subsided and she once again reached out to her partner. Instantly Misha was there; only as a presence, though. An emotional signature and not yet a voice.

"Misha."

She felt him open a little more. He seemed to be

both calling and hiding, confused, coming awake from under drugs. He both beckoned and resisted her.

After a time she asked languidly, "Why did you pull out back there?"

His resistance was instantaneous.

"What's wrong?"

He drew further away.

"What are you afraid of?"

He hesitated.

"Trust me. Let me feel your body."

Still no voice from him, but the response was definitely no.

"I let you feel my body—why don't you let me feel yours?"

No answer, but he was still there.

"Misha, what's wrong with you?"

"They . . . they . . ." Misha's voice sounded inside her head with startling clarity. Val opened her eyes for a second just to make sure the voice wasn't Frank's. No. The shower was still running.

Misha didn't finish his thought with words but she could feel an aching sorrow from him. He was fighting to keep something from her, maybe something from himself, too, something so horrible that he could not face it. He was cringing inside a body he no longer wanted to inhabit. She could plainly detect that the accident had cost a terrible price, though she couldn't tell exactly what it was yet. But he was fighting to keep the fact of the loss as far from his consciousness as possible.

"I've been sleeping a lot," he said, far away in his misery.

Val could think of nothing to comfort him. She wondered what he had lost. She remembered with a chill that his cock had felt painful from his point of view; oh, Lord, she thought, maybe that's what he lost. No wonder he won't face it.

Maybe that wasn't it.

Maybe he was paralyzed; maybe blinded. She was

sure it was something awful, something that was the result of the accident.

"Who are you?" he finally asked as if to change the painful subject.

"If I tell you, will you let me know what's happened to you?"

"No."

"Please. I let you experience my body."

"You don't want mine, I assure you."

"I can help you. I can take it; I'm strong."

He was silent.

"Besides, don't you want to find out more about this telepathy?" Val could feel him giving more and more of his sensations to her. She could feel his arms were bound. Was this some king of kinky witchcraft game? No, his arms weren't bound, but merely restrained. Curiosity nagged Val.

"They tied me up because I tried to kill myself."

"Why?" To Val there was no rationale for suicide.

"You should see what he did to me."

"Let me see, then."

"Bastard paramedic mutilated me."

Val's heart wrenched. Maybe it was his face.

"I remember you thought you were making a movie. You told the paramedics to call the guild."

"It's a lousy script. I want off the picture."

"Are you an actor?"

Silence.

"You have to finish your contract, you know," she said, carrying the metaphor to its conclusion. "There's never any way to get out of a contract like this one. Don't you see?" Val was just beginning to see herself. "You're throwing yourself out of your body—that must be why we're connected, somehow. But it's not time for you to die."

"No way—none of that astral projection telepathy crap. Uh-uh."

"Then how do you explain us talking as plain as day like this?"

"You're not real," he answered quickly as if he had

66

been working on an explanation. "I'm unconscious. You're something my unconscious dreamed up to entertain my frontal lobes until I figure out a way to kill myself."

"My name is Leslie Valentine," she responded with equal certainty. "I was born in Glendale Memorial Hospital in March 1956. I live in a pink apartment house on Moorpark with Frank Surrell who has every intention of being a movie director. My phone number is five-five-five-HONK—"

"That's ridiculous."

"Frank figured it out to help me remember. I have trouble with numbers sometimes."

"I mean the situation. If you're real then that means . . ." He sounded frightened.

"It scared me at first, too. I'm beginning to kinda like it now." She sent him a delicious memory of the best climax she'd ever had—the one she had just experienced with him. He shied away.

"What's wrong?" she asked, afraid again that it was his cock. Just about anything but that, she prayed, anything but that . . .

"I, uh, told you. I'm unconscious."

"A catheter!" she said with relief.

"Yeah."

"Sorry."

"When it's out we'll have another go at it, okay, Val?" She received a definite furry sex feeling from him that rekindled the nerve endings she thought were sated.

"By the way, why don't you use your first name?" he asked.

"God, you're nosy. One roll in the hay and you think you own a girl."

She felt the smallest stirrings of humor in him. Nothing so direct as a laugh, not even a mental grin; just a ripple of humor that gave Val a wonderful feeling of accomplishment.

"You're going to live, Misha."

"No, not like this—" She felt a flash of the misery

67

from him, like a deep pit that threatened to swallow them both. That rational corner of her mind warned her again that this might be more than she could handle, but she pushed down the thought and reached out to hug him.

He still wasn't going to let her in on his loss.

"There are many reasons to live," she offered.

"Name one."

"We just did it—well, I just did it—but I'll bet you can enjoy it, too, when they take out the plumbing."

"A telepathic fuck."

"At least we don't have to worry about getting a colorful disease. Or pregnant."

She could feel him on the verge of getting ready to trust her, to open his eyes and face whatever he was going to have to face.

"Come on, Misha," she coaxed from the spot behind her eyes. "Come on, baby," she added aloud, not very loud, but loud enough.

"Of all the shitty—" Frank was saying, dripping water on the bed as he looked down at Val.

Fuzzily she opened her eyes, feeling wrenched, feeling Misha fade away. She had the instant, freezing awareness that her finger, though relaxed, was still snorkled down between her legs.

"So, I don't satisfy you," Frank shouted, sputtering like an angry machine. "Why didn't you tell me? Why did you have to fake it?"

He stood over her, trembling in hurt and anger, waiting for her response.

CHAPTER 9

Val rolled out of bed and stood.

"I wasn't faking, honey," she said, touching his chest beneath the orange velour towel draped around his neck. Her voice was sexy as she laid her cheek against his shoulder, "I'm just full of the devil this morning."

"It's me you're full of," Misha whispered like a breath in her mind. He was unseen but so audible he could have been standing right behind her. Frank obviously had not heard him, but Val felt a persistent image of Misha cupping his groin against her ass. For a moment, it felt like she was sandwiched between the two men, one real and solid, the other only sensed as skin on skin. It was too much. Val pretended to push back a strand of her unbraided hair to see if she and Frank were truly alone. They were, of course. "You satisfied me. Honest," she soothed.

"You're just saying that." Frank morosely toweled his thatch of Irish-brown hair.

"No," she assured him, hugging him again. "I'll take a shower and—" He suddenly grabbed her in his arms and half dragged her into the shower. They laughed and lathered each other like children until he tugged her pubic hair so hard it brought tears to her eyes and she had to beg him to stop. He pulled her close to him again, without passion.

"I don't want you to ever do that again," he muttered into the wet thicket of hair behind her ear.

"Do what?"

"You know."

She turned on the water and adjusted the temperature, then faced him, making it clear she was ready to ball again.

"No," he said emphatically, turning from her to wash the suds from his body.

"Why not? You're hard as a rock."

"To punish you," he said as he looked back over his shoulder. "You've got to promise you'll never do that again."

"I don't see why." She turned off the water.

"Because it's like you don't need me."

She stepped toward him, but he rebuffed her another time, making a definite statement with his back. He stood just beyond her reach as he put on a terry bathrobe, and didn't turn around until he had the sash securely tied. She could see his hard-on simmering down. It had to be serious for this man to deny his impulse.

"It's like you have another man on the side."

Frank never recognized his own perceptions because he considered himself rational, unpolluted by intuition. "Only worse than another man. It's like you don't need anyone."

Just expressing it was difficult for Frank. He left the room.

Val dried off slowly. She thought about what Frank so perceptively said about her having a lover on the side. She could hear Frank rattling a skillet in the kitchen and felt peaceful despite their confrontation.

It was as though Frank were outside, unable to assault her inner fortress where she had this wonderful, sexy, sad man named Misha imprisoned. . . .

She shook off the fantasy. It disturbed her. She drew two circles on the steamed bathroom mirror so she could regard her own gaze.

"Misha?"

At first there was no response, as though he had drifted off to sleep. Did he pick up on her fantasy of having him chained, all to herself inside her fortress? It seemed a kind of sick thing to imagine, and she hoped he hadn't seen it. Evidently he hadn't. She felt his mental equivalent of a yawn, then his distinctive voice, its tone implying that he had withdrawn on purpose: "I don't like your boyfriend."

The sound of his voice was again so close Val had to look around to see if he were not hiding behind the shower door or in the linen closet.

She wrapped the huge towel more closely around herself and sank to the tub edge, staring into space. After a while she asked silently, "What the hell is happening to us?"

"That's exactly what's happening to me. Hell. I'm in hell."

"And me?"

Out in the hallway Frank yelled that coffee was ready.

"Coming—" she called, then asked silently, "am I in hell, too?"

"No." Misha's voice was shaking. "I think you're my ticket out, though."

Val wiped sweat from her face and smelled with little appreciation bacon cooking in the kitchen. She could feel Misha waiting for her response.

"You're my secret valentine . . ."

He's all alone, Val thought. Except for me connected with him in this special way . . . like it was meant to be.

"You want breakfast or not?" Frank demanded from another country.

"Valentine?" Misha's voice was on edge, tinged with anxiety when she didn't immediately answer. "You still with me?"

"Yes." Val said in the spot behind her eyes and out loud, too. She felt as though she were in a no-woman's land between the two male voices, tugged in opposite directions. It felt ironic to be able to answer both Frank and Misha with the same simple word.

Yes.

Tanna, who was a few minutes late to work Wednesday morning, would have bet a hundred-dollar bill that

71

Michael was actually waking up, though he shouldn't for another twelve hours.

She had been standing at the foot of his bed watching him for the past five minutes. He was in a light sleep—he must have the stamina of a Clydesdale to reach for consciousness so soon after the double whammy he'd received

I love a fighter, Tanna thought.

And a lover, she had observed. Not many men could sustain a hard-on with a catheter up their prick. He was quiet now, though. Every second or so his lips would move, but he didn't speak out, as though carrying on a dream conversation. It gave Tanna the creeps. Once he gestured with his right hand—Tanna had taken off the leather restraint to turn him.

A moment ago he reached as if for something or someone just outside his grasp.

Now he was just lying there.

Suddenly he called, "Valentine—you still with me?" It made Tanna jump as though she'd been slapped. She stepped closer.

"Michael," she said with professional gentleness.

"Yes," he answered.

"Hello."

He opened his eyes.

"I'm in a hospital," he said, dry-lipped and drug-lucid.

"Yes." She lay her hand on his forehead; no fever. His eyes were clear. He appeared alert. She'd seen it happen before: Sometimes they just wakened.

"There was an accident," she said tentatively, watching him for the slightest sign of a violent reaction. She felt personally responsible for his suicide attempt and was not about to let it happen again.

Only his left hand remained restrained and he was awake; she might not be able to get his right hand back into the cuff, and she would have to reach past him to hit the buzzer for help.

But he was quiescent. "I remember," he said, slowly lifting his right hand above his face. The Band-Aid on

72

the slashed wrist was coming loose where the strap had rubbed it. "You don't have to tell me. I was awake once before."

Tanna reached over and refastened the tape, her breast lightly touching his bicep. He looked at her to see if she was aware she was turning him on.

"What'sa matter, honey?" She tapped his raised arm meaningfully, covering her own anxiety that he might get violent at any moment, with the tough black-mama routine she saved for problem situations. "You ain't scairda titty?"

He lowered his hand calculatingly to her uniformed breast.

"Later," she said, stepping back out of reach.

"Honest?"

Tanna regarded him frankly.

"Sure, if you promise not to try any more funny business."

With both thumbs she smoothed down the Band-Aid on his wrist to emphasize that funny business meant attempted suicide.

He pulled with his left hand at the restraint.

"You'll take this off?"

"You promise you'll be good?"

He managed a smile. "What's your specialty?"

That surprised Tanna. This one had a lot of spunk. "I guess you'll just have to wait to find out, won't ya?" she said as she licked her ample lips, laying it on thick.

"I'm not into bondage," he said wryly, rattling the bindings on his left hand.

"You've got to promise me."

"Promise." He gave her a lethargic but thoroughly engaging Boy Scout salute.

She untied the left restraint.

"I want to take a piss—the regular way," he said, looking around the room, trying to sit up, mumbling something like "honk" to himself over and over. He seemed befuddled now. He'd probably go back to sleep soon.

73

"Too early for that." She pressed his shoulder down. "Maybe this afternoon."

"A telephone . . ."

"All your calls have to be cleared through Dr. Raymond."

"Who the hell—?"

"The boss here—Sunnyrest Convalescent Hospital."

Michael laughed soundlessly at the joke, nodding as though he should have known. "Good old Uncle Lazlo and his tax write-off—"

"Your uncle's in China."

"And I'll bet I'm incognito until he gets back, right?" He snorted cynically, still trying to sit erect. He used her arm as a lever. "Look, do me a favor—" When he saw the bandages on the stumps of his legs the sight froze him.

"Uh . . . uh . . ." he stammered, gesturing at what was left. "I . . ." He pawed a little at the bandages as if looking for an itch.

She saw him starting to slip, not physically. His eyes glistened. He might faint, throw up or slug her. You never knew.

"Michael," she said earnestly, trying to gain his attention. "It's going to be okay." He would have none of it, and shook his head to indicate he knew ever so much better. But she had misperceived the emotion behind the blank look on Michael's face as he rocked forward, rhythmically scratching his legs.

"Uncle Lazlo wants to take care of this one personally," he said more to himself than anyone who might be listening. "Wants to make sure I'm going to be a good boy, play the hero, bring no shame to the family." He snorted again. "The old fart may even turn a buck on this." Now he gently rubbed the bandages.

"He's due back tomorrow," Tanna said lamely. She felt out of her depth; Michael was referring to deeper, older wounds than the merely physical.

"How long have I been here?" There was something snakelike, even wicked in the glance he threw sideways

74

into the nurse's eyes. He was patting the stumps now. It was a childlike gesture.

"Three days."

He looked calculatingly down at his stumps and back at her again. "It's been longer than that. The ends are itchy. I'm healing."

It was chilling to Tanna that he showed so much purpose while on so much medication. She decided that it must be the result of the trauma; he was reacting as though he were still in physical danger, and he had the unnatural adrenal strength and perception of a soldier whose life is on the line on a battlefield.

"Well, how long since the accident?" he demanded shortly. She realized this man was used to having servants, getting immediate service, encountering no frustration.

"Two weeks."

Tanna stood as she said this. She was watching his every move as if she had caught his continual, electric vigilance. What am I getting myself into, she wondered to herself.

But her face was serene and beautiful, professional.

When Michael saw her standing away from him he reached out in a swift, accurate clasp that lightly encircled her hand. They were still like that for a moment. All that moved between them were their eyes locking together; no words were necessary. Tanna knew she could easily pull away. His hand was only gently imprisoning hers. He was doing it on purpose, asserting dominance right away.

She didn't move to free herself.

"Well?" he asked.

"Well—?" she managed to bridle, injecting her voice with black-mama strength. She pulled out of his grasp with more force than necessary and put her offended hand on her hip in a sassy grind: "What?"

"Are you going to get me a telephone or not?" he demanded.

"All your calls have—" she started to rattle off by rote.

"That means incoming calls, sweetheart. To keep the sweating masses out. Come on." He waited. "Consider it therapy."

"It's against orders. Sorry." At first he didn't move, then he suddenly looked away from her in a sudden mood change, a symptom of the battle he was waging against the drugs. It must be exhausting for him. Empathy snared her again; she stepped closer in her desire to help him.

"He didn't have to do that," he said unexpectedly, looking beseechingly up at Tanna, who was frozen by his hypnotic eyes.

"I could feel my toes." He sounded perfectly rational. "I could feel my toes but he cut off my legs anyway."

"People often feel ordinary sensations instead of pain with this kind of injury. It's shock."

"Bastard," he said, giving no indication he had heard her.

"It's going to be okay," she said, reaching to touch his hand.

"Call that number for me," he whispered hoarsely. He touched the plastic label with her name on it. "Tanna," he said with satisfaction. "What a lovely name. What a lovely lady."

Tanna knew in the cells of the marrow in her bones she could help this man, that she wanted to help him no matter what.

"What's the number?" she asked.

"Uh," he said, thinking, letting his head fall back. "Five-five-five-HONK." He was really tired now. He was chuckling as if to an enervating joke. "You get it for me."

Tanna moved the phone and jack cord from a credenza. She saw herself in a wall mirror, and saw Michael watching her with heavy-lidded eyes.

"Who do you want to talk to?"

"Just get it, just get it," he said with mild impatience.

"Don't you tell anyone I'm doing this." Her heart was pounding.

"Five-five-five-HONK," he said dreamily.

Tanna punched up the number and handed the receiver to him. It rang a couple of times before a man answered.

If a man answers . . .

But Michael couldn't hang up. He had to know. The memory of Val's voice was too real. He had had intuitions before, hunches that certain people were going to call just moments before the telephone rang. He had always had a phenomenal kind of left-handed luck that got him out of bad places in the nick of time. Sometimes he felt he could read women's minds especially, like a book. Not so well with men; not so well with Uncle Lazlo, for instance, but there had been a couple of times when he knew what the outcome of a deal would be before it was even suggested. Maybe telepathy.

But never anything like this. Like goddamn radio. He bit his lip remembering Val bringing herself off and him riding her body, feeling every sensation as if he had been right there with her—hell!—as if he had *been* her.

No, Michael couldn't hang up when the man answered.

"Who's this?" the male voice growled.

"Uh, Val at home?" Michael asked, expecting the guy to say there was nobody there named Val. Michael felt the words come out too fast. He was suddenly hyperventilating like crazy, feeling crazy, totally bananas, crazy and crippled and too foolish for anything but pity.

He closed his eyes so he wouldn't have to see what that bastard did to him and listened in the dark when the man on the other end of the line said, "Just a minute—"

Michael blinked and nearly dropped the phone.

The nurse, Tanna, was looking at him as though she

77

expected him to grow tusks. Jumpy as hell. Great bod. Positively prehensile lips, the sweetheart.

You dumb jerk, you've just used telepathy to screw some chick—sure you did, and they just painted the White House purple! Look at you, sitting here like a frog after someone's dinner, like some shit traffic statistic, and all you can think of is getting into the nearest female—

"Hello?" The voice that interrupted his careening thoughts was hesitant and distorted as phones make human voices, not nearly so clear as it was on their own intimate channel; but Michael knew with certainty whose voice it was.

"Hello?" she said again.

"Val—" he blurted on top of her hello. "It's me, Michael."

"Who?"

"It's me. Misha."

There was a long silence. For a second he thought the connection was broken, but she finally said, in another tone of voice entirely, as if a different conversation were in progress, "Yes, Randy—"

Michael detected the unmistakable click that meant someone had just picked up an extension on the line.

"Of course I can meet Brenda at one. How about the Blue Earth in Westwood—? Good. Bye," Val said formally and hung up.

Michael held the phone receiver for a second, then started laughing to himself.

Tanna took it away from him as she tried to hear what he kept repeating. "It's the craziest thing, it's the craziest thing," he said, but it was hard to understand the words because he was giggling so strangely.

CHAPTER 10

So it was real.

She had been pretty sure before but now she was certain. She wasn't having a breakdown. It wasn't a sick fantasy.

Benign satisfaction settled on Val. For the first time in what seemed like years, she felt calm, rested, perfectly in tune with the music of the atoms around her.

Misha is a real person, she thought triumphantly, a real person connected with me as certainly and as unequivocably as daylight is to dark.

Every yearning in her abundant heart, reinforced by thousands of movies and rock songs, was in sympathy with this new reality: She had stumbled onto her soulmate.

The concept had mesmerized her since early adolescence. The idea that one day, out of the blue, she'd turn around and he'd be there, just as thunderstruck as she. They'd take one look and move unimpeded toward each other through a crowd of strangers. They'd touch and never be apart again.

But none of the men she'd met had been *the man,* so Val had always deferred the dream, allowing the attractions of other men to dazzle her for intense periods of several hours to a few months. She truly loved each of these other men in some special way—the way she loved Frank at this moment even though he was ugly as he surreptitiously hung up the kitchen extension.

It didn't matter, suddenly, that he had been eavesdropping on her. The serenity that certainty brought Val invaded every nook of her being, washing out all negative judgments from her. All her life she'd been waiting for this moment, waiting for *him.* She certainly never expected that he'd come by telepathy. Her mother did confide to her once that she and Val's father often anticipated each other's words. Val heard the same thing from other couples, though people were sometimes reluctant to talk about it. Many love songs seemed to be expressing the same idea, that people who are meant for each other were connected in more than a merely physical way.

It was supposed to take years to happen, though. Here was Val, basking in the joy of having it out of the blue and she hadn't even met the man in person yet.

She must've had a funny look on her face because Frank was looking at her strangely. He shrugged when he realized she had been observing him eavesdropping.

His shrug, like a guilty child's, touched Val deeply. She understood Frank was confused and frightened, just as she had been up until a moment ago when she heard Misha's voice on the phone.

Wordlessly she met Frank in the kitchen, feeling only the most tender emotions for him, but knowing there was going to be no way out except to hurt him, eventually. She had been with Frank two years, longer than she'd ever lived with any man. She looked at his face, snagging his eyes with her own, seeing perplexity there.

"I'm sorry, baby," he said into her ear as he held her. "I'm sorry I was sneaking around on you. It's just that you're acting so funny."

She patted him affectionately on the back, but didn't speak. As he hugged her she idly touched the dirt in her hanging plants to see if they needed watering. They didn't.

"I feel like you aren't being honest with me."

"You don't trust me?" she said, pulling away from him.

"I trust you, but you're acting funny. I just want to know what's going on. I'm worried about you." He had a way of slumping down, although he was taller than Val, and looking up at her kind of hangdog, round-eyed and suppliant. It was too blatantly an appeasing

80

gesture, an irritating way for him to try to appeal to her.

She broke away from him and sat on the chair near the window where a puddle of sunlight warmed the seat. She put her hands around the mug of coffee he had set before her place. Steam tickled her nose. The sun felt good on her thigh.

Frank left the room but quickly returned with a kimono. He tossed it to her and went back to the stove.

"Nobody can see me," she said, but put on the robe.

"You're acting crazy, I tell you—running around naked, talking to yourself, staring into mirrors—it's creepy," he said, fussing with the eggs. It chilled her to think he must have been watching her when she was alone in the bathroom talking to Misha. That probably looked pretty weird.

Funny, she didn't mind Misha spying on her in a far more intimate way. . . .

Misha, she called silently, are you listening?

She could not detect his presence and that made her sad.

"So, you're meeting Brenda for lunch," Frank said over his shoulder, trying to change the subject and sound casual. He managed only to sound uncomfortable.

"I guess you know that. You were listening."

Frank looked helplessly at her. "So I apologize." He found a spatula and returned with it to the stove. "Don't order quiche. You can't eat like that. You're gaining weight."

Val regarded him in what had to be a new light. She wondered if Misha were also watching behind her eyes, but she still could not detect that he was with her.

"Find out why Brenda lost that toothpaste gig for you—rattle her cage—she didn't push you after that breakfast cereal gig."

"She has something for me at the Valley Stage."

He looked at her piercingly, taking a stance that broadcast disdain. "A *play?*"

"It's a chance to work with some terrific people—

81

that director who did that thing you liked so much at the Beverly Hills Playhouse. I'd get to do a Tennessee Williams lead—"

"Val," he interrupted, gesturing with the spatula. "Stop. Think: no money. No audience. No real exposure. Nothing. Zilch."

"Prestige—"

"Okay. Prestige. Strictly small beans, girl."

"But a lead."

"Brenda is paying off some old crony, throwing you away." He slid an egg onto a plate and placed it in front of Val. "Make her explain why she didn't swing that toothpaste ad for you. Eat your egg."

He took a basket of brown vitamin bottles from a shelf and set it down beside her plate, then proceeded to take out B-complex, L-Glutamine, vitamin E and a mineral combination. He took the caps off.

"I'm not hungry."

"All your appetites are satisfied, huh?" he cracked.

"Frank, drop it."

"Promise you won't do it anymore."

"How can I promise a thing like that? I mean, my whole life's ahead of me—"

He slammed his fist onto the table with enough force to topple two of the vitamin bottles. Capsules rolled all over the table and onto the floor, but he ignored them. "I can't stand it—knowing you do that after we make love," he roared.

"I'm sorry. I didn't do it to hurt you," she said, trying to catch a white capsule as it rolled off the table edge. "It's just a harmless diversion."

Frank let his shoulders slump minutely, still leaning on the table where he had hit it.

"No reason for you to browbeat me," she said, "to force me into some stupid promise—to listen in on my phone calls. Hell, Frank, you know I'm working my ass off. When do I have time to fool around?"

He slumped further into a chair. "I know you're working hard, baby. It's just that, well, a man has his pride."

"You mean to tell me you never jacked off, not even once in the time we've been together?"

"Well . . ."

"Okay. So, get off my back."

He reached for her hand. "I'm sorry."

She patted his hand perfunctorily.

"I know," she said as she stood. "You always are."

"You haven't eaten."

"I'm late."

"You don't meet Brenda until one."

She fanned her fingers in the air. "Nails. I told you I'm having them porcelainized at ten."

She left the kitchen, scooping up several of the vitamins that hadn't rolled onto the floor.

Frank stared morosely after her. He roused himself, hating himself when he was at her feet like this. He looked into the hallway where her shadow moved across a wall as she dressed. She lifted her lovely arms and slid into a shirt, and the sight of it thrilled him as much as it had when he first met her.

I'm so crazy about this woman, he thought miserably, I get it on just having her shadow near me.

"Val," he said and made a tentative move to go to her. The moving shadow stopped him, busy with some small gesture. She was humming in a contented way that did not include him.

"I love you," he said. But she must not have heard him because she didn't answer.

Tanna put the phone back into the credenza.

Michael had stopped giggling and seemed to be settling down to sleep it off. Whomever he had so briefly spoken to on the phone had certainly boosted his spirits. Tanna regarded the man she was going to spend sixteen hours a day with for the next few weeks.

He was drowsy.

"Before you go to sleep, Michael . . ." she said. She twisted the window shade rod to close the narrow louvers, and approached the bed. "You've got to turn over."

"No."

"You've got to." She slid her silky hands under his back between the cotton hospital gown and his skin. She felt a film of electricity between their separate flesh.

Come on, girl, she reminded herself, thinking of her vow. But she knew it was already too late.

"Help me, baby," she urged, her fingers pressing up into his back muscles, gently massaging against his weight. He was strong, in amazingly good shape considering what he'd been through. UCLA had taken good care of this patient.

"If you don't turn over every couple of hours you'll get decubitus . . ." She purposefully loaded her throaty voice with dire implications.

"Don't like the sound of that one," he muttered under the arm he had flung across his face.

"Bed sores."

She gently slapped his hip in the direction she wanted him to turn. On his stomach all his energy seemed to flow from him. His eyelids fluttered. He found one more giggle on the edge of consciousness. "Craziest thing. Secret valentine . . ."

His circulation was good. The buttocks were firm—not as much tone as she'd bet he was used to keeping; from the shape of the thigh muscles, she'd guess he ran a lot.

That's going to help you get back on your feet again, she thought, immediately struck by the inaptness of the expression. Still, maybe he could do it. If anybody could, this body could. She knew of a couple of bilateral amputees who had accomplished the arduous, painful adjustment to two artificial legs. But without knee joints the task would be Herculean. The best results he could hope for would never approximate normal unaided walking. But, she countered to herself, anything was possible with the new technology and a determined human spirit.

When she retied the restraints on his wrists he groggily protested. "You promised."

84

"Only until the doctor says it's okay," she said softly.

"Don't leave," he commanded, groping for her hand.

"I'm right here."

"I'm so cold. I've been cold ever since I got here."

Tana shivered. He was right. These places were always cold, even the newer ones like Sunnyrest. She pulled her sweater around her shoulders, and went to the closet. She unfolded a blanket over him, sickened anew at the sharp dip in the covers where his strong legs should have been.

"It's my feet that are cold," he said, just about out. "Isn't that funny." A mirthless chuckle. "My feet are cold."

"I know," she said, bending so she could whisper in his ear. "Sweet dreams, darlin'."

CHAPTER 11

"Love the sign, hon—it's dignified," Hugh was saying as they entered the back door of Maxine's new office. It was dark and cold in here after being closed up all night. As she removed the key she looked up with a groan at the sign the painters had finished on the window.

There was a long, elaborate curlicue on the last *s*.

Hugh walked to stand in front of the window beyond which Ventura morning traffic already whizzed. "Yes." He nodded emphatically, to Maxine's unseen distress behind him. "It reminds me of the Declaration of Independence." He went out of the front door and stood outside nodding his approval.

"Oh no." She stared at the sign. "That bastard . . ."

"That sign is perfect for this office and location," Hugh said as he reentered.

85

"You really think so?" She stared at it again.

"Yeah. Wouldn't say so otherwise."

"Well . . ."

"What's wrong?"

"The curl on the *s* seems a bit much to me."

Hugh regarded it again.

"I like it. The effect seems just right. Like I say, dignified." He ambled over to the wall socket Maxine had been trying to fix the day before, taking off his suit coat along the way. He draped it neatly on the back of a chair and took a screwdriver set from one pocket.

Maxine went to the phone as she continued to frowningly regard her new sign. She found a number in a desk index and punched it quickly, watching the sign as though she expected it to crawl away.

"You bent the screw, honey," Hugh said over his shoulder.

The number she had dialed put her directly into an office in the Van Nuys County Building, one of the most frequent numbers she used. She spoke a bureaucratic code that slipped her through to the exact desk she wanted. "Station reports," she said, walking up behind her husband, who was on his knee at the outlet. "The hardware store won't open until ten," he said as he glanced at his watch.

Waiting for her connection, Maxine said, "I guess I can just put a file cabinet in front of it. . . ."

"No," Hugh replied, standing. "Might as well fix it now." He touched her elbow. "Let's go get a cup of coffee—"

"Hi, Connie—" Maxine said into the phone. She took Hugh's hand and led him to the counter in an enlarged closet where she had put the coffeepot. Hugh looked dismally at the coffee fixings—not what he had in mind.

"Yes, Connie—If I can get on this right away I can finish my first official case on my first official day." She walked from him toward the desk, where she found a stubby pencil and the back of an envelope. "Why, Connie, that's terrific—congratulations—when's the big day?" A couple of pauses more and she got to the point. "I'm trying to run down a station report from one of your paramedic units—probably a fatality, maybe two. Happened during the storm, one night, let's see—" She glanced at her record-calendar to see what might have been a date. The girl said one of the last nights of the storm. "It might be the twentieth or the twenty-first," Maxine said when she saw a note on the page for the twenty-first that she connected with the rain—she had had to drive Ben to his clarinet lesson at four that afternoon, had made a note to pick him up if it was still raining. It had been the worst night of the storm but the last, Maxine remembered.

"Yeah," she continued. "I figured it wouldn't be in county records yet. I knew you could help me, tell me at least where I might start."

She glanced up at Hugh, who stood looking between her and the wall socket. He reached out and tried the light switch but nothing happened. He scowled at the light fixture overhead.

"Okay," Maxine said, listening intently, then jotted a concise note. "Okay. Connie, you're a doll." She hung up and grabbed the notepad.

"Is that the toilet I hear running?" Hugh asked, his head cocked.

"The sink leaks. Just a faucet. Hugh, if I get over to Connie's office immediately, I can go through reports for the last three weeks. She'll be processing them for the rest of the morning, then they disappear to be eaten by the computer, which may take days." She was finding her purse as she said this breathlessly, heading toward the door. "How long do you figure you'll be here?"

"Hell, I might as well fix everything that doesn't work," he said as he walked toward her.

"You're so good to me."

They met in an easy embrace.

"Got to get my girl launched right."

She leaned against him for a moment, allowing herself one more hug. "I've got to get out of here. Thank

87

you—" She looked up at his face. His collar was tucked. Gently she straightened it and gave him a kiss.

"Oh, that girl—Val—she's supposed to be here at ten-thirty. I should be back, but if I'm not, tell her I'll have the information she wants by noon."

He looked agreeable. "I'll be here until about eleven, I suspect," he said, listening to the drip from the bathroom.

Maxine closed the door between them and walked quickly to her car. She felt excited, a little dangerous. It had been almost too easy.

Val thought for sure as soon as she was alone in the car she would feel Misha reaching out to her. But it was very quiet.

She called and got that open-line feeling in her head, but Misha wasn't on the other end sending back. It was as though he were *there* but not *here*. Like he was asleep in the same room and not available for interplay.

"Misha, are you sleeping?" she asked out loud.

No answer. She was driving the switchback curves of Coldwater Canyon now, as though she and the old Citroen were on a well-worn track. This was her favorite route for getting over the hill and into Hollywood or Westwood.

Val tried not to worry about Misha's absence. This is the time to think clearly about what's happening, she told herself. The thought of Westwood reminded her that she wanted to go to the UCLA research library. She hadn't done much reading since graduation from the Theater Department nearly five years ago, but she had kept up her alumni membership so she could take books home. Maybe this sort of thing happens more often than she knew. She knew the university was doing sleep research and laboratory work on ESP. Maybe telepathy wasn't so strange after all.

"We can talk to each other," she said out loud to collect her thoughts, "but only when we both want to. He's not with me all the time; no need to worry about that. I'm not with him all the time. He can prevent me from feeling his body and I can do the same with mine."

But, she thought with a return of the thrill of it all, we're still connected, like a bond has been forged. She called to him again, in her mind, and received a fuzzy image she was sure was from him; a woman bending over him in white. The image was gone and the feeling was left behind, like an aroma or an aftertaste. Something about a broken promise: You promised not to tie me up again.

A nurse. A hospital. Val concentrated, letting the hypnotic hum of the car carry the thoughts. There was little traffic on Coldwater this late in the morning; she was supposed to meet that detective at ten-thirty. That gave Val more than forty-five minutes to drop in to Brenda's office and cover herself with the lie she told to Frank.

She considered what she was going to do about Frank. Best to wait, she told herself, until I find out what's wrong with Misha. She knew, though, that she wasn't going to stay with Frank, not now. It would never be the same with him again.

Misha?

Still no answer, but she could feel him near her, a kind of floating feeling from him. Sure, she told herself, he's sleeping. But he got the message about where I'll be at one. We can finally connect in the flesh.

She was feeling edgy at the weirdness of what was happening. It would be good to get this thing on a real footing, on a down-to-earth basis.

Brenda's office was just minutes away.

By the time she pulled into the little parking lot behind Brenda's gingerbread house, she felt calmer, even though Misha was still not in contact with her. She had come to the decision that she must find out who he was. Maxine was her best bet. She'd get a complete name.

Michael, a woman's voice had called him in the vision of his childhood, lost in the snow. Misha must have been a baby name. But his real name was Michael. Michael Christopher something. She could almost remember from the vision. Why did she have the persistent feeling she knew him from somewhere?

She shut off the ignition and looked up at the high window of Brenda's office above her.

The window, from the inside, was a jungle.

The 30-by-60 louvered window in the old house above Sunset faced northwest, the preferred exposure for many houseplants. Spiders, ivies, Charlies and their traveling companions, the Wandering Jews, completely curtained the only window in the huge beamed room that had once been Tallulah Bankhead's parlor.

These exuberant plants were watered weekly by one of the Beverly Hills extras, a maid from Dinkman's, and that was it. They had never been trimmed, clipped, pruned, edited or disciplined in any way. The only law these plants knew was to occupy as much glass surface as could be snatched from a neighbor. Only centimeter chinks amid the jungle admitted the peachy O. Selznick light. Real spiders, the arachnids, lived here. One old-time TV writer who had been Brenda's client since "Your Show of Shows" had sworn he once saw a grass snake insinuating itself along the peduncle of a spider plant, taking a last bit of pleasure from the westering sun. He had never been able to prove it, but a snake in Brenda's window wasn't hard to believe.

Behind the green snarl of survival, no doubt relishing the metaphor, sat its authoress, the agent Brenda Felicia Padron.

The daughter of a Filipino princess and a German diplomat, this woman was rumored to have come to Hollywood with one of the big-time German directors. But, the story goes, Garbo took one look at Brenda's screen test and vowed that if this child stayed, then she, Garbo, went. Brenda was supposed to have been that incredibly cinegenic in the thirties. Now all she had left were those bones, those magic cheekbones, and this great old house overlooking the Strip. For forty years she had been an agent, was actually one of the inventors of Hollywood agenting by practice if not by patent, mostly for actresses and dancers who specialized in musicals, and later, inevitably, commercials. She kept a few writers in her stable—like the man who saw the grass snake—but that was mostly just out of cronyism or curiosity. She'd made her reputation with young, perfect girls, the crème de la crème in a town used to sour milk, chalk water and Cool Whip.

At this moment her regal, thrice-lifted face and her outlandishly mu-mued person occupied the Chippendale wing chair in front of the Louis XIV table she made her desk by sheer dint of will against the disarray of scripts, portfolios, dog-yummie cartons, theater programs, publicity packages, paper-clipped contracts and hundreds of scribbled memos. She was also on the phone.

"I see, I see," she was saying, her throaty Marlboro voice husking into the ivory telephone receiver, talking to the vet about Bruno, her Yorkshire terrier, who was dying of cancer.

It was ironic that she told the vet, "I see, I see" because that was probably more correct than if she had said, "I hear, I hear." While she had turned her phone amplifier up as far as it would go, she still could only barely hear what he was telling her. At that the man was screaming; his tinny voice coud be heard across the room, and still Brenda was frowning to catch a word or two.

Randy, her secretary, came in softly in his $200 kid Gucci's, wrinkling his nose and forehead at the squeaking noise from the phone. Most of the time he did the phone work, since Brenda's hearing had gotten so bad. But about Bruno, her precious baby, she wanted to speak in person. Randy stood waiting respectfully beside his boss's flowered and flounced elbow. She glanced up, indicating with her huge eyes that he should speak.

Knowing she was only reading his lips anyway,

Randy whispered with exaggerated pronunciation, "Here's the Latimer contract—messenger just brought it."

She nodded—she had caught the most important words.

"Frank Surrell is on the other line. Should I get rid of him?" Randy asked her in a loud stage whisper. He was paid a great deal of money by Brenda to put up with her eccentricities. He loved his job, and so he didn't rock any boats by suggesting, as did her last unfortunate secretary-assistant, that she should get a hearing aid. Everyone around her knew that Brenda would pretend she did not understand when that suggestion was made. She was an expert lip-reader, and mostly ran into trouble on the phone.

No, no, Brenda gestured, closing her eyes, suspending her long, dragon-blood-red fingers in the air. "I'll talk to him," she mouthed, took a long drag off her cigarette in its practical, filtered holder and listened for exactly ten seconds more to the verbose vet.

"Very well, Dr. Manz," she intoned, signaling that the conversation was at an end. "Good day to you," she said deliberately and put down the phone button.

"Lemmie speak to the asshole," she continued to Randy, dropping her voice another octave and settling in as if for a feed. As she listened she glanced up at a TV set across the room, its sound turned off. She was only superficially interested in the "Price Is Right," which was just starting. She left the set on throughout the morning, through "Password" reruns, and "Family Feud." She'd glance up with mild interest when a pretty woman's face flickered in a commercial. But not until eleven-thirty would she take out the padded Koss headphones—the only way she could hear the program. "It was "Search for Tomorrow." From then until one everything on her schedule would hang. Randy knew to get all morning business taken care of before eleven-thirty—all afternoon business commenced after the soaps went off.

"Frank's on nine," Randy said, exaggerating as he

always did for Brenda so she would understand him. There was only a trace of fashionable lisp in his voice as he took himself and his silk ensemble out of Madame's office.

"Frank, dear heart, what can I do for you?" She always spoke very forcefully into the phone to encourage others to do the same.

"When you see Val at lunch today, tell her to give me a call, okay?" he yelled. Actually she could hear Frank's baritone fairly well, but out of spiteful habit she made him repeat.

"What's that, dear?"

It infuriated him, but he complied.

Brenda had never understood what Val saw in this lump of a man. Maybe he would, maybe he wouldn't ever be a director. Who was he, anyway? Oh well, Brenda sighed, at least he had kept the girl balanced. That was Brenda's client philosphy: Find them a rock of a personality—preferably a man—to feed them, keep them anchored to the ground and get them to rehearsal on time. At least Frank Surrell had served that purpose for one of Brenda's favorite clients, in whom she saw a lifetime of 10 percent of many residuals.

"Sure, Frank." She had no idea what he was talking about, but she could smell a squeeze a mile away. She flipped through her daily calendar to today, Wednesday. Lunch was taken up with the developer over at Akashic Records. They had some new money and were out to diversify from MOR rock into commercials to make more use of their recording artists. They had already cut singing commercials for several area radio and TV stations and were ready to try out commercial products. They'd gotten a couple of accounts and had to make them good or lose them.

Because of Brenda's love of soaps, lunch never started until one-thirty. Her clients were well enough established that she could indulge her soap addiction.

"Any other messages?"

"Be sure she leaves the quiche alone—you are going to the Blue Earth, aren't you?"

93

"Huh—?"

"The Blue Earth—you are going to the Blue Earth?"

"I don't know," Brenda said sharply. "Val's taking me." She allowed a tone to creep into her voice that indicated without doubt he should get off the phone.

"Oh?" was all Frank said. Brenda was trying to keep it general. "Well, make sure she gets the low-cal plate or something."

"Anything else?" Brenda's voice dripped disdain, but she was mildly amused at his unsophisticated attempt to pump her. And mildly annoyed at Val for putting her into this position without a warning. Still, she liked the girl and was always glad to help her. She did wonder what was going on, though. Was Valentine getting ready to dump this turkey? Nasty way to go about it. She'd have to have a talk with her. Frank was one of those shifty-eyed creeps who'd go berserk over something like this. Val seemed to think she operated on some kind of magical immunity, as if she believed she were charmed and not liable for her mistakes.

"Naw," Frank said suspiciously.

"Very well, darling. Good-bye," Brenda signed off and hung up on him before he had time to add anything.

She was surprised when she looked up to see Val through the glass partition that separated the outer office from Brenda's own, behind a huge hanging batik that allowed Brenda to see out but nobody to see in.

"Val, darling," Brenda said suddenly over the intercom. Val looked up as if to the voice of God and walked on her practiced dancer's legs into Brenda's office.

Now, Brenda was nearly deaf, but she had the eyesight of a falcon. Even through the batik she had seen that Val looked like hell. Shadows under her eyes as if she hadn't been sleeping well. Her mouth was drawn down, death for a woman who must be photogenic.

Even like this the girl was incredibly beautiful, not in the classic way, but in a warm, American way. The fatigue she obviously was feeling gave her a wan, wistful look that was not unbecoming, but it was certainly not the current zestful, brimming aliveness that was the bottom line in commercials these days. Too Victorian, like a blurred old photograph.

"Let me guess," Brenda said coyly as Val walked closer. "You want to take me to lunch."

Val looked surprised only a second, then figured it out.

"To the Blue Earth, I suspect," Brenda finished.

"My agent is getting psychic on me," Val responded with a conspiratorial grin.

"So, sister, what's going on with your love life?" Brenda cracked, slipping into her mother's native patois. Brenda had been educated at the best girls' schools in Europe but used her mother's island persona when she wanted to intimidate. The exotic never failed to intimidate Americans.

"That's a funny question to ask me." Val took a chair close to the ornate gilt table. She knew of Brenda's false pride about her deafness; like all those Brenda let close to her, she respected it and made it as easy for Brenda as possible.

"Frank sounds like a cheated man to me."

Val had a funny look on her face but she said, "No."

"Well?"

"Are you going to let me take you to lunch today?" Val asked.

"You may. Of course, I won't be there." Brenda fluttered her calendar pages. Val had a sudden insight into Brenda: She brandished the calendar like a weapon—the old law in Hollywood was: "You're only as important as the person you'll have lunch with today."

"Previous appointment. Maybe I can get a job out of it for you. Akashic is going into the commercial business. They snagged a big oil company account so it's good-bye rock and roll, hello thirty-second spots."

"Frank doesn't want me to do that play."

95

Brenda shrugged. Inside she was furious. She had schemed to get Val into the director's mind, and now that dumb shit Frank could blow it all.

"Oh," Brenda said without a trace of her feelings about the play. "I'm to make sure you don't order the quiche."

"He *didn't*—"

"I'm to make sure you get the low-cal plate."

"Thank you," Val said, bowing a little. She knew Brenda wouldn't let go of the play that easily. She'd wait for another time to push it.

"There's something at Ritcher and Raye tomorrow morning. They're looking for a girl your type to do a series of dog food commercials." Brenda regarded her directly. "Ever dance with a dog?" She scribbled a memo.

That funny look on Val's face again. She hadn't taken it as a joke, which she could have. She took it as Brenda had meant it, meaning Frank. But Val didn't say anything, and for once Brenda couldn't read her. She was keeping it close, whatever it was that was bothering her. She reached for the slip of memo paper in Brenda's claw.

Brenda held on to it. "Do you need to talk to me, Valentine?"

Val shook her head, but still Brenda held on to the note.

"You look like you need someone to talk to, sweetie-pie," Brenda said smiling cadaverously. "What's going on?"

"What could possibly be going on? You're keeping me so busy." Brenda barely caught that because Val looked sheepishly away, so her lips could not be read.

"I told you your luck would change when you started calling yourself Valentine."

"You're always looking for ulterior motives," Val said. She took the paper, memorized its message and put it in her purse.

"How long I know you?" Brenda demanded. "Two, three years. I never see you look the way you do—

your hair's a mess—why do you insist on those childish braids? Look at your nails. Not caring."

"I have a lot on my mind."

"Is it going to get in the way of work?"

"Have I ever let you down before?"

"No, but I see signs." She regarded her client suspiciously, her exotic eyes wise and white-rimmed around jet black irises. "A girl comes out here, struggles until some people pay some attention to her, then she goes off the deep end. A man. Drugs." That's what Brenda suspected, actually.

"Something. Alla time something."

"You know I'm not into anything kinky."

"So you say." Brenda shrugged. "Look, sister—my mama was what you call a sorceress in her country, you dig? A *bruja*. Anyway, she got the evil eye, the second sight." She stabbed her own chest with a dagger fingernail. "Well, I got it too." She walked cannily, slinkingly, around the table and pushed aside a pile of papers with her ass and sat down. "I look at you and I see something." She took Val's chin in her hand, tilting it for the best light.

With her other hand she drew a circle in the air over Val's face. Val, during all this, was mesmerized as she always was by this woman, part sophisticate, part witch.

"I look in these eyes and I see something different, something strange." She stared dramatically into Val's eyes. "What is this thing?" she demanded, leaning back for a moment, giving Val back the use of her face.

"I don't know what you're talking about," Val said a little testily. She was never comfortable under Brenda's scrutiny; this time the old girl's remarkable accuracy of perception scared her, but she'd be damned if she let it show.

"The camera will see this strange thing, I think," Brenda said with an oddly gentle inflection. She was farsighted, so she gave Val another once-over, leaning even further back over her desk to get the child in focus. Val looked surprised; ah, yes, Brenda thought with the delight of a hawk spotting a gopher. Now I have her admission that something is happening—not in words but in her honest little face, which has this way of telling all. "You are surprised that I say the camera will see your new strangeness?"

"The camera will see exactly what I let it see," Val answered quietly. She had decided a long time ago that these people would never tell her how to do her work. Only her own instincts and her director would tell her what acting was or how to go about it. Parasites like agents, business managers and promotion men were hired. She must keep in mind that people like Brenda, no matter how commanding their counsel, worked for her and not the other way around.

Brenda was undaunted.

"You are a brilliant actress," she said, matching Val's soft tone, foregoing the tinsel endearments and native song-and-dance in favor of plain speech that Brenda hoped would convey her genuine concern. To prove that she was sincere she vacated her superior perch on the $5,000 table and drew up another chair so she could face Val on an equal basis. "I am proud to represent you, but I do not only consider you a client. You are my friend, and I hope I am yours. That is why I say I am concerned about an alteration in your personality that is clearly evident."

Part of Brenda's charm for Val was her ability to slide in and out of her native accent. Now she sounded like a diplomat, well-oiled and polite.

"I've just been working too hard and sleeping too little." Val relinquished that much information under Brenda's relentless probe.

"Don't mistake my meaning, child. I see this difference in your eyes that is frightening to me—see here, it is putting goosebumps on my arms." Sure enough, Val saw gooseflesh rising along the woman's hairy arm. "Old stories in my mother's country of Luzon in the Philippines tell about the *anito,* the ghost-who-walks, the spirit that finds a lonely person to haunt. If I did not know better I would say the ghost has found you."

98

"That's the most insane—" But Val was trembling.

"You have bad dreams, yes?"

Val was amazed.

"I thought so."

"You go to church and say fifty Hail Marys. Light a candle."

"Brenda, that's superstitious nonsense."

"Maybe so. You listen to what I say."

"It's only that the dreams keep me awake. I'm just not getting enough sleep."

Brenda pawed around in a desk drawer and came up with a gold chain that had a small medallion on it. "Here," she said, offering it to Val. It was a lovely piece of workmanship; Val couldn't remember Brenda ever giving her a gift. She took it gladly.

"A Saint Christopher's medal—why thank you, Brenda. It's beautiful." It looked very old, very gold. Probably an antique.

"You keep it. *Wear* it. It keeps you safe. And you will get your hair done before the dog food thing." It was not a question.

"Sure." Val backed out.

Brenda regarded her favorite client as she departed. Frank was wrong, Brenda decided. If anything, Val was losing, not gaining weight. She had a haggard look about her.

Brenda ground her teeth together; perhaps she should not have scared the girl. Perhaps she should have been more gentle. The agent stood and walked to her jungle window. With a dragon-blood-tipped finger she parted the veil of Wandering Jew foliage and peered out, still bruxicating noisily with her expensive dentures, her eyes glittering like a snake's.

Val was getting into her car. Must talk to her about that heap. She's getting too successful to drive around in such an old car.

Was it too early for a Mercedes? Probably. She was making good money but not the big time yet. Until Val dropped the cutesie-pie act she'd never get mature parts. She was still playing teenagers.

Damn, Brenda snorted. She wished she could get Val a nice juicy soap character, something that could become a launch vehicle. Brenda's antenna always vibrated around Val. She was sure the girl had star-stuff. But she had that innocence, and now was probably into something weird, probably drugs, Brenda suspected. She knew Frank was into pot and probably coke. Brenda had a low regard for directors. Persons who always wore blue jeans were low-lives in Brenda's estimation, without the true glamor of Hollywood. All of them were on something. He'd probably gotten Val on to something. In addition she had a stubborn streak that was positively self-destructive.

Brenda remembered with a shudder a party once when she overheard Val tell a producer how much she someday wanted to direct. Brenda had immediately pulled her client aside to read her the riot act.

"Never, never, under any circumstances repeat what you just said to that man."

"But I do want to direct someday."

Brenda hushed her.

"Never again. Such a remark means the kiss of death to an actress in Hollywood."

"It means I'm serious about my work," Val had countered. "It means I'm smart—"

"Smart-ass is what it means. Look, sister, these men—" Brenda had gestured with her ten red daggers at the posh Beverly Hills room choked with good-looking or ugly, but powerful men, and the few, mostly beautiful women among them.

"These old boys have no intention of admitting women directors except as tokens. No matter what the feminists do. Long after they have elected a woman president, these men will oppose women directors. Remember that. Never express a desire for it. They will call you a ballbreaker and blacklist you."

Val's eyes had narrowed with independent spirit.

Brenda held up five fingers. "This many women directors," she said, pausing dramatically, then adding with a flourish, "on the whole planet."

100

Val opened her mouth to speak: She knew of at least twenty women directors with network credit in the United States.

"Grow balls if you want to direct," Brenda replied, stopping her.

Val saw that she could take it or leave it. It was not a point of argument, and Brenda never heard her express a desire for the ridiculous, unfeminine aspiration again.

But she knew Val would defiantly jump at the chance if directing were ever offered to her.

Brenda remembered that defiance now as she looked out of her window. The agent stood gritting her teeth, watching Val down below toss the Saint Christopher's medal across the rearview mirror with casual disregard.

CHAPTER 12

One compensation for taking the shit a successful independent TV producer had to take was being chauffered all over Beverly Hills and environs in one's own silver blue Rolls-Royce Corniche, equipped with a $17,000 video system and a wet bar.

Lazlo Evan Stafano eyed the little TV screen where millions of small dots were adding up to one big headache, sipped his brandy and thought of the unfortunate accident that had befallen his asshole of a nephew.

Ms. Peach distracted him momentarily by jiggling her expensively shod foot. She was scribbling numbers into her ever present notebook as she watched the screen where fragments of Lazlo's first feature movie were transferred to tape for editing purposes.

He looked away from her, staring out through the filtered glass of the car window at the passing palm trees. Not only was he struggling to pull this picture together—the first U.S. feature to be shot in China in forty years—now he had to deal with Michael. For this reason he had cut short his China stay. He had planned to come back Thursday, but Peachie got him a flight a day early. Just thinking about his nephew—who was also his fifth son, by adoption—made Lazlo Stefano's ulcer hurt. If the kid had been a bastard before, he was going to be nothing short of a pain in the ass now. Best thing was to ship him off as quickly and as quietly as possible to Geneva. The question was how to get Michael to go along with the plan. Too bad the little shit was so uncooperative, after all Lazlo had done for him. Could make some hay out of this accident. Ever since he had heard about it, when Peachie called him in Peking via diplomatic telephone, Lazlo had been beating his brain trying to figure a gimmick. He'd heard about a Texas sailor who'd lost both legs but was petitioning the government to give him captain's papers anyway because he could get around on his boat so well. If Lazlo could sell a pilot, it would kill two birds; give the public the kind of offbeat hero they could love and pity, plus get Michael work, which he'd need now. Otherwise, best to keep him under a lid. He was bound to shoot his mouth off. The money-eating hospital Lazlo bought eighteen months ago was finally paying off. Peachie proved her worth with that idea. If he spilled the beans there, it would be to hired employees who could be shut up. Old Raymond would say or do anything to retire in peace. Certain of Lazlo's bookkeeping practices would be of interest to several governmental agencies. He shuddered to think of Michael telling these secrets under sodium pentothal.

Since some of those questionable bookkeeping practices were used with Michael's name as an employee with phony overtime compensation, it was in Lazlo's best interest to keep any secrets Michael might divulge in the family, so to speak.

These thoughts had put Ms. Peach's boss in an uncharacteristically quiet mood. He turned his gaze from the passing panorama of the city back to the TV

102

set. He nestled back into the rich chamois folds of the seat cushion. Inside the cool yachtlike luxury of the moving car, a hidden vibrator hummed as it went about its business on the tight muscles in his upper back. All the time in China, this was what he missed most. This was really the only pleasant thing he had to come home to.

Since Rosa's death a few years ago, Lazlo had turned all his energy to solidifying his company's position. For the past five seasons he had averaged two hit series per season, the result of hard work, unadorned cannibalism and the bookkeeping dances the rest of the industry copied the way they copied his shows. Almost everyone who knew him hated Lazlo Stefano. He prided himself that he owned their fear.

"What about the accident?" he finally said to Peachie. "Did Aaron check out this guy who did this thing to my nephew?" He was referring to his first son, his attorney. His second two sons, Simon and Leo, were his accountants and Philip, his fourth son, was a PhD candidate to the Annenberg School of Communicatons at USC where he was doing theoretical work on computers and rating systems.

"He talked with the paramedic who got Michael out of the wreckge."

"Are we going to sue the fucker?"

She shook her head emphatically.

"Aaron says there's no doubt in his mind," she reported. "The doctor who supervised the paramedic confirmed it. At great risk to himself, that medic saved your nephew's life."

Lazlo made a sour sound.

"Here's Aaron's report—those are copies of the original document Aaron intercepted. For a hundred he got to a county clerk before the data went into the computer. We let the information on the dead girl go on through." Peachie watched Lazlo for any appreciation of the quick and efficient coverup his son and she had achieved, but the old man was grimly silent.

"The insurance settlement was generous," Peachie

went on. "Her family won't make any trouble. Michael probably just picked her up in the barrio someplace."

To that Lazlo scowled deeper. Peachie agreed with him. The uncle she was rather fond of. The nephew was something else.

Michael possessed the one quality which would do Ms. Peach in. She wanted madly to fuck him, and he knew it, so she never would. It would have given him power over her, which, if combined with the uncle's power in a friendly, normal uncle/nephew way, would greatly curtail the power Peachie had over Lazlo. Therefore, Peachie loathed Michael, and made sure she encouraged war between the two men. She had already arranged standby medical, all first-class of course, for Geneva. She knew Lazlo and other members of the Stefano family went there for rejuvenation and plastic surgery. Michael's own nose had been broken and reset to create a more cinematically he-man image. Geneva was the logical place to send the prick for recuperation. A nice long recuperation.

Peachie was a little worried about Lazlo as she covertly watched him staring at Aaron's report. All the way from LAX he had been subdued like this.

She knew he was mulling over whether to press for action against the paramedic and the entire county. But, always the pragmatist, Lazlo would accept Aaron's cool analysis. He had no intention of taking on the county of Los Angeles unless there was hope of winning. He finished Aaron's report.

He looked at her, or rather at her ankle.

"God, Peachie," he finally said slowly, "you've got great legs, you know that?"

She stopped jiggling her foot.

He sighed, bringing to that sigh the sound of hundreds sighed in vain before it. As far back as he could remember, about the only thing he had wanted and had not been able to get, was into Peachie's pants. It was a bewildering phenomenon that he, a rich and powerful widower, had not balled this woman. In his

104

worst moments he figured he was finally starting to get old.

Peachie favored him with-the merest of glances over her clipboard, as bewitching as any geisha over a fan.

"I'm all but puking on those rushes," she said mildly, to change the subject to something as equally unpleasant but not as discomfiting to herself. It wasn't that she was glad this had happened to Michael, but as far as she was concerned it couldn't have happened to a nicer guy.

Lazlo regarded the flickering TV screen, while Peachie thought about his nephew. This should take the arrogant prick down a peg or two. Something he couldn't buy his way out of like he had all his spoiled, indulged life. Peachie's own childhood in the slums of Baton Rouge fed her vehemence against him.

When Lazlo finally spoke, Peachie had almost forgotten that she had put down the rushes, the raw, uncut film of his colossal dream project. Since Lazlo had worked on a movie about the Boxer Rebellion in the early sixties, he'd dreamed of producing the blockbuster, definitive picture of China's great upheaval.

"It's my lead. He sucks," Lazlo replied. "Look at him. This is a picture about the Chinese Revolution— he makes it look like 'Star Trek.' Well, we can save it in the cutting room."

He looked away from the screen in distaste. Outside a bunch of rowdy black kids on minibikes advanced on the Rolls as the chauffeur pulled into a crosswalk. The kids couldn't see inside, but one of them ogled Lazlo's shadow in a grotesque parody of someone looking into a fishbowl. Then the little shit flipped the regal finger at the automobile's occupants. Up front on the other side of the interior glass partition, the driver floored the monster, showering the punks with gravel and burned rubber.

Lazlo Stefano absorbed the little bit of street theater, expelling a long-suffering Serbian sigh that must have come down from his great-great-grandfather, and stared out through the celebrity-shielding glass. Peachie almost felt sorry for him. It was times like this when she almost bought Lazlo's con. He seemed burdened by the weight of world history and the disrespect of smartasses.

But, Ms. Peach quickly, silently reminded herself, Lazlo Stefano's Byronic moods always preceded terrible, bloodless beheadings, devastated careers and even a suicide or two along the way. She had told him of Michael's attempt when he got off the plane. It had, of course, infuriated him. He insisted they immediately drive out to the valley and see the kid, unannounced. "Show him I'm there in his hour of need, all that crap," was the way Lazlo had put it. He was willing to let bygones be bygones if Michael would cooperate.

"We haven't spoken in six months, you know, Peachie," Lazlo reminded her. He didn't have to. She had been in the office during that last violent argument between Lazlo the producer and Michael the actor, that had left the open wound between them she hoped would never heal. It had been Michael who stormed out of the office, refusing to do any more of the dumb-shit scripts his uncle chose for him. He wanted something serious to sink his teeth into, some great part that would put him through his beefcake phase quickly into his leading-man phase. But Lazlo refused to change a winning run. He wanted to put Michael into more action adventure parts, with as little clothing on as he could get by the censors.

"Are we there?" Lazlo asked, suddenly impatient in one of his mercurial mood changes. Peachie ascribed her boss's personality to his being a double Gemini; she knew to steer clear of him when necessary.

"Soon," she replied.

Lazlo reached decisively and switched off the TV set.

He stared at the dimmed tube for a moment, pouting like a Buddha. "Gimmie what's-his-name—who's cutting this turkey, anyway?" He had gone through three editors in two months on his revolution epic.

"Mark Shapiro," she said officiously, hiding behind

her cool façade the hot fear her boss of twelve years could still put into her. She knew instinctively he must never see that fear. The uncensored, raw power at his command was like a vacuum which sucked in all life forms unfortunate enough to get in his way.

"The one you chose personally," Peachie said lightly.

She glanced professionally at her notes as if tallying running times, skillfully avoiding Lazlo's eye lest he observe a trace of doubt: Because he was taking so long to respond to her dig, she was afraid she might have strayed too near Lazlo's undefined but unbreachable line. She owed her remarkable employment record to gunner-timing, flawless organizational ability and an uncanny knack for turning the little word *no* into an art form. As long as she kept him off her bones she could move around him almost as she wished.

He had not yet interrupted his observation of the most expensive real estate on the planet whizzing by his window. He had insisted on buying Michael a present—hence the side trip down Rodeo Drive on the way to the hospital. Lazlo thought a nice watch would do, one with a stopwatch function which would imply to his nephew that he was thinking of future professional use, despite this terrible accident. After all, blood was almost as thick as contract ink, wasn't it? He and Michael shared both. Lazlo wanted to say he'd give Michael a job, some kind of a job.

Lazlo still had not responded to Peachie's remark about his chosen editor. Now he slowly pivoted his dour face in her direction, taking exquisite care in leveling a dramatic, woebegone gaze—much like Orson Welles, he imagined, at his most tragic when the Hollywood philistines were tormenting him. Lazlo nodded sagely and made low, assertive noises in his throat. "*Et tu*, Peachie, *et tu?*"

Peachie gave absolutely no hint she ever doubted her own instincts. She was looking up a phone number. "Ah," she said brightly.

"Here's Shapiro's number," she said. Warmed by her power over this ugly little man, she reached across his space for the telephone. He relieved her of the receiver with the most openly provocative stare he could muster as he watched her breathing. After a moment the other party came to the phone.

"Mark, my boy," Lazlo said with resinous sweetness just sticky enough to blur the distinction between invited guest and entrée, "come up to the office for lunch."

At first there didn't seem to be anyone in the detective's office. Val tried the front door, even tapped lightly on the window pane beneath the completed sign. She was about to turn away when she saw a shadow of a man standing in a far corner and then a bit of his elbow behind a door frame.

She saw that the back door was open, so she walked around the small building and into the open doorway, calling, "Halloo," to the man she had seen.

He called from another room and they met in the main office area, she blinking in the gloom after the bright sunlight, and he holding a screwdriver and a handful of washers.

For a second he stared at her as if utterly surprised. Then he said, "You must be Val—Maxine should be here any minute."

Val smiled and he smiled back, then got self-conscious and looked down at the tools in his hand. He gestured toward the bathroom. "Fixing a faucet—" he explained.

The tall, distinguished-looking man stood grinning at her, his expensive shirt-sleeves rolled up, with plumbing tools in his hand. "Oh—I'm Hugh—" he extended a hand, saw the grease from his work and pulled it back. Meanwhile Val reached out to shake hands with him, so she was left with her hand sticking out.

"Hugh Wise. Maxine's husband."

Val nodded, looking around.

"The ceiling light doesn't work. That's why it's so dark in here."

"Am I late or early?"

He glanced at his watch, then looked back at her.

"Right on time."

"Do you have any coffee?"

"Oh, sure." He gestured at the alcove where he had plugged in the coffee machine. "Matter of fact, I think I'll join you—" he said, dropping the screwdriver and knocking over a stack of Styrofoam cups.

He laughed to himself and bent to pick them up. The girl stepped back. He noticed particularly how nice and long her legs were even though she was a petite woman.

"Well, there has to be some creamer around here," he said, opening drawers.

"Okay for me. I take it black," she answered, pouring a cup of murky liquid into a cup.

"Me too."

She sipped and he sipped.

"Maxine's checking out some facts about your case."

"Oh, she's working on it already?" The girl appeared interested; she leaned a little closer.

Hugh walked into the office and sat at the chair behind the desk where Maxine had placed the row of family portraits. "My wife's really good at finding people," he said, "and you, uh, your case, is kinda special to her," he said, watching that perfect face for a trace of emotion. It was distracting that she was so compelling to look at; she seemed very open, almost childlike, but he knew that was almost always manufactured. She must be in her late twenties, old enough to have lost real innocence. But she certainly knew how to act it unless she really was that way. He found that hard to believe in one so beautiful and an actress by profession.

She looked puzzled. "Why special?"

Hugh cocked his head and looked shyly away. "I think, now that I've met you, that you remind her of someone. Also, you're her first official case since she went into business—that's officially today," he laughed. "That is, if I can get the lights to work."

"Who do I remind her of?" she asked, a trace of

frown between her lovely eyes. Hugh thought he might have detected some distress in her question. What was she afraid of?

Hugh looked at the family pictures of himself and the boys. "There's one missing," he said, looking puzzled; he knew how much Maxine adored that portrait of their daughter Melodie. She had kept it with her since the child's death, the only memento of her.

"Anyway," he continued, looking at Val with what she thought might be a wistful glance, "on first appearance, with your hair braided like that, you look like our little daughter Melodie." He gestured at the pictures. "I don't know why her picture isn't out here . . ." he added, thinking. It just occurred to him that Maxine might have put Melodie's portrait away on purpose. That combined with her reaction to what he had to tell her last night—maybe she was more depressed than he thought. Opening the office had been a strain on his wife, who worried more about her family's health than her own. He just couldn't think of any other reason why she would leave Melodie out like that.

"Is that good or bad?"

"Melodie died of leukemia when she was eight."

Val sighed and sat back on an office chair. "I'm sorry."

"No, please; I didn't mean to make you sad," Hugh said, almost jumping to his feet.

There was no way he ever wanted to distress this girl. There was something about her, something he could not pin down. It wasn't so much that she resembled his daughter, whom he knew he had romanticized in his memory. Val didn't look like the child close up. It was just the braids and the pointed chin that did it. Close up she looked entirely womanly; but with a sweet openness of a child still hiding inside. Hugh had never met a woman over nineteen who had that quality. Val did, and he thought that was what reminded him, and probably Maxine, of their dead child.

She was saying something about the loss of a child.

"I mean, I've never had a kid, but I can imagine that's the worse kind of loss in a family . . ." Her voice trailed off apologetically.

God, I'm staring at her like a fool, Hugh thought.

"Well, I think I'll get this back in and clean up," he said, heading toward the bathroom. Val followed.

She stood in the doorway, looking down at him gently as he bent over to do the work.

"Now, I'll just turn the water back on," he said, reaching for the faucet handle beneath the sink. It wouldn't budge, so he applied a wrench to it. The old metal crumbled in an explosion of spewing water that drenched him and hit Val in the face. They both made noises of exclamation and bumped into each other in the doorway trying to get out.

Hugh ran slipping back through the office to the open back door where his gestures said there must be a main shut-off valve.

Val stood in shock, her arms out as sheets of water still sprayed behind her in the bathroom. Evidently Hugh had been successful because the spray diminished to a trickle.

Every surface in the small bathroom was dripping water. There was nearly an inch on the floor at one end. A large stack of toilet paper rolls was drenched.

Val turned from surveying the damage as Hugh reentered the office, still slinging water from himself. He looked up at Val sheepishly. "What a mess," was all he could think of to say.

She stood grinning at him, every curve of her body accentuated under the sopping clothes. Her grin widened and she burst out laughing. It was contagious and he joined her. It felt good to laugh with her, to make fun of a dismal situation that he was going to have to remedy in the few remaining minutes he could spare; find a plumber who could make an emergency call. Probably was going to cost an arm and a leg. Shit. What were they charging now—$50 an hour, $15 bonus for emergency?

Damn. This business venture of his wife's had already set him back nearly $50,000, what with the office lease and a car and a thousand incidentals. It was worth it in the long run; Hugh had complete faith in his wife's ability at her specialty. He'd often considered she had some kind of psychic ability, she was so good at finding people. She hated that, of course, because she detested anything occult. But Hugh believed in her; had insisted she go into business, and now, he chided himself, was no time to worry about money. Not when there's this glorious girl within arm's reach of me, laughing, giggling, holding herself with such pleasure.

Just then the phone rang.

"That must be Maxi," he blurted, bumping into a chair as he caught it on the second ring. "Hon—" he said quickly, then, "yes, she's here now." He looked over at Val, who was trying not to laugh. Hugh started laughing again.

"No, it's okay—I just this minute busted a pipe under the sink—" He paused, mouthing no, no, as if soothing a child while Maxine said something Val couldn't hear.

"No, no, everything's fine, sweetheart. Don't worry, I'll get a plumber—" He glanced at Val and had to turn away to keep from laughing again. Behind him, Val exited through the front door. As Hugh listened and replied to his wife, he watched Val as she went to her car and removed her gym bag. His eyes followed her as she walked quickly, still drenched to the bone, back across the proscenium of the front window the way Maxine had watched her the day before.

"It's just a busted shut-off valve. No big deal," said Hugh, moving to keep Val in view as she approached the open door. She was taking a towel from the bag as she entered. There were goosebumps on her arms.

She rubbed her face, chest and arms then handed the towel to Hugh, who took it with a beaming smile.

"Yeah," he said into the phone. "Sure—love you— here she is—" and he abruptly handed the receiver to Val, whose teeth were chattering.

112

"Sorry I stood you up," Maxine said, "but I think I've found out something funny about that accident—"

Val's face and demeanor changed abruptly from relaxed joviality to concerned interest. The goosebumps stayed. Hugh noticed the change and stood drying his shirt as he watched her.

"I found a death certificate that is dated two days after the report of the accident in which the death occurred—the body was found downstream at the bottom of a canyon on Mulholland Drive."

Val didn't move.

"The flood took the wreckage of a late-model 450 SL about a quarter of a mile before it lodged against a debris dam. That's why it took so long to recover the body."

"Who was it?" Val asked, thinking to herself, oh no, is it possible that Misha is dead? For a horrible moment, there flashed in her mind the old ghost stories about a person who is dead without realizing it. Maybe that's what was happening. . . .

"Girl named Jan Hernandez," Maxine reported crisply. Val slumped with relief onto the desk chair. She sat openmouthed and chattering, her mind racing, listening to Maxine. What had Misha called his passenger? She remembered the first dream in which she heard voices, the dream she had had while parking out in front of this very office. She looked at the curb where a delivery van was now parked. In the dream, Misha called his passenger Jan.

"They don't think she was driving, yet I haven't been able to find paperwork on any other person from this accident. You sure there was a man driving that night?"

"Yes," Val answered simply, feeling the weight of evidence behind that small word. There was no doubt in her mind that there was a man driving that night.

"Well, I'm going to talk to a paramedic who was on duty that evening. It was the twenty-first, by the way."

Val nodded dumbly.

"Val?" Maxine said in the tinny telephone voice.

113

"Yes, I said, yes. That's great, Maxine. You sure do work fast.".

Behind her, Hugh walked back into the bathroom.

"I think I can have the name of the driver by this afternoon. Can you come back to the office about three?"

"Sure—"

"Oh, I found out one more thing," Maxine added just as Val was about to say good-bye. She was freezing and could hardly wait to get to the gym and put on some dry clothes. She had about an hour to kill before going to the Blue Earth; even if Brenda couldn't make it, Val wanted to be there so Misha could call her. Might as well use that hour at the gym; Tuesday's yoga class started at eleven.

"What?" Val asked.

"The Mercedes—it was maroon, by the way—belonged to a movie production company."

"Which one?"

"Stefano Productions. Does that mean anything to you?"

CHAPTER 13

The name fell into place with the solid fit of the last piece of the jigsaw puzzle. Stefano. Michael Stefano.

"The whole family's in the business," Val managed to say, making it sound like shoptalk. "The old man sees himself as a kind of tycoon of tit-and-car-chase TV shows. His nephew is Michael Stefano, an actor. Works primarily for his uncle, except for the last six months. There's a running feud between them. The nephew is under contract but the old man is pissed at him and won't put him in any show. That's one story. The other story is that the nephew got smart-ass when he was hot and refused to do any more of his uncle's schlock shows. He tried to buy his contract, but the old man is trying to teach him a lesson in familial obedience. Meanwhile the nephew hasn't worked in six months. He's living off residuals."

Her mouth was running on automatic. Inside she was having conflicting emotions about this disclosure. She'd never met Michael Stefano, but what she knew of him didn't attract her. "Of course," Val said when she realized Maxine did not have the additional information of a first name, "Stefano has some other sons, I think." It sounded lame.

Val took a deep breath, wondering if Maxine had hung up or was simply listening intently. "I guess that's what I wanted to know . . . no use you spending any more time on it, since his name is all I need."

"You think it was this Michael Stefano? Don't you want to find out what happened to him?"

"I'll bet he's in a hospital someplace . . ." Val said smugly.

"Still . . ."

"Thank you, Maxine. You've been great."

"Still, I'd like to find out who's keeping the lid on the accident. You'd think a celebrity like that, the newspeople would eat it up. Eric Estrada, Ann-Margret, Jim Stacy, Richard Pryor—when they got hurt it was big news. But I haven't heard anything about this man."

"Well, Michael Stefano isn't that well known. He only starred in one klinker of a series—I forget the name, 'Buddies' or 'Partners' or something like that."

"Then who would want to keep it quiet?"

Val considered that one. "Maybe Michael Stefano."

"I guess you're going to go say an Ave Maria for him and the dead girl," Maxine said.

"This must seem like religious mumbo jumbo to you," Val said.

"No, it seems like bullshit," Maxine replied calmly in the phone receiver. Val looked at the detective's husband hanging his damp shirt on a hanger. He picked up the towel and started drying his bare chest. Actually he wasn't at all bad-looking for an old guy. He had a trim figure, though she guessed he was probably at least fifty-five. She wasn't good at guessing ages. "Did you hear me?" Maxine asked.

"Yes," Val replied. "You think I'm lying."

"I think you're not telling the truth," Maxine said pleasantly in Val's ear. "There's a difference."

"Right now I'm reaching for my checkbook. How much do I owe you?"

"A day's fee. One hundred. My only expense was a twenty for the information from my contact." Maxine's voice was cool.

"I'll leave it with your husband. Thanks again, Maxi—I really appreciate it."

Val hung up the phone and picked up her things.

"Well," Hugh said as he walked in from the bathroom, "did you find a time to get together?"

"You were right—she's really good at finding people. She found the name I was looking for." Val handed him the check. "I told her I'd leave this with you, Mr. Wise."

"But—"

"Thank you again."

"I'm sorry about the mess—"

"No problem—my gym is right next door. Nice to meet you."

"Yes—same here, uh—"

But she had closed the door. Hugh walked to the picture window where the sign painters had put his wife's name in gilt letters.

He watched Val hurry in her clinging garments to the door of the woman's gym. He sighed and chewed on a finger he had nicked with the wrench, wishing there was some way he could see that girl again.

As she hurried to the gym she was trying to contact him. She called his name over and over in her mind.

116

She was so distracted she had to pause to remember her membership number as she signed in.

She hurried to the locker room, still calling him in her mind. "Misha . . . Michael . . . where are you?"

He might have been there. She could feel his presence, like before, but he was either shutting her out or was asleep on a level where she could not reach him. She listened as she peeled off the soaked clothes, listened for his voice.

She put the skirt and blouse she was wearing on a hanger she found in the locker and asked the gym attendant if she could hang the outfit up in the laundry room. The heat there would dry it by the time the yoga class was finished.

She climbed the stairs with a line of other leotarded women, found a place in the dance studio and settled into the lotus position. She was glad she had come here; she desperately needed the serenity of the stretching exercise. The teacher put a record on the stereo and set the needle in place. Soon the dim room was filled with the shimmering sitar music. She stood and began the exercise.

She let her body follow the Salutation to the Sun as she'd done a thousand times before. Her thoughts were somewhere else, probing, probing, calling out to him.

"Misha . . . ?"

She was in the front row of women doing the slow dance of celebration to the sun. In front of her was a floor-to-ceiling wall of mirrors.

She felt something. She'd snagged a thought from him, a slippery moving thing that was hard to hold on to. He was on the verge of waking, drifting. She was sure she heard the word *toe*.

Val closed her eyes. Instantly in her mind, through half-open eyes, she could see a glow that was not present in the dark dance studio where she was working out. The eyelids fluttered; beyond them she could see bars of light and shadow on a tiled floor.

She knew she was riding his body as he had hers.

*   *   *

117

Michael lay without moving on the bed. Soft morning light slanted through the window, sliced into light-dark-light by louvered blinds pulled halfway up. His eyelids fluttered but he was completely awake. He had been awake for several minutes. He could hear orderly bustling noises through a doorway slightly ajar to the right.

He was alone.

He was thinking about toes and how he'd never given much thought to toes before. From somewhere in the past, probably from his Aunt Rosa, he knew the French word for toe, *le bout. Ou est le bout?* Where is my toe? He repeated the phrase in his mind, over and over. The toe is in the boot. *Le bout est dons le bote. Bout*, boot. It seemed funny so he laughed because it was so depressing to think about the answer, *le bout n'existe pas.* French made it sound better than English: The toe is no more.

"This is not happening to me," he started to wail, but heard something that left his cry unfinished.

"Misha . . . ?"

Omigod, he thought, so I didn't hallucinate her—the phone call, that goofy number, those things I thought were dreams . . .

He closed his eyes and the next moment was looking out through fluttering eyelids from a low perspective in a dim room. Vaguely he could see a wall opening into reflected walls . . . mirrors.

"Val?"

"Misha . . ."

He knew he was inside her head looking out through her eyes. He saw other moving female shapes around her. Val was working out in the front row in a roomful of mirrors. For the first time he was dimly aware of what Val looked like. Her reflected self was a beautiful body, small-boned, but strong, with glorious legs and a good face that would age very well. He especially liked her hair.

"I was afraid I had lost you," she said slowly in time to her movements. Her voice exuded relief.

118

"No," he said, resigned. "I'm still here." In this room, he thought to himself. Most of me is here. He was having trouble keeping awareness at arm's length. Pretty soon he was going to have to throw off those covers and confront what that bastard paramedic had left him.

Val felt all this emotion boiled down into a concentrated lump of misery and self-pity from him. It was only edged with pain. Michael suspected they had lowered the dose of medication they were giving him. It was almost impossible now to sleep; the effort was giving him a headache. He was starting to feel a dull tension around his knees, not agony, not what he might have expected. Were he playing this as a rôle, he would surely have gone for the drama of pain. But the mundane reality was more like a pulling tension, a muscle cramp.

Val was stretching, back arched, arms high overhead. Her entire body tingled with exertion.

"Oh," he sighed in her mind, "it's so good to feel toes again—"

"Misha—you're hitchhiking on me." She didn't say she was also riding him.

"Feels so good."

"Misha, you should ask me before you do this." Her voice inside his head was insistent. He could distinctly feel all the toes on his right foot the way he had felt them right after the accident. He could wiggle them, but he couldn't feel any of the rest of his lower legs. Just his right toes. The toes were not in pain. Pain he could have understood. But this prickling sensation was more terrible than pain because he couldn't relieve it. It was infuriating suddenly to be tickled in this manner, as though his right foot were covered with ants. . . .

"Ugh—" Val whispered in revulsion, slapping at her right foot.

She was struggling to scratch her foot on the carpet; she would have sworn there were bugs crawling all over her right toes, as though she had stepped into a bed of ants.

119

Her little outburst—she was still kicking her foot—brought her looks and whispered admonitions to be quiet from the other yoga students, so she left as quickly and as quietly as possible. The inclination to scratch was irresistible. In the alcove she rubbed the top of her foot along the carpet. The yoga teacher saw her leave, but cast her eyes back under her lids, as serene as a twentieth-century female Buddha can be.

"Val?"

She heard his incongruous voice in her inner ear as she walked, favoring her right foot, which still prickled. There weren't many women in the gym this early in the morning, but even so the locker room reflected a cross section of the population in this varied community on the north side of the Sepulveda Pass: young, old; healthy, ill; fat, thin and lots in between.

"Sorry," Misha said.

"Were you responsible for that crawly feeling on my foot?" she said out loud, immediately catching herself. An older woman nearby thought she was speaking to her and she smiled in response.

Mustn't start talking to myself, Val told herself. They'll lock me away for sure.

She lifted her foot onto the bench between the lockers and began vigorously scratching all around the toes and instep.

The woman stood staring at her while scratching one pendulous breast. She was probably in her late sixties and must've had a formidable bosom when she was younger. Now her tits looked like cantaloupes in loose bags that hung nearly to her navel, a testimony to gravity. She was grotesque but fascinating because she appeared totally unselfconscious here in her haven of the gym. Val loved this about the place. It was truly a sanctuary here, where a woman could separate herself from the organized, perfumed, fabricated world of men outside. In here it was all flesh, peacefully somnolent and asexual. Not only did all this undisciplined anatomy not offend Val; she loved the place because no judgments were made here. Svelte girls who worried

120

that their clavicles were too pronounced (as yet a fatal flaw untouched by cosmetic surgery) and heavy great-grandmas who only worried anymore about germs, co-existed here.

This woman was a germ worrier, Val detected immediately. She knew exactly what the woman was thinking seeing Val scratch her foot like this.

"Foot went to sleep," Val said apologetically.

"You're supposed to wear thongs at all times in here," the woman laid down the law.

Oh well, so much for Val's idea that this was a sanctuary of nonjudgment. She smiled and nodded and the woman ambled off, her towel thrown around her shelf of shoulders. There was something simian and lovable in her stroll toward the showers.

She could feel Misha's reaction was quite the opposite. He saw nothing lovable about the old woman.

"What'sa matter?" Val asked archly in her mind. "You only want to see one kind of woman, the young and beautiful? The other kind of woman, the others with stretch marks and the old used-up grandmothers, you don't even want to think about."

Oh boy, Misha thought to himself in a place Val couldn't hear. I have to get a feminist. Just my lousy luck.

Val felt something from him, not words. The feeling she got from him was disgust.

Val was alone for the moment in the corridor between lockers. Then another woman stepped onto the scales a few feet away at the end of that row. She moved the weights with a shapely arm, but Val could plainly see when she lifted her hand to move the weights that she had only one breast. The neat scar of a mastectomy lay on her empty chest just above the nipple line. The remaining breast was firm and young; the woman could have been no more than thirty. She unselfconsciously found her weight on the scales and stepped out of sight.

"Isn't it terrific that she has accepted her body

despite that operation?" Val asked, sensing some kind of message there for Misha if he would just listen.

She felt a choking sensation from him, like a rising gorge of revulsion. "Mutilation is an obscenity," he said tightly. "She should hide it."

"Seems better to me that she accepts it and goes about her life."

"Nine people out of ten would say that, but those same nine look away when they see someone like that."

"Is that what you're afraid of, Misha? That I'll look at you and turn away?"

"Most people will. You did it yourself—"

"What are you talking about?"

"You saw a crippled veteran collecting for wheelchair basketball in Westwood the other day. He called out, 'Hi, beautiful,' but you just looked away."

"How do you know about that?" She was ashamed; he was right.

"I . . . I don't know," he said, sounding genuinely perplexed.

Val was removing her leotard. She was sorry she had not been able to finish the yoga class, the second in a row she had cut short. She had decided to steam a while, spend a leisurely time in the Jacuzzi, then go to the library. No use bothering with the Blue Earth, since Misha and she were in contact without the awkward instrumentation of the telephone.

"I've been to that restaurant," he said after a while.

"I knew you were going to say that," Val said quickly. "I had a flash memory of you walking through the restaurant door with a beautiful girl."

"You can see my memory."

Val turned to face the tall mirror between lockers.

"We really are reading each other's minds," he said in wonder.

She had the strange sensation of being herself and looking at herself as someone else. She had once had a similar feeling, creepy and weird, the first time she saw her image on a TV screen. But this was even stranger, because she could feel the other person slipped inside her body.

"I want to make love to you," he said. "Like we did before."

"I . . . I can't." She looked around. "Not here."

"Go sit on one of the jets in the Jacuzzi. Pretend it's me fucking your brains out—"

She grinned at the mirror, at him watching through her own eyes. She turned around slowly, letting him admire her, sensing his lust. With her back to the mirror, she looked coyly over her shoulder, some of her hair veiling her face. She reached out with a pink tongue and licked a strand of it into her mouth. Then she turned slowly around, still sucking on the strand of hair in a classically provocative pose right out of *Playboy*. She couldn't know it but he hated that, her sucking on her hair like a toddler or a whore.

"Don't do that, baby," he said.

She used the strand of hair as a brush to stroke her cheek.

"It's like a little kid . . ."

She pouted. "You don't like me?"

"Oh, I like you, all right."

"Tell me who you are. I want to know who wants my body."

She felt a warm glow between her legs. If she weren't looking, she would have sworn a man's penis just brushed between her thighs.

"Misha—"

"Hurry up, woman—get in the pool. I'll be with you."

Someone opened a locker nearby, so Val turned to pick up her towel. Misha? she thought, but he was silent. She went to the shower room and took the first one available. She stepped inside the shower stall and closed the door.

She leaned back against the cool damp tiles. She felt his breath in her ear; it made her shiver. She turned on the water and adjusted the temperature, getting the water as stingingly hot as she could stand it. She quickly lathered and rinsed off. Twice she felt his hands on her flesh, gently pressing, but he did not speak.

She hurried to the pool room and stepped into the swirling, boiling waters.

"Let me feel how it is for a woman," he whispered in her ear. A shiver went down her spine, despite the scalding water around her. Almost instantly she was about to come. The entire lower portion of her body was tingling with the sensation. She sat down on an underwater ledge and leaned her head back on the pool rim.

"Ahh," he said, "you're my secret valentine . . ."

The woman with the cantaloupes was at the other end of the therapy pool. They were the only two women using it at the moment. She was watching Val, who looked like she might have gotten light-headed, sitting down suddenly like that.

She had seen someone faint in the therapy pool before. She decided to keep a close eye on the girl—you never knew.

Before long the older woman detected Val's hands just below the water's surface; the girl was shivering all over, just like . . .

Val was startled momentarily by the sudden nearness of the woman climbing out of the pool at her right. Val blinked her eyes open, her pleasure interrupted, as the woman stood—a great pink body dripping water—and bent over as she stepped out and whispered a harsh admonition close to Val's right ear: "You ought to be ashamed doing *that* in a nice place like this—"

She sloshed out before Val could reply. "Well, that takes care of that for me," she said to Misha, who apparently had been through the little episode with her.

"Jealous old biddy. Probably froze her pussy years ago," he muttered.

She left the hot pool and lay down on a chaise longue near the windows. Eyes closed, relaxing under a towel, she asked him, "How is this happening to us, Misha?"

She had almost said, Michael, but caught herself. She didn't want him to know she knew who he was. Maybe he would volunteer that information and let her be with him.

"I don't know. I've tried to figure it out. Tried to do this with other people—"

That stung Val briefly. She had never thought to put their telepathy to any such scientific test or to open it to a third party. Somehow, she'd thought of it as just theirs.

"Who?"

"Oh, just some of the staff here—the orderly."

"That pretty nurse?"

As a matter of fact, Michael had spent five full minutes trying to mentally communicate with Tanna, but all it got him was a headache and a funny look from her. She had left the room a few minutes ago and had not returned.

"Anyway," he replied. "I can't reach anyone else. Why you, I wonder? What do we have in common?"

"We're both actors," she suggested, then wished she hadn't.

"How did you know that?"

"You told me. I sensed it, the way you sensed the wheelchair incident in my past. The way I lived through your accident with you."

"How did you see the accident?"

"Dreams. For three nights I dreamed your car going off the road. Then yesterday I dreamed you speaking to me and I dreamed you as a little boy lost in the snow, then someone found you—"

"Aunt Rosa. Aunt Rosa rescued me."

"I relived it with you. I felt you thinking, repeating the words of some grownup, someone you overheard talking to herself about you. 'Michael is going to be a terror,' the grownup voice said. In the same way I knew you were an actor. When they put you into the ambulance you asked for the Actor's Guild."

"Jesus—a cosmic union grievance. It'd be funny if it weren't so weird."

"It's scaring me, too. I mean, I want to meet you in person, so it isn't so weird, understand?"

"Slow down, slow down," he said, thinking, Damn—a woman who talks too much. All the millions of women walking around L.A. and I have to get hooked up with one who runs off at the mouth. Just like Jan, he thought, recalling his doomed passenger for the first time. He had been getting tired of her anyway; nagging him all the time.

But to Val, he said, "Have a heart. I'm not a whole man anymore."

"You still have what counts."

"Well, yes, but . . ."

"Look, what you're doing is eavesdropping on me and it gives me the creeps. I admit I did it to you a little back there, but you are mostly shutting me out. You can't ride me if I can't ride you. You know who I am . . ." she continued, toying with the idea of telling him she knew his whole name now, thanks to Maxine. Something told her not to crowd him, though. "Maybe you're just some senile old man waiting to die in some dark room, some kind of voyeur sneaking up on me—"

She felt instant denial—strong and virile—from him.

"It's just not fair," she finished. "It's just not fair—"

"Stop it, please. First, I'm not dying. I'm . . ." It seemed difficult for him to go on, more than merely painful. "The truth is, I don't want to admit what's happening to me, and if I let you see through my eyes, I'll have to look, too."

"So, how long can you sleep? Your body wants to wake up, get well, get it over with. Open your eyes now, with me here to help you."

He hesitated, eyes fluttering, but she could now see again through his lids, like before in the brief moment of making love when he was open to her.

Just then, someone entered Michael's room.

CHAPTER 14

Val was with him as he turned his head to see Dr. Raymond and Tanna.

"Well, well. Good to see you awake," the doctor said with professional joviality. He walked to the bed; Tanna followed with a tray of chrome instruments. The doctor reached with a clean pink hand still damp from washing to a cord switch, instantly bringing the patient into full illumination. Michael blinked in the glare, his heart pounding with the sudden intrusion into her private world.

"It's okay—I'm here with you," Val said from that secret world only the two of them shared. Michael had to admit it felt good having her with him, real good. He felt propped up by her strength.

Tanna had not taken her eyes from Michael since she entered. Her demeanor was totally professional, however, except for that secret glance.

"Time to begin therapy, Michael," Raymond said. He lay his hand on Michael's left thigh. Michael could feel the warm outline of the handprint on his supersensitive skin through the gauze. But instead of letting his gaze be drawn to where the hand touched, he watched the doctor's small bright eyes.

"I'm going to remove the bandages from the stumps now."

Michael felt cold at the sound of that awful word: *stumps.*

Back in the pool room at the gym Val sat upright on the lounge. Her shoulders were hunched over and she shivered with more than a chill. So, she thought. That's it.

Both legs.

Tears streamed down her cheeks to mingle with the water drops that were evaporating on her chest. Never to dance again, she thought. Never again to lock legs around a lover's back. Never again to jump for the sheer joy of it, but especially, never to dance again. She wondered if she could bear that, if she were in Misha's place.

"Please don't turn away," she heard him beg. She lay back down.

The doctor removed the chrome scissors from the tray so that he didn't see Michael close his eyes and move his lips. But Tanna saw and wondered what he was saying to himself with such intensity.

"The young medic who saved your life did a first-class job. He cut only what he had to—the rest was a disjointing, really. So, you are left with usable stumps that can be fitted with prostheses—"

Michael glared dripping daggers at him.

Val whispered in his head, "The worst part's over."

Michael's lip twitched cynically. Again, only Tanna caught the gesture. Michael saw pleading in her eyes, pleading for him to be sensible and listen to the doctor.

"We'll start you in a wheelchair, of course," the doctor continued. "Perhaps this afternoon if you feel like it. Miss Henderson can help you learn to get into the chair and get around by yourself. We have a lovely roof garden where you can get some sun."

The scissors snipped coolly against Michael's skin. He would not look down, but could follow the progress of the unwrapping by the tracery of the cold blade.

"Oh yes. It looks, clean, very clean."

Michael felt the doctor's soft hands around the new curve of his knee. It was tender, incredibly sensitive, but so far there was only muffled pain. He felt as if he could discern the whorls of the doctor's fingerprints, the skin was so sensitive.

". . . lucky in many ways," the doctor was saying softly as he began working on the right bandage.

"I know it doesn't seem like that to you now, but

128

you're lucky to be alive. They're going to give that medic a medal for risking his life to get you out alive."

Shit, Michael thought. If I get my hands on him, I'll give him something, but it won't be a medal. Something *metal*.

But he made no outward response. He adamantly stared ahead, his arms crossed defensively across his chest. The doctor was trying to catch his eye. Just outside the ring of bright light, Michael saw Tanna's sympathetic face, her eyes shimmering. Suddenly he wanted to smash that pretty face. Her eyes were telling him to listen to the doctor, and Michael did not want to be lectured in any way.

"Look," Raymond commanded, gently slapping Michael's thigh.

"Misha—it's not so bad," Val was telling him as he stared at his lap where the doctor finished unwrapping the other leg.

Actually it *wasn't* so bad. He felt kind of numb.

Val, perceiving through Misha's eyes, saw him glance again at the pretty nurse's luminous eyes. The nurse—Val could almost read her nameplate in the shadows—was nodding agreement to what the doctor was saying.

"No reason why you can't live a life normal in almost every way," he droned on in a monotone as he tossed the gauze into a metal container.

"Kid I saw on television the other night, lost a leg up to here." He demonstrated. "Skiing, motorcycles, swimming—everything. That's the spirit."

He very carefully snipped away the thread of a suture. Michael felt the sting that activated a sharp shooting pain centimeter by centimeter up to his groin.

"Sorry about that," Raymond said sincerely, pausing before he removed another. "We'll toughen you up, though—the whirlpool bath will help, so will exercise—"

There were more stings, but none as bad as that first one. The doctor kept on talking as Michael watched him.

"You know who Al Capp was?" the doctor said, tweezing out another suture. Michael bit his tongue and didn't move.

Back in the gym Val sat hugging her legs up to her chest, her head resting on her knees, eyes closed. Unconsciously she stroked her knees with her hands.

"The cartoonist who invented L'il Abner. He lost a leg when he was a teenager. I'll never forget what he said about it. He said he had to learn to live without resentment or embarrassment in a world where he was different. He said he learned to be indifferent to his difference. Isn't that great? I've never forgotten it."

Raymond's words were not making any impression on Michael. He was staring, marveling at the fact that he felt no emotion as he looked at the doctor's hands examining him. Then the physician bathed his own hands in alcohol and pulled the sheet up over Michael's lap.

So you won't have to look at the awful sight, you hypocritical bastard, Michael was thinking as Raymond sat casually on the edge of the bed, continuing to speak in his sincerest tones to the young man staring back at him. "It's too bad, of course, that they couldn't have saved the knee joints— It would have been easier to wear prostheses—"

"That's artificial legs you're talking about, huh?" Michael spoke for the first time since Raymond and Tanna had entered.

"They've made some remarkable progress in that science—" the doctor started to continue with his sales pitch.

"No way," Michael said flatly.

"But surely you'd rather be able to get around on your own than sit in a wheelchair for the rest of your life—a young man like yourself in the public eye—"

"Piss in the public eye."

Dr. Raymond looked aghast. "But—"

Behind Raymond, Tanna was struck with dismay.

"Nobody sees me like this. Nobody."

"But your uncle—"

130

"Fuck my uncle."

The doctor backed away from Michael, feeling his boat rocking.

"I'm not going to live like this," Michael said bitingly, his voice raised and strained. Bunch stepped into the room at the sound of the loud voice, arms folded menacingly.

Michael sat back and took a deep breath. Tanna beside him looked as if she might cry. Raymond glanced at Bunch, who was on overtime because another orderly called in sick. It was the end of a double shift for him. When Raymond saw Michael restraining himself, he nodded that Bunch could leave.

"I understand you're upset," he said, turning back to Michael. "This is a terrible thing that's happened to you, but it's not the end of the world." Raymond's look told Tanna to stay with Michael in the room, then, wiping his face with a starched handkerchief, he followed Bunch.

Tanna leaned close to Michael to touch his face with a cool hand.

It felt good; he closed his eyes.

"Would you like to try the chair now?"

At that moment Michael felt Val pull away from him.

He opened his eyes and looked around the room as if someone had just turned off the air supply to his spaceship; as if he could tell by the sudden absence of a purring noise.

"Val?" he called, frightened, out loud.

Tanna watched him with fear and interest.

He shook himself, aware suddenly that he had called someone's name. He looked around, as if surprised to find himself here.

"Who's Val?" Tanna asked as she sat down on a chair beside the bed.

He let his head fall back on the pillow and did not answer her. He had to think, had to find out what had happened to Val. Why did she suddenly pull away from him like that. All the time he went through the ordeal with Raymond, she was here just as she had promised. Why did she leave when it was all over?

"It's a beautiful day outside," Tanna was saying, far off but right next to him. "Why don't we go up to the roof and enjoy it?"

"Gimmie a minute," he said, closing his eyes. "Just a minute to think." He was not tired, but suddenly needed to try to become clearheaded. He knew he needed to get physically better so that he would be able to sort all this out, find out what it was he had here. But right now he needed to find Val.

Tanna backed away and sat down on the chair. She watched and listened for a few minutes while Michael lay apparently dozing. Once or twice his lips twitched in some dream argument. Once or twice he almost called out that name.

Val had pulled away from Misha and was slowly bringing herself back to the chaise longue in the echoing pool room. A small class of older ladies practiced swimming exercises at the shallow end.

She listened to the sounds bouncing off the walls. Through her closed eyelids Val could see shifting patterns of light reflected from the glittering pool surface. The air was humid and cool; a breeze blew in from a open window on the sunward side of the building.

She was still shaking from the experience of being joined with Misha in his body. She ran her hands along her thighs where gooseflesh ran in a chill when she thought about it.

One of the swimming ladies squealed with delight when she was able to do an exercise correctly. The others laughed with her in their high echoing voices. It helped Val concentrate on the here and now.

What would you think, she wondered to herself as she watched the cavorting grandmas, if I were to tell you what I've been doing while you play water ballet.

She turned over on her stomach and folded her hands under her chin.

It was peaceful lying here, among many sisters, part

of this group and yet alone within it. But she wasn't thinking of the swimmers as she stared at them. She was thinking of why she had pulled so suddenly away from Misha.

Suddenly his voice interrupted her thoughts of the nurse's nameplate.

"Val, I miss you—where are you?"

She didn't respond immediately, but considered the emotional quality of his call.

"You promised you wouldn't turn away from me."

She closed her eyes.

"Valentine . . . ?" his voice said, with a different tone, a bedroom tone.

She stirred on the lounge and crossed her legs. Water droplets were evaporating on her skin. They tickled.

"I know you can hear me," he whispered in her inner ear. If any of the ladies had been watching Val they would have seen a smile on her lips.

"Let me be with you, Val."

She covered her eyes with her hands.

"Don't shut me out, not now that you've shown me how much I need you."

"It's pretty heavy, Misha," she finally said.

"God, I'm glad I didn't lose you."

"No."

"Well, now you know."

"Yes. Now I know."

"Does it make any difference?"

"No. I told you that you haven't lost what counts."

"I can't live the way I am."

She didn't know how to answer that one.

"Right now, you're the only reason I'm alive."

"You're not seeing things clearly."

"Let me be with you for a while."

"I don't want to be together all the time."

"But I need—"

"I don't mind being with you sometimes, especially in sex. But I want to meet you as a person, as a man

133

with a body I can snuggle next to after we make love. I want someone *real*."

He started to answer, but in that quick-tongued way of hers she interrupted his response.

"And I want my own space. Like right now. I kept my promise to you—I didn't turn away when you needed me to help confront this awful thing that's happened to you. Now I need time to assimilate all that's happened. I need to be alone."

"This is what women always do—" he said, furious but restraining himself. Across the room Tanna saw him tense up and pull the covers closer around his face. She didn't like him mumbling to himself like this. It wasn't right. It wasn't something to indulge him in. She'd give him another five minutes of this retreat into fantasy and then it was up on the roof for some sunshine.

"Besides," Val continued, "my period's starting."

"That always turns me on."

"Sometimes me too. Not this time. I shouldn't have used the Jacuzzi—as soon as I get up from here I'm going to flood." She was slowly sitting up on the chaise longue, draping the towel around her waist.

"Please, Misha. Let me have just a few hours to think about this. I was terrified when you didn't answer me. I was beginning to think I had hallucinated you. I'm glad I didn't—but I need to be alone."

"Well . . ."

"Say, until this evening. Say until midnight."

"You're thinking about Frank."

"I'm trying to decide what to do about Frank, yes."

"He thinks you're crazy."

"He's always thought I was crazy."

"Get rid of him."

"It has to be done right."

"If you love me, get rid of him *now*."

"I am going to leave him but—"

"I can't stand to think of you sleeping with him."

"It will only be that."

"Please—I can't wait until eleven. They want me to

134

get in this fucking chair. God, I hate being so helpless—"

"You've got to get well."

"I can't do it without you. If you leave me now—"

"Misha—I love you. I'll come to you—in person—this instant."

"Soon. Let me have some time . . ."

"That's all I'm asking, too."

"Until seven then. Let me be with you at seven."

"I'll be with Frank."

"I won't distract you. I just want to be with you."

"Okay. Seven."

Val pulled away from Misha again, bringing herself fully into the present and the place where her body already sat. Her loins felt full, heavy. She knew her period would begin within the hour if not sooner. She felt physically depressed and edgy; now she realized that had been part of her problem all day, all week. It had sneaked up on her because of the excitement of the telepathic experience.

But Val was happy. She hugged herself deeply into the towel and stood slowly. She walked to the locker room, realizing that now she had the whole afternoon free. She decided to call for an appointment with her favorite hair cutter in Westwood, and then spend the rest of the afternoon at the UCLA library.

She felt truly happy now that she knew where Misha was in addition to his full name. She had pulled away from him suddenly because she didn't want him to know she had seen the name of the hospital on Tanna's name tag, as well as the room number on the door behind her.

". . . but you didn't have to be rude to that old man," Tanna was saying. Michael was getting the hang of the wheels—he was moving around the room, bumping into things, snagging on the bed and on the cables of the machinery.

He didn't answer Tanna, but maneuvered close to

135

the bed, where he removed the light blanket Tanna had spread over him. She watched him methodically cover up his lap, tucking in the edges of the blanket, lumping it on the foot supports.

"Michael—what are you doing?"

He continued making the blanket just the way he wanted it.

"It's not going to do any good hiding it. People here won't stare at you—they have their own misery. Just accept it."

He finished tucking in the blanket to his satisfaction as though he hadn't heard her. "I've got to get out of here—I'm going stir-crazy."

But to himself he thought, You stupid cunt. I don't have to accept this . . . I just may have found a way out . . .

He thought with a chill how he could just reach out and connect with Val. Funny how each of them could do that, just connect or disconnect, like magnets or something. One end attracts, the other repels. Some crazy thing like that. He was still too muddled to work it all out. He wanted to work it all out, figure what he could do and could not do.

He repressed the desire to mentally reach out to Val as Tanna opened the door. He did not want to spook Val by getting too anxious, not when he was just figuring out what he had here. A stubborn woman, that's what he had. Why couldn't it have been another man, someone more rational, or someone more compliant like Tanna? He tried in that instant to contact Tanna with the telepathy he still had no idea how to control. He tried to think of a hole bored into his forehead shooting out a beam of light to hit Tanna smack in the old third eye. That's how the yogis were supposed to do it.

"What for you looking at me in that tone of voice?" Tanna demanded, slipping into her black-mama routine.

He laughed bitterly and shook his head.

"Come on this way," she said as she took the chair

136

handles in her hands. Michael gripped the wheels himself so that she could not push him further. He looked back at her until she removed her hands from the chair.

"Only one place I need you to push me baby," he said and wheeled forward. His dexterity with vehicles was already giving him an air of confidence with this one. "And I think we just may take that trip tonight."

"The elevator," she said demurely, not a trace of the secret smile he expected to see on her face. He looked for that devious, erotic look in her eyes, but when she looked down at him he saw something else.

Oh well, he consoled himself. Fear had always been a pretty good substitute.

Almost three weeks since he'd felt the sun.

It hit him in the face with a jolt as they exited the elevator onto the roof of the four-story building that housed Sunnyrest Convalescent Hospital.

Michael let the sunlight have him. It felt so good. He leaned back in the chair, closing his eyes. Suddenly it didn't matter if he propelled himself or Tanna did it. So long as she got the message, she could push him once in a while. She saw the sun was making him dizzy, so she took the handles of the chair.

They moved toward a group of trees potted in giant redwood boxes. Moving through the sunlight and fresh air with his eyes closed, Michael could almost imagine himself on the chairlift at Mammouth, going up for another run. He could smell the pine trees. Then the gasping laughter of what sounded like a bevy of old elves broke his skiing fantasy. He couldn't help but be drawn in by their exclamations of delight that bordered on awe, then on horror.

"Look at that one—she's spreading out her legs— omigod—I think my heart's going," one old man's voice croaked mockingly.

"Morrison—it's my turn—"

"You guys are hoggin' the glasses," said another, more petulant.

137

Michael opened his eyes as Tanna wheeled him closer to the trees. Now he could see the old men in their pajamas and bathrobes, two of them in wheelchairs, too. The other three sat in the deck chairs that matched an umbrellaed table.

They were as different as five old elves can be. The old geezer demanding the glasses was in a chair like Michael's.

"Come on—hand it over," said the croaker, also in a wheelchair, the one Tanna had sought out last night for a vitamin B shot. "Them's my glasses and I demand you hand the damned things over immediately."

Reluctantly Morrison gave him the beat-up binoculars.

Goldman took them imperiously, raised them to his eyes and adjusted the focus. "Ahhh."

Morrison simpered. "She was just about to put suntan lotion on her privates," he whined.

"Women don't put suntan lotion on their privates," said the petulant one who sat drinking coffee from a Styrofoam cup at the table. "It'd give 'em cancer of the *curvex*."

"What's she doing now, Reg?" Morrison asked.

"I'm looking at the fat one behind the potted palm," Goldman said, still focusing. "Jeezus . . ."

Michael propelled his chair toward them.

"That old broad is sixty if she's a day—" said the guy with the glasses. The others around him frowned. A couple of them were trying to see with the naked eye, but the roof where the girls lay was too far away to see much without the binoculars.

One old man elbowed another when he saw Michael and Tanna enter their circle. The men became quiet, all except Reg Goldman, who was unaware of the interruption.

"If she's a day—" he repeated.

It was Tanna who worried them. They were afraid that if their game were discovered by the hospital it would be stopped.

138

Someone elbowed Goldman, who snarled, then saw Tanna.

"Oh, Miss Henderson," Goldman said, looking at the glasses.

Tanna smiled. "Gentlemen, this is a new patient. Michael, these are my rooftop swingers." She grinned at the men again, to let them know their pastime was safe with her.

She told Michael she would be back in a few minutes, then she left him soundlessly, her clean white nurses' shoes sparkling across the dark surface of the roof.

Every one of the men's eyes was on her as she departed. As soon as she was out of sight, Goldman regarded Michael.

Michael now saw that the old man was missing a leg, too.

Goldman saw him looking at him. "Oh," the old man said, "they've been hacking pieces off me for years." He saw the look of surprised horror on Michael's lean young face. "Diabetes," he explained. "Shuts off the circulation."

Michael nodded, while the other men took up the glasses.

"You?" Goldman was for once more interested in something else.

Michael shrugged and looked shyly up. Goldman eyed the carefully folded blanket on the young man's lap. He couldn't tell what it was hiding, but he already knew from scuttlebutt.

"I know how you feel. But you'll get used to being an amp."

Michael looked grimly away. The sky was an unbelievable blue flecked with the merest smattering of cloud over the Tarzana Hills. A sea breeze must be blowing this way.

Goldman was watching the others fight over the binoculars. He was aware, though, when Michael looked over at him. "That's what we call ourselves—amps," Goldman informed him.

He saw Michael wasn't going to talk about it.

Goldman, who remembered his own seething anger right after his first operation, wasn't one to push the subject. After a while the breeze came up and ruffled their hair.

"You want to see through the glasses? They're mine, you know."

"What is it, some kind of hotel or something?"

"A gym. A woman's gym," Goldman giggled. "Two floors below, about a block away. There's a straight shot to the roof where they sunbathe. So far, nobody knows about it—the potted bushes hide us."

"You're kidding." He thought to himself, it couldn't be the same one.

"No. Come on—" He expertly spun his wheelchair around like a kid popping a wheelie on a bike. "Hand me the glasses, Bud."

"But, I just—"

Goldman snapped his scrawny hand and the old man handed over the glasses. Goldman glanced back meaningfully at Michael to let him know who was boss here and gave the glasses to him.

Michael swept the lower roof with the frail lenses. What he wouldn't give to have his Zeiss eight-forties in his hand right now. They would bring out details lost with this antique set.

The gym roof was virtually paved with browning female bodies, lounging like sleek cats in the sun. There must be forty-five or fifty women down there, most of them stark naked. The sight of them stirred his cock; a mild twinge of pain accompanied it. The entire lower part of his body was sensitive now that he was recovering from the medication.

"Like that, eh?" Morrison called out behind him.

"Hmmm," Michael responded. He squeezed his thighs together. The blanket had fallen aside and the old men snickered behind him. Michael looked down, and then back at them. He grinned and started to laugh, too, his mind shell-shocked with the overabundance of women so close yet so far away. He imagined them to be a platter of sweetmeats trimmed by the parsley of the potted trees around them. He could almost reach out and take the one he wanted.

At the glasses again he stopped on one long black body. Like Tanna, he thought with a little thrill when he remembered what she had promised. He moved the glass leisurely along a line of women, biscuits simmering under their cocoa butter.

His view ran over the edge of the gym roof. He was looking at the parking lot lined with automobiles the way the roof was lined with women. He was about to swing the glass back to the more preferable gathering of bodies, when he saw a petite young woman moving through the parking lot. She had ginger-brown hair done up in pigtails that reached just below her shoulders. He couldn't make out her face because she had angled away from his line of sight, but she moved with the grace of a dancer on a lovely pair of legs.

He knew immediately who it was. He followed her with the glasses as she approached an old gray Citroen and unlocked the driver's side door. In a moment the car belched ominous-looking fumes from its exhaust pipe and backed out of its parking slot.

When the driver aimed the car at the exit gate, Michael caught a flash of gold. Something was hanging from the rearview mirror. But he couldn't see what now because the car was too far forward, its windshield pointed toward Ventura Boulevard. He chuckled to read the bumper sticker: I BRAKE FOR ANIMALS. He figured as much.

His eye followed her car to the exit where she had to wait for a line of cars before she could enter traffic. Michael thought, I said I'd leave her alone until seven. I promised her . . .

Still, he couldn't help thinking about being with her. He wondered if it were possible for him to connect with her without her knowledge. It was a titillating thought, peeking through her eyes as she innocently went about her business. The ultimate in voyeurism.

141

He vaguely heard one of the old men behind him asking for his turn at the binoculars.

He ignored him and concentrated on the girl in the car. Just then he saw what she couldn't see—a van bearing down on her as she pulled out into the street. The van's driver was blinded by another vehicle and couldn't see Val in the Citroen moving into his line of fire.

"Val—" he called inside his head, "look out—"

CHAPTER 15

Val heard Misha's voice and then everything went black.

It seemed like the time it takes to blink and she was awake again, head aching, about to retch. She forced down the bitter bile in her throat as the car bounced to a stop against the curb.

She had not fallen over; her hands were still on the wheel. In fact, they were gripping the steering wheel. That may have been what kept her sitting upright. Did I pass out, hit my head, or what?

The van whizzed by.

"Sorry—" she heard the driver yell as he passed, but she didn't look up. She was trying to figure out what had happened.

Val thought she might black out again when she couldn't feel her hands. She could see them, but it was as if they had gone to sleep. Then the circulation, or whatever, returned. They tingled unpleasantly.

"What happened?" she asked nobody.

"Van almost hit you—" Misha answered in her mind, and it startled her.

"Misha, I thought you were going to leave me alone until seven."

142

"I heard you scream . . ."

"You grabbed the wheel?"

A man who'd been hosing down the sidewalk just behind her and had seen the near-accident leaned down to ask her through the driver's window, "Are you okay?"

Val rolled down the window hurriedly and answered, "Yes, yes, thank you—"

"That bastard almost hit you—" the man said, backing off. "You sure you aren't hurt or something?"

"No—just shaken up," Val smiled convincingly, taking charge of the steering wheel again, parking the car at a less vulnerable angle relative to oncoming traffic.

The man walked off and Val sighed and leaned back against the headrest. She knew what this meant; Misha had been watching through her surreptitiously.

"No," she heard him in her mind. "I didn't break my promise. I just heard you call. I knew you were in danger."

It touched Val deeply.

"Thank you, Misha," she said aloud. She opened her eyes and saw the St. Christopher's medal swinging on the rearview mirror. She reached out and stopped its pendulum movement with a trembling hand.

"I couldn't let anything happen to that beautiful body of yours," Misha said. She could feel him fading.

"My Saint Christopher . . ." she answered.

"My secret valentine," he said. "I'll be with you at seven."

And he was gone.

"—he just passed out—"

"—fainted dead away—"

"—must've been the sight of all that pussy—"

"—Jeezus—get him outta the sun—"

The old men fussed around Michael, who was coming to with a slant of sunlight in his eyes. He squinted and turned his head away. They were holding him up in the chair, moving into the shade of the umbrella.

"What happened—?" It was Tanna's anxious voice

coming closer. Michael could see her now; she was so beautiful, her expression so full of exclusive concern for him.

"Must've been the sun," Goldman said.

"I can't reach them," Morrison said behind the group. "He dropped them on a ledge just out of reach." He looked up and saw Tanna.

She was hurrying to Michael's side. She knelt down and looked into his eyes with the lids held back. He must have fainted. She cursed herself for leaving him alone. She had to slow down, not push him so hard. But she was so afraid of those fantasy episodes.

They would take him away from her if they thought he was psychotic. She was so sure she could reach him, bring him back from the terrible pit that yawned in front of him. She didn't want them to take him away, but if the fantasy episodes continued she would have to report the behavior. A psychiatrist would be on the case soon, anyway, but if they thought he was dangerous they'd put him in a psychiatric hospital.

"Michael—"

His eyes rolled.

"It's okay," she assured him as she stood. She'd get him out of the sun. Too much in one day. She pushed his chair toward the elevator while the old men watched behind her.

Morrison gestured obscenely.

"The glasses are gone, eh?" Goldman asked.

"Yeah."

"Well, shit."

It had surprised Maxine for Val to call her Maxi.

Then she hung up so suddenly, it made Maxine mad. She was ready to drop this whole thing, too. Penny-ante job like this. If it weren't her first official case, she wouldn't have bothered.

But the girl had gotten to her.

Whatever compelled her to refer to Maxine as Maxi, anyway? She supposed the name suggested it; still,

144

since Hugh stopped calling her that after Dad's death, nobody else had, either.

Maxine was driving west on Ventura. She turned right off Ventura and began looking for the address she had found for Scott Rand.

She knew the minute Val had told her to drop the case, she wouldn't. Now she had to know what happened, and why Val so suddenly wanted to forget the whole thing, when yesterday she'd been in such an all-fired hurry to find out about these people. Good old Connie. Even after Maxine lay the $20 bill under her purse, Connie had told her the paramedic who could answer all her questions was on vacation. He wouldn't be back at the station in the hills where he was assigned until next week. Because Connie had worked with Maxine before when they both were employed by the county, she didn't mind helping her now that she was an independent. She told her the paramedic's name. "Up to you to find out where he lives," the twenty-two-year county employee told Maxine. "I have to draw the line somewhere."

They had left the coffee shop in the county building with warm good-byes, Maxine with the name of someone who could answer her questions and Connie $20 richer. This had been a lucrative case—$120 so far.

The address of Scott Rand's apartment house was in this block. It was a tree-lined suburban street with huge apartment houses and condos on each side for miles.

She found the right one and parked on the street.

It was a security building, but when she talked to the pleasant young man in 24-B by telephone while the sour guard watched, Scott was completely willing to talk to her.

She was allowed through the gate and down corridors of blue carpeting, a plush, human warren with what seemed like hundreds of doors leading mysteriously off the main hall.

Twenty-four-B meant the twenty-fourth apartment

145

on B floor of the main building. She walked and walked, took an elevator and suddenly was there, regarding a door like the hundreds of others.

It opened after one ring and she was suddenly confronted with the smiling blond countenance of Scott Rand, 195 pounds, six feet three inches of pure American he-man who probably still called his mama every other day and maybe even went to church on Sundays.

"Come on in," he said in a friendly baritone. Maxine entered his modern singles apartment full of raw wood and leather and many green plants at every window. It was a pleasant, masculine-looking room, comfortable and clean, as if he had been trained in the military, but had loosened up enough for civilian comfort.

As he ushered her into the high, beam-ceilinged living room, Maxine saw that he had something spidery and fragile in his huge ham of a hand. He saw her looking and said, "A 1922 Ford delivery truck."

She saw that it was a model car. Tim had gone through a stage when he was about nine of wanting to put together every model kit ever invented, but he'd outgrown the urge. She looked around the room and saw in one corner a huge old table covered with many boxes of all kinds of models. Shelves behind the table were crammed with hundreds of model cars, each one a masterpiece of craftsmanship. She examined a little sportscar and admired it.

"I love these things," Scott said charmingly. He was a true giant, a huge young man, strong as an ox, it looked like. It fit that he was a paramedic.

"What can I do for you, Mrs. Wise—you said something about an accident."

"You were on duty the night of the twenty-first—last month?"

"Yeah," he said, moving to his high-intensity lamp. He picked up an emery board and began sandpapering a part of the most fragile plastic the size of a fingernail.

She watched him, fascinated, as she talked.

"A man and a woman went off Mulholland Drive

west of Park Lane Circle—the woman's body was recovered two days later."

He was already nodding his head, ready to answer. "Yeah, that was a rough one—"

"What happened to the driver of the car?"

"Oh, I got him out—hated to have to amputate under those conditions—" He saw her questioning gaze.

"Both legs," he said, frowning.

"Had to—that car was going over the side—had to cut him out." He filed the plastic part down to his satisfaction and fitted it against the chassis he was building. When he saw it almost fit, he sandpapered it more and then applied some glue and set it in place.

"Let me show you," he said in a good-natured way. Maxine liked this man immensely. She felt as she often did in the presence of firemen or policemen that she was grateful for these brave people who would risk their lives to save her if it was necessary.

He plucked one of his hundreds of plastic models off the shelf. "I don't have a Mercedes of that model—but this'll do." He showed her the beautiful little maroon touring car in the style of the twenties. He set up a cardboard box to represent the steeply inclined hillside, and hooked the back wheels over the edge so that its nose pointed downward.

"Now," he explained, "just as the car left the road"—he made the model swing out in an arc above the make-believe canyon of boxes—"it flipped over so that this is the way it landed, upside-down."

He moved a bottle of paint thinner into place so that it prevented the model car from sliding further down the embankment.

"When it hit, the passenger was probably killed immediately because that side of the car hit first. The driver was probably trying to get out at that point. He was caught here—" Scott lay two beefy fingers under the miniature window glass of the driver's side. "We were losing the wreck—water was pouring down that slope."

147

"Did you make the decision to amputate?"

"I gave my radio report to the physician over at the hospital who works with us—he said take 'em off to save the guy."

"He would have died, huh?"

"That car went over the side minutes after we got him out."

She thought for a moment.

"Did you recognize the driver?"

"No. Should I?"

"I just wondered." She hadn't seen a TV set in the living room.

"Is there going to be trouble over this—Dr. Mason will back me up one hundred percent, all the way. He's the doctor on the two-way who supervised the surgery."

"Oh no—nothing like that. I'm a private detective as I told you, working for a witness to the accident."

"Oh."

"She's religious—wanted to pray for the victims."

"A witness, huh?"

He scowled and set aside the model.

"What's wrong? She said she saw it from the road."

"Well, maybe, but the road had washed out up ahead, and we didn't meet anyone going up—I don't see how anyone could have been there without my seeing them."

They both thought about that for a moment, then he said, "Course I wasn't doing much sight-seeing at the time." He grinned that charming grin again and Maxine smiled back, thinking of her own sons and how proud of this one some mother must be.

"Well, I appreciate your taking the time to talk to me," Maxine said, getting ready to leave.

"Anytime. I don't mind cooperating. Like I told that lawyer who came by a few days after this accident—"

"Lawyer?"

"Yeah. He asked the same questions you did. Wanted to know who authorized the surgery. My su-

148

periors said I could talk to him. Stefano, his name was."

If Maxine's ears had been capable of twitching, they would have.

CHAPTER 16

Something about Michael's miserable situation reminded Lazlo Stefano of his own father.

The old man had come to America in the year 1900 after offending his huge Serbian family by marrying a Hungarian, considered an enemy of his people. Despite his exile, when World War I was born in his native city of Sarajevo, born out of seething Serbian discontent at Austria's arrogant push east, Lazlo's father returned to fight the patriotic fight in 1914, the year Lazlo was born. He left behind in America a young emigrant wife and an infant son named for his maternal grandfather and surnamed for his Serbian father. Of course the father was killed early in the fighting that spread like an ink blot across the map of Europe.

That his father would have died for a country he no longer inhabited was an incomprehensible and idiotically romantic notion to the son, Lazlo. Even as a boy he could remember thinking that his father had been a fool, an unlucky romantic fool. Lazlo spent his early years on the streets of a big Eastern city where Stefanovich the elder had settled, playing stickball and learning how to fight to survive. His mother, who had been disowned by her family, too, moved to California and died of a broken heart when Lazlo was ten. He was raised after that in state institutions and various foster homes. All because his father had gone off on an idealistic cause. Despite great potential, the old man had just been plain unlucky all his life. That ill fortune must have skipped a generation and settled on the grandson, Lazlo's nephew Michael.

Despite all his opportunities, the kid seemed dogged by a kind of lopsided luck. He was born to wealth, but lost his parents at an early age. He was always charming and good-looking, but he had a mean disposition that had spoiled him before Rosa got to him, and she spoiled him rotten. Lazlo had never been able to reach the kid, so he resorted to force, which never worked with Michael. In rebellion he separated himself from Lazlo's other sons by making himself his uncle's enemy. That made him foolish in Lazlo's eyes as well as unlucky.

Most of Michael's bad luck, Lazlo thought to himself as he sat waiting alone in Michael's room for his return—most of his bad luck he brought on himself. Like this accident. Michael had wrecked three cars and was always paying off traffic fines, asking his cousin Aaron to get him off the hook with some misdemeanor or another. Lazlo had hoped he'd settle down by his thirties, but Michael seemed determined to become the proverbial black sheep, just as his grandfather had been the black sheep in another generation, time and place.

Lazlo checked his watch. He was still irritable with jet lag. He hated to wait on anyone, but knew that in this case, it was all he could do. Dr. Raymond had told him that his nephew was in therapy and would be out in a minute.

Ms. Peach had stayed in the car with the driver. Lazlo had just walked up to the hospital's main desk and asked what room Stefano was in. The nurse he asked disappeared and returned with old Raymond, whom Lazlo had chosen to run this place because he could be counted on to cooperate in whatever Lazlo asked.

Raymond wished that Lazlo had called, but he couldn't very well chide the man who owned the place, so he patronized as much as he had to and took Lazlo immediately to Room 20 where he left him to wait for his nephew's return from physical therapy.

The room was unpleasant to Lazlo. It was dark. Michael's bed, freshly made since he'd left for whatever it was he did in physical therapy, looked like a plate of vanilla ice cream, cold and uninviting. Light coming through the blinds was sliced up like an RKO picture from the *noir* period, a style thematically and artistically opposed to Stafano's technicolor temperament. This was the first time Lazlo as owner of the hospital had been inside its doors. The place looked clean enough, but with a disinfectant tinge that unconsciously reminded Lazlo of the toilet in one of the orphanages where he lived after his mother's death.

Despite being orphaned at ten, Lazlo's life had been touched by luck, but of the other kind than his father's. His mother had moved herself and son to the then small city of Los Angeles where she had heard she could work as a seamstress for the movies. She never got the chance, winding up instead in the downtown garment district where she finished her life over a sewing machine for a bathing suit manufacturer.

But the move brought young Lazlo to his opportunity. The second orphanage he lived in, after the abortive foster homes, was in Highland Park, one of the first L.A. suburbs close to the studio locations in Silverlake that long predated the massive lots farther out. As a boy Lazlo rode the Red Car, a now defunct trolley and train line, out to the studios. Gates were easier to climb in those days. Lazlo remembered fondly, thinking back over his big break into movies. He wrangled a pennies-a-day job as a sandwich gofer for one of the lunch wagons that supplemented the commisaries. That was when he was fifteen. A year later he was on salary as a gofer for the director of a picture that was never released. The career of Lazlo Stefano was literally off and running, even though the year was 1929. Lazlo almost did not even experience the Depression as he moved from job to job in positions of greater and greater responsibility. His natural administrative talent was an asset and he was a quick study.

Lazlo was proud of what he had accomplished from nothing, and he was pissed that his nephew had done so little with so much more.

Now Lazlo sat in the plain hospital room he owned as a tax shelter, hating every minute of it, waiting for Michael.

Until the kid rolled through the door with the pretty black nurse behind him, Lazlo had been prepared for confrontation. Now, seeing that lean, handsome face drawn by convalescence, Lazlo was weakened. He felt his own age, which he had been able to deny for some time because of favorable genetic makeup, expensive preventative medicine and plastic surgery, stealthily slip into the room on those silent wheels. Someday I'll be like that, he thought with an interior groan he displayed with a deeper frown between his eyes. Sick and helpless, moved about and kept alive by machinery. . . .

He shook the awful image from himself and stood to meet Michael.

The two men connected with the psychological impact of two coupling railroad cars. Even the nurse was jolted by the sparks that flew between the uncle and nephew.

Michael had been lethargic when he first entered. Now electricity animated him. He wrested control of the wheelchair from the nurse, who started to follow him into the room.

Michael looked back at her. She knew without asking who Lazlo was.

She instantly got the message and backed out of the room, closing the door on their privacy.

Michael seemed to gather his resources before inching the wheelchair toward his uncle, who had sprung to his feet.

It wasn't often that Michael saw his uncle uncomfortable. He had so much power he could usually set things up under his explicit conditions. But here was other territory.

152

Lazlo swallowed and rubbed his palms along the fine material of his pinstripe-suit trousers. He suddenly felt like he was towering unnaturally over Michael, imprisoned as he was in that chair. A stray quiver of revulsion rippled Lazlo's features.

Michael caught it. Even though his lap was covered by his carefully folded blanket, his uncle was staring at the spot where his legs would be. For some reason that look of undressed revulsion gave Michael pleasure, a perverse pleasure, because it supported his thesis that he was now worthy of revulsion. He smiled grimly.

"You, uh, look like you're recovering," was all Lazlo could say as he sat back down.

Michael crossed in front of Lazlo to the window. He opened the blinds so that more light filled the room, then he spun around with a quick hand motion the way he had seen the old man, Goldman, spin his wheelchair around up on the roof.

"Yeah, I'm just fine," Michael replied, his voice dripping irony.

He locked the brake on the chair and sat with his hands folded on the blanket covering his lap, his eyes leveled on his uncle.

"There's a guy walking around who did this to me," Michael said with a burst of feeling. "I want Aaron to go for his ass."

Lazlo was already shaking his head.

"What do you mean?" Michael demanded, then immediately lowered his voice. His uncle was getting redder in the face, a sure sign he was just barely holding his own temper in deference to Michael's injuries.

"The guy checked out," Lazlo replied. He took Aaron's multipage report from his inside coat pocket.

"Tio—" Michael whipped off the blanket. "He cut off my legs. See?"

Lazlo looked like he might puke.

"For no fucking reason," Michael continued as he watched his uncle struggle to compose himself. Michael could see minute lenses of sweat reflecting the light from Lazlo's balding head. He thought silently that the old man looked really old. What was he? Must be at least sixty-five, sixty-six. He's always tanned and in superb condition. Still balling three, four times a week? No, probably not that in a month, Michael observed. There were blue bags under the old man's eyes. That gave the nephew almost as much pleasure as seeing the revulsion at his injuries on Lazlo's face. "He cut off my legs because he was afraid that wreck was going over and he didn't want to go with it. Hell, he isn't even a doctor."

"He saved your life," Lazlo said with amazing evenness, determined not to be pulled into a screaming fight with his nephew. He leaned back in the chair, forcing himself to remain calm. He wished to God Michael would pull the blanket back over himself. Christ Almightly.

Lazlo gestured with the stapled report in his hand.

"The supervising doctor authorized the amputation by two-way radio. That paramedic must've been good. They are going to give him a commendation for saving your life—" Lazlo was looking, shifty-eyed, at the report. Michael could tell he was both trying not to look at Michael's legs and trying to look out of curiosity. He finally pulled the blanket over his lap and adjusted it so that it completely covered the lower half of his body.

Lazlo's hands were trembling minutely. Michael detected relief in the old man's expression now that the blanket was in place.

"Michael, I sympathize with you totally," Lazlo said as he tossed Aaron's report on Michael's bed.

"Like hell you do. Look at you. You can't even look at me."

It was too much of a challenge. Lazlo looked directly at him. "I'm deeply sorry for what's happened to you and anything—anything—I can do to help you, I will."

Michael slapped the brake and spun away from Lazlo. He wheeled to the window and stared out, hugging himself.

"Just tell me. What do you want?" Lazlo came as close to pleading as Michael had ever heard him.

"I want satisfaction," Michael answered, rocking himself miserably. "I want the bastard who did this to me."

"Revenge won't change things. You've got to get well, go on from here."

Just like in the movies, Michael thought with the taste of vomit far back on his tongue. He stopped rocking. His face hardened.

"You can't just give up—that suicide thing—that was terrible. Promise me you won't try that again."

"What'sa matter, Uncle Lazlo—do you already have your writers working on the script?"

Lazlo registered surprise. Michael knew him too well.

"What will it be, dear Uncle? Let's see—what are the possibilities?" Michael asked rhetorically as he wheeled back around to face his uncle. " 'Legless Lawman' maybe or 'Amp Patrol'? That's what we call ourselves, we amputees. Surely your boys can come up with something catchy for a title, huh? Have you already pitched it to ABC?" Then Michael caught himself with elaborate surprise, as if he'd just had an idea. "No, it wouldn't be ABC, would it? It would be NBC with its sporting cripples and blind runners, and all their other incredible, heroic freaks?"

Lazlo drew back at Michael's vehemence. Here was cynicism not even Lazlo would embrace, though he *had* already decided to pitch his series idea to NBC. At least, he silently consoled himself, his nephew had learned his marketing well.

"My son," Lazlo said with an air of long-suffering patience, "you overestimate my interests in the television business. Right now, you are my only concern." This approach he had borrowed from old Louis B. himself.

Michael chortled sarcastically.

"If I did find a project for you, it would be only for your best interests, to give you work, to take your mind off—" he gestured at Michael, suddenly embarrassed again by that blanket.

"So," Michael said with surprising calmness. "You *have* been thinking about a story."

Lazlo shook his head. "No, it's out of the question. To do such a story you'd have to have a completely different attitude."

Michael knew his uncle better than that. But he let him go on talking while he straightened the blanket on his lap.

"No. Jim Stacy could do that kind of part. He's a hero. But the way you're acting I'm not sure I want you to be anywhere near the public. That suicide business—you dishonored your name."

That stung Michael, despite the fact that he surmised his uncle was trying to manipulate him. Stacy, an actor who lost an arm and a leg in a motorcycle accident a few years back, had made a heroic recovery and had acted in many pictures where his handicap was used in the story line.

"Good, because I don't want anyone to see me like this." For the first time since Lazlo had seen Michael in the chair, he showed a vulnerability. Lazlo couldn't miss it and it touched him despite himself. The poor kid. His life was wrecked now. Jesus, what could he do? Lazlo was chilled by a flash memory of a legless begger who had been a fixture on the Hollywood sidewalks when he was a boy. The guy got around on a little truck made from roller skates. It was an ugly memory that did not fit with anything he knew about his nephew.

"I think the clinic in Switzerland would be a good place for you to get well, don't you?"

Michael shrugged.

"Of course, when you decide to come back to work, I do have a couple of ideas."

Michael waited for him to continue. He knew this was what Lazlo had come to talk to him about.

"You know," the old man said, deal-making in his voice, "you were always bugging me to direct . . ."

Michael looked at him with genuine interest.

"Perhaps this is the time to get things started, get you into the guild. You could work out the rest of your contract learning with Al or Crazy or one of my other guys."

Michael flashed interest.

"I'll have Peach send some material over," Lazlo said. Michael shrugged. "Come on," his uncle coaxed. "We'll have some fun."

Michael shook his head. "This thing," he said, indicating the wheelchair, "can you imagine it on a set, getting tangled in the cables."

Lazlo tossed aside that suggestion with a wave of his hand.

"Use the dolly tracks," Lazlo said, referring to the board ramps on which the cameras roll.

"No. I don't think so."

Lazlo watched him, trying to think of something that would rekindle that spark of interest he sensed would eventually save his nephew. "I bought you a little present," he said, slipping his hand into his pocket where he carried the beautiful watch he and Peachie had bought earlier. "You can time scenes with the stopwatch."

Michael took it from the velvet box. It was a fine instrument, clearly one that cost more than a thousand dollars. Michael examined it, but he really didn't see it because his eyes were filling with tears and the one thing he must not let happen was that his uncle should see him crying.

"It's beautiful. Just beautiful."

"Don't worry about anything. I covered for you. You're in China working on this picture—God, I wish you were. Anyway, I had Peachie call Piro—he's supposed to pack some clothes to send to you."

Michael nodded his thanks, but he couldn't speak.

Lazlo was pained by Michael's tears. It hurt to see him cry almost as much as it hurt to see the blanket on his lap and he thought he could stand it no longer, seeing this wild, arrogant young man brought so low.

He reached out to pat him, but Michael backed out of reach, unwilling to let Lazlo's hand touch his leg.

"Anything you need? They taking good care of you here?"

Michael nodded, his breathing now liquid as he turned his face away from his uncle's sight.

"Nothing you want that you don't have?"

"A phone."

"Huh?" Michael was so choked up Lazlo couldn't make out what he said.

"A telephone," Michael repeated. "They won't let me make any calls."

"Just be careful what you say, huh."

"Sure, sure."

"Aaron's got everything real quiet. Don't make trouble."

Lazlo walked to the door. "Try to understand about the paramedic." He could see Michael tense up, though he couldn't see his face. "He could've been killed, Aaron says."

Please go, please, please go, Michael begged silently. He was determined not to cry out loud in front of this parent of his. It was the only strength he could hold on to, to deny him the sight of his weakness.

"And, Michael, think about shaving the beard. You look like a dope dealer, or a record producer, or something."

In his misery Michael thought achingly of Val, wishing she were with him to help him withstand this sadistic old enemy who would not give him a chance for the one thing he now desired—revenge on the paramedic—and also wouldn't leave him alone.

But when he looked, Lazlo was gone. He had left Aaron's report on the bed. Michael picked it up, read a paragraph and threw it across the room. The pages came apart and fluttered to the floor.

"You take good care of him," Lazlo said to Tanna, instinctively sensing in her exactly what Michael needed. "You give him anything he wants, anything he needs—"

She nodded to this short, ugly version of Michael, this uncle of his who had so much power, who owned her very livelihood. He looked rumpled despite his expensive suit, rumpled, tired and old.

"You understand my meaning, my dear? Anything he wants. And see if you can talk him into shaving off the beard." He glanced at Dr. Raymond, who with Carson had waited outside Michael's room for Lazlo.

"He needs her more than he needs your drugs, you old quack," he said, laughing without a trace of mirth. He threw his arm around the doctor's shoulders, and as they walked down the hall Tanna heard him saying something about getting Michael a telephone. Carson scowled, threw a dirty look at Tanna and walked off.

Tanna smiled to herself and slipped into her patient's room.

He was sitting in front of the window, his fists rhythmically hitting the chrome wheels. She walked up behind him and lay her hand on his shoulder, but he shook her off violently as if her touch burned.

She stood back, ready to wait all night if necessary.

It had been months since Val had visited the UCLA library. That wasn't because she didn't like the peaceful setting among the trees and buildings of the huge campus. She loved it here, always had since she had been an undergraduate memorizing lines out in the sculpture garden. Life after college seemed to have little time for such luxuries.

Now she walked with fond memories past the reflection pool where the somber statue of a woman playing with her stone nipple still stood.

Val walked up the short flight of steps to the library entrance and moved through the card catalogs with the keen sense of having retained her old research skills. She used to get the best grades on college papers, finding out about some obscure Elizabethan playwright, or digging out costume information for the plays of Euripides. That was when she still believed she'd someday be able to direct. She loved keeping the whole play in her head, pretending even now, although privately, to block out action and cast characters.

She found more references on telepathy and related subjects than she had expected. When she located the books in the stacks she was able to quickly pick out ten or so which were written for the layperson.

Standing in the long check-out line, she thumbed through a couple of her selections.

"Can you control another person's movements telepathically?" asked the authors of *Handbook of Psi Discoveries*. "Scientific tests indicate that some people can . . ."

Val stepped up a space in line as the others ahead passed through the check-out gate. She looked through another book. Someone with a penchant like her own for marking library books had underlined the sentence, "Telepathy may spring into evidence as the result of trauma or serious physical injury."

That gave Val an idea. She set the ESP books to one side of the large check-out desk and stepped out of line. She moved back toward the card catalog again; there was another subject she could research for Misha.

There weren't many books in this library on amputation, though there were references to the medical library. But Val didn't want to learn to perform the operation. She just wanted some information on the psychology of recovery.

She took the elevator to the third floor, searching out a couple of books that might be what she wanted.

One, complete with a number of alarming pictures, informed her that one in about 250 Americans had lost an arm or leg, and that 98 percent of them suffered from phantom limb. Amputation was considered a major psychological as well as physical trauma. Many new amputees were depressive and even suicidal.

It was really depressing because it described Misha to a tee.

She set aside that book and took up another that was far more entertaining and hopeful. This one had the intriguing title of *Best Foot Forward*. Val, who was an avid Lucille Ball fan, was familiar with the actress's movie of that title, but this book wasn't the same story. It was instead the incredible story of an English pilot named Colin Hodgkinson who lost both legs during World War II and went on to fly hundreds of missions and eventually survive capture by the Germans.

Sitting at a desk beside a tall window, Val started reading the absorbing book by the extraordinary hero. Not five pages into it she was sure it would help Misha.

"Young men," the major wrote, "believe such things always happen to someone else."

Val stared out of the window, feeling her own thoughts churning. Down below students were clustered in pairs or small groups at an outside eating area. It was a peaceful academic scene with pretty people in the bright sunshine, sparkling leaves all around like a border on an antique manuscript.

The book had given Val another idea.

Since Misha was an actor with a track record and an uncle who produced TV movies, maybe they could buy the rights to the major's story. Misha could star in it. It would be just the thing to bring him back, and Val's commercial sense told her it could be a big success.

It was a terrific idea, she just knew it. She had to get this book to Misha.

She read a little more. The major had lost his legs on his qualifying solo flight and had gone back into the cockpit because he was determined not to let his fear of flying ground him. While he was recuperating his fiancée came to see him, to tell him that she "wanted time to think things over." But she was really saying good-bye.

"There is a class of human being for whom amputation is not nice," Hodgkinson wrote about the heartbreaking rejection. "Double amputation was of a sudden something obscene . . ."

Val closed the book and thought about Misha's reac-

161

tion to the woman with the mastectomy scar they'd seen in the gym. It reminded her of Brenda's stubborn refusal to deal with her deafness, how she made others accommodate her and how it finally resulted in the worse handicap of being cut off and misunderstood.

Misha must fight the inclination to pretend he's the way he was before. Val knew she had to help him despite himself.

She took the major's book to the check-out desk, where there was an even longer line than before.

She took a place at the end of the line behind a girl with a single book. The girl didn't speak but she smiled wanly at Val as if to commiserate with her over having to stand in line. When they stepped closer to the check-out gate, Val set the major's book on the desk edge while she pulled the other books she'd left there toward her.

The girl ahead of her brushed against the major's book and knocked it to the floor. She picked it up for Val, and as she stood Val saw her pleasant expression change to undisguised distaste when she saw the pictures of Major Hodgkinson (called Hoppy by his squadron) learning to use prosthesis.

"How gross," the girl said, her pretty lip curled. "You a medical student or something?"

It made Val uncomfortable and a little angry. How dare she react like that to something a person couldn't help. Then she remembered her own reaction to the veteran she'd seen collecting for wheelchair basketball. Misha was right; that was the way he said most people would react.

Val shrugged to the girl. "Life goes on."

The girl pushed her book across the desk to be checked out, but over her shoulder she said to Val, "I'd rather be dead."

Val was really glad Misha wasn't with her to hear that.

She couldn't get the girl's reaction out of her mind.

162

She thought about it all the way home. She made a cup of coffee and took all her books into the den. She set aside the major's book for a thorough read later on, and spread out all the texts on telepathy in a smorgasbord of facts and figures, ideas, speculations, explanations and personal experiences. She marked pages and cross-referenced, learning more about telepathy than she had ever thought there was to know.

One particularly interesting book called *Stalking the Wild Pendulum* by Itzhak Bentov suggested that more and more people will have psychic abilities in the future.

What if others, hundreds or millions of other people started having telepathic experiences, Val wondered. What would happen as people got used to hearing someone else in their heads? What if you didn't want to hear a particular telepathic communication? What if they found a way to put commercials out into the air waves like that? How could anyone stay sane? It could be a curse. On the other hand people would be less likely to lie, to cheat or steal. Maybe it would bring people closer together.

She thought about Misha intervening in that near-accident this afternoon. At the very least she would have been hurt because that van would have hit the driver's side of her car if it hadn't been for Misha. He reached out to save her and now she must do the same for him. She knew she would get some of these books to him and they would give him hope. Major Hodgkinson's book would give him a model. He'd see that the anguish he was going through was part of the healing process and he would get well, maybe even walk again.

She lay the book she had been reading, *Journeys Out of the Body*, on the ottoman in front of her chair, then lay the pencil she'd been marking it with in the crack between the open pages.

In the back of her mind all afternoon had been the question of how to use her knowledge of where Misha was. She could send the books over by messenger. Or she could take them herself.

She liked that idea best.

She found the phone under some scripts and called information, then called the number for the Sunnyrest Convalescent Hospital. A switchboard operator answered.

"This is the Encino Florist Shop," Val said officiously. "We need to confirm a delivery for a patient, Stefano, Michael C."

"Just a moment," the operator said and clicked over.

She came back on the line immediately. "We don't have a patient registered under that name."

"But I'm *sure*," Val began earnestly, then changed her tone back to disinterested clerk. "We were given this hospital as the delivery address, ma'am."

"I'm sorry. May I take your name and have our administrator return your call?"

"Uh, no, never mind." She hung up, her heart suddenly beating loudly as if she were a child playing telephone pranks. So, she thought, they aren't giving out his name. That fit with what Maxine reported about a discrepancy in the documents for Michael's accident. Perhaps his uncle had hushed up the incident until he was sure of Michael's cooperation, considering their well-known feud.

Well, it appeared that it was going to be difficult to just walk in and see Misha. Val's unconscious must've been anticipating this snag, because she had a solution. Her mother and father were on his long retirement vacation, their first overseas in their thirty-one years of marriage. They were due back from the South Pacific in two weeks, and had left their keys with their daughter so she could keep an eye on their Glendale home.

Val recalled fondly that her costume trunks were in Daddy's garage. The fragile costume history of Val's career all the way back to her first tap dance recital was in those trunks.

She jumped up from her favorite reading chair, forgetting to turn off the light above the many books she left lying marked and dog-eared on the floor.

She had a plan now that she knew where her man sat crouched and hiding, waiting for her love to come and save him.

CHAPTER 17

Maxine drove home slowly through the deepening twilight of Wednesday evening. The boys were at some kind of game, and Hugh was in the den watching the news. She joined him, sitting on the arm of his chair without speaking.

When a commercial came on she said, "Sorry I'm late."

She bent over to kiss his forehead. "Thanks for fixing everything at the office."

He lowered the volume with a channel wand.

"Sorry I made such a mess," he said, returning her kiss.

"How was court?"

"The judge recessed until next week. Their chief witness has the measles, if you can believe that—"

"Adults do get measles. They say it causes—" She realized what she was saying, but continued, no way out of it now. "—sterility. Or maybe that's the mumps."

He hugged her to let her know it was okay. After a time he asked, "What'd you say to that girl today? She left in a hurry." He took Val's check from his pocket and handed it to Maxine. Maxine had called Lazlo Stefano's office late that afternoon. She left a message with his secretary, pretty sure she wouldn't get to talk to him. Probably sic a lawyer on her, she thought.

"I guess I found out what she wanted to know." Maxine looked down at Hugh, who had tilted his face back to watch her. "What did you think of her?"

His eye darted to the silent TV screen where another commercial appeared.

"I was only with her a minute before you called."

"But you must've formed some impression."

"I didn't know you wanted a professional evaluation."

"Well, not professional, exactly."

He upped the volume when the newscaster's face appeared after the commercial.

"If you'd like for me to come up with some conclusions about, say, her stability, why don't you arrange an innocent meeting or something."

"She's closed the case."

Hugh let the volume creep up just a fraction. Maxine needed no more of a hint, but she kept talking. "Her teeth were chattering—did she get wet, too?"

Hugh gestured at the TV set. There was a short news item about the case he was working on, a mere mention that it had been recessed.

Together they watched in silence as the talking head read the news story; then when the anchorman turned it over to the weatherman, Hugh said without looking away from the screen, "Why don't you ask her to the party?"

"Boss, you calling from China?"

Michael could hear the Pacific Ocean behind his houseboy's voice. He must have answered the extension beside the sliding glass door for the surf to sound so loud over the phone. Michael could almost smell the sea: He longed to be in his Malibu home.

"China?"

"Ms. Peach say you shoot a picture in China. Make big deal."

"Ms. Peach is just a bundle of information, isn't she?"

"Huh, boss?" Behind Piro's voice Michael heard a sandpaper growl and whimper.

"How's Caesar?"

"He miss you—won't eat."

"Take good care of my baby," Michael said. He heard the solid sound of Piro's hand slapping the Doberman's flank. The dog whimpered and barked.

"He hear you—lick phone—"

"Listen, Piro, I'm not in China." Michael leaned back on the clean sheets, pleasantly smooth to his bare back. Turn over, Tanna signaled, and he obeyed. As Michael continued talking to Piro, she began massaging his back.

"I was in an accident—"

"You okay?"

"Well, I'm better. I'll be home soon. Meantime, I want you to bring some things to the Sunnyrest Hospital on Ventura—clothes, pajamas, bathrobe—"

"I already pack for China."

"Yeah; and my telephone file. The big Rolodex with all my business numbers. Oh, and my binoculars. They're in the hall closet with the camera equipment—"

"Oh, yes," Piro said happily. "The one we use to take the movies of the girls."

"That's the one. Good man." Tanna got to a particularly sore muscle in his shoulder and he groaned.

"You sure you okay?"

"I'm getting better all the time, Piro. I can't think of anything else. My guitar, I guess, some shirts."

"Shoes and socks, huh? Which shoes you want, boss?"

"Uh, you decide, Piro. You decide."

Val wasn't home Wednesday night when Frank returned after a bitch of a day that had gone into overtime.

He carried several film cans as he walked through the dark apartment, knowing Val wasn't there but calling her name anyway. The place had two bedrooms. The master they used for sleeping, and the smaller they divided as a kind of office and editing room.

They both had realized at the beginning of their relationship that each needed private space. Val did a

167

lot of reading in connection with whatever part she was playing. In between the commercials she usually danced through, she worked in local theater groups and every once in a while landed a part in a series or in a made-for-TV movie.

She was always rereading some classic play. Lately she'd gone through everything Isben wrote, often learning whole scenes, playing all the parts.

Frank was always cutting some film project on the sly around union rules or legitimately free-lancing spill-over jobs from the lab. Also he had been cutting his never-completed masters thesis for more than eight years. When he was bored he'd go in and tinker with the thing, knowing in his heart he'd never finish it but playing around with it anyway. His side of the room contained a metal desk with a frame counter on it, a simple desk chair, a swivel lamp, film strips taped to every wall surface almost to the ceiling, boxes of hundreds of marked film cans and two editing machines.

He set the film he'd brought home tonight on the antique Movieola he had taken in lieu of payment on a small job last month. It was busted, but he liked looking at it because it was from the early days of movies. The other editing machine was more modern but still an oldie, army green and noisy to operate. It was his primary working tool.

Val's side of the room was a more cozy office with a huge upholstered chair, a side table stacked with scripts and books, a small rolltop desk she'd had since she was a teenager and an ottoman in front of the chair. There, snuggled under an afghan crocheted by her Great-aunt Floreta, she would read or memorize for hours under the glow of a hanging lamp.

That lamp was on in the otherwise dark flat. On, as if Val had been reading late into the afternoon as the light outside failed, when something—perhaps something in the book she was reading—compelled her to get up and go somewhere in a hurry.

Frank walked casually to the chair. The material

was cool to the touch, so she had been gone more than a few minutes. Yet the chair and the afghan still held her impression.

An old clock on the bookcase on the far wall tick-tocked in a melancholy way. He half expected to turn and see Val standing at the bookcase, but when he looked he saw he was alone.

He felt slightly guilty being on her side of the room. They had a strict hands-off policy about two things—each other's mail and these separate but joined sanctuaries. To rummage around on her side of the room, to disturb the arrangement of the books she had obviously been reading, to find out what subject had so fascinated her that she left these dozen texts scattered all around with pages marked—that was some kind of violation he felt guilt for. He knew how furious he'd be if she so much as touched a single fragment of film taped to his side of the wall. But he'd never listened in on her phone conversations before, either, yet he'd been doing that recently. He rationalized that this was a special circumstance and he had Val's best interests at heart.

He crouched down to see what passage she'd been reading just before she had set this book open here on the ottoman.

Frank picked up the library book. He knew of Val's habit of marking library books, but usually they were bound copies of industry magazines, or various published plays in paperback.

But this was something different. It was *Journeys Out of the Body* by Robert Monroe. Two others left open on top of the ottoman were *Parapsychology* by Rene Sudre and *Mental Radio* by Upton Sinclair.

Upton Sinclair? Frank wondered, *the* Upton Sinclair? He saw on the flyleaf that it was. The playwright and his wife had conducted numerous telepathy experiments which Sinclair claimed were successful. Einstein even wrote the introduction to the book. That impressed Frank, but the other books scattered on the floor, arranged in a semicircle facing the chair, seemed less reputable. They were all on the subject of telepathy, consciousness or possession. One recalled Ken Russell's film *The Devils*.

It was *Bibliotheque Diabolique*, a nineteenth-century discussion of the devils of Loudun. Val had bracketed a quote from one of the priests involved in that famous possession case, Father de Surin. Frank couldn't resist reading aloud the strange report from the lips of the no doubt crazy priest as he told it in 1635:

" 'I could not explain to you what went on in me at that time and as this spirit linked itself to my own without depriving me of consciousness . . .' " Frank intoned sarcastically as he sat hunched on Val's chair.

" 'But making itself nevertheless into another myself as if I had two souls, one of which is dispossessed of its body and the use of its organs and stands aside watching the action of the new soul that had entered.' "

Some of the sarcasm bled from Frank's voice as he finished the quote, " 'When I wished, by the action of one of these two souls, to make the sign of the cross . . . the other turns aside my head very quickly and stuffs my finger between my teeth to gnaw at it with rage.' "

A chill ran up Frank's basically Irish spine. The clock ticked on.

"What in God's name is Val into?" he wondered aloud. He lay aside the old book and looked at the others arranged on the floor. From where he sat he could read several passages she had underlined.

"O the power of thought," one chapter heading quoted Lord Byron, "The magic of the mind."

Frank picked up a heavy bound volume, relatively new, one that he remembered seeing reviewed somewhere important, *The Times*, or one of the news magazines. It was *Handbook of Psi Discoveries* by Ostrander and Schroeder:

"Researchers at the Maimonides Medical Center in Brooklyn have established the reality of telepathy in dreams and pursue it on a government grant," Val had underlined.

Telepathy in Brooklyn, Frank thought. That had to

be the living end. Another waste of taxpayers' money as far as he was concerned.

He caught an author's name he recognized on another volume.

He knew of Val's vestigial Catholicism in conflict with her rebellion against the Church. That conflict left her with a fondness for one of the Church's least-favored sons, Teilhard de Chardin. The book that lay open belonged to Val. She'd had this copy of *The Human Phenomenon* since college. Hardly a page of it was without the adoring defacement of her neat hand-written notes.

One passage she had underlined with yellow ink oddly tied in with all this other crap on telepathy:

". . . as mankind patterns its multitudes . . . the psychic tension within it increases . . . How can we fail to see that after rolling us on individually—all of us, you and me—upon ourselves, it is the same cyclone . . . which is still blowing over our heads, driving us together into a contact which tends to perfect each one of us by linking him organically to each and all his neighbors?"

Val had circled "driving us together."

Sweet Jesus, Frank subvocalized. If she could find justification in de Chardin, Val would believe the Earth was flat. Frank personally had never seen what de Chardin was getting at. Too obscure for him. But he knew Val loved the mystical paleontologist.

He sat staring at her books, trying to determine how bad it was. This could all be preparation for some role he didn't know about. Maybe Brenda had conned her into doing *The Crucible, Dracula, Blithe Spirit, Bell Book and Candle* or even *Finian's Rainbow,* for all he knew.

No, he told himself, shaking his head. It's those dreams. Those fucking dreams. She had told him she thought she heard someone calling from the dreams.

"Christ," he muttered, slapping his fist, "I've got to get her to see the shrink."

Just then he heard the front door open.

171

"Frank?" her sweet voice called.

Frank hurriedly replaced the de Chardin book, but in his haste he dropped it and lost her place. He left it there and walked back over to his side of the room. He picked up a strip of film as though he had been looking at it with Val's light behind it.

The clock on the shelf struck a note: seven o'clock.

"Hi," she said breathlessly as she entered. She regarded the striking clock as she came over to Frank with a package from one of those all-night drugstores. Over her other arm was folded what looked like a white dress.

"Where you been?"

She looked around her chair.

"Oh, out and around. Went over to Mom and Dad's, bought some shoes. Frank . . . ?" She turned with wide eyes focused on him.

"Did you move any of these books. There's one missing . . ." Then she saw the de Chardin on the floor facedown. She picked it up.

"How dare you," she said simply.

"I was interested in what you were reading. Sorry I lost your place."

"Since when are you interested in anything occult?"

He shrugged and shoved his hands into his pockets. "That's pretty interesting stuff."

"You're spying on me again, aren't you?"

"I mean, that devil stuff is pretty interesting," he snorted, starting to snicker.

"How dare you violate my space, Frank Surrell."

From behind her eyes she heard Misha's voice say, "Give him hell, Valentine."

It startled her.

"You said seven, Mama," Misha whispered as she stared back at Frank's guilty eyes. "You said I could be with you after seven."

Val shivered as if chilled and took a step toward Frank.

"How would you like it if I moved this little piece of film?" She grabbed a strip that was looped several

172

times in a canvas bin behind the working editing machine. Frank stepped toward her.

"Here comes the bastard," Misha hissed in her mind and she jumped back, taking a handful of film strips that came loose from their taped moorings on the wall.

"Now you've gone and done it," Frank yelled. He reached out to take hold of her arm, but she wrenched free. He had stepped into a cardboard box full of film cans that spilled onto the floor.

"Let me have him," Misha said in her inner ear. She saw the snarl of menace on Frank's face and in that moment hated him.

Everything went kind of red then black after that, and the next thing she knew she was lying on the floor, a film can pressing uncomfortably into her spine.

Frank was sitting on her chair, the phone in his hands, talking softly to someone.

"Yeah," he said, unable to see Val coming around.

"I tell you, she became another person there for a minute, some kind of maniac, strong as hell——" He looked around the decimated film collection. The room was in disarray and when Frank turned against the light Val saw that his nose was bleeding blackly. He patted at it with a stained handkerchief. Val could see his bruised hand trembling. She caught the word *schizo*.

She rose to a sitting position and caught Frank's eye with the movement. He stared at her.

"Tomorrow." He paused, listening, nodding finally. "Okay. three P.M. Yeah. Bye, Phil."

He replaced the phone receiver without taking his eyes from Val as she struggled to rise in the shadows.

A few blocks away Michael lay trembling in a sweat-soaked bed. He let go of the bed rail he had been gripping with white knuckles. Bunch, the orderly, had fallen asleep in a chair. Michael lay there. pulling a more controlled breathing out of himself. With each breath he let go of the rail some more until he was leaning back on the pillows. Each time he took on

173

Val's body he had to let go of his own. Reentry was difficult, but he was learning.

Oh, how he was learning. His face was strained and sweat-mottled, but there was a narrow smile on his lips Bunch would have seen and been worried about if he hadn't been snoozing.

Michael breathed more normally. He lay his arm across his eyes.

"Oh boy," he whispered to himself with extreme satisfaction. "Oh boy, oh boy, oh boy. I can do it. If she's the slightest bit willing, I can drive that little girl like an eight-cylinder turbo charge."

Only one problem, really, confronting him, he thought, his mind racing. The problem was how to get rid of Frank.

Soon.

CHAPTER 18

"I have no intention of arguing with you," Val said as she left the bathroom.

Frank was in one of his let's-get-it-all-out-in-the-open moods.

"No argument. Just a calm, rational discussion of events."

She was brushing her hair in front of the beveled mirror over her chest of drawers. She could see Frank behind her on his side of the bed, his light turned out. She couldn't actually see his black eye, but she could tell exactly where it was from his position in the gloom. She was trying to sort it all out. Misha was gone. He abruptly pulled away from her sometime back there when she blacked out and she hadn't heard his secret call since. That had been more than three hours ago. Frank had to be at work by six tomorrow, Thursday, so he wanted to get to bed early. Val had been exhausted, and agreed.

"A—" Frank was saying, ticking off his points finger by finger, "you are acting more crazy than anyone I've ever seen, and, B, you won't admit it."

"I'm not crazy. I told you, I've considered that possibility, and I know that's not what's happening here."

"I know what you think," he said tightly. "All those books, those dreams, that shit. You think you're hearing someone in your mind, don't you? Telepathy, that's what you think it is. Psycho-whatsis."

"There's no way to prove anything to you and you won't take my word, so I'm not going to talk to you about it," she said, not looking at him as she filed her nails. He was going to keep on, baiting her for a fight. He was so transparent. He thought that if they fought they would make up afterward. He knew already, without words, that she had no intention of fucking tonight. She had a raunchy, pit-smell to her even though she had bathed. He knew she was menstruating, a turn-on for them both, but she was putting out wave after cold bleak wave of rejection that infuriated and pained him. Still he hoped to provoke another fight. He had decided secretly that he liked this violent, sexy new Valentine. He wanted to see her in operation again, fists flying, blood in her eye. It gave him an erection just thinking about her like that, but the covers hid it.

Val knew anyway.

"I suppose it's a man," Frank said sarcastically. "This telepathic playmate."

She ignored him. She had earlier considered staying at Mom and Dad's house. How she wished now she had done so.

"You're oversexed, Val. Left-handed people always are. You've invented an imaginary playmate to get yourself off." Those were both guaranteed fight-starters that had provoked several past arguments.

Val's lip twitched. Her nails were ragged. She hit them with a slicing motion of the emery board. She was determined not to take any bait.

"I thought you were going to get your nails done."

"The manicurist was sick."

She had that audition at eleven in the morning, just barely time to get her hair done. She hadn't been able to get an appointment this afternoon; all that was available was a nine A.M. tomorrow slot that would leave her only minutes to get to Century City for the audition after a quick cut and blow-dry.

She forced herself to recall the appointment time, the address of the shop, the name, age and personal history of her hairdresser, all to keep herself distracted from Frank's salvos.

"You're really sick, you know that?" Frank snarled, getting pissed off that she wasn't answering.

Val wished fervently that Misha would come to her. She looked up past Frank into the mirror at a window open on the other side of the bed. A breeze was moving the drape. She could smell that particular sweet smell that came with the natural overcast accompanying these early spring evenings and mornings.

"You're going to see Phil if I have to drive you there myself."

Val chewed the inside of her mouth.

Frank moved around in the covers, settling deeper into them.

Misha, where are you, Val called in her mind.

"Come on to bed," Frank said. "It's getting late." He had already set the clock. It was just past ten.

Val lay aside the emery board and walked toward the bed. On the way she picked up the headset and snapped on the TV.

"Oh, Val, not tonight."

She climbed into the covers, plumped her pillows and settled down to watch the news. Under the headset she departed from Frank, the TV screen beyond her feet ignored.

Frank burrowed into the covers until he was nothing more than a flannel blob, while Val sat there staring into nothing. She didn't call Misha. She just sat there waiting attentively, in case she heard him calling her.

*   *   *

"Hey, ol' buddy," Michael said into the receiver. In the background he could hear rock music, people laughing and talking like a party. His buddy Claud loved to have parties in his Hollywood Hills home.

"How's it going, baby—you outta circulation," Claud said. "Come on over, we got a few girls, a couple cases of wine, some hash—"

"I can't," Michael said, resting back as he spoke. Tanna was reading a book in the chair by the window. He could barely make out that it was a current best-seller. "I'm in the hospital."

"Taking the cure?" the cynically knowing voice said.

"A minor operation." Michael saw Tanna look up at him from the book she was reading.

"Deviated septum, huh? That old cocaine finally ate your nose out, huh?"

"Yeah. That's what it is. Hey, listen, I have a favor to ask."

"Anything. I owe you for that time in Mexico."

"You have anything outta town for a friend of mine, needs to get away, you know. He's a good director, but he'll take anything you got."

"Hell, Michael, I don't know. Things are slow right now."

"I want to help my friend out so bad I'd even pick up half his tab. He's that good a friend."

"Hmmm. This guy hot or something?"

"No, nothing like that. He's having woman problems, you know."

"What's he done?"

"Docs, video, some news stuff that won some prizes. He's good."

"Well, I might have some pickups on an oil-rig doc due in next week. Santa Barbara. But it's a really numbnuts job. Drive up tomorrow, shoot on Friday, have the stuff back to me for processing. Got to be in the man's hands bright and early Monday."

"Santa Barbara?" Michael said, focusing on Tanna reading.

177

"Afraid that's all I have right now. Got that only because some guy croaked. Christ, you never know when your number's coming up."

"Right. Well, thanks. I have Surrell's number—that's his name, Frank Surrell, you probably heard of him. Five-five-five-HONK."

"What's that?"

"His phone number. Five-five-five-HONK. H-O-N-K."

"Got it. I'll give him a call right now. I have to confirm, you know—"

"That's his home number."

"Say, by the way, the word's out you and your old man patched things up. You working for him on this China picture?"

"Uh, supposed to, yes."

"Maybe now you can talk to him about my script, huh?"

"Oh, sure, Claud. Soon as I get back on my, uh, feet, again."

"Yeah, get well soon. We'll go whorin'."

"Yeah."

Michael hung up the phone and sat brewing in his satisfaction. Tanna caught his eye. She smiled at the erotic sparkle she saw there.

Val didn't hear the phone ring, but she felt Frank's movements as he sat up to answer it. She stared ahead, superficially seeing the TV screen, the colors and movement, but not partaking of it. She could hear Frank's muffled voice through the headset.

"Val, Val," he was saying suddenly, pulling at her, taking the headset from her ears. "You won't believe this—"

"What?"

"That was Claud Davis on the phone. Claud Davis—he called *me* to help him out. Some pickups on an oil-derrick documentary up in Santa Barbara—holy cow—there's going to be a problem at the lab—they're swamped right now—"

Val almost made the mistake of asking why Claud Davis would call Frank, but she held her tongue. Frank *had* been working hard.

"The regular guy dropped dead. They need the footage Monday."

"When do you leave?"

"I'm supposed to meet the cameraman tomorrow afternoon. Val—" he said, turning to watch her. "Go with me."

"Oh—" She shook her head.

"Come on. It's just what we both need—get out of the city. Get some fresh air. The beach'll be great. Come on, honey," he said tenderly. The adrenal rush of opportunity was pulling the corners of his mouth into an unnatural grin.

"I can't, Frank."

"Val—it'd do you a world of good."

"You made that appointment for me tomorrow afternoon," she said cannily, knowing what his answer would be.

"We'll cancel it. Phil would be the first to agree this trip will be better for you than three hours of therapy."

"No. I have too much to do."

"What?"

"Brenda says I'm a natural for this thing tomorrow. If I get it, I'll be locked in for a week or more."

"Hmm."

"This sounds like an opportunity for you, Frank."

"Boy, is it ever. He called *me*. Can you beat that? I've been trying to get him to look at my stuff for months, then, out of the blue, bang, he calls me like an old friend and begs me to help him out. I can't believe it."

"You never know when luck is going to strike." Actually Frank had been trying to get everybody in town to look at his films.

"That's for sure," he said, simmering with pleasure. It was an emotion that did not go well with his usually dour countenance. He appeared hyper, shaky, a little out of control.

He put the phone back on the bedside table and slunk back down into the covers, grinning to himself.

Val regarded the silent TV set. Near her hand was the headset with tiny voices inside it like bees. Val switched off the system with a remote control wand. A hard point of light centered itself on the glass screen, and the high-pitched buzz faded from the air of the bedroom. Val turned off her light and lay back in the darkness.

"I suppose you have a headache?"

"I'm working on one," she replied.

"I sure would like to celebrate."

Val ached with desire, but not for this man.

"Val?" Frank said.

Misha, where are you now? Val cried silently.

Frank's hand touched her skin.

There was a trace of bitchiness in Val she wished she could direct to her silent companion. Where was he? How dare he just leave her without a word, scaring her like this. He needed to be taken down a peg or two, pulling that macho shit.

On that fragment of revenge she turned to Frank's mundane warmth, secretly hoping Misha would suddenly come to her and be jealous.

"You want some help, Mr. Stefano?"

"Uh, no, uh—" Michael stammered. He had been impotent with Tanna so he'd been jacking off, or rather trying to under the covers with his back turned on the world.

Bunch's stupid, kind face loomed over him, wide and innocent and childlike. Michael hated him.

"Uh, thanks, no, Bunch." Shit, Michael wondered, why am I feeling like this? Like I was a little kid and Lazlo caught me—

"I'd be glad to help you out, if you want me to."

Michael wasn't sure for a second if Bunch meant it. Maybe they were talking about different things.

"I don't think you can give me the help I need."

"Oh yes," Bunch said brightly. It irked Michael that

180

he was so open, so friendly. He couldn't figure out the guy's con. "I know just what you need—" With that he reached purposefully out and yanked back the blanket Michael had pulled up to his nipples.

His penis was painfully hard, red and utterly dry. Michael felt totally vulnerable; he actually shrank back against the bed, grabbing instinctively for the covers. The actual feeling was all around his navel, a cold slimy soup of sensation that bordered between agony and delight. Like an elevator drop when you're three years old, he thought. Rosa's laugh echoed down the halls of memory.

"It's okay," Bunch said, his voice completely devoid of lasciviousness. His strong pink hands lightly touched Michael's thighs. Slowly, methodically, he began massaging, kneading, rolling the flesh between the fingers, harder and harder until Michael cried out in small pain. Bunch's grip loosened.

"You just lean back now, Mr. Stefano. I'm good at this."

"No," he heard the patient croak, pulling the sheet up.

Bunch swiftly reached down between his own legs and pulled a chair under his ass as he sat down. It was a polished action, done many times before. Orderlies were like bartenders, Everyman's shrink. He leaned close to Michael, who was scrunching down in the covers. His legs were hurting like hell. The stumps were throbbing with the painful knit of cellular growth. Bunch's touch had activated all the nerves in his lower body. He was glad he could pull up the covers; he didn't want Bunch's hands to bring his climax. "Go on, get out."

"You gotta relax, trust me," Bunch was saying in a soothing voice. He used his big hands to emphasize his points, slow and sure. He wasn't stupid, just slow, Michael thought.

"Course, if you want me to call Tanna, I will."

"It's okay. Just leave me alone."

Eager to comply, Bunch got up from the chair and left.

Michael breathed relief.

CHAPTER 19

She didn't hear from Misha until the next morning, a bright, cheerful Thursday, on her way to the beauty salon.

She was pulling away from an intersection after the light had changed when she saw that a bee or wasp or some kind of large stinging insect had gotten itself trapped in the car. It buzzed furiously in the narrow place just this side of the windshield. Val hated bugs and she was afraid of a bee sting. She always got sick after bee stings and didn't want one while she was driving or at any other time. She grabbed a map from the holder and started flapping it toward the bug, which she now saw was a wasp.

"Kill the fucker," she heard Misha's unmistakable voice in her mind.

"Misha—"

"It's going to get you."

Val rolled the window down.

"There—I can hear it—get it while it's landed."

"No," she said, scooping at the insect while keeping her attention on the road. Finally the wasp slipped out into the brilliant morning air.

"That was dumb, Val. Why didn't you kill it?"

"Where were you last night? I was terrified."

"I saw that bastard coming at you, and I couldn't let him hurt you."

"You scared the shit out of me."

"Good. He'd better keep his hands off you."

A diesel honked at the nearby left.

"I heard that," Misha said, "to the left, a big semi."

"That's amazing."

"I can feel your foot. Your right foot on the pedal."

"Stop that—it gives me the creeps. Listen—Frank's made a shrink appointment for me."

"Well, you're not going to keep it."

"No, but I haven't told Frank that." She pulled into the parking lot of the beauty shop and went inside, the secret conversation continuing without interruption. A couple of times Misha even made comments about what was happening in her objective reality.

"I hate the smell in these places," he said as Val was escorted by the hostess back to the station of Charles, her regular hairdresser. While she waited for him to return from wherever he was, Val sat in the plastic-covered barber's chair and talked in silence with Misha.

"You can smell it?" she asked, incredulous.

"Yeah, that ammonia smell."

"It's from the permanent-wave solution, I guess," she said, playing with her straggly hair as she watched herself in the mirror.

"I can see you," he said.

She smiled for him.

"God, you're beautiful. Don't let these butchers change a hair."

"I have to get it cut. See how shaggy it's gotten?" She held out a lock of curly ginger-colored hair.

"Yes, yes, beautiful Valentine," another man's voice said behind her, and she looked up to see Charles coming at her with his hands flexed, already reaching to touch her hair. "You've let it go a long time," he admonished like a dentist.

"A swish," Misha said behind her eyes.

"No, just sensitive," Val replied silently, smiling up at Charles. "And he's really good."

She felt the mental equivalent of a snort from Misha.

Charles led her back to the shampoo bowls and washed her hair with his own expert hands because the shampoo girls were all busy with other customers. It

183

was a delicious experience for Val for Charles to wash her hair, a duty usually beneath him.

"Yeah," Misha said, "he's good all right. Strong hands. Lots of exercise."

"Misha. You always think the worst."

"Hmmmph." What she heard was not a sound, but was a muffling of sound that set up a small vibration on the inside of her skull.

He was quiet while Charles rinsed her hair and added a conditioner, the cold liquid trickling all over her scalp.

Actually Val's hair only needed shaping. Its natural curl lay perfectly with only the least amount of blow-drying. Charles knew just the look she liked to keep; he was proud of this rising young actress who wore "his" hair.

"So," Misha said a while later, while Charles was using the blower, "tell me about Frank. What'd he do?"

"You scared him pretty bad last night. I guess he's never seen me as mad as I was, coming at him. His eye was black and his nose was bleeding."

"I'll kill him the next time he puts a hand on you."

"Frank means well."

"Oh, come on, last night you wanted to break his face in."

"I have to admit I was mad."

"Mad—lady, you were furious."

"But I wouldn't have hit him. I want you to promise you won't do that again."

"Hell no. You think of yourself as nonviolent, don't you? But you wanted to kill him back there. You can't lie to me, Val. Maybe to yourself, but not to me."

"I don't believe in killing."

"You'd kill if you had to, to save yourself."

"I don't know. I doubt that I could kill even then."

Charles pulled extra hard and Val made a sound of protest.

"Sorry, darling—"

"Prick," Misha exclaimed. Then to Val: "You'd kill. If your life depended on it, you'd kill."

"I'd find another way."

"Let the wasp out through the window, right?"

"No use killing an innocent creature. It's just being what it is. No use killing it for being a wasp."

"The fucker could cause a wreck that could kill you."

"But it's so easy to just free it."

"Easy to say with a bug. You can feel self-righteous over saving its little life. But in a pinch you'd kill without batting an eye, just like any other human being who wants to survive."

"Survival's not everything. The way you survive—how you think about yourself—that's important, too. I'm glad I didn't kill that wasp."

"You idealists are all alike. You just refuse to take the reality of human behavior into account. The world is the way it is, not the way you want it to be."

Charles was turning her chair around so she could see the lovely cut he had given her. He was a magician with a razor. She hopped out of the chair and gave him a kiss as she slipped a five into his pocket for a tip, then walked to the front of the salon.

"How's the world ever going to get better if we don't believe it can?" Val answered as she paid the cashier.

"Dreamer," Misha chuckled. Val didn't answer and there was a lull in the conversation.

"So, where are you going now?" he finally asked.

"I have an audition at Ritcher's—you know them over there?"

"I don't have too many contacts in commercials," he said, and Val couldn't help but detect some superiority from him. People in the business looked down on people who made commercials. But it still remained the most active film area, one that used more actors, directors and other production talents than movies and entertainment television. "Who's casting?"

"Favio Bernstein." She left the salon and hurriedly walked to the car.

"Good old Favio."

"You know him?"

"We've worked together. He's directing too? What's the gig?"

"Dog food commercial."

"Uh-oh."

"What's the matter?" she asked, as she started the engine.

"He'll pull something."

"Like what?"

"Oh, I don't know. Something unexpected. He probably had them train the dog to run up and pee on your foot, just to see how you come across with the animal. He'll get your reaction on film, probably, and they'll use the film to determine who gets the part."

She was driving east on Wilshire Boulevard. Traffic as usual was a soup and required her concentration. But inside, as she drove, she carried on the interior dialog.

"You're awfully cynical, Misha, you know that."

"I had a good teacher."

"Who was that? An acting coach?"

"No. My uncle."

"Lazlo Stefano's an infamous man."

"He deserves his reputation. I don't know a meaner human being."

"What's he like? Will I get to meet him?" She discretely avoided asking if she was ever going to get to meet the uncle's nephew.

"Too bad you wanted to be Garbo yesterday afternoon. You could have seen him in glorious action."

"What do you mean?"

"He came to see me. To bestow his generosity on me."

"I thought he was in China." She followed the trades religiously.

"He came home early to deal with me, I suppose."

"Sounds like he cares for you."

"Oh sure—says to call when I'm feeling better. He refuses to go after that son of a bitch who did this to

186

me. If I don't cooperate and play the hero for the publicity people, he'll keep me locked up forever."

" 'I could be bound in a nutshell and count myself king of infinite space,' " Val quoted.

"What's with the Shakespeare?"

"Hamlet."

"I know what it's from. I guess I'm just surprised you know."

"Thanks."

"It's not what you'd expect from a girl on her way to try out for a dog food commercial."

"I take my work seriously. I trained for it and studied all aspects of it."

"Serious actress. What else you done? Any real acting?"

"You sound sarcastic." She did not tell him her biggest part had been in a cereal commercial where she danced on a giant spoon.

"No, I don't mean to. My uncle's visit just put me down, that's all."

"What did he say to you?"

"Oh, what you'd expect. I'm supposed to be brave and pick up the pieces, all that hero crap."

"He's right."

"I can't believe you're siding with him."

"It sounds like he wants the best for you."

"Oh, yeah. Uncle Lazlo has always had my best interests at heart. You want to hear a little story about my uncle?"

"Sure." She still had a good ten minutes of driving before she arrived at the audition studio. Plenty of time to make it, she thought as she glanced at her watch. There was something reassuring in this silent conversation. She always did her best thinking while driving. Something about having her conscious mind occupied with mundane chores, it freed her thoughts. Talking to Misha was like thinking fast, and she liked it.

"He raised me. You probably know that. After my mother and father died. He probably identified with the orphan. I'll give him credit for that. He already had four sons, but he took me in and gave me a good home, fed me, educated me, all that he did. I had the best of everything, the best clothes, schools, money, cars—all the things kids growing up want and need and more. On my twenty-first birthday he called me into his office—it's full of all the real stuff from the old studios of the thirties—no reproductions.

"Fabulous junk all around him, junk Louis B. Mayer and Thalberg had in their offices. He got right to the point. He handed me an envelope with ten thousand dollars cash in it. My mother had started a small account for me when I was born that matured when I was twenty-one. This was that money. Here it was. Period. I was just graduating from college, and I had only the vaguest ideas about what I wanted to do in my life. I thought I might want to direct, maybe some acting to learn the craft."

Misha took a long breath and continued. Val drove along without any trouble, listening to him as if he were her own private radio station.

"Uncle Lazlo shook my hand, handed me my money and said I was on my own. He cordially wished me luck and said I would someday thank him for forcing me to sink or swim alone. Make a man out of me. He said he hoped I didn't expect any favors just because he was my uncle."

"He did give you a job with his company, didn't he? I mean, he produced your series."

"That was years later, after I'd made a name on my own back in New York, off Broadway, television commercials, that sort of struggle. I went through it just like any kid from the sticks." Just like me, you mean, Val thought, but didn't express it. He was playing on her empathy. "I went through that ten thousand in eighteen months. I worked at odd jobs, struggled to get auditions, find an agent."

"But your name helped some."

"My uncle has a lot of powerful friends in the business. They knew his method of weaning sons. He did this with all of us except Aaron. From the beginning Aaron was going to be his right-hand man, his counselor. He personally trained him—Aaron's another story."

"Tell me."

She was pulling into the parking lot at Ritcher & Raye's on the east side of Santa Monica Boulevard. Across the way the towers of Century City loomed against a clean blue sky.

"He named his first son Aaron on purpose."

"I don't get it."

"Aaron was Moses' spokesman, in the Bible. My uncle cold-bloodedly planned how his first son was going to work for him when he was a man. The kid had no say in the decision. His life was planned for him from the day he was born. Lazlo didn't miss a trick."

"Aaron must've gone along with the program."

"He was brainwashed. He is totally my uncle's creature now. Lazlo owns his balls."

"Lots of parents do that to their kids. For their own good."

"It's dictatorial."

"Well, he left you alone, didn't he? I mean, I wish I had been left alone with ten thousand when I graduated from college. Most people never get that."

"My mother gave me that. My uncle never gave me anything. All the time I was growing up he saw I was the cute one. His own sons are business types, good solid ugly men. He planned all along that I would be an actor rather than a director which is what I really wanted. He worked it all out and manipulated me exactly the way he wanted to. When I was broken in, he put me on contract, but I have only some say in what I do. He is still trying to make decisions for me. He sees himself as a goddamn godfather, with everyone in orbit around him."

"He sounds like a lot of parents I've heard of," Val said, getting out of the car.

"You want me to stay with you for this?"

"I'm glad to have you with me. I just wish you felt

189

that way about me." She entered the cool reception area and gave her name to a secretary.

"I want you to be with me. Soon. Real soon. I'm getting used to this, I think. I can handle the chair fairly well."

"You really mean it? Soon? When?"

"Maybe this weekend."

Val's heart quickened with anticipation.

As the secretary showed her where to go, Val had an awful intuition about Misha, that he wasn't being completely honest with her. She had a flash for some reason of that nurse with the sparkling eyes.

"Misha, you're not . . . married or something, are you?"

The studio was full of people, mostly beautiful young women in dancing costumes. There were a few men here, most of them sitting in a row of theater seats above the dance floor. Among them Val recognized Favio.

"Hell no. You know I'm not."

"No girlfriend or anything like that?"

"No."

"What about that girl who died in the accident? What was her name—Jan?"

"I don't even know her last name. I just met her at a party."

"Hernandez."

"What?"

"Her name was Jan Hernandez."

"How do you know that?"

Someone had started playing a piano that echoed in the huge studio. Most of the room was empty. This was a television studio, not a rehearsal hall or mirrored dance hall. The area being used for the audition was lit by spotlights suspended from the high ceiling on girders.

"How did you know her name?"

"From your dream about the accident. I heard you call her Jan, just before your car went over the side."

"How do you know her last name, Val?"

Val was certain he'd know if she lied. It was almost

impossible to hide an emotional reaction. When they were connected like this a lie was ridiculous.

"I looked up her death certificate."

"There hasn't been time."

He had her. "Misha, I care about you," she started to explain.

"Come on, level with me."

"I hired a private detective to look up an accident during the storm, somewhere in the Hills. I knew a man and woman were involved."

"Jesus. Who is he?"

"It's a woman. Her name is Maxine Wise."

"Why did you do this?"

"I think we should be together. I mean really. I think it's time to make it real. I feel like I'm losing contact with everything around me. It's taking over my life."

One of the men from the seats stepped to a microphone that buzzed and crackled.

"Okay, girls. Line up." There was a general rustle and wrinkle of feminine voices as the dancers formed a line along the edge of the lighted space. Boards had been laid down on the cement floor, so there was a lot of creaking and clomping as twenty-five women's tap shoes rang against the wood.

Val hung back from the herd. She loathed cattle calls like this. In that moment she hated Brenda for getting her involved with this indecent exploitation of human beings. All the girls were so pretty, so perfect. Not a crooked tooth or pronated ankle among them. Val wanted to walk out of the building and never return to anything like this again. Why did they make it so degrading?

"You were hurt when I tried to connect telepathically with a third party, yet you brought in a third party without telling me," Misha said.

In the background the man at the mike was instructing the dancers what was expected of them. He wanted five rows of five, and as they formed up, he told them he wanted to see a simple step in unison. Val had so far not seen any dogs.

"I shouldn't have done it," Val said silently, knowing she was not going to audition. "I was wrong, and I apologize."

"You sound so solemn. Don't sweat it. Aaron'll take care of it. Maxine Wise?"

"She doesn't know anything. I paid her and she's dropped the case."

"Don't worry about it now. What's Favio doing?"

Val looked over at the theater seats where Favio and his staff were huddled. The piano player had found the melody, a familiar pet food jingle. The dancers were fairly well formed, but the choreographer told the taller girls to take the line furthest from Favio's point of view.

"He's talking to his people while they warm up the dancers."

"Go over to him."

"I don't want this job," she said, looking around for a way out. The red light was on above the heavy metal door that was the only exit. Cameramen were pulling out their machines.

"I can assure you, you'll get the part. Just say and do exactly what I tell you."

"No." Val could see, far above on one wall, the lights of the control studio.

"What do you mean, no."

"I mean I hate this."

"Go on," he urged. "Nobody's looking. Just walk over and sit behind him a few rows. You probably can't get out of here now anyway."

"Nothing weird, Misha," she warned. "I don't want you to just take over or something." She felt positive response from him but no words.

The men in the shadows were turning their attention to the chorus. The routine the director gave them was simple. Most of the girls had the step as two TV cameras moved experimentally around them.

"Okay, okay," said the dance director away from the

mike. The piano cut out mid-bar and the dancers rattled to a stop. He showed them another couple of steps and nodded to the accompanist.

Val walked quietly to the seats and took one.

"Get closer to him," Michael coached, "and let me see through your eyes." Favio Bernstein stood in the shadows and was watching the dancers out on the lighted floor.

From this perspective Val could see the group of men watching two small TV monitors set up in the aisle.

"I can see better through your left eye than your right," Misha said idly as if tinkering with the controls of a TV set.

"I suppose your eyesight is perfect."

"Twenty-twenty."

"Okay, kids," said the choreographer, waving toward a wall. "Line up over there by height. I want each of you to take that routine from this point"—he stepped on a white X taped to the floor—"to there." He pointed to another X about twenty-five feet away. "Go through the entire routine twice as you move to that far point. The piano will continue after each set. There will be no break between dancers."

The girls were dutifully lining up.

Starting from the first X, the choreographer took the routine across the boards in the manner he wanted. The piano found him and kept up the jingle. He misstepped once and chuckled as he trotted gracefully back to the microphone.

"Well," he said sweetly, "of course you'll do it much better than a clumsy old man, but you have the idea." He clapped his hands briskly. "Now, are you ready?"

The girls all answered yes with big smiles and exaggerated nods.

Val had a good shot at the TV set.

"Mr. Bernstein is ready to see you dance now," the choreographer said deferentially with a little bow toward the shadowy figure by the seats.

He clapped his hands again for absolute quiet. The

floor manager crouching beside a camera with a red light on held up four fingers and the choreographer stepped away from the mike. The piano started and the floor manager, listening with glazed eyes to his instructions by headset, sliced the air. Bernstein pointed to the first girl and she started dancing across the boards.

Over and over the piano threw out the jingle and the girls whirled and tapped in front of the cameras, red lights blinking on and off as the director up in the control booth sent various shots to the men in the seats. None of them were watching the girls live; all eyes including Val's were on the TV monitor.

Her discomfort forgotten, she studied each face and body as the dancers danced their hearts out.

A person either has it or they don't, she thought. That ability to transcend the clanking technology of TV and project something of him or her self through the tube, into the electrons and finally through a receiver into people's minds.

Val loved auditions, usually. They offered a challenge, like tests or research at college. Over the years she had developed a mental attitude of arrogance backed up with practice. More and more often she had callbacks. But now, suddenly, auditions seemed disgusting. Each girl thought she was so good, the best. But back here, watching coolly as the images moved on the screen, she saw that most of them were flat, even though they all were professionally adequate dancers. It wasn't the dancing these men were looking for.

They were looking for something in the face, in the manner. Val knew she had it. She had known since the first time she'd seen herself on video. Actually she had known since she first began to dance, even before she knew of the strange transformation that came over people in front of a camera. Warm, responsive people in person often came off stiff and cold on the tube. Val had never had to wonder how to do it. It was the thing that Brenda knew about her, what she called star-stuff.

Many great performers did not have it. They could command a stage in Vegas or New York, but on film they were uninspired. They couldn't transcend the tube. Val could. Something of her went into the lense and electronic innards of the equipment that turned the images of faces or tomato catsup equally into millions of dots on the screen. When all those dots that were Val's image came on the screen, there was something else there that made one feel like she was in the room.

The dancers were still going at it. Nearly all of them had taken their two little turns at the wheel. Didn't the piano player get tired playing those few bars over and over and over?

"Wonder when they're going to bring out the dog?" Misha said as clearly as if he were sitting in the seat next to her.

"Maybe they're going to play around with the images, make them dance backwards like the Purina cat food cha-cha."

"Yeah."

The last dancer tapped out across the spotlight. She misstepped, but like a trooper kept on. She never found the beat, though, and even before she was finished, the choreographer was clapping close to the mike. The piano stopped abruptly and all the lights on the cameras went off.

"Thank you, thank you," he said, too close to the mike. "We're going to take a short break and come back and do it one more time." He moved quickly to Favio, and the women started breaking into more casual postures, gabbing, adjusting shoes, while the overhead lights went on and the spots blinked off. There was a table in view now with a large coffeemaker and stacks of Styrofoam cups.

Val saw the light blink off over the door. She stood and walked toward it via the least public route.

"You're crazy not to talk to Favio," Misha said. "None of these girls has what he's looking for. You do."

"Sweetheart—" Someone said aloud near her just as she was reaching for the door handle. "Why didn't you dance for me?"

195

Val saw it was Favio who had broken from a smothering group of hangers on and intercepted her.

Misha said, "Say and do exactly as I tell you."

"Say, aren't you the girl who danced on the spoon?"

Val nodded.

"I'd like to see you dance—you okay?"

"Tell him you don't do cattle calls."

Favio stepped closer to her. He was a lean, aging Southern Californian with a brilliant tan and hard blue eyes. He was bald, but good-looking.

"I don't do cattle calls."

"Brenda didn't tell you what this was?"

"She didn't tell me it would be a cattle call."

"The routine—would you do it for me?"

"Sure."

"Milton—" Favio called to the choreographer, who came running. "Look at this face—"

"What's your name, honey? Haven't you done something?"

"I was the dancer in the Crispy Flakes commercial last year."

"Oh, yeah, the big spoon—" he grinned up at Favio. "She might do. Want to see her? Hey, why didn't you audition?"

Misha instructed her to tell Favio to make a private appointment with Brenda.

Val thought, "But that'll insult him."

"Do it."

"I'm sick—" Val said, touching her waist. "I'm sorry—but may I dance for you another day?"

Favio took her elbow. "Of course—" He glanced at the choreographer, who nodded. "Would you like to lie down?"

Wonder why he's being so nice? Val thought.

"I told you he would like you," Misha said. "Keep on with the hard-to-get routine."

"May I call a cab?"

"No, thank you—I have my car," she said and groaned a little to make it sound right.

196

Favio held the door for her. Milton looked over the milling, expectant dancers.

Favio started to follow Val.

"What about the next take?" Milton asked.

"Yeah. Do it," Favio said over his shoulder.

"You really do have an interesting face—what's your name, by the way?"

"Valentine," she said, walking with him down a long hallway through sets and props. Nearby was a huge sliding door standing open in the sunshine.

"Oh yes. Brenda showed me your tapes. You're good."

He touched her elbow and smiled suggestively.

Oh, no, Val thought, not another one of those.

"He's a cunt man," Misha said with a sneer. "Play up to him."

"Hell no," Valentine said silently.

"Thank you, Mr. Bernstein," she said politely at the open door.

"I'll be looking forward to seeing you again, Valentine."

She walked away with the feeling of his eyes on her. In her car she relaxed a moment.

"You had him, and you didn't use it—"

"That was awful."

"Why didn't you play up to him?"

"I don't like to do that. You're going to have to accept me the way I am."

"With your looks and body, you're crazy not to eat him alive."

"We're really different people, Misha. Don't try to make me be like you."

"I just want to help."

"I appreciate that. But I was doing okay on my own. That kind of help I don't need."

"Okay. I apologize."

"I accept."

"But I'm right, you know."

"Let me be alone for a while, Misha."

"Sure, Val. I need to call Aaron, anyway. Try to

197

patch up whatever damage may have been done with that detective."

"I told you she's off the case. Leave it alone."

"You endangered us, you know."

"How?"

"Just don't tell anyone else about this, okay?"

"You mean the telepathy? I haven't told anyone about that. I just told Maxine I wanted to find out the names of two people I saw in an accident."

"I'll bet she thought you hit-and-ran."

"I told her I was a witness but didn't report it. I said I wanted to make up for not calling the police or something by praying for the people who were hurt."

"She couldn't buy that. She'll keep snooping until she finds out something. Aaron will stop her."

"You'll just make her more suspicious. She's smart."

"You leave it to me. Let's be together later on. Go to the gym, why don't you," he suggested. "We'll make love in the Jacuzzi again."

CHAPTER 20

When she left a message with Stefano Productions late Wednesday after talking with the paramedic, Maxine didn't expect to talk with The Man himself even on the phone. So she was surprised when his private secretary returned her call to say Mr. Stefano would be delighted to meet with her in his office at 11 A.M. today, Thursday.

Maxine had never been inside the offices of a movie studio before. She didn't know what to expect, but she knew something about the art deco period and was impressed with the furnishings. The office itself was in a plain stucco building on a movie lot in Burbank. Lazlo had bought as much of the furniture and decorations from the old studios when they broke up as he could find, and used it to decorate his production staff suite.

Ms. Peach told her courteously to sit on the round beige couch, Mr. Stefano would be right with her, and did she want some coffee? Maxine said yes and waited for the great man to summon her.

Presently she was ushered into an inner office where Lazlo held court behind a huge blond-veneer desk. He stood politely until she sat down and Ms. Peach left.

"Well, well," he said, rubbing his hands together. I've never met a woman private detective before. It's Ms. Wise, right?"

"No actually, I'm married. Mrs. Maxine Sarah Wise. My initials are interesting, though."

"A Mrs. who is also a Ms." He nodded while a young man of perhaps seventeen, not a servant, but with an elaborate coffee service, entered the room.

"Mrs. Wise, this is my grandson, Benjamin."

Benjamin smiled shyly and went about pouring coffee. Light flooded into the room from a huge picture window behind Lazlo who played the host by handing Maxine the cup after she had said she took it black. He poured cream into his own cup and nodded to the young man, who quietly left the room.

Lazlo turned to study her when the boy left. "My eldest son's oldest boy. Learning the business."

"I understand all your family is part of your company, Mr. Stefano."

"Please. All my friends call me Lazlo, Mrs. Wise." It was hard to imagine this imperious little man having close friends who chummily called him by his first name, but she didn't want to insult him.

"Please. Maxine."

He nodded extravagantly and took a sip of coffee, savoring it. It was delicious, Maxine thought, exotic.

"My own blend," he explained when he saw her enjoyment.

"Now, what may I do for you?"

"Uh, you invited me here, Lazlo."

"To ask what I may do for you, Maxine."

"But, I could have spoken to you on the phone. I just have a couple of questions to ask about a car that belongs to you." She consulted her notebook.

"A maroon Mercedes, I believe. As a private detective you would be asking questions about the accident that car was in three weeks ago."

"Specifically about the driver."

"Let's see," Lazlo said, consulting notes of his own. "Formerly a police officer—"

"An investigator—I didn't have a badge."

"Specializing in missing persons, specifically runaway teenagers, that sort of thing."

He leaned toward her with piercing eyes. "You've been snooping around about one of my children."

He leaned even closer. "I don't appreciate your doing that."

"I'm working on a legitimate case."

"The implication is that I don't take care of my family. I'm sure you understand, Maxine, being a mother yourself."

"How do you know that?"

"I too have done my homework. I know you've had three children; two are still living. Boys, nineteen and twelve. In fact, one of them has the same name as my grandson. A coincidence, don't you think?"

She shrugged.

"We have much in common. I'm sure if someone implied you are not taking care of one of your children, you'd be upset." He stood abruptly, pacing deliberately around the salmon-colored office with its gold, white and brown decorations from another era, very light on his feet for his age and weight. She watched him, fascinated.

"Now, I've been taking care of my family for all my life. It is my only occupation. We happen to be in the picture business, an especially sensitive business to the wrong kind of publicity."

"I merely want to find out if your nephew was driving that car."

"That's none of your business."

"Accidents on public roads are anyone's business, only there aren't complete public records of your nephew's accident."

"Because of the nature of my business my friends have helped me keep it quiet. Surely you understand."

"I have a client."

"Not any more. I happen to know Leslie Valentine closed the case. You've been snooping around on your own. I request you stop. I'm prepared to tell you everything if you will sign this agreement not to repeat it to anyone." He handed her a one-page agreement that had been drawn up by a lawyer.

"I would want to relay the information to my client."

He gestured toward the agreement.

If she signed it she'd be admitting slander if she spoke of the matter to anyone other than her client. They had thought of everything. Something was paper-clipped to the agreement. When she looked under the paper she saw a check for a thousand dollars.

"Is this a bribe?"

"Consider it a retainer."

He handed her a pen and she signed the agreement and gave it back to him with the check still attached.

He sat on the edge of the desk.

"My nephew was seriously, permanently injured in the accident you've been investigating. He's not taking it well at all. In fact, he tried to commit suicide." He looked woebegone and pitiful, a parent worried sick about his kid. "You understand, you have children."

"This must be very hard for you."

"My nephew is an actor. Perhaps you've seen his work."

Maxine nodded, but could not recall anything he'd done.

"Anyway, he was messed up pretty bad in that accident."

Maxine grimaced. She hated to think of such an accident happening to one of her sons or to Hugh, or to herself. It was too horrible. In some ways death was preferable.

"The life he knew is over. But he refuses to accept what's happened to him. I raised this boy. I know him. He's going to need a lot of help and privacy, away from a morbidly curious public, to recover."

Maxine's heart went out to this man who was, after all, only trying to help his child. She empathized with him completely. "I understand."

"I'm so glad," Lazlo replied, truly consoled. He touched his plump hands together. "You are not a stranger to family tragedy, I believe."

Her look said, Yes.

"Please, please," he said. "Take the check."

She touched it gingerly. "Only as a retainer, but I can't imagine how you'd use the services of a private detective."

"Oh, you'd be surprised," he said with a dramatic, diabolic twinkle in his eye. "The movie business even more than most requires unorthodox methods." He chuckled to himself and smiled at her, charming as only an ugly man can be.

She'd heard so much against movie people. It was a delight to find a gentleman among them. But he'd never met Val or he wouldn't have called her Leslie Valentine. Was he merely using a name somebody had given him? Who could that somebody be?

As she drove to her office her thoughts flicked from Lazlo to Valentine. There had been something in the girl's response when Maxine told her who owned the Mercedes, something that suggested Val deduced the name of the driver too soon.

Maxine hated to admit it, but it was becoming more and more likely that Val had been involved in a hit-and-run accident. She could hardly wait to question her further.

Maxine pulled into the office lot and hurried inside because she had seen a deliveryman at the front door with some flowers. He was just turning away when she opened the door.

They were beautiful roses.

As she thanked the boy she was thinking they might be from Lazlo. He had been such a gentleman. She stood in her office doorway opening the envelope.

They were from Hugh. What a wonderful surprise, she thought. As good a man as he was, he'd sent her flowers only once, the night he proposed. He had the traditional husband's memory for special dates and anniversaries, so roses from him were unexpected.

Maxine stepped toward the inside of the office. She saw the sign with the long offending tail on the s. She quickly set down the flowers and rummaged in a box still unpacked behind her desk until she found a package of single-edge razor blades.

She regarded the sign outside again. Very carefully, so as not to damage the part of the letter she wanted and not to ruin her nails in the process, she made a thin cut where she wanted to remove the decoration. Then she methodically went about scraping off the unwanted paint.

Val observed herself in the mirror. The nurse's uniform looked just right. The white shoes were perfect. She had no white stockings, but she knew more and more nurses all the time were wearing regular panty hose. The only thing missing was a hat. She had piled her hair on top of her head in a prim bun and it looked okay, but it needed a cap to be just right.

Maybe she could make one. She found some stiff lining material in her sewing things. She sprayed it with starch and ironed it until it shined. In her old jewelry box she found a tiny pin she'd had when she was a cheerleader in high school, an enameled metal insignia. From a few paces it could be an emblem of a nursing school. She cut the starched material into a simple straight rectangle she then bobby-pinned to her hair. She stuck the broach in one corner and observed the effect in the mirror.

It looked very good.

She could pull it off, she just knew it.

*   *   *

As Tanna entered with his medication and a huge bouquet of flowers from Lazlo, Michael was sitting near the window playing the guitar. He was diligent but not very inspired, she thought as she set the flowers on the credenza. Michael didn't look up but started singing softly along with his melody.

Tanna saw from the remains on the lunch tray that he was eating heartily. She was glad for that anyway. She knew he was depressed. He had been impotent last night. He had told her he liked being sucked off, but he wasn't able to come after an hour of trying. She knew he was miserable when she left him, and from the sound of his song, he was still miserable.

She brought the medicine cup and a glass of water to him. He finished that bar and looked up at her. Without speaking he took the medication and drank the water in one gulp, handed her back the cup and resumed playing where he had left off.

She rolled the food table into the hallway, closed the door and sat on a chair to listen to him. He had a so-so voice she suspected he had too high an opinion of. It sounded like he'd been playing only a few months.

Presently he set aside the guitar and wheeled around to speak to her.

But he didn't say anything, just looked at her for a minute.

"What's wrong?"

"I want to try again," he said.

Involuntarily she glanced at the door. She had hoped to spark him but not in the middle of the afternoon.

"Nobody'll bother us," he said.

She looked away for a second.

He looked down at his fingers, rubbing them because the guitar strings had made them sensitive. Three weeks away from playing and one loses the calluses.

Great wounds, he thought, make one vulnerable to the smallest pains and failures.

"That never happened to me before," he said, clearly speaking of his impotence last night.

"You've never been this sick before," she replied tenderly as she stood and drew the nylon curtain between them and the door. He watched her return to the chair and touch his hand on his lap.

He moved his hand so that her palm lay on the blanket above his penis. He slowly pushed back the satin edge of the blanket until her hand lay against his flesh.

Michael was surprised and delighted when she slid gracefully off the chair and onto her knees before him.

Val drove up the boulevard to the hospital, but the parking lot was full, so she went to the lot next to the gym. It was only a block or so away.

She felt very proper in her nurse's uniform. Looks from a couple of passersby told her she was just right.

She got the books from the backseat and locked the car. Her purse didn't look like anything a nurse might carry, but it would have to do. She quickly left the parking lot and headed toward the intersection, where she had to wait for the walking green. Her heart sank when she heard someone, a woman, calling her name.

She turned to see Maxine running up to her. She reacted to the uniform.

"I have an audition in an hour," Val said. The cover story was a natural. "Do I look the part?" Maxine wouldn't know that one seldom auditioned in costume.

"You could fool me," Maxine replied, shielding her eyes from the sun over Val's shoulder. "Val, I want to talk to you—"

"I'm in kind of a hurry."

"I found out more about that accident."

Maxine couldn't tell what the look on her face meant—surprise, maybe. Distress quickly shielded by cool. But she couldn't hide her curiosity.

"Why don't you come by the office after your audition?"

"Okay, but it might be late—five-thirty or so."

"I'll be there until about six."

"Great, Maxi. See you then."

"Uh, do you mind not calling me that?"

"I'm sorry—"

"No, it's okay. You couldn't know, but it reminds me of my father. His death was a blow to me."

Val smiled apologetically. "Your husband says I also remind you of someone else who died. I guess I'm just destined to make you sad."

"Please, that's not true. I mean, you did remind me of Melodie at first. You looked vulnerable, worried when I first saw you. Mother instinct, I guess."

"Listen, it's nice to see someone who cares," Val said, aching to get away.

"I'm keeping you," Maxine said, backing off politely.

"See you," Val replied and they parted. She actually liked Maxine. Under other circumstances she'd love to get to know her, compare experiences. A private detective and an actor must share some perspectives on human behavior. But the timing for such a relationship was off.

Val did not want Maxine to see her enter the hospital. Jesus, Val thought. All I need is a Jewish mama. How could she get rid of this nice lady? What in God's name had she found out now?

Maxine was watching her, Val was sure. When she glanced back she saw she was right. Maxine waved and walked toward her office.

There was a row of small shops along here, between the gym and the hospital in the next block. A sign in a window gave Val an inspiration and she turned to go inside the open door. It was a florist shop. An old woman with bright blue hair asked in a respectful tone of voice if there was anything she could do for her. The uniform made a difference, Val thought as she asked to see the roses.

"They are beautiful," she said. "Send a dozen of the red ones to this patient, please." She wrote Michael's name, room number and the name of the hospital a couple of doors away.

While the clerk was writing up her credit card ticket,

she chatted to Val, asking how long she'd worked in the hospital.

"I don't work there," Val said. "I'm from County." Val knew it would be difficult to trace a single employee at County General, a gargantuan public hospital.

The old lady had a cousin who'd died there, so she mentioned it, adding, "But I'm sure you people did the best you could. He was old."

She told Val the roses would be delivered later that afternoon.

"I don't see nurses buying flowers very often," she said as Val scribbled a note to send with the roses: *Get well soon. Love, your secret valentine.*

Val smiled. She could see over the clerk's shoulder that there was no sign of Maxine on the sidewalk. As she replaced her card she said good-bye to the woman and stepped just outside. She put on sunglasses for an excuse to stand there a moment to see if the coast was clear.

Then she walked briskly into the hospital. She had a touch of stage fright, expecting the hand of a uniformed guard or someone else to stop her. But nobody paid her the slightest attention. In fact, a girl in white, probably an aide, nodded to Val as she stepped onto the open elevator. Val smiled to herself and pushed the second-floor button.

In the quiet muffled space Val felt suddenly elated. Finally, she thought, we are going to meet. This is the first day of a new life. It wouldn't be easy. Misha had to get well. She had to break with Frank. The elevator door opened. She looked around for the room.

Room 20. When she had seen the name of the hospital on Tanna's pocket label, Val had also seen the door open behind the nurse. She had clearly seen Misha's room number and a NO ADMITTANCE sign hanging on a thumb tack. There was nobody in the hallway, so she walked over to see how the rooms were numbered and followed them up to 19 then 20.

The door was closed. There was a NO ADMITTANCE sign on it.

She shifted the psychic phenomena library books to her right hand and opened the door with her left. It was very quiet all around, but as she slowly opened the door she heard the murmur of voices inside.

A nylon curtain had been drawn around the only bed in the room. The window beyond the curtain threw a glow. Two people were silhouetted in that glow in an unmistakable position of lovemaking, the woman bent over the man's lap. She heard Misha's distinct voice say, "That's it, baby, that's it, right there, ooh, yeah."

Val threw the curtain open.

CHAPTER 21

For a flash of a moment she saw the pretty nurse in uniform on her knees on the floor in front of a dark-haired, handsome man in a wheelchair. He saw Val first, then the nurse looked up while her mouth was still encircled around his cock, but it slipped out as she abruptly stood.

Val stood there for a paralyzed second. The books in her arms fell noisily to the floor as she whirled around and ran from the room.

"Who the hell—?" Tanna was sputtering as she dashed to the door. "Who was that?" She looked back at him.

"I dunno," Michael said, drawing the covers up around himself, pushing himself down into the nest of the blanket. But he knew, he knew. Shit. He reached out to Val immediately.

He could feel her pain and humiliation turn into anger as she ran down a flight of stairs.

*   *   *

Val didn't wait for the elevator. She found a door marked EXIT and took the stairs to the first floor. The stairwell opened into the alley behind the hospital. The air felt good outside. Val thought there for a second she might faint. Seeing him like that, being serviced, it was terrible. All thought of Misha and herself together was fading.

She should have paid attention to her intuition, she thought. She suspected something like this, but still the shock of seeing it made her feel hysterical, out of control the way Frank sometimes got.

She ran in the crepe-soled shoes to the front of the hospital. She walked in the direction of the gym, praying that Maxine wouldn't be around. She didn't want to see anyone, she just wanted to run away, run as far and as fast as she could.

"Valentine, don't run away from me—"

Frank, oh, Frank, please don't be gone yet. She couldn't remember a specific time when he said he'd be leaving for Santa Barbara, sometime this afternoon. She saw a phone booth and hurried into it. Please be home, she begged Frank in her mind. She could feel Misha calling her, calling her name while she heard the phone ring.

"Hello?" It was Frank. She nearly cried with relief.

"I'm so glad I caught you," she said. "I've decided to go up north with you."

"Please, Valentine," Misha begged in her head, "please let me explain—"

She ignored Misha's silent call and said to Frank, "If you still want me to."

"Want you to? Baby, you know I want you to. Hold on a minute—" She could hear Neil Young singing on the stereo behind Frank. He loved not having to go in to work this morning. She was suddenly filled with happiness for this man who had been her friend and lover for so many years. He was a good man, despite the fact that he was hard to live with. He was kind to her, fair to her—and he had absolutely never cheated on her.

209

"Honey—you still there?" he said, coming back on the line after muffling the phone while he talked to someone. "I already picked up the cameraman. His name's Rooney—you're going to love him—he's got some great stories to tell."

"So how much time have I got?"

"We're leaving in an hour—but don't sweat it. We have all night to drive up. We aren't going to start shooting until morning, anyway."

"I'll be right home. I'm at the gym. It'll take me just a minute to throw some clothes in a bag."

"Val, please—" Misha begged.

"This is going to be a wonderful trip for us both," Frank said, sounding more happy than she had heard him in months. She said good-bye to Frank with Misha's voice calling inside her head.

She didn't answer.

Michael was trying to locate the exact spot in his brain that controlled the telepathy. Val was just not answering.

He stopped calling her and concentrated on Tanna bent lovingly over him again. Such a wonderful lady, so eager to give him pleasure. She demanded so little in return. All the textures inside her mouth were touching all the sides and tip of his penis like a living glove. She knew exactly what she was doing. So many women, Michael mused, distracted from his attempt at telepathy—so many women thought it felt good merely to have the penis sucked. But that wasn't the way he liked it. What felt the best to him, whether genital or oral, was what he thought of as yielding resistance. He liked to feel his penis was forcing the penetration. He wanted resistance but not too much.

This lady was the best at it he'd ever experienced, so good he suspected she had been a hooker. Why, he wondered again, can't I telepath with *this* lady? He tried calling Tanna's name again and again mentally. Tanna held back and sat up, her lips glistening, her hand in place of her mouth on his cock.

"Why'd you stop?" he asked, blinking his eyes open.

"You're not here, baby."

"I guess I'm not in the mood anymore."

"That was just someone who opened the wrong door. Don't let it upset you. Try to concentrate, you know what I mean."

"I guess you want some, too."

"Not necessarily. Not the way you mean."

She saw his look of puzzlement. "I earned my way through nursing school by working as a sex therapist."

"Oh." He had not expected to hear that. "I thought you were too good to be true. What's the difference between a sex therapist and a hooker?"

"Concern."

"I've known some awfully sweet hookers."

She shrugged and stopped stroking him. "A sex therapist helps a person overcome a problem that keeps them from enjoying sex."

"But you don't get involved, right?"

"We're not supposed to." She looked down as she wiped her hand on the sheet.

"You don't like me just a little bit?"

He tilted her chin up. Her eyes were glistening, wet.

"I can't help you if I start to like you like that."

"So," he said, breaking contact with her hand, "I'm just a case. A charity fuck—" he chortled bitterly, never thinking of himself as that before, though he had thought of others that way. What was left of his hard-on went limp. He pulled up the blanket.

"No—" Tanna was saying.

"I guess a man left like this can't expect anything else—Well, tell me, Henderson," he said, looking directly at her, "do your services come with the bill my uncle will never get, or are you a la carte?"

Tanna looked at him for a second or two, then stood up and walked out of the room.

He was immediately sorry for hurting Tanna's feelings. But he didn't call her back because he couldn't explain it all to her. How could he explain that the anger he was directing toward her was meant

211

for Val for sneaking up on him like that. In costume yet, the cunning bitch.

Really got her eyeful.

As furious as he was at Val, though, he knew she was more than angry. He lay back on the pillow, closed his eyes and called her. She was like a brick wall. He knew she could hear him but was purposefully shutting him out. He decided to try to reach her by a more conventional channel—her home telephone. Maybe he could reason with her, make her understand Tanna was just part of his recovery. He was entitled to some pleasure after what had happened. They had denied him revenge, they were all trying to force him to expose himself to public pity. All I have left, he reasoned as he listened to the phone, are a few moments of sex to keep my mind off what's happened.

When Frank answered he was surprised. He expected him to be out of town by now on Claud Davis's little shoot.

Michael hung up without speaking.

Frank thought it was just a wrong number and had forgotten the call by the time he rejoined Rooney, the glib, red-haired cameraman, in the kitchen. Finishing a beer, Rooney picked up his story where he'd left off when the phone rang. "The director refused to post bail until the next morning—but he had to do it finally or lose a day's shooting time." While he talked, and occasionally sipped at the beer can, he expertly rolled a dozen cigarettes. Frank was already sampling the smoke, a powerful Hawaiian marijuana bud. In a few minutes Val came hurriedly in. After quick introductions she went off to pack.

She could hear Rooney's voice starting another story as she took her overnight bag from a shelf in the bedroom closet. Even now she could hear Misha calling her. She was determined not to answer, to teach him a lesson. As she threw clothes into the suitcase, she was crying. She felt so humiliated, so cheated on. How could Misha do it? Here they had this wonderful connection and he was willing to destroy the relationship by cheating.

"Valentine, please answer me," he said in her mind. "I know I've hurt you, but please let me talk with you. I'm sorry, please forgive me . . . You gotta understand how it is for me right now."

Val set her mouth and wiped the tears from her eyes. She washed her face and combed her hair, but did not look into the bathroom mirror. She didn't want to give him any opportunity to connect with her. At this point she thought she'd never speak to him again. To hell with him and the telepathy.

She knew she'd soften up, however. But she planned to punish him sufficiently before she did. She pulled on an old college sweater and looked around to see what she wanted to take on the trip.

Val was a quick packer, so she was ready to go before the men were. They smoked some more and finally got on the Ventura Freeway by six. There had been an accident near Thousand Oaks, so that slowed them down. Santa Barbara is a coastal city about seventy-five miles north of L.A., close enough to drive in one push. But Rooney's pot was having its effect. They had major munchies by the time they reached Oxnard, so they stopped at a famous seafood restaurant to gorge themselves on lobster and cracked crab.

They stood on a windy pier to watch the sunset. She let Frank hold her, but she felt far away. He didn't seem to sense her distance, however, he was so elated over the job. By now he and Rooney had traded dozens of location stories, dropping famous names like crumbs. Even though they had only just met they found their personalities compatible. Val was very quiet; that in no way interfered with their jovial chatter. They were trying to top each other with outlandish stories of things that had happened to them while shooting movies.

"Valentine?" Misha called, but she did not answer.

It was dark by the time they were on the road again, with another thirty miles or so to go. Rooney's

Volkswagen was a cozy little cabin on wheels, the air inside it thick with smoke. The cassette player blasted rock and roll. Rooney and Frank kept throwing stories at each other. They ignored Val completely. She was half-awake in the backseat, declining the joint when Frank offered her a toke. She was drowsy from events, rich food and the stoning smoke around her.

She dozed with Misha's voice pale and faint in her mind. Once she felt the car had stopped. Small noises were pinging around her in the darkness when she opened her eyes briefly to see she was alone in the VW parked outside a roadhouse. She could hear country music coming from inside the small building where a beer sign blinked on and off in a single window. She just closed her eyes and went back to sleep. Misha's voice was still there but very weak now.

She knew she wanted to answer. As she drifted deeper into sleep she was startled awake again by the thought that he might be in trouble. No, she countered to herself. If he wants to be with me, he's got to learn he can't cheat. She wasn't against an open relationship—it just wasn't what she was looking for. He had to accept that, or they couldn't be together. She had to make the point to get the relationship off to a mutually beneficial start, or not at all.

"Valentine . . ."

It was difficult not to answer him, he sounded so much in need.

Reluctantly she closed the doors and windows of her mind. She shut her eyes and let the heavy hand of fatigue muffle her ears.

She went to sleep with the sound of his plaintive voice calling her name.

CHAPTER 22

Carson was not in a good mood. Since she lost Tanna as her swing-shift nurse, she was shorthanded. When one of the regular night nurses called in sick, Carson had to cover for her, herself, after a full day of work as nursing supervisor.

So when Tanna and another night nurse stayed out longer than their scheduled meal break, Carson was waiting for their return.

Tanna and the other nurse had gone to dinner at a salad bar up the street. The girl was newly engaged and Tanna didn't have to talk much as her companion told her about the wedding plans.

She was glad she could play audience to her friend. Inside she retreated into her own thoughts. Her mind was on Michael. She knew he hadn't meant to be cruel. He was still sick. Allowances had to be made. She knew logically that much of his hostility toward her was displaced anger at what had happened to him. He was bound to transfer like crazy—and she was the closest person to him right now.

It was part of the accident profile. He'd swing between fury and depression as he gradually got well. He'd make progress as he grew to accept. He could even learn to walk again if someone were there to care and to help.

But, damn, his words had hurt.

These had been her thoughts as the girl across the table went on about a cute apartment in Van Nuys and a new car from her prospective in-laws. It was a warm late-evening as they strolled back to the hospital. Not until they reached the front door did they realize they had stretched their hour to an hour and a half.

"Uh-oh," Tanna said as they entered, gesturing at Carson standing nearby watching them.

Carson looked at her watch as they passed then parted, the other night nurse to her station and Tanna toward the elevator and the second floor.

"I don't have enough staff to watch out for your private duty, too, Tanna," she said, stepping onto the elevator with her.

"I apologize," Tanna said simply, trying to make the door open sooner by sheer mental effort. It was awful being shut inside the small elevator space with this woman.

At the second floor Tanna didn't wait for the door to completely open before dashing out. Bunch was waiting for her, it seemed, or waiting for the elevator. She knew immediately by the look on his face that something was wrong.

"Your private duty," he said, already walking toward Room 20 where the door was standing open.

"What's wrong?"

"Don't know. Is he an epileptic or something?"

Oh no, Tanna thought as she ran into the room with Bunch and Carson on her heels, not another seizure.

It was immediately obvious something was wrong with Michael.

He was just lying there. His eyes were rolled back in his head and his breathing was so shallow she couldn't see his chest move. She could barely feel a pulse. She popped the buttons on his silk pajamas and listened for his heart. There was no reason for this patient to be dying. No reason at all. He wasn't even critical anymore. He was young, with no history of heart or nervous problems. His wounds, while major, were healing. He'd been healthy and athletic before the accident, so his body was in prime condition. He had even seemed to have begun adjusting to his condition.

He couldn't be dying.

But he was.

His heartbeat was very slow. There was too long a time between beats, almost as if he were fading away.

Bunch and Carson were momentarily frozen at the door. They saw Tanna clasp her hands above her head as if preparing for a karate strike, gather her strength and slam her fists onto Michael's chest with a powerful blow. She bent close to him and called his name. She listened again for a heartbeat, but she heard none. By the time she climbed onto the bed and straddled the patient, Carson and Bunch had bounded into action. Carson ran for the telephone on the bedside table while Bunch dashed out of the room for the crash cart.

Tanna didn't hear Carson's voice as she told Dr. Raymond that he should hurry down because Stefano was going sour. She gave him a few curt details in answer to his questions and hung up the phone. She turned and saw Tanna aiming a couple more blows to the patient.

Tanna listened again to his heart. There was a definite beat now, not as strong as it should be, but it was there. Still straddling him, she bent to whisper in his ear.

Val woke up in the VW. She saw the diner's lights. There were a few people inside, maybe off the buses, or truckers or locals. One big semi was pulled up on the other side of the buses.

Among the customers Val saw Frank and Rooney still engaged in an animated conversation they had not interrupted all the way up from L.A. Frank was in movie-freak heaven, swapping location stories and getting paid in the bargain. Fragments of their stories swam in Val's brain; they might as well have been speaking some foreign language; all she had absorbed was the emotional content of each anecdote from their tone of voice.

Val sat up in the snarled blanket. She was stiff from sleeping in an unnatural position. Despite the slumber, she did not feel as though her body had renewed itself. She had a terrible headache in the spot behind her eyes, no doubt from the tension of resisting Misha, as well as from the low oxygen content of the car. She was vibrating unpleasantly all over with the feeling of moving at 60 mph in a small car with bad shocks.

She wasn't completely awake, but she was sure she had heard Misha's voice just before she opened her eyes. Could he still be calling her? Surely as she got further from him, the telepathy would fade.

"Val . . ."

This time his voice cracked. That sound stabbed right through her. She instinctively knew he was in trouble. He sounded *pastel;* it was the only way she could think about it. Transparent. Jesus, she thought. He may be dying.

"Henderson—" Carson shouted. Tanna didn't respond. Carson shook Tanna's ankle, but the younger nurse only kicked out at her and continued kissing the patient's lips. Carson sucked air in outrage and backed toward the door, sputtering.

Abandoning decorum to administer cardiac resuscitation was one thing; breathing into the lips of a dying person—that was part of the job. But this, this was obscene. She looked once more to insure she was seeing what she was really seeing, then Carson left the room, forgetting to close the door behind her.

Presently Bunch shoved the crash cart into Room 20, looked up and saw Tanna break her passionate kiss. The patient's eyes were open and he was kissing back. Tanna heard the cart hit the door and looked up at Bunch's startled face.

"It's okay, Bunch—Mr. Stefano was having a nightmare, that's all. Please close the door on your way out."

She turned immediately back to her patient, who looked dazed but certainly not in danger. Bunch could plainly see the guy was hard as a rock at Tanna's hand.

When he had gone Tanna whispered to Michael, "Oh, love, don't ever scare me like that again."

She lay her head above his heart, which was beating

218

in a normal way. "What happened?" she heard him ask with her ears and through his bones under her ear.

"You had a convulsion, I think."

"That's not all."

She looked at his face. Color had returned to his cheeks. His lips, which had been gray before, were thicker and pink, opening to hers. They lay there kissing for a while before he urged her with his hands to kiss him elsewhere.

Tanna felt she had saved his life. His response warmed her through and through, but as she lay her lips against the head of his penis she heard him say something. She glanced up to see his eyes were closed, his lips moving. She couldn't hear what he was saying, but it was repeated, the same word, and it might have been a name.

"Valentine?" Misha's voice sounded far away.

Christ, she swore at herself. What have I done?

She called to him. At first there was no answer, then faintly she heard him ask, "Is that you?" This time his voice cracked with hope.

"You sound terrible. What's wrong?"

"I thought you left me forever."

She was silent in the settling car.

"Val?"

"You cheated on me."

"I know. I'm a shit," he said, fading. She called him but he didn't answer. The open-line feeling was here but he wasn't. There was nobody at the other end.

She sat still for a while, listening. She began to cry silently, her eyes burning. "I've killed him," she said out loud.

She saw Rooney and Frank inside the cozy little restaurant, laughing. They were having a ball. Rooney lifted his hands in a frame, fingers and thumbs framing an imaginary shot.

Val closed her eyes and called Misha again. She put everything she had into it. There was no answer. It was a pit of loneliness.

She wiped the tears away and found her purse. Very quickly, even though it was dark, she wrote Frank a quick note on the back of a utility bill envelope: *Dear Frank, don't worry about me. I'm taking the bus home. —Val.*

It was humid and cool outside. She was glad she had put on a heavy sweatshirt now. She walked to the bus with the motor running and asked the driver if he stopped anywhere in the San Fernando Valley.

"Express to L.A.," he said, closing the baggage compartment door in the side of the bus. He looked up at her and stood.

"Course," he said, smiling, "I don't have but three passengers—they won't mind if I let you off at Sepulveda—only take a couple of minutes."

She managed a smile of gratitude and paid him the fare through to the city. He said apologetically there was nothing he could do about that.

The bus looked empty at first, but as she got settled in the roomy front seat she saw a few people scattered toward the back, all apparently sleeping.

The driver boarded and a last passenger returned from the snack bar. The driver closed the door with a whooshing sound. Val leaned her forehead against the window. The glass was cool. Her breath fogged the pane. She watched the restaurant window grow smaller and smaller until even the beer sign blinked out of existence.

The road surface against the tires vibrated up through the body of the bus and into her skull.

"Misha, I'm coming to you—hold on—I'm coming to you now—"

Tanna lay back beside Michael. She was still completely dressed, though rumpled.

"Thank you," he said. "That was wonderful."

She hugged him for an answer.

"You sure you don't want me to return the favor?"

"I'm sure."

"You're not a dyke or something?"

220

Shocked, she looked at him and shook her head. "No," she said emphatically.

"Don't get me wrong, I love what you do," he said, stroking her lips. "But you women are always complaining that we don't consider your pleasure."

"It's nothing like that," she said vaguely. Sooner or later she was going to have to confess the reason she had such empathy for her amputee patients. "I'm just not ready, that's all. Then it becomes more than nurse-patient."

"So," he said, pouting. "You won't let me be a man to you, only a helpless patient."

"It's not like that, I tell you," she said earnestly. "It's not professional for a nurse to love her patients like that."

"Okay, then, you're fired."

She looked horrified.

Carson sprang to her feet at the back exit when she saw Raymond's Cadillac pull into its slot. She met him at the door. Without a pause they headed toward the elevator while Raymond asked her a few perfunctory questions.

"I tell you, he wasn't breathing—he was white, lips blue. He's dying—I've seen it many times, and I tell you he's dying."

"That's not the usual response of a man his age when a woman like Tanna climbs into bed with him, Carson."

"I've never seen such shocking behavior from a nurse—instead of following procedures . . ."

"But you said she administered several blows to the chest," Raymond said, stepping off the elevator onto the second floor.

Carson saw Bunch look up from the magazine he was reading in a chair just outside Room 20. He stood.

"You shouldn't, Doc," he suggested respectfully to Dr. Raymond when he saw the older man was going to push open the door.

Carson opened the door and walked into Michael's room.

Tanna, still in uniform, but stretched out beside the patient, her shoes kicked off, looked up first. Michael saw her glance and followed it.

Carson and Raymond entered the room, while Bunch stayed outside looking in. "I told you, you shouldn't go in there."

Tanna jumped to her feet and began smoothing out her uniform.

Raymond looked at the patient, who was sitting up, arms comfortably behind his head.

Raymond turned wordlessly to Carson.

"But—" she said.

"What's going on here?" Raymond asked Tanna.

"Mr. Stefano had a nightmare, Doctor. If Mrs. Carson had stayed a moment longer she would have seen him wake up."

"I'm okay now, Dr. Raymond," Michael said mildly. He looked tired, but completely conscious.

"May I see you outside, Carson," Raymond said and left without further comment. Carson looked at Tanna, then followed him.

"Now, will you come to bed with me? All night?" Michael asked as the door closed.

She shook her head.

"But I fired you. Now it can't possibly be a matter of professional ethics."

She laughed at his simplistic attack on her scruples. What would he say if he knew the real reason for her reticence? "The answer's still no," she said. "For now, just let me help you get well. In time, we'll see." She smiled, but inside two things worried her—his possible turn-off when he saw she had no clit, and his own condition. She couldn't figure out what had happened back there. Did he have a seizure or what?

It had happened so quickly, he had responded so well to her touch, it was hard to remember. He looked in perfect health now, had even complained in the last few minutes that he was hungry.

"You've got to get some sleep. Tomorrow's a big day."

"What's up?"

"The prosthetist is coming by to see you." When she saw momentary puzzlement, she added, "The man who will fit you—"

"Oh no. No way I'm going through that. I told you."

She stood regarding him, curled self-protectively in his blue security blanket, adamantly refusing to deal with reality.

"You've got to stop this."

"You want me to play hero, just like Lazlo and—" He didn't finish the thought and Tanna didn't wait for him to.

"Look. I'm a nurse, but I never saw anything like what happened to you back there. Michael, you nearly died. Your heart was stopping. If you keep on like this, you'll kill yourself. The only way to survive is to get up out of this bed."

"I'm not going to clomp around like some damn machine."

"Then you're going to stay in that chair the rest of your life?"

"I want them to make me look like a normal person with both legs but who just can't walk. I want them to fit me for show, so I won't be a freak. Will they do that?"

"They'll do whatever you want. It's your decision. But you should get up off your ass and walk."

"You and I both know there's no way I'll ever be able to walk normally."

"You could try."

"I'm not going through that agony. You tell them."

"Okay."

"Then you can make an appointment."

"They're doing some amazing things these days—space science."

" 'The Bionic Man' I'm not."

She saw it was useless to argue. Later she'd try to reason with him.

223

"I'm going to stay here tonight, in an unused room up the hall," she said. "If you need me, just have Bunch wake me up."

"Sure, sure."

"I mean it—just call and I'll come to you."

"Go on. I'm okay."

"Get some sleep."

"Yeah."

She leaned over to kiss him lightly on the face. He did not watch Tanna leave. Already he was calling Val.

"Go to my house in Malibu," he urged her. She was on the verge of sleep on the bouncing bus seat.

"The bus will stop at Sepulveda and Ventura," she said. "I have to go home and get some sleep."

"Take a cab to my house—Piro, my houseman, will pay your fare. I'll call him. What do you say, baby? You'll love my house. It was in *The Times* a while ago. Especially my bedroom. We'll be together there . . ."

"Wake me when the bus stops in Encino," Val said as she leaned over to the driver, who smiled back at her.

She curled up and went immediately to sleep. The last thing she remembered was Misha's voice whispering his address inside her head.

Michael stayed with Val until she was deeply asleep. He came back into his body sitting up in his bed, apparently sleeping. He was immediately awake and alert. He saw Bunch snoring in a chair by the window. His mind seemed to be working with its old clarity for the first time since . . .

He reached for the food table where a notepad was already open. He picked up a pencil he'd been using before, started writing furiously. He would not have been able to explain his compulsion to write about feet, he just knew he had to do it, had to work out in his mind just what he had lost. Since he had begun to wake up, it was all he could think about. He found a pencil and scribbled for several pages, listing all the things one needs feet to do.

He looked up, biting the end of the pencil as he considered the human foot.

Mysteriously ugly instead of tantalizingly beautiful, out of reach after the age of two or three, the foot is often despised by its owners. To the Chinese feet were abhorrent, so much so that women bound them into unidentifiable balls for decency's sake. Such delicacy required a rich husband and a lifetime of agony, but thousands of Celestial Court ladies lived the life of a cripple to attain the appearance of having no feet. Michael possessed a portfolio of erotic thirteenth-century woodcuts. One he was particularly fond of, because of its anatomical precision, showed a Chinese woman spread-eagle like a ripe oyster, her *jade gate*, as the Celestials called the clitoris and labia, about to be unlocked by her husband's *jade tool*. The gem euphemism wasn't for prudity; the Chinese prized rare pink jade because it resembled human flesh, and sold the common green stuff to Westerners. The drawing was explicit enough to be in an anatomy textbook; the woman's sex was open and exquisitely detailed, but her unspeakable lower appendages were hidden under ankle pantaloons.

Less aesthetic cultures merely ignore it, shoe it and mention it only if the foot hurts. It's something one uses and doesn't think about. Until now.

He could feel his right foot this minute. Funny how phantom limb showed up in the lower foot and toes, a needlelike pricking. Foot's gone to sleep. That's how it felt.

He recalled his absurd sense of loss over the running shoe during the accident. It all flashed back with the clarity of 35 mm film. He'd never forget how the medic ignored him when he said he could feel his toes.

He spat out his pruney thumb, took a firmer grip on the pencil and proceeded to fill several notebook pages. He wrote quickly, adding to his list of things one needs feet to do, and was scribbling frantically when he finally stopped with a cramp in his hand on number fifty-two: reaching for something that's rolled under the couch just out of arm's length.

Bitterly, he added one more thing to the list of things you need feet to do, fifty-three: skiing. Goodbye to skiing.

"Shit," he said, setting aside the notebook and pencil. He picked up the medical dictionary he'd asked Tanna to get for him. He had dog-eared several pages and underlined several definitions.

Bone: The hard, tough, elastic material which forms the skeleton of vertebrate animals, composed principally of calcium salts. One of the individual segments of which the vertebrate skeleton is composed, in the adult human body numbering 206.

Foot: The terminal part of the leg or posterior extremity in a primate, composed of 26 bones, the largest number of bones in any one part of the human body.

More than a fourth of the bones in the entire human body are in the feet, Michael calculated. I've lost more than a fourth of my body, that's what it means. How much did a leg weigh? How tall am I now? He had been six two the night he picked up Jan Hernandez.

I'm probably about as tall as Val, he thought. A shrimp.

"I don't have feet anymore," he said out loud.

Bunch, who was snoozing in the chair beside the dark window, snorted, blinked and then said with his eyes closed, "That's right, Mr. Stefano."

He settled back for more slumber.

"Get lost, Bunch." He was working two jobs. He used this shift to recuperate.

"Tanna's not due in until—" He roused himself enough to peer at his watch. "Jezus, not for two hours yet. It's only five A.M., man, go back to sleep."

"Get outta here. You're snoring."

Bunch stretched and ambled to the door. "You want Tanna? She said I was to call her if you wanted her—"

"I just want you to get the hell out."

He left, but did not close the door completely. They were still afraid Michael would try to ace out again.

Not now, he told himself. Not now that I have my secret valentine.

He reached out to Val. He could feel that she was still on the bus—the rolling movement, everything dark, the smells of exhaust and sweat of the nearby snoring passengers.

He did not call her. She was asleep. He just stayed with her, greatly comforted to be part of her slumbering body. She was curled up in the seat. He could feel her legs, especially the right foot. It was cramped. It would be sore in the morning if she didn't move it.

He concentrated.

Presently the girl in the front seat of the bus stirred. The bored, drowsy bus driver caught the movement in his mirror as her shapely legs stretched out and settled into another position.

The screech of the bus brakes wakened Val. The driver spoke to her and she got out. He waved and drove off in a blast of exhaust. Sepulveda and Ventura is a fairly busy corner even early in the morning. There's a big hotel up the street and an all-night gas station on one side of the corner. Val was relieved to see a cab over near a coffee shop where the lights were on and customers were sitting around the counter.

She crossed the street and saw a cabbie in the car. She told him the address Michael said was his house in Malibu. The sleepy cabbie pulled out with squealing tires and was soon on the Sepulveda pass of the San Diego Freeway. Just after the Westwood off-ramp he turned right onto the Santa Monica Freeway. Val was aware of the meter running into higher numbers.

Val settled back into the seat as the speeding car moved through the artificial glow of freeway lamps. The city beyond the cab window was a blur of light. She may have dozed. It seemed like a second later the cabbie was saying, "Here we are, lady—"

She gave him almost all her money and got out with the sounds of surf somewhere nearby. The address was in brass numbers imbedded in a high stucco wall with lance points running along the top. Beyond it flowered bushes hid a luxurious house. There was a high wooden gate, a light, a simple speaker and an on/off button near a potted plant.

"God, it's good to be home," she heard Misha say in her mind.

She pressed the button. Somewhere deep in the bowels of the house she heard a faint bell and the muffled barkings of a big dog.

"Did you call your houseman?"

"I rang, but he didn't answer."

"Terrific," Val said with a sinking feeling. The dog's ominous bark grew louder. She was exhausted, could hardly stand, she was so sore and tired. "Why don't you call him now for me?"

"There's a gate key under the potted ficus—I'll call if he gives you any trouble." She found the key and entered a small patio.

There was a jungle garden here and a fountain. A light came on and a heavy oak door cracked. Immediately the long ugly snout of the dog shot out with a vicious snarl. Val jumped back, even when she saw a chain held the dog in check. Presently a short brown man appeared, holding the heavy chain against the powerful pull of the Doberman. He was slavering now, growling and barking a single fierce note, throwing saliva about as he tried to break free of the chain and go for the throat of this intruder.

Val felt her heart pound against her ribs. She wasn't usually afraid of animals, but there was so much menace in that snarling muzzle, in those bright hard canine eyes, she wanted to run.

The short man blinked at Val.

"What you want, honey?"

The dog lunged; it seemed the little man could not hold him, but he was unperturbed and quite strong. He saw Val's fear. "Don't worry. I got him—Caesar don't like chicks. What you want?"

Val swallowed. "Michael gave me a key—said I

should drop by if I was in town," she stammered. Misha said in her head, "Home . . ."

The dog settled down to a guttural vibratto, barely sitting on his pony-sized haunches, ready to spring if he felt the slightest lessening of tension in the chain.

"Goddamn crazy time to drop by."

In her head she heard Misha warn, "Watch him—Piro's a smartass."

Piro seemed to be making a decision as he looked from her eyes to the key in her hand.

"He said I was welcome . . ." Val hated the note of pleading in her voice.

"Come on," Piro said suddenly, making the dog jump to four paws again. The dog had not taken his stare from Val. "I put you in the guest room."

Misha whispered secretly, "Tell him you want the sea room."

"The sea room," Val blurted. "I want to sleep in the sea room."

Piro and the dog led the way inside the dark house. There was a faint light somewhere to the left, but even in the dimness Val could see it was a magnificent place.

"I just change sheets. That's boss's room. You can't sleep there." The dog threw another growl/bark over his shoulder at Val.

Misha said, "Tell him to shove it. Say, 'Shove it, Piro,' just like that."

Val's gift of mimicry was unerring. It had a peculiar effect on the houseboy and the dog when she said, "Shove it, Piro," in Misha's unmistakable inflection. Piro stopped as if leashed and looked at her oddly. The dog shook himself of all viciousness. His chain rattled on fine Mexican tile as he wagged his stump of tail and crawled to nuzzle Val's foot. He whined and gave her a happy little bark, looking up into her eyes with the total devotion of a one-man dog.

Val felt Misha speaking with her lips. She didn't fight him. "Good dog, Caesar," her voice said. Her hand touched the warm velvet muzzle. The dog's ham-sized head and neck leaned against her thigh. His pink tongue moistened her fingers. Without doubt, he had recognized Misha in her voice, picking up with infallible animal sensitivity the message that Piro could only suspect. The houseboy dropped the handle of the chain and, still staring at Val, bent to pick it up. His eyes narrowed and he said in a hostile voice, "Who the hell—?"

He started to take a threatening step toward Val, but the dog stood alertly between them, growling suddenly in Piro's direction.

Now it was Piro's turn to stammer. "He never like chicks before."

"The sea room . . ." Val said in her own softer voice. The dog's ears jerked as if on puppet strings. The animal moaned and took a tentative step toward her. He sniffed. There was bewilderment in the sound he made as he cowed his hindquarters and backed off. "Caesar knows I'm here with you," Misha whispered. "Poor old boy can't figure it out."

Piro was wide-eyed. The dog leapt behind him and watched Val from that shelter. Piro pulled on his chain as he finally said, "It's over here," and led Val down a shadowed corridor.

He said no more as he directed the dog into what looked like a kitchen beyond a swinging door. Val then followed him through the maze of glass and wood and creamy sand-colored carpeting toward Misha's bedroom.

CHAPTER 23

Like most really fine things, the beach house was extremely simple. It was basically a series of redwood boxes laid on pilings, with glass between the beams. It was a deceptive simplicity, however.

It was an expensive structure, calculated to capture as much ocean view as possible, full of wood, metal, Mexican tiles and textured materials. It was sparsely furnished. The carpets were all sand colored. There were seven skylights.

The master bedroom opened to the sky with three of them, free-form shapes that captured three islands of heaven centered above the huge waterbed. As one entered the room, the bed seemed to be floating on the sea—an illusion created by a mirrored pedestal. Directly behind the bed lay the Pacific and a wide expanse of western perspective. Beige and brown predominated, and most of that in woods. Any color in the room had to come from whatever humans happened to bring with them.

Val's faded blue jeans and shirt looked like an ink stain in one corner, reflected in a panel of mirrors.

Val was thinking, It's a real nice room, as she entered. Behind her Piro efficiently set down her slim bag and stood grinning. He couldn't be waiting for a tip.

"This is his room?" she said for want of anything else to say. Anything to wipe that silly grin off the guy's face.

Off in the distance she heard Caesar howl mournfully.

"This the place," he said in a heavy accent she guessed was Filipino. She was familiar with the accent because she'd once met some of Brenda's relatives.

231

He was kind of cute, but there was something that she didn't like about him. She couldn't pin it down.

"This will do fine," she said, taking possession of her room by walking around a little bit of it. She looked up and saw the skylights just filling with early dawn light. There were a few clean clouds in one sector high enough to catch the fiery pink of the early sun.

"Sheets are clean," he said, walking over to the bed. His touch made it stir faintly.

"Where's the bath?"

"Over here," he said, running into a space between the mirrors that had seemed hidden because of the reflection. Now she saw that it was the entrance into a spacious bathroom that opened on one wall to a small exterior garden enclosed in a snug high wall that had ivy climbing over it. Ferns gave the light a green tint. The plumbing was all black porcelain with exquisite Mexican tiles in golds, browns and siennas.

"I'll take it," Val said, whirling around, making a joke. But Piro had stepped very close to her, so that her nose practically brushed his.

Since entering the bedroom, Val had not heard Misha. Now his voice was close to her ear. "Tell the bastard to fuck off."

"Excuse me," she said pointedly to Piro, "I want to be alone now."

"You a very pretty lady, you know, baby."

"Look," Val said, not waiting to hear what Misha might say. Piro's look of expectancy told her that he was used to some kind of arrangement with the ladies his boss brought home. Maybe the ones who just showed up were fair game, some kind of tip from employer to employee. "I'm an old friend of Michael's and—"

"I know all his friends. I never see you before."

His hand was reaching out to her, so when Misha said, "Let me take care of this," she didn't hesitate. It felt so good to just turn the difficult situation over to him, but she wanted to see what was happening, so she

232

silently told Misha, "You can talk to him—go ahead—but I don't want to pass out—"

Her hand caught Piro's firmly.

"Get lost, Piro." It was an icy dismissal.

What Piro saw was this little girl, cute little cuntie, open her sweet red lips and utter a phrase he'd heard before, spoken in just that tone of voice, although in a deeper masculine pitch. His eyes widened and he didn't fight her hand. She was amazingly strong: Her grip was hurting his wrist. She had a left that wouldn't quit, no sirree.

She just stood there seething red energy, her body tense with wound-up action, fists clenched, but in utter control. Piro decided she was into some Oriental martial art he didn't want to learn the hard way. But the uncanny similarity to his boss unnerved him. He figured it was just a good imitation.

"Hey," Piro said, backing out with a nervous laugh, "you do Kirk Douglas, too, baby?"

"I told you Piro was a smartass," she heard Misha say as the houseman left. She followed him to the door, and as it closed softly she was grateful to see it locked from the inside. She shot home the bolt and turned around to survey this wonderful space, which included what seemed like the entire Pacific Ocean, that had been given to her. Her stomach felt a little weak. She clutched it, thinking for a moment that she might throw up.

"He has permission to hit up on any ladies who just show up here."

"And sometimes sloppy seconds?" she asked, sitting on the edge of the waterbed. The rim was air-filled, unlike the kind with hard supports. She had barked her shins more than once on wooden-framed waterbeds. She looked around for a closet. She wanted to take a shower and get out of these filthy clothes.

There was a feeling of surprise from Misha.

"What's the matter?" she asked. "Aren't nice girls supposed to know about things like sloppy seconds?"

"No comment."

"I think I'm going to be sick. I don't like working myself up to a fight like you did back there with Piro."

"You get sick at your stomach whenever someone confronts you?" He sounded incredulous.

"I hate to fight." Then: "Where's the closet? I need a robe."

"Near the bath," he said mildly. "Hostility's a turn-on. Did you see old Piro's face? He knew who was talking to him, the superstitious bastard."

"Sometimes you're disgusting."

Val was opening up two double doors of a cedar-lined walk-in closet. There were six rods filled with hundreds of shirts, suits, trousers, fur jackets, specialty clothing. On one wall were hundreds of pull-out boxes with transparent ends that displayed individual pairs of shoes. Val looked quickly away lest Misha be saddened by the sight of all those shoes.

"On the costume rack are some interesting things. Help yourself."

She moved several hangers.

One rod was obviously for costumes exclusively. She pulled out a velvet doublet.

"Have you done Shakespeare?"

"No, but I played an Elizabethan duke at the Renaissance Faire one year." As a spectator, Val had been to the elaborate commercial reconstruction of a seventeenth-century country fair that was held in the hills north of Los Angeles in the spring each year. The fair was in fact a huge set, where hundreds of actors played out elaborate parts from history and their own imagination in the style of the 1600's.

"What's this?" Val asked of another vestlike leather shirt. What caught her eye were the elaborate Indian patterns of glass beads sewn on both sides. It was an amazing garment, obviously handcrafted.

"I've never seen anything like it," she said, touching the intricate beads. There must have been literally thousands.

"I wore that in 'Pard'ners,' " he said as she turned it over to admire the stitching. She knew his series only

234

by reputation and did not want to comment on another actor's work.

"What's this on the back?" There was a cleverly concealed pocket that opened at the back of the neck. There was something inside it.

"The scabbard. Take out the knife—it's a beautiful weapon." Val pulled on what she saw was a bone handle followed by a wicked-looking blue blade. The metal was thick on one edge and extremely sharp on the other. The entire graceful curve of the knife must have been ten inches.

"That's how I did the trick in the opener," he said proudly. "It was a very difficult trick—I worked on it with a coach for weeks."

Despite its slimness it was heavy. "Careful," he warned. "That blade'll slice a finger and you won't know it, it's so sharp."

"It's horrible—"

"I forgot. You don't like things like this."

"I can appreciate it is a fine thing, but it looks so lethal."

"It's authentic. The prop man on that show collects antique knives and guns. This one supposedly belonged to Geronimo. Smell it—"

She sniffed the cool blade, which was dull except for the shining edge reflecting back the overhead light. The smell was unusually acrid.

"Supposedly the blood of a hundred white men aged the metal."

Val shuddered and carefully replaced the knife. There was a cleverly designed strap and a brass fitting to secure the weapon. She snapped it closed. Once in the scabbard, the knife was not detectable.

Val held out the vest to marvel again at the beadwork.

"Two seamstresses worked for three months exclusively on the beads for it," he said. "Try it on—it weighs a ton, doesn't it? But the designs are placed so that it just feels good and snug."

Val slipped it on her shoulders. It was huge on her.

235

"Let me see you in it—the mirrors—"

Val trotted out into the bedroom and admired herself in the vest. She had thought he had been watching through her eyes since the confrontation with Piro, but he said, "Let me see you, Valentine." Her eyes got what she now thought of as that twinkly look.

She stood very still in front of the mirror. Finally he said, "It would look better if the only thing you were wearing was the vest."

She smiled at him as if he were standing right there in front of her eyes, and not merely looking at her through her own in the mirror.

"I think I'm going to keep this, if you don't mind," she said wickedly, clutching the vest close to her breasts, turning small circles away from the mirror. But it made her dizzy and she stopped spinning.

"What's wrong?"

"I think I'm just exhausted. I haven't slept except for a catnap or two since yesterday morning."

"See the wooden panels beside the mirror?" he asked.

She walked to the spot. It appeared to be as he said, a series of rectangular panels, but when she examined them more closely she saw that they were the fronts of drawers with ridges along the bottom of each panel to pull them out.

"Second drawer from the right, top," he said. "Something's there to help you sleep."

She gazed down at the pharmacopoeia in the deep drawer. There was everything: several kinds of hash and a hash oil in small bottles like perfume flasks; a tin of what looked like purple sansemillia bud, a fine California marijuana; and at least fifty medicine bottles with everything from ludes to speed to cocaine.

"See the small blue glass bottle?"

She unscrewed the lid and poured out a few innocent-looking white pills.

"Take two and you'll sleep like a baby, but don't take any more or you may sleep a lot longer than you'd like."

In the bath she found a glass and downed the sleeping pills. She wandered around some more, touching surfaces until the bed summoned her. She lay back on its rolling surface.

"You're on the bed," she heard Misha say.

"Hmmmm," she answered. She really wanted to take a bath, but she could hardly keep her eyes open. Maybe just a nap then a good wash.

"I want to make love with you."

"I must have some sleep."

He did not speak for a few moments. By the time she heard his voice again, she had dozed off and the sound gave her a start. She blinked awake, seeing the miraculous dawn in the three skylights directly above her. Tangerine and mauve clouds moved quickly in a sprightly wind.

"I must sleep."

"Val?"

Her eyes fluttered again and she dreamed that Misha called her from far away, then from closer and closer until he was on the bed beside her, stroking her face with his thumb, kissing her lips.

Scott Rand was finishing the intricate paint job on the beautiful little Ford truck he'd been building when Maxine visited him. The radio was on. He was sitting at his work table under the glare of a high-intensity lamp, painting a miniature delivery sign on the tiny door, when he heard the front doorbell ring. He was mildly annoyed, To look right this decoration should not be interrupted, but should be completed in one hair-thin line. Scott had amazingly steady hands. Despite the insistent bell, he finished that section of his pin-striping and carefully set his little masterpiece aside. With the brush still in his hand he went to see who the hell could be here at such an early hour. On his way he glanced at a clock. It was just past seven.

He was surprised, but pleasantly, when he opened the door and saw this beautiful chick standing there. She was about so high to him—wouldn't have reached his chin with the top of her light brown fuzzy hair. She smiled bewitchingly with a lovely mouth that made Scott forget entirely about the beautiful curves of his model.

"Hi," she said sweetly. "You don't know me, but I know you. I want to thank you for saving my boyfriend's life a while ago—"

"Uh, how did you get in?"

"The guard was asleep—"

"Yes, it's kinda early."

She threw back her head and laughed, then stepped up to him. Without warning she flung her arms around his neck and planted a lingering, juicy kiss on his resisting then relaxing lips.

She finally broke the kiss. "Thank you."

"It's not often I get an in-person thank-you note," he blushed, smiling back at her, but he was fumbling with the brush, with his hands.

"I just had to deliver this message in person," she replied, glancing around the cozy room.

"Uh, can I get you a cup of coffee, or something?"

"Why, yes, thank you. That would certainly wake me up. I'm sorry I had to come by so early, but I have to be at work early . . ." Her voice trailed off as she followed him into the kitchen.

"I can't help but notice the beadwork on your vest—what is it? Indian? South American?"

"American Indian, kind of," she answered. She was staring at him, still smiling with those beautiful lips. There was something entirely provocative about her, something expectant and waiting. She stood very still watching Scott prepare the coffee.

"Sorry, all I got's instant."

She just smiled. It made him uncomfortable, horny, he decided, and he had no idea who this strange girl was.

"Who did I save, and don't I know you from somewhere?"

"The man you saved is very important to me. They say you will get a medal for saving him. I think people

238

should always get what they deserve. I mean, I'm extremely grateful . . ."

Scott blushed, turning beet red as he fumbled with the coffeemaker.

"I mean, *extremely* grateful," she said pointedly, unmistakably provocative.

"Uh, do you take cream and sugar?"

"Lots of cream," she said with heavy emphasis.

"Instant," he smiled again, feeling a little foolish. Here was this terrific-looking broad standing here broadcasting on all wavelengths. He was getting an erection, but he hid it behind the island stove.

"I feel like I've met you or seen you someplace," he said hesitantly.

He quickly looked away from her dazzling eyes as he poured the steaming water into the cups. He was thinking, Here I am pouring coffee for a girl who just walked in, kissed me and now makes it clear she's ready to thank me genuinely. Like it happened every day. When he looked up again, she was staring at him with those luminous hazel eyes. She licked her lips. Oh, God, Scott Rand said to himself. It was not a prayer.

"I was about ready for a cup of coffee myself. I worked all night."

"You saved people's lives all night?"

"No—I'm on vacation, but I love to build models—" he gestured at his work table, but she only gave it a perfunctory glance and was looking at him again so that he had to look away.

"I know where I've seen you—"

"You do?"

"You've been on TV. Not news—no, don't tell me—commercials. I've seen you in some commercial."

"You have me confused with someone else." For the first time since she entered his home so unexpectedly such a short time ago, she seemed to cool, to darken. She even slunk back in the shadows as he brought the coffee cups into the living room near his workbench. He had it in mind to show her the model truck.

239

"This is what I was working on," he said. He turned around but she had not followed.

He heard her voice, deep now with what he assumed was desire: "Your work must be a turn-on—I mean, having all that power of life and death over people. All the praise, all the commendations."

She had not moved from the kitchen area, a good fifteen feet from where he stood turning back to see her. Oh, Lord, he thought, still holding the coffee cups, she's taking off her blouse. It did look that way. The beautiful girl stretched out her arms as if she were unbuttoning her blouse from the back, her elbows bent at her ears. "I have a commendation for you, too."

Then the girl made an incredibly swift move with the right side of her body; in a shaved second Scott saw the dull blue blade whizzing at him. The coffee cups saved him, though painfully. He was holding them at his nipple level when his body's instincts took over. He threw his arms up to protect his face while falling backward to one side. Coffee scalded him. The knife struck but not in the throat where it would've hit if he hadn't shielded it with his arm. He heard the girl screaming in a banshee voice, "You bastard, you blood-sucking butcher bastard—" as she turned and fled from the apartment.

Full of adrenaline his heart pounding with sexual energy wrenched into defense, Scott reached in a deliberate, swift movement and yanked the extraordinary knife from his bicep, where it had penetrated only a couple of inches at a lucky angle. He hardly felt it.

It was the scalding coffee that hurt like hell.

Scott sat there on the floor for a few seconds studying the blade, recovering, holding his wound to stanch the bleeding; the blade must've nicked an artery. Blood was jerking out between his fingers in small spurts. But it wasn't critical. He saw the open front door.

At that moment he remembered exactly the commercial he'd seen the girl in.

It was one of those silly dumb things you don't

240

watch except that they're so dumb and sometimes the girls are great-looking.

That's why he remembered the commercial, because it was a breakfast food thing and this pretty girl in braids was dancing on the spoon, a giant spoon in a giant bowl of corn flakes. It jogged a memory from childhood. A thin smile of accurate thought interrupted Scott Rand's grimmace of pain.

" 'And the dish ran away with the spoon,' " he said.

Damn, he thought suddenly. Some nut just walked in here and tried to kill me. He looked at his blood, a sight no less shocking because he was a medic. This was his blood, an entirely different matter from the buckets of the stuff he slogged through professionally.

"Christ!" he said. He decided, though reluctantly because the girl was such a dish, he'd better call the police.

Crazy broad running around like that could hurt someone.

There was just one thing Bunch was afraid of and that was height. He stretched his arm out as far as possible, trying to grasp the binoculars that lay several inches beyond his considerable reach. All the time, from above, Goldman was shouting, "That's it, boy, you almost got it—a couple more inches—come on, you can do it—"

But he couldn't. The truth was that Bunch had no intention of letting go of the windowsill, not even for the fraction of a second it would take to snatch the glasses and pull them in.

He crawled back inside the window on the floor just below the spot where the old men watched the girls. He could hear Goldman admonishing Bunch to try again as he closed the window.

"What are you doing?" Dr. Raymond demanded behind him. Bunch's heart almost stopped. The old man had a habit of wandering around "his" hospital, but it never failed to startle the orderly for him to suddenly appear.

"Nothing, sir," Bunch said, locking the window hardware.

"Who's that out there?"

"Mr. Goldman dropped his glasses on the ledge. Can't reach them."

Raymond nodded. "Well, maybe he has an extra pair," he said and wandered off to open the door of an empty room, peer inside and close it without comment.

Bunch shook his head at the old man's behavior. He heard again as Goldman called his name. "You get 'em?"

"There's no way I can reach your binoculars, Mr. Goldman," he said a little later when he joined the group on the roof. "I'll get myself killed. I'm a big man. I'd fall hard."

Behind him the other old men played gin at the table.

Goldman mumbled his thanks but Bunch could see him deflate just a little. He'd been doing poorly since his favorite pastime had been interrupted.

"Maybe your daughter will give you a pair for your birthday."

"Yeah. Maybe."

It just broke Bunch's heart to see him so dejected. He remembered Goldman's daughter, a leggy, long-haired young woman who had risen to the top in a big advertising company. She always sent baskets of fruit.

"You know, I think I know where we might borrow some glasses, just for a few minutes, though," Bunch said. Goldman's face lit up like a candle.

"You do? Where?"

"Now, it'll just be for a minute, you understand. It's not for keeps." Bunch stood.

"You just wait right here—"

He left Goldman grinning in the early morning sunshine.

CHAPTER 24

"Maxine Wise?"

"Yes."

"You don't know me—I live with Valentine, Leslie Valentine."

"Oh, yes. Frank, isn't it?" Odd, Maxine thought, that I should remember his name from that snarled telephone conversation with Val.

"Have you seen her?"

Something in his voice communicated his anxiety, even though he thought he was in control.

"Not since late yesterday—why?"

"It's very important I reach her—she's . . . she's in trouble. It's very personal, but she might be in danger."

"I left a phone message for her yesterday, but she hasn't returned it." Maxine realized that's how he knew to call her. When Val stood her up yesterday afternoon, Maxine had left a message on her home phone.

"If she does, please get in touch with me as soon as possible."

"Maybe if you could explain. . . ."

"She's—she's in a bad mental state right now. She needs a doctor, maybe even—"

He seemed to be struggling with the thought. "Well, she shouldn't be by herself right now."

"I'll tell her you called if I hear from her."

"No—she doesn't want to see me. She ran away from me. Look—for her sake, help me get to her. I found the address of a Sunnyrest Convalescent Hospital near her phone. You know about that?"

"All I can do is tell her you called."

"But don't you see——" he screamed. "She's running from me, from help. She's crazy, don't you understand?"

"Listen, I don't know you," Maxine said in a no-nonsense tone of voice. "My relationship is with Val, not you. The best I can do for you is give her your message."

"Goddamn it——"

Maxine hung up on him, thinking, What an unpleasant son of a bitch. But before she forgot it, Maxine wrote the name of the hospital in her notebook.

Frank sat there looking at the buzzing receiver. He swore at the woman who had hung up on him. He was tired, been up all night. When he got Val's note he had been ready to go back to L.A. and commit her, but Rooney convinced him to finish the shoot before he went back. If she was sane enough to write the note, Rooney reasoned, then she'd be okay for the short time it would take to do the job—no use getting a rep for unprofessional behavior like going home without the footage. Well, he got the footage. Then he got immediately to their empty apartment. Val hadn't been there; there was this woman's message on the phone machine.

He replaced the receiver and was thinking maybe Val had gone to her mother and father's house, when the phone ring startled him.

"Yeah?"

"Frank, where is she?" It was unmistakably Brenda.

"I don't know," he sighed.

"Ritcher and Raye have been calling all morning. They loved her, but I've got to get her to a meeting at one this afternoon. This could be her big break, Frank. She could be the Doggie Sweet girl."

"Lotsa luck, Brenda. She's gone nuts on me. Ran off, God knows where. She thinks some guy is talking to her, you know, mentally——"

There was no response from Brenda. Frank figured she was about to say, Huh? but she didn't.

"Did you hear me?"

244

"I knew there was something wrong with her. I figured you got her into drugs or something."

"Well," he replied self-righteously, "she's into something all right. I've got to get her to a shrink."

It was his first conversation with Brenda in which she did not ask him to repeat a single phrase. "I'll work out something with these people," she said, "but for God's sake get her to call me—"

"Sure, Brenda," Frank said, contemptuous of the old bat and her commercial perspective. He felt superior to her. He'd always suspected she wasn't good for Val. After she got some rest and was ready to work again, he was going to find her another agent.

He hung up almost as abruptly as Brenda had previously hung up on him. He was making a list of all the places Val might be in addition to her parents' home.

First on his list was the gym.

Val woke on the beach.

The dawn she had seen earlier in Misha's skylights had turned into a sunny day. Nearby some kids were playing with a kite that bounced on the upper reaches of a spanking breeze. She lay back on her sandy pillow and watched the red and yellow paper diamond dance against the blue sky.

Judging from the sun, it must be after noon. She roused herself, brushed sand from her clothes. She saw the beaded vest and it made her think of Misha.

When she called he didn't answer. She got to her knees and stood, stretching out all the kinks. She was groggy. The interrupted sleep on the bus, then the sleeping pill and a fitful dream-filled slumber had failed to refresh her.

How did I get out here on the beach? she wondered, looking at the children as they ran off up the sand with their kite leading them before the wind.

She squinted in the light. She felt sore, expended, as if she had done great exercise. Her right arm muscles ached. She rubbed them and stretched again but the knots were still there.

She knew she had dreamed something powerful, but she could not recall any part of the dream, except something about a model truck. She looked around. Her own footprints led from here back to the tree-shaded deck of Misha's beach house.

The houseman was standing there at the rail, watching her.

She started walking toward him, and as she got closer she saw him frowning with emotion. He backed away from her, watching her every move. She knew instinctively that this man was afraid of her. She stretched her arm again, to unknot the muscles, and she caught the unmistakable ducking motion of someone who doesn't want to get hit. The look in his eyes confirmed it: He was terrified of her.

She didn't speak to him. Her dislike of him last night had ripened. Now she loathed him.

She found her way to the master bedroom through the house. The door was locked, so she walked around to the deck again.

Though she didn't have a clear memory, somehow she knew now she had walked outside through a sliding door. She found it, still open, the drapes stirring in the breeze.

She looked around the luxurious room. Her eyes were sore, gritty. The bed had not been slept in. That bewildered her. She stood there staring at it, registering that in fact she had not slept here. She frowned with the effort of trying to remember where she went to sleep. The drug drawer was still pulled open over by the mirror.

She looked up at the skylights.

"Misha?" There was no answer and Val felt almost for certain he was asleep.

She smelled herself at an armpit and made a scowling face. She slipped off the vest and lay it on the bed.

She felt chilled and hugged herself as she turned completely around on the spot, looking at the room. It was beautiful but it made her frown. Things were not adding up here.

Her thoughts were interrupted by the sound reverberating throughout the house of a large door being slammed.

She followed it to the area where it sounded like it came from and found herself in a large well-appointed kitchen in sparkling order. Through the heavy back door she saw a compact car, maybe a Toyota or Datsun, backing rapidly out of a driveway that wound behind the garage and out onto Pacific Coast Highway several hundred feet north of the gate she had entered. Piro was driving with Caesar in the passenger seat; and as the car passed the kitchen window, she saw that it was full of possessions—boxes, a TV set, other personal items like clothes on hangers wired together.

Apparently Misha's houseman had resigned.

She did not feel comfortable in this house alone. She locked all the doors she could find and found her purse. Misha said last night there was a car in the garage.

She left via the back door and entered the garage. It wasn't a Mercedes, but to Val the cute little TR-6 was the most beautiful car she'd ever seen. He had said there was an emergency key in a magnetized box in the front bumper. She pawed around, breaking a nail, but couldn't find it. She found the key in the ignition, and suddenly she knew she had driven this car recently. She had to figure out about the garage-door opener, but found the control immediately. The key turned over in the ignition and for the first time in a long while she felt good. She had wheels again. She could almost forget the nagging doubt that she had misplaced hours in the morning, hours in which something had happened while she was asleep. She wanted Misha to be with her to allay her fears, but he wasn't here. The consolation of the gym beckoned, away from the world, where she could think, sort out all her feelings. She felt dread at finding out what had happened, but she pushed her dread back and wouldn't think about it. Soon when Misha came to her she would ask him.

Maybe he could remember the nightmare that troubled her, for surely it had been a nightmare.

Her body cried in ten places. Her right arm and shoulder were especially sore. She could hardly wait to get to the gym as she backed out of the garage, turned around in the wide driveway and headed for the gate she had to open to enter Pacific Coast Highway.

She took the time to close the gate and after that barely stopped for lights in her rush to get to the gym. Today it would be a true sanctuary.

When he first saw the sports car pull into the gym parking lot, Frank didn't realize Val was driving because it was so unexpected. He knew her old car was parked back at the apartment. He thought maybe she had walked the mile or so to the gym, and was prepared to merely wait outside in his car, watching the front exit.

So when the sports car pulled in from the street, he saw it but didn't know Val was in it until she got out. She was walking in the front door as Frank jumped out of his car and followed her.

Inside she was bending over the receptionist's desk as he came up behind her, taking her by the elbow just as she was turning to enter the door with the MEMBERS ONLY sign. He surprised her and was able to grab Misha's car key from her hand while someone passed beside them and into the locker room. Val was wrenching free, but Frank held on tighter.

"Stop it, Val—you're acting crazy—"

"Frank—give me back that key."

"Whose car is that out there? What's going on, Val?"

She tried to pry his fingers loose from her arm. The receptionist behind them was standing, addressing Frank: "I'm sorry, sir, but you'll have to leave."

He ignored her. "Come on, Val, you're going with me now."

"Stop it—" Val ordered, pulling from his grasp.

"You'll have to leave, sir," the receptionist said,

touching Frank's arm. He turned to shout at her and Val took that opportunity to hurry through the door. She was gone before Frank realized it, and he quickly followed her, with the receptionist calling after him, "You can't go back there—this is a women's gym—"

In the hallway that led to the locker room, Val was aware Frank had followed her. As she ran to the further door she called over her shoulder, "Frank, now who's crazy—Get out of here—"

She really thought he'd turn around at that point. He was usually shy about women and would not put himself in such a position. She went into the locker room and had found a locker when she heard someone scream, "There's a man in here—"

Forty-five or so women started asking questions or shouting, depending on whether or not they saw Frank. He was moving along the rows of lockers looking for Val among the naked and half-naked female bodies. One particularly fat woman whirled around, stark naked, and fainted when she saw him. Someone else tried to catch her and Frank ran into their tangled bodies.

He saw Val and went for her just as a large powerful gym attendant strode up to him and ordered him to get the hell out. She grabbed his arm and started to lead him to the door but he turned on her and shouted an obscenity at her. She responded in heated Spanish. For a second they appeared to be starting to fight, but Frank backed off when she was joined by a couple of other women who were not yelling or trying to get away. Someone near the door was yelling, "There's a man in the locker room," as she hurried out.

Frank had grabbed Val again and was trying to pull her toward the door. The women came up behind Frank and pinned his arms behind his back while dragging him to the door. He kicked and lashed out at them, but there was no way he could overcome six or seven strong adults determined to throw him out.

Val had gotten to her feet from the crouch she was in when he yanked her. She stumbled back and realized it was Maxine Wise she had bumped into. Maxine caught her in her arms and pulled her away from Frank's sight. Val was crying now, more from the struggle than from any concrete emotion.

She followed Maxine into the foyer where they had first found the privacy to talk.

"You look like you're in trouble," Maxine said in a friendly voice.

"God, you said it—"

"That's Frank, I assume?"

Val nodded, catching her breath. Far off they could hear Frank yell her name. Then a door slammed.

"What's the matter?"

"I went up north on a location with him, but I changed my mind and came back unexpectedly on a bus. He worries about me—even though I left him a note and said he shouldn't—"

"Do you have anyplace to go?"

Val flashed on Misha's house. It was a beautiful place to be, but now that Frank had the key to Misha's car he could easily find the address of the owner from the registration. He'd follow her for sure. Her own place was out of the question, though she wanted to go by there and pick up some clothes and her car.

"I could go to my parents' house—they're on vacation," she said tentatively but knew Frank would look there, too.

"I have a spare room. You're welcome to it for as long as you like."

"Why are you helping me?"

"I told you—it's the maternal instinct."

"I think I'll take you up on your offer. Thank you."

Maxine cracked the emergency exit door. From there she could see Frank standing outside the building. Someone, a man in a business suit and most likely manager of the gym, was sternly talking to him. Frank's arms were folded adamantly across his chest. He didn't look like he was going to budge.

She closed the door.

"There's just one thing I want from you," she said. "Tell me the truth. What's happening?"

Val looked pained. She glanced around.

"Go on. There's nobody here but you and I."

"You won't believe it."

"Try me."

Val took a deep breath. "I've fallen suddenly, madly in love with a man who is a true soulmate—you know the meaning?" She stepped closer to Maxine. "He feels like my other side, you know? I can't live without him, all I want is to be with him. It's the first time in my life I've loved—"

Maxine felt sour. Damn her. Just another little whore trapped by her own game. Maxine felt self-righteous at having found a husband of unquestionable loyalty to protect her from such excessive desire. This is nothing but a jealous-lover case. Val had probably been tailing him the night of the accident, saw him with another woman. God, she may have even participated in the accident somehow, maybe even caused it to happen. At most she watched her faithless lover plunge over a cliff without calling for help. At last Maxine felt the mystery evaporate; the moment when the truth stood out unobscured and the innocent girl turned out to be a classic scorned woman bent on revenge.

"Who is he?" Maxine asked, knowing exactly who he was, but wanting to hear Val say it.

"You know who."

"What I can't figure out is why you hired me," Maxine said. "If you knew him, then why did you need me to find out about him? You could've just called his house or something, since he was an acquaintance."

"You've got it all wrong," Val said with a wide-open gaze that almost sucked Maxine in. She seemed so completely honest, but what she was saying just didn't add up. "I've never met Michael Stefano," Val lied minutely. No use to mention the awful scene at the hospital. It couldn't possibly count for a true meeting anyway.

"Then how could you be in love with him if you don't know him?"

"Oh, I know him. I didn't say I didn't know him; I just said I hadn't met him."

"You're not making sense, Val," Maxine said, genuinely concerned for Val's mental state. Maybe her boyfriend was right, even if his tactics were a bit crude. Maybe Val did need professional help.

"Look, do you mind if we continue this conversation later?"

Maxine cracked the door again. The manager was gone but Frank was still waiting, sentrylike, just outside the front door. She quickly closed the emergency door and nodded to Val.

"I'll honk three times," Maxine said, about to open the door.

"You still have on your leotard."

Maxine laughed and together they returned to her locker where she changed back into street clothes.

"You really have me curious," Maxine said as she found her sunglasses. "How do you know someone you haven't met. You pen pals or something."

Val was sitting on the bench. There were several other women dressing and chatting nearby. Just below the level of the general hum in the locker room, Val said softly, "I know him because I'm telepathic with him."

Maxine looked blank.

"You know, telepathic. I speak with him in my mind."

Maxine sat down. "You mean you hear voices?"

"Much more than that. Sometimes he uses my voice. Sometimes he can see through my eyes. Once I saw through his. I didn't know who he was at first. I knew of his accident because I relived it with him telepathically through a dream. Then I started hearing him call me. I knew you wouldn't believe I saw an accident by telepathy, so I said I witnessed it and ran away. I didn't say how I witnessed it."

She waited for some response from the detective.

"Well?"

Maxine looked up.

"I don't know what to say."

"You don't believe me."

Maxine squinted. "I believe you believe it."

"Well, that's more than I expected from you, I guess."

"Come on, let's go," Maxine said. She could hardly wait for Hugh to hear this. He'd have some scientific explanation for what was happening. Some kind of massive psychotic episode the girl was going through. Maybe he'd be able to help her. Maxine hoped so.

"Three honks," she said at the door. The gratitude in Val's smile was unmistakable. Maxine left, taking with her a glow of what she supposed the feminists called sisterhood.

Tanna watched Michael sleep. He was deep in slumber, almost as though he had been heavily sedated. It was late Friday afternoon; he'd been sleeping since that morning. Bunch said he had stayed awake all night.

When she had left him last night he seemed okay, had even agreed to meet with the prosthetist today, but when the man had arrived for the appointment, Michael was so deeply asleep she had decided not to wake him. She checked his drug chart again; he had not been given any more than the mild painkiller and muscle relaxer Raymond promised he'd keep him on as long as Michael behaved as though he didn't need something stronger.

But here he was, sound asleep at six in the evening.

She picked up the notebook from the table. He had made a list of more than a hundred things he needed feet to do. Some were bitter, some merely sad. Others on his list were humorous. She looked at him again.

His lips were moving in a dream. She bent close to hear what it was he was saying but she couldn't make it out. She stood regarding the man. She kissed her fingers and touched his lips with them, then backed into the chair near the window. She could hear the traffic down below in late rush hour. It was getting dark. A beautiful sunset streaked the sky.

She decided to stay with him, just in case.

"So, is this telepathic partner with you now?" Maxine asked as Val hurriedly threw a selection of clothing into a large lightweight bag. She was anxious; Maxine knew she was afraid Frank would come in at any moment.

But her nervousness made her talkative.

"No," Val replied, "he doesn't like you."

"Val," Maxine said, handling the bag while Val took her overnight case, purse and the afghan from her chair in the den, "do you know what projection means?"

"Look," Val said flatly, "I minored in psych. The main reason I hired you was to find out if there had been such an accident, otherwise I'd know I was going over the edge." She set down the case at the front door and walked back into the kitchen. Maxine followed after putting down the suitcase. "I knew you'd think I was nuts. Just like Frank."

When she entered the kitchen Val was watering her plants. There was something poignant in the way she went about the task as though everything were okay and she was just going away overnight. Poor kid, Maxine thought, hoping Hugh and she could persuade Val to seek professional help. Maybe even commit herself.

"Don't you think my own sanity was the first thing I questioned?" Val had four or five plants hanging in the eastern-facing window of the small but tidy kitchen. She was methodical in her watering, making sure it didn't drip.

"You really believe you're in telepathic communication with this man, don't you?"

"I know it," she said, finishing the last plant. She put the pitcher away in a closet and made sure the back door was locked.

She saw Maxine watching her and shrugged. "Habit, I guess."

There was no sign of Frank outside, but when Val got inside her car she was dismayed to see the fuel gauge on empty. "I'll have to park it at a station overnight—can you bring me back in the morning?" Her regular station was nearby but closed at six. She knew from past experience when it was this low she couldn't get far.

"Sure," Maixne said, privately thinking about the fact that it was six-thirty and in two hours her home would be full of friends wishing her well on her private detective agency opening, and in the morning she'd probably be hung over and sleep until afternoon.

Val was privately thinking how dumb she was to have forgotten to fill the tank of the Citroen. She felt like she really wanted to have her wheels near her to keep away from Frank, but finally convinced herself it was best to park it and have Maxine bring her back to it later.

She followed in her station wagon as Val parked in the first gas bay of the station across the street from her own office. She got out to help Val put all her things into Maxine's car.

"Are you sure," she asked as she caught her breath, "that it's not just those funny cigarettes you've been smoking?"

Val hoisted her overnight case through the rear door of Maxine's car and closed the lid. "That was a lie, Maxine. I don't smoke pot. I just used that as an excuse to explain why I didn't report the accident."

Maxine thought about that as she got back into the driver's seat. When Val slammed the passenger door she said, "I told you, you wouldn't believe me." She didn't appear angry about it, just resigned.

"Do you blame me?"

"No. I'm claiming a crazy thing."

Maxine headed for home.

"I've been thinking about how crazy it sounds. I mean, I never even had good hunches before, no history of ESP of any kind, and here I am telling an almost complete stranger that I'm a telepath."

"I'm not judging you. Honest," Maxine said when she saw the skeptical look on Val's face. "Strange things happen. I worked in law enforcement long enough to know that."

She turned down her street.

"By the way, I forgot to mention it, but Hugh and I are throwing a small party tonight."

Val looked distraught.

"Don't worry, you don't have to come downstairs if you don't want to."

Val was grateful. "I think I could sleep for three days." She knew she had slept but it seemed not to have refreshed her. Why was she so tired? Why did her right arm ache so?

Maxine had been about to comment that she looked like she was falling out on her feet, but out of good will thought better of it.

"Take a nice hot bath, a sleeping pill and sleep all weekend if you like."

"I'll skip the sleeping pill, but the rest sounds like what I need." She lay her head back on the headrest as if to prove her point.

"I have a million things to do in the next couple of hours," Maxine said. "I'm taking my boys over to my mother's for the night. You'll have a bathroom all to yourself right by the guest room. It's far enough away from the rest of the house to keep the party from bothering you. Course, you may feel like partying after you get some rest."

Val didn't answer and Maxine thought she was asleep. She saw as she approached her house that the caterers were already getting set up from a marked van parked at the curb.

"You think you've got it all figured out, don't you?" Val said quietly, her eyes still closed, her head back, relaxing. "Nothing can surprise you. You've seen it all, done it all." Val's speech was flat with fatigue.

Maxine *was* rather proud of her experience. It had been a full forty-two years.

"But someday, something's going to happen you

can't explain, something that will take your breath away," Val continued in a weary, dreamlike voice. Maxine turned off the ignition after pulling into the driveway. "Something that violates all the laws you've built your neat life around." Val didn't seem to be aware the car had stopped.

Her words made Maxine uncomfortable. She didn't like being around drunks, drug addicts, or people who had not gotten enough sleep. They were all incoherent.

"We're home," she said brightly to arouse the girl. Val rolled her head to look at Maxine. She saw that Val was chewing absentmindedly on one of her braids like a little child.

Maxine almost cried out in memory. Melodie used to chew on her braids, too. In this subdued light Val looked so much like the dead child it brought stinging tears to Maxine's eyes.

She quickly exited the car so Val wouldn't see and had Val's bags out by the time the girl joined her.

Val grabbed hers and Maxine's purses and the overnight bag, while Maxine took the suitcase into the side door that entered the kitchen.

The TV set could be heard down the hall. It was that same show they always watched at seven o'clock, that Western. She showed Val the hallway to the stairs and left her on her own while she went to get Ben and Timmy ready to go to Grandma's.

They protested that their favorite show was just coming on, but Maxine shooed them out to get their stuff together. They had permanent toothbrushes at her mother's house, but still took schoolwork, pajamas and other things along when they stayed overnight there.

Maxine reached to turn off the TV set but hesitated when she saw the name Michael Stefano flash under the actor's face. She stood watching with the sound turned down as he crouched in his role of an Indian and flung a knife expertly, almost pinning the villain to the tree trunk. It was the logo of his show. She'd seen it before, but it hadn't registered until this moment that this man was the object of Val's bizarre search. She stood there until the logo changed to a commercial, then switched off the set.

She delivered the boys to her mother's ten minutes later and was back at her house in time to take a shower and dress for her party.

CHAPTER 25

Michael woke early Friday evening bored and restless, complaining of cabin fever. He found his binoculars missing and that left him even meaner. So Tanna took him to the Jacuzzi pool, thinking that would relax him. They talked while they soaked.

"Tell me why I feel feet I don't have anymore."

"You feel because your brain hasn't forgotten." She reached out to him across the water and lay her hand on his forehead. "Here," she said, moving her hand to the crown of his head. "Back along here." She took her hand away, but he caught it and held it just under the surface of the whirling water of the Jacuzzi pool.

"It's like a computer model. Your brain has a program of the body you've grown over the years. To your brain's model you still have feet."

"But why pain at the toes, and so little pain at the stumps?"

"The brain is registering pain at the terminal end of your leg. To the brain that's feet. It's a wiring problem."

"I'll always remember."

"Probably. But it'll diminish over the years. This," she added, indicating the water around them, "is great, so's exercise."

He pulled her toward him in the water. "Lotsa exercise," he said. With his teeth he pulled down her bathing suit strap, but she protested and pulled it back up again.

"Why are you teasing me?" he demanded in sudden exasperation.

"You're rushing things."

"How can you distinguish between"—he kissed her meaningfully on the lips—"and this . . ." He slipped his fingers in around the leg of her suit, but she backed off and swam away. He watched her swim with an impressive stroke to the far end of the therapy pool, about ten feet. Carefully he scooted along in a sitting position on the bench under the water. Once he nearly slipped off into the deep water, but he caught himself, realizing that the four-foot level would probably fill his mouth and nostrils with the hot mineral water.

Tanna was instantly beside him. He saw she understood and was grateful she didn't speak about it. He felt stupid and childish to be frightened of such shallow water.

She pushed off and dog-paddled to the far end of the pool. He followed her, buoyed up by the tingling water. He found it easy to swim.

"See?" she said as they met, "there are still a lot of things you can do."

"You must've seen my list."

"Only about a hundred things you can't do right now. You can shorten the list when you learn to walk again."

He sat on the underwater bench and pulled her into his arms.

"You're the horniest man I ever met."

"You've known a lot, huh?"

She shrugged suggestively. "You, too."

"No, you're the very first," he said mockingly.

"Who's Val?"

He moved to let a jet of water thrash his lower back.

"Who is she?"

"Nobody."

"She must be somebody to you. You call out her name all the time."

259

He looked piercingly at her. "I swear I've never personally met anyone named Val."

She could almost believe him, but she knew he liked to play games.

"You call out her name in your sleep."

"No, you must be mistaken."

"I've heard you. So has Bunch."

"Bunch is always asleep—how could he hear anything?"

She regarded him a long time. Finally he looked up at her but he didn't speak. "You know what?" he said.

"What?"

"I sure would like to get out of this place for a while."

"Against the rules."

"Maybe go out on the boulevard, get a pizza. What do you say?"

"I say it's time you got out of here before you turn into a prune."

The wheelchair was on a ramp that led from the pool edge into the middle channel of the water. She pulled it over to him and he got into it. It was easy in the water.

"Come on—what do you say?" He gestured at the clock on the wall of the room as they left. "It's not even nine on a Friday night. We could catch a movie."

"It's against the rules. And your uncle's orders."

"I need to get out—"

"Maybe tomorrow," she said. "I'll ask Dr. Raymond."

She made a note to remind Bunch to keep a special watch on Michael. Now that he was definitely getting better he was surly and nasty. They returned without speaking to his room, where Bunch was removing the last of the IV setup and the monitoring equipment. Tanna went off to get coffee.

Michael watched Bunch untangling and looping tubes.

"You took the binoculars, didn't you, Bunch."

"Mr. Stefano, I did, but I can get them right back to

you. I was going to bring them back right away anyway." He was backing out of the room.

"What did you do, hock them?"

"No, it's not like that. It was for Mr. Goldman—"

"I don't give a shit about some old Peeping Tom. I can have your job, you know that?"

"Why would you want to—?"

"Word gets out you're a thief, what other hospital will trust you?"

"I didn't hock them. I can get them right now, if you want me to."

"Yeah," Michael said, leaning back, looking out of the window at the traffic below on the boulevard. "Why don't you do that."

Less than a minute later Bunch returned with the glasses. He handed them to Michael, but Michael ignored him.

"Why don't you close the door, Bunch."

"Huh?"

"I've decided to let you help me."

He let his bathrobe fall open to reveal his limp cock.

"Look, I brought you back your glasses. What more do you want, Mr. Stefano?"

"I want you to help me. Like you offered before. Now. So, close the door."

Bunch looked down at him in the sliced light from the blinds. He sucked on the inside of his mouth and bit his tongue.

"I, uh, have a fever blister."

"I ain't particular." He wagged his cock at Bunch.

Bunch was still holding the binoculars. He looked at them, at their fine workmanship and detail.

"You can keep them," Michael said languidly.

Bunch tossed the glasses onto the bed.

"I don't want them."

"You come back here."

Bunch stopped at the door. "No, Mr. Stefano. The other day I'd help you out. I felt sorry for you, I really did—" He saw Michael's face grow angrier. "I'd help any man if I could, I ain't ashamed. But now, looking

261

at you not even willing to share your binoculars with some old men who don't have anything left but dreams—well, Mr. Stefano, I don't care if you do get your old man to can me—you can stick them up your ass."

Michael screamed an obscenity at him and wheeled fiercely over to the door to slam it. He hit his fist against it and screamed again, "You'll have to move to China, you asshole—"

He wrapped the bathrobe around himself and wheeled back over to the window. It was getting dark outside. He thought about Val and reached out to her. "I need you . . ."

Val stirred on Maxine's big bed. It was dark. She could hear party sounds faintly but it seemed like a dream. Her eyelids fluttered and she might have wakened but she didn't. Somewhere down a corridor of her mind she could hear Misha. He called her, too, and he was preferable to a party where she knew nobody. She would follow him instead. She needed to pee anyway, so she followed his voice to a dark bathroom, did what she had to and stumbled back to bed.

"Let me be with you," he whispered.

"Let me sleep just one more hour." She should have been rested after sleeping this morning, but had been bewildered ever since she had wakened on the beach.

"I'll be with you," he answered and she drifted off again.

"I'm sure she's okay," Maxine answered Hugh, in the midst of the noisy party. Most of the fifty or so people here knew each other, having worked in law enforcement with Maxine or Hugh.

"But you said she was acting weird. I think you should go up and check on her." It was after eleven and the party was going strong.

"Why don't you?"

"I think I will, just to make sure she's all right."

Maxine turned him around and pointed him toward

the stairs just as a newly arrived couple came up behind her.

"Maxine, darling—so sorry we're late—"

Hugh was surprised to find the girl lying on top of the spread of his and Maxine's huge bed. Maxine said she was in the guest room, but she must have gotten up to go to the bathroom and gotten lost in the dark hall. She was sound asleep, arms and legs flung out like a bird in flight on the blue covers, completely naked and as lovely as a statue.

He stood in the open doorway with the light from the hall throwing his long shadow across the carpeting and the corner of the bed where the beautiful girl lay. He stood there a long time looking at her perfect body, her lovely breasts and flat stomach moving slightly with her dreaming breath. He thought as he set down the drink he'd carried in, that she was the most beautiful human being he'd ever seen. He was content to just stand there drinking in the sight of her on his bed.

Just then her eyes blinked open. In this light she seemed confused, maybe even frightened, and he was just going to sit on the edge of the bed to comfort her, tell her everything was all right, and see if she wanted anything to eat or drink from downstairs.

It was all dreamlike for Hugh. He sat on the bed and saw her eyes in the hall light. Without thought he bent over her and kissed her. She didn't resist but instantly flung her strong legs around his waist. He was immediately, burningly horny. He had in mind a gentle petting maybe, nothing to worry about at all, but the girl seemed suddenly fired by his passion. She squirmed beneath him and wouldn't let him break the kiss. He didn't fight her but scooped her up in his arms and rolled with her across the wide expanse of bed.

Frank pulled up outside the large ranch-style house in Sherman Oaks. The woman Maxine, whoever she was, had left her address on the phone machine with her message to Val last night. Frank was pretty sure

Val wouldn't be going to a party, but what the hell, he hadn't been able to find her anywhere else. He'd tried everything, every place he could think of where she might go. He was furious when he returned to their apartment and found she'd been there and taken her car. But it looked like she didn't take much else, so he was pretty sure she'd be back.

Then he'd listened to the messages on the phone machine. There were another two or three gradually more frantic and then coldly curt messages from Brenda. She was angry with Val not getting back to her for the commercial job. No other messages were on today's tape, but Maxine's message last night was still on the machine. She gave her address and told Val she forgot to tell her she was invited to a party tonight.

It wasn't far away, so Frank got there a few minutes after eleven when the party looked like it was just getting started. People were smoking out on the front patio. They seemed a happy group, Frank thought as he looked for a familiar face among the drinking, laughing crowd. He stopped at the caterer's table in the living room of the house and stood there eating canapés, drinking wine while he looked around. He didn't know anyone here. How did Val know these people, he wondered? Who was Maxine Wise?

Maxine was in the kitchen helping the waiters get some ice—they had run out and were taking her stock from the freezer.

After she'd taken care of that, she glanced at the clock. It was nearly midnight and she hadn't seen Hugh for a while. She wanted to get him to go down to the boulevard and get more ice because she was sure there wasn't going to be enough. She asked some guests if they had seen him and when they said they hadn't, she decided to go up and see if he were talking to Val.

Frank was helping himself to globs of liver pâté on fine pumpernickel bread at the food table. A bright-eyed older woman was loading up her own plate nearby, so he leaned over casually and asked, "Wonder where our hostess is?"

"Oh," the woman said helpfully, "I think I just saw her go upstairs." She sawed at a loaf of bread with an inappropriately heavy knife, then used the same cleaver to spread pâté on her slice of bread.

Frank followed her gesture and pushed through the crowd to the stairs. The lights were off up here and it was quiet. Frank walked down a long hallway where a ceiling light burned at one end. To the left he saw a bathroom and stepped inside to take a quick leak.

Hugh moaned her name as the girl dug her finger-nails into his shirt and the muscles beneath it. She tongued his ear then bit the lobe hard. It urged Hugh on as he sucked her breast in return. Their struggle knocked an ashtray or something off onto the floor.

The girl was breathing through her teeth now, each breath a hiss of passion. She clawed at Hugh's pants zipper while he unhitched the belt, then she rolled over on top of him and sat forcefully on his erect cock. She was crying out, making fierce little noises that had no human speech to them. Hugh lay back and let her go; before very long he was coming like a jet into her, while she kept ramming him harder and harder, then abruptly stopped and didn't move. Hugh looked up at her. She was looking over her shoulder toward the door. Hugh followed her gaze to see Maxine standing there silhouetted in the light from the hallway.

Maxine wasn't moving, so the girl had a moment to spring to her feet. She walked boldly toward Maxine, who was standing there with her mouth moving, but without words coming out. Just as the girl approached her Maxine whirled around out of Hugh's sight. The girl followed her into the hall.

Hugh was struggling to find his pants when he saw the girl's arm and shoulder from around the door. She appeared in silhouette with Maxine in tow. Hugh sat there unbelieving as he saw the shadow of the girl lean forward and kiss Maxine passionately on the lips, take

265

her hand and lead her into the bedroom. Beside the bed Maxine tried to break the kiss but the girl, possessed of strength beyond her petite frame, wouldn't let her go. She held on to Maxine's head from behind while she kissed her, pulling her hair while her other hand explored Maxine's plunging silk neckline.

The girl broke the kiss and stood there playing with Maxine's left nipple while Maxine stared at her in the shadows as if hypnotized. She was thinking, all in a rush that mixed with arousal, I may be gay and didn't know it all those years, but damn, I swear I am responding to someone else.

She tried to see closer into Val's bright, unblinking eyes. Val seemed to be glowing. There was a wild smile on the girl's face that didn't seem to belong to the person Maxine knew.

"Val—?" she asked hesitantly.

The eyes narrowed, cloaking themselves, and Maxine was sure there was someone else there, though later she would forget that part of the experience and attribute her response to sexual frustration during these weeks of Hugh's impotence and to the drinks she'd had at the party.

The incomprehensible feeling translated into fiery desire.

For an instant Maxine started to flee.

"No—" the girl barked. "You know this is what you want—" Hugh was startled by the harsh sound to her voice he remembered as soft.

Maxine would've protested. Her hair was disheveled, her blouse torn. Hugh looked at the girl kissing his wife again in a slow, imprisoning embrace. It stirred him more than the sight of the girl alone on the bed and he stood on his knees with his pants unzipped, reaching for them both. He was thinking deliriously that this was a Maxine he'd never seen before and she was sexy as hell. He didn't think any more as he pulled the two women down onto his bed with him.

Neither protested.

*   *   *

266

Frank stepped out of the bathroom and continued on down the hall, where he thought he heard voices.

To the right was what looked like a bedroom. There was someone in there, wrestling on the bed, and for a second Frank stared in curiosity at the writhing shapes. "I'll be damned," he thought, "there are three of them going at it in there."

He chuckled to himself, and just then one of the three in the room cried out in a fit of passion. He recognized the voice though she sounded hoarse.

"Val—?"

He slammed his hand on the light switch just inside the bedroom. There in a pile of coats on the bed was Val, a tall, gray-haired man with his pants down and a good-looking mature woman who seemed to come awake the fastest of the *trois* in the harsh light.

Frank couldn't take his eyes off Val. She was sitting there dumbly staring into space, blinking, looking bewildered.

He stepped to the bed, grabbed her hand and pulled her to her feet. The other woman was struggling to her feet and the man was already off the bed, zipping his pants.

"What the hell is going on here?" Frank demanded as he pulled Val to him. "Get your clothes on—"

Maxine, who recognized Frank from the gym parking lot, was pulling her blouse together across her breasts. She said to Frank, "You—get the hell out! Who asked you here?"

"Come on, buddy—" Hugh was saying, his hand on Frank's elbow, but Frank spun away from him and slugged him. Maxine ran to Hugh as he fell to the floor with a bloody lip.

With Val still in tow Frank stumbled to the door.

"Where are your things?"

She started to protest. She looked groggy, squint-eyed, as though she had just waked up.

"Come on, come on, where are your things?"

She gestured hesitantly toward the guest room and Frank pulled her to it and inside. He put on the light and saw her bags sitting open on a bench near the bed. He pulled out a silky dress, one of the few pieces of clothing Val had thrown in the bag when she and Maxine had left her apartment.

Frank quickly helped Val to get into the dress. He took a pair of sandals from the suitcase—they didn't match the dress, but he wasn't bothering with such niceties.

"Frank, wait, what's going on—what—?" Val sputtered, gesturing toward the hallway and the bedroom they had so suddenly left.

"Just shut up and get dressed."

She pulled on the dress obediently, frowning as she seemed to be trying to sort out what had happened, as if she didn't know.

"What was I doing in there?"

"That's my question, bitch," Frank yelled, zipping her dress at the back. It was a pretty dress for a party, but Val's hair was messed up and her lipstick smeared. She looked, in fact, as though she had just wakened.

She was getting into the shoes when Maxine and Hugh came into the room. Hugh immediately tried to restrain Frank, who merely ignored him. He had hold of Val's arm and was pulling her past the couple and into the hallway. Val grabbed her purse on a chair and followed Frank because there was little else she could do. She stumbled and told him to stop, but Frank was intent on getting down the stairs, through the party and out of this house.

Maxine and Hugh were talking to themselves, as if planning something, but Frank didn't pay them the slightest mind. He pulled Val toward the stairs and they descended. He held tightly to her hair.

By the time they reached the floor, Frank had taken a more loving hold on her arm so they didn't look suspicious moving through the party guests. Hugh and Maxine appeared at the head of the stairs and started down.

What happened next was so quick only Maxine and Hugh saw it from their vantage point on the stairs.

Frank and Val were moving through the crowd, nobody around them the wiser about their conflict, but Maxine could see Val struggling to get away. As she passed the food table she grabbed the large cleaver Frank had seen that woman use to cut the bread loaf, and wrenched free of Frank. She was already around the table where she saw French doors open to a small unlighted and therefore empty patio outside.

Frank called her name, but over the general hubbub of the party it was not distinct. Maxine saw Val whirl around at the doors and fling the knife at Frank. It was very fast. Only Maxine saw the blade strike him. With the party going on innocently around him Frank dropped to the table where he poured blood from his severed jugular vein into the crystal punchbowl.

It was only when he fell over sideways that he caught anyone's attention. The crash of the punchbowl and the condition of the man bleeding into it pulled a scream from someone nearby.

There was a frozen moment of silence in which nobody moved. Maxine remembered later seeing the glass curtains at the French doors moving in the breeze, and thinking, Thank God she got away. She had slipped out without anyone seeing her in those first few moments of shock.

So at a party attended by at least a dozen cops, plus several parole officers, social workers and newspaper reporters, not one person thought to chase the culprit until it was too late.

Val, meanwhile, took advantage of the shadows on the side of the house to walk quickly away. She crossed the lawn under some kind of flowering tree that filled the night air with unbelievable perfume.

She was fully awake now, with that sweet smell in her nostrils, like a funeral, she thought.

Misha, oh, Misha, what have you done now? she asked silently.

He didn't answer. She didn't feel him with her any longer.

CHAPTER 26

Behind Val couples and small groups were clustered in the lights from the porch. It was a cheerful, somewhat middle-aged group. Most of those outside were smoking; Val caught the distinct aroma of pot. Figures, she thought cynically. Everybody knew cops could get the best grass; Frank was always talking about it. She had not been seen, but she was paranoid.

Run, she told herself, but run with caution. Don't cause a commotion that will send them after you. She walked briskly in the cricket-filled darkness. Her shoe heels clacked on the cement. She stepped off onto the nice middle-class lawns so she would make no noise. Once a dog barked, but for the most part she was alone.

She knew the Valley but was unfamiliar with this cul de sac neighborhood. All the streets looked alike, with their modern lamp standards between oleander and hibiscus bushes.

Finally she saw the deserted boulevard. She headed east in the direction of the station across from Maxine's office. She had had a premonition she should've brought her own car. Damn that she forgot to fill the tank. She had let the needle in that fuel gauge get to empty before, and knew from experience there was less than a mile's worth of gas left in the tank. Only a couple of convenience or liquor stores were open within a mile radius of where her car was parked.

She would have to stay awake all night, stay alert for Misha's presence. Since she woke up watching Frank die she had not felt her silent partner near. She dared not call to him.

Yet even with the revulsion she felt at the very

thought of him, Val was lonely for Misha. She was starting to cry, but stopped herself. She looked down at her hands as she walked along the quiet boulevard. These were the hands that threw the knife that killed Frank.

But *I* didn't kill him, she reminded herself. God knew the real situation, even if nobody else did. Please hear me now, she prayed with her eyes open. I know I haven't had much to do with church, but I've always believed in You. I've always tried to obey the commandments and do the right thing. I answered a call for help, didn't I? I took on another person's problems and offered love, just the way the Bible says we should.

Well, she did have to admit she had gotten something from it, from a purely selfish point of view. Even now her loins ached for lovemaking with her secret partner. She hated to lose that incredible sexuality she had with him. Ordinary sex would be pale now, in comparison. She would always wonder what it would have been like if they had made love with their bodies while telepathically connected.

Snared by desire, she told herself. Snared by lust and love.

But there's some honor in being able to love at all. There had to be. As for belief in God, well, just because she dropped the Church didn't mean she didn't believe in God.

It's so hard to keep believing in anything in this world. I kept believing in love and look what it's gotten me.

No, she countered to herself. It's better to be able to love than not. Oh, Misha, it could have been so perfect. Why did you have to fuck it up?

She stopped that line of thought lest it summon him. She was pretty sure he couldn't take over all of her body at the same time unless she was at least slightly willing. She had to admit she had hated Frank last night. That emotion had given Misha his entry. And the paramedic—the night of the attack she still only vaguely recalled, she had taken sleeping pills—precisely so she could lose consciousness for a blissful time. I opted for unconsciousness, she thought. I handed him my body, that's what I did. So, she consoled herself minutely, he did need to have some compliance on my part to take over and the takeover required recovery time for him afterward. After the aborted attack on the medic, she hadn't heard from Misha for five or six hours. How long he'd need to sleep off the energy drain from killing Frank she could only guess. Maybe the same, maybe less now that he was getting more facile in taking over. But she figured she had at least a couple of hours before he would be whispering, calling her with that clear voice only she could hear.

Under other circumstances Val liked being out at night on the streets of the city like this, when the only other people in the early-morning hours were night-people—streetsweepers, graveyard-shift workers, hospital personnel, whores and pimps, musicians and . . . cops.

There was a patrol car right over there at that donut shop. The two cops inside were on a break, stuffing donuts down to punctuate a vigorous friendly argument. They weren't even looking in her direction, but she felt cold to the bone as the walked through the intersection. A woman in a silky dress out in the night like this was an invitation for all kinds of trouble.

So paranoid. I'm an outlaw running for my getaway car, she thought. It was so comical she had to laugh at herself stepping quickly on the ringing sidewalk, nearing her destination.

She walked to the gas station, so very glad to see her old car waiting for her like a loyal horse. She practically kissed it as she hurriedly opened the door and climbed in. It was so good to be inside the familiar cocoon of the Citroen which had seen her through some crazy times. Nothing as crazy as this, she thought. It was such a lovable vehicle with its baroque styling, its little quirks, its tattered driver's seat upholstery coming loose at the seams from a thousand pressures of her body. She felt its hominess around her, thinking, This car has been a friend to me. Machine or not. Look at me now, she chuckled, am I with a human friend? No, I'm in my own little wheeled sanctuary, my old friend, my car.

She shivered and glanced over at the glassed-in office where a CLOSED sign on the door informed her the place would be open by 7:30 A.M.

Sitting there in her comfortable old car she thought again about being an outlaw. She looked around, expecting to see the patrol car creeping up, but the street was deserted.

I'm running from something worse than the police, she told herself. She shuddered to think she was some kind of special criminal who'd broken more than man's law. Somehow she had fallen into a network of discrepancies that let her speak with another human being without benefit of the usual human senses. It was beginning to feel more and more like she had made some grave mistake, broken some psychic law as immutable and as unforgiving as gravity, so that a fall was inevitable. No, thinking like that will leave me without belief in my right to survive, she insisted in her own defense.

My only mistake was loving unwisely.

She kept thinking, consciously talking to herself as she stepped out of the car and into the cool night. In the trunk she found a ratty beach blanket that had been there almost since she bought the car second-hand a few years ago. It was filthy but she shook it out, glad to have it.

She tossed it in the front seat and looked at the station building. There was no sign of a restroom, so maybe the women's room entry was outside. Maybe, just maybe, if she had any luck left at all, someone would have forgotten to lock it overnight.

She took her purse and keys and ran like a shadow to the other side of the building. The door was locked but she immediately spied an open window. The screen came loose and she hoisted herself inside, feeling like a

273

kid again. She stepped on the lavatory, then jumped to the concrete floor. No lights, of course; she didn't dare with that patrol car on duty up the street. But some nightglow fell in through the window. She saw her silvery face as she washed it.

She peed, so thankful to be able to do so before climbing back into that car. She knew she could lift her skirts behind the station, but it would have been terrible to have to, to have to make herself so symbolically vulnerable, with her pants down.

Running was still her best hope. Surely she could put enough miles between herself and Misha to keep him from taking over. Was there any alternative? While she brushed her hair, barely able to see in the mirror, she considered what alternatives friends or family offered her.

Her parents were gone until the end of the month. Most of her old girlfriends had fallen away in her single-minded assault on the TV industry; Frank didn't like women around anyway because he was always working at the apartment and preferred to have his movie-crew buddies as social contacts rather than people outside the business. She didn't have a best friend, not since high school. She didn't know anyone at the gym well enough to confess what was going on. That left Brenda. She thought briefly about calling her agent, but decided against it. Brenda had to use a device on her telephone that amplified voices, and still she couldn't hear. If Val called her at night at home, Brenda would most likely not understand or simply not answer.

So, her car really was her only friend. She collected her toiletries from the lavatory surface and left by way of the door.

Back inside the Citroen she locked all the doors and climbed into the backseat. She kicked off her shoes and loosened her bra. She had to stay awake but there was no reason she couldn't be comfortable. The satin dress would be ruined but she didn't want to be found here naked. The men who worked in these places were probably used to opening up with drivers sleeping in line, at least since the gas shortage. But a naked woman might bring the police.

Her watch didn't have an alarm, so she would have to rely on her usually accurate time sense to waken her. Val hung the tiny watch on an ashtray handle. She could see the time in the light of a streetlamp—1:37.

She really tried to stay awake, lest Misha sneak up on her. Perhaps fatigue would allow him entry as her willingness and drug stupor had done before. She didn't want to take the chance. She was pretty sure she was safe for the next few hours, but she could not know anything with certainty. She probably had until the station opened.

She pulled the blanket around her. The night had started out balmy, perfect Southern California weather. But now it had turned cold and it took a moment to get warm.

She had been wide-awake after she washed her face. But now, snuggled into the blanket that was taking on her body heat, she began to fade.

Her head snapped up from drowsing twice before her eyes finally closed. The last thought she had before sleep claimed her was that she must not answer Misha's voice, no matter what.

After the police left, the party pretty much broke up. Maxine didn't encourage anyone to hang around. The last few people to leave were still talking about what had happened. The police and the ambulance had gone long ago, but when they stepped out on the front patio to say good-bye in the refeshing air, Maxine saw a patrol car still parked at the curb, the cab light on, two cops filling out reports. She could make out the sound inside their closed car of the two-way radio, a mournful sound to Maxine who had been at many accident and crime scenes. The sound was always connected in her mind with tragedy.

"Well," said one of her departing guests, Castanian, one of the deputies she used to work with when she was in the juvenile bureau. Maxine had started her career many years before as a uniformed officer. After her first child she resigned and returned later as a contract investigator assigned to the missing persons bureau of several sheriff substations. Castanian, a sheriff's deputy in the juvenile division, had been an acquaintance for many years.

"Not everyone provides such an interesting floor show with their office warmings," he rattled.

His wife groaned and dragged him away. She long ago learned to put up with his grisly humor, but he always went too far. "Come on Cass," she begged, "you got the early duty."

Hugh and Maxine stood there watching the stragglers climb into their cars. Maxine saw in the front porch light that a car had been driven across the dicronda lawn. Hugh had not seen it yet, and she didn't want him to. That lawn was his pride; he had fought cutworms and drought and the high cost of water for three years to nourish it. The entire corner at the driveway was ripped up and two long tire tracks had taken out parallel strips of sod, then backed over themselves to rip out even more.

She reached into the hallway and switched off the light. Castanian over at his car parked on the street and yelled, "Hey, who turned out the lights?"

But he had plenty of light from the streetlamp. Maxine pressed her hand in the small of Hugh's back and he gratefully stepped inside, all hosting chores complete.

They held each other just inside the door. Finally their breathing settled into matching rhythms and their clothing rustled as they reluctantly parted.

She had never seen his face so tender as it was at this moment looking down at her. All during the questioning by the cops he and Maxine had both skirted any reference to what had immediately preceded the killing. Since he and Maxine were the only two witnesses, and since their thinking processes were so familiar to each other, they didn't even have to agree beforehand. They told the police exactly the same story without any reference to Val and Hugh embracing on the pile of wraps and purses piled on their king-sized bed.

Now his gaze was open to her and all that they had not said to others flooded between them.

"Can you ever forgive me?" he said, his voice cracking.

She was about to cry with love for this man. He was ready to take it all on himself. How did I ever deserve someone like you? she asked herself. She took a deep breath, already knowing what to say.

"I haven't been totally honest with you."

He looked confused. He was all ready to confess and find himself back in his wife's loving arms.

"I set that girl up," Maxine said, unable to keep her eyes still. "I knew the minute I saw her that she would turn you on. She's a nice girl, a beautiful girl, but kind of dumb in a sweet way. I knew you'd love her."

Hugh took a second to digest it. "You weren't kidding about Sarah and Abraham, were you?"

"I knew that if that girl didn't stir you, then you probably were really sick. That's all I was worried about. I know you love me, even if some other body turns you on." She felt there was more to say but it was all tumbling out incoherently.

She looked at him helplessly.

"I guess I'm about the luckiest man alive," Hugh said, sending the word *alive* into her mouth with his kiss. He held her for a long time, until she relaxed and let him have her weight, gave in to him. Then he slowly began to press his body against hers, from the knees up. He was methodical about it. There was nothing hurried about his movements, nothing hesitant about him in any way. She started to say something when he finally broke the kiss and was nuzzling her neck, causing the little hairs there to stiffen. She started to say something about how she was just thinking she must be the luckiest woman alive because she certainly

277

didn't deserve a man like him. But he put his lips back on her and forcefully prevented her from speaking.

For a second time that night Maxine was thankful she had had the foresight to send the boys over to her mother's during the party. They weren't due home until tomorrow afternoon, a blessed Saturday.

Hugh had a hand cupped around a breast when she suddenly remembered that Val had left her car parked near the office.

"I'll bet that's where she went—God, how could I have forgotten—"

Hugh did not interrupt his fondling or his nuzzling of her ear as he said, "She was out of gas—that's why she left it. The closest station open this late is in Hollywood. No, she's hiding someplace, but her car would be the first place she knows we'd look. She's too smart for that."

"Still, I ought to call the police and tell them about her car," Maxine said, not really wanting to do that to Val.

"You don't want to do that," Hugh said in her ear, forcing her backward into the dark living room. Even with the lights out they could tell the place was in a mess. Nothing had been cleaned after the party.

"God, we should clean up now—I don't think I can face this in the morning," Maxine started to say but Hugh half dragged her to the huge couch, swept away napkins and a couple of paper plates with his arm and threw her down.

There they proceeded to fuck royally for a long, long time. It was wonderful, just like old times, nothing had changed. Maxine's heart sang, all her parts sang. She even called out to Hugh just as she was coming— oh, Lord, it had been so long—she called out his old nickname to him—"Huge, Huge"—and her screaming brought him completely inside her. It was perfect, just perfect.

Then as he was coming mightily he called out. Maxine was already past her peak of pleasure so the experience could not be spoiled. Even so, it hurt when Hugh called Val's name instead of hers.

But, Maxine thought, I guess I deserve it.

CHAPTER 27

Before the accident Michael had been in the habit of rising at dawn to run on the beach. With the lowered medication his old patterns of behavior were returning. Bunch was snoring away as Michael focused his binoculars out the window of his room.

He knew Val had to be in her car, and he knew she had parked it near Maxine's office last night with the fuel gauge on empty. He could see the deserted parking lot from here. He swept the quiet street with the glasses. He felt terrific. Even though the attack on Scott Rand had failed in its primary goal, the act of attacking had a therapeutic effect on Michael. He felt sweetened by it, maybe even charmed, the way he always felt the second before he heard the word *Action!* just before the camera started rolling. It was a feeling of power, of being totally in command of a situation. Now that Frank was disposed of he had only to implement the plan he felt righteous in carrying out. Val would just have to understand he could not live like this. It was unacceptable. Karma or fate or just plain luck had given him her body to use. She would eventually come around to enjoy the benefits of having a not-so-silent partner.

He smiled with satisfaction when he saw Val's car at a station. He couldn't see inside because of the angle to his best view but it was Val's, all right. How many people in fashionable Encino drove an old gray Citroen with an I BRAKE FOR ANIMALS bumper sticker?

Momentarily he closed his eyes and tentatively

reached out for her. He was ready for any response from her and he was certain she was in that car. He opened his eyes, made a happy little sound and focused the eight-forties.

"Val . . . ?"

She pulled for consciousness as if from a great depth. She was more crouched than lying in the backseat of the Citroen, one moment sound asleep, the next wide-awake with a sour taste in her mouth, grit in her eyes and Misha's chocolate voice thick in her mind. Even now—how strange—he was desirable.

"I know you can hear me—where are you, girl?"

She bit her lip and struggled to sit up. Outside Saturday had dawned cold and gray. The Citroen was the only car waiting for gasoline at the station, which had not opened yet. There was some traffic out on the boulevard, but nobody had come to open the pumps.

"Are you asleep?" his voice asked. "I can feel you near."

A car pulled into the gas station and drove around back.

Val watched as the driver got out and entered the station office with a key from his pocket.

"Come on, come on," she whispered out loud, eyes following the attendant as he puttered around inside the glassed-in office area. He had brought in a paper bag from one of the donut shops and now sat at the old desk with his feet up, opening the steaming Styrofoam cup. Val swallowed dryly.

"I can feel you but you seem so far away," Misha said. Her lips begged the gas station attendant to hurry up. She took her watch from the ashtray handle where she had hung it last night; it was past 7:30.

Still the attendant dawdled, sipping at his coffee and munching on what looked from here like a chocolate glazed donut. The sign on the door definitely said the station opened at 7:30 A.M.

"I know, I know," Misha said sweetly. She closed her eyes and sat there very still, listening to her dark companion. "You're upset about last night. About Frank. But Valentine," he said softly, with such feeling she had to remind herself not to respond, "Frank was going to kill you. He was in a rage, a jealous rage because he had figured out about us."

Val was shaken by a shiver. Wet streaks were rolling down her cheeks as she listened to Misha inside her head, her teeth nibbling at her bottom lip as if to keep her mouth sealed against him. She was fighting both him and her desire for him.

"I saved your life, sweetheart." His voice was so kind, so loving, and it was saying all the right things, but she knew her memory of Frank's death was the true reality and she must not let Misha have what he wanted. She had to hold out against him. To let him win would be to contribute to a terrible evil. One had to fight the demon, even if he was a beautiful demon. Why was evil always pictured as ugly? It was much more evil and dangerous when hidden under beauty.

She must hold out until she could get away from him. She thought about honking to make the attendant hurry up, but knew that would probably just make him slow and surly.

She looked around but the attendant was not in the office now, and on its rear wall she could see a door opening into the garage area. The attendant appeared, nonchalant, holding his coffee cup as he returned to the desk, where he stood for a moment studying a stack of papers one by one.

The tears streamed down Val's face. Her nose was running and she sniffed and wiped liquid from her upper lip and cheeks with a corner of the ratty beach blanket. Sand that went unnoticed last night in the dingy folds stuck to her face, compounding her misery. She wiped at it, looked at her hands all gritty with the dark beach sand she had long ago captured with the blanket.

"Frank would have killed you, and that would have killed me, too, Valentine, because you *are* my life now."

281

The awful memory of Frank's face came back to Val. She thought she might gag. The startled look on his poor face when the knife hit his throat.

She stared at her hands, the hands that certainly had thrown that knife. Frank's face flashed in her mind again, frozen in his last word, her name screamed. She blinked to rid herself of the awful image.

"Just think. Like no other lovers the world has ever known, we'll be together forever."

She pushed back her hair and started to unwrap herself from the blanket.

"Just because you're not answering me, doesn't mean you're not there. I know you can hear me. I can feel you, like I was inside you. Remember the way we make love?"

She stretched out her legs.

"Ahh—that feels so good—"

Wide-eyed, she looked around at his voice, so confident, so sure of himself. She rubbed her right calf.

"—stretching your legs out like that. Uhh, charley horse in the right calf. I guess it isn't strange I can feel your legs so good, considering . . ."

Fear squeezed more tears from her eyes as she hugged herself against his assault. Her jaw was trembling spasmodically as if a great cold had entered and was freezing her from the inside out.

A blur of movement over by the office window caught her eye. The attendant was lighting a cigarette.

Val gathered her energy together and hauled herself into the front seat. Every muscle seemed to have been affected by her cramped sleeping position.

"Your body's tired. The muscles are sore. You slept in the car, didn't you?"

The rearview mirror caught her glance. Her eyes were dark-shadowed by troubled sleep. She saw the St. Christopher's medal Brenda had given her. It was a small protection but she put it on.

"Let me see through your eyes."

She reached up with a trembling finger and touched the skin beneath one eye.

282

"Let me touch with your fingers."

She covered her face with both hands and sat that way very still, listening to him, wondering what chance she had of holding him off.

"Imagine what it's like, Val. What if our places were reversed and I was stretching out my beautiful dancer's legs over there and you were over here with your legs cut off. Trapped for the rest of my life if Uncle Lazlo has his way about it."

Val's hands slipped slowly down her cheeks and neck. The gas station attendant was flipping over the CLOSED sign to read OPEN. She watched as if her intent watching would make him move faster, as the attendant walked to the pumps carrying a green flag and a ring of keys. He put the flag in a holder and approached the driver's window as she lowered it.

She found her gas tank key and handed it to the attendant.

He was a good-looking kid with twinkling eyes. "Hi," he said as he bent down to speak to her through the window.

"It's past seven-thirty," she couldn't resist saying as she handed him the key. "Fill it with regular."

"That low-octane shit is going to eat out your valves," the sparkly-eyed attendant said, close to her face. "If it hasn't already." He gave the hood of the Citroen a doubtful glance.

"How can you be so cold?" Misha wanted to know inside her head. "Shutting me out like this."

The attendant gave her a wink and stepped around to unlock the tank cap.

"For selfish reasons, you need to be in contact with me, too," Misha went on as she stared ahead while the attendant went about filling the tank. "Think of all the things I can do for you. All my contacts. You're where I was seven years ago. You can benefit from my experience. I can help you to get the right parts, make the right business decisions."

Val found her credit card. The attendant gave her the eye through the windshield as he wiped it clean.

"And," Misha continued insidiously, "you know I'm a better driver than you."

The church up the street, the same one she had entered and departed from so suddenly a few days ago, started chiming out the half hour.

"See? Right on time," the attendant said.

"Val?" Misha whispered behind her eyes, "I know you can hear every word I'm saying."

"Hey—you okay, honey?" the attendant asked solicitously, close to Val's face again.

She nodded and handed him the credit card.

"Check under the hood?"

She shook her head to indicate she was in a hurry and he went off to write the ticket. But he kept glancing back at the pretty, distraught woman who was biting her lip and crying silently.

Across the street Maxine entered her office. She had wakened early with Val on her mind. She knew what time the station opened where Val parked her car last night and so creeped from a warm Saturday sleep-in bed to come down on the long shot of finding her. When she parked beside her office, she heard the phone ring inside and hurried to answer it. Through the window she saw Val's car at the service station as she picked up the phone. "Yes?" she said into the receiver.

She recognized the voice immediately. It was Castanian, the last guy to leave the party last night. "I expected to get your answering service—your home machine is on," he said. "You're up early for a Saturday." She asked him what was up, thinking he just wanted to gossip about the killing, but instead he told her there was an arrest warrant out for Val.

"What possible charge?" Maxine asked incredulously. It was too early for paperwork on the killing last night.

"Not about that brouhaha at your place."

"What?"

"Assault with a deadly. A county paramedic named

Scott Rand said she tried to knife him. He's okay, but he said she was crazy, a screamer. He recognized your gal from a commercial."

"Another Hollyweird crazy," Castanian snickered.

"Let me call you back, okay, Cass?"

She practically hung up on him as she walked toward the front door of the office. There was only light traffic on the boulevard, so she jaywalked, heading toward Val, whom she could now plainly see.

The attendant, who had the name *Tony* embroidered on his uniform pocket, was handing her the credit card holder so she could sign the receipt.

"You stayed here all night, didn't you?"

She wrote her name shakily but didn't respond.

"You in trouble? Maybe I can help you out," Tony said, smiling suggestively.

She took her card and receipt and handed him back the plastic holder and the carbon. She started the ignition.

Misha said, "Val, it won't do any good to try and get away from me. The books you brought say telepathy isn't affected by distance. . . ."

Val grimly considered this as she pulled the Citroen away from the gasoline bay. Another car had pulled into her place but the attendant was watching her drive out until the other driver had to honk to get his attention. Val had glanced in the rearview mirror to see that and so when Maxine appeared at her window it was surprising.

Val started rolling up the window.

"Val—let me talk with you—please—"

Maxine saw that the door was locked. She tapped on the glass, but it didn't take long to see Val was not going to stop and talk.

"I know how upset you must be—"

"It's Maxine—" Misha said in her head. "You're talking to Maxine. I can hear through your ears, Val—

entine. Let me be with you, help you fight that cunt. We'll fight all of 'em—"

"—you were terrified. Frank was crazy—" Maxine was saying.

Val put her foot on the gas and killed the engine.

Maxine saw she had only a moment to try to get Val's attention. Her hands were against the window glass as she pleaded.

"Hugh and I will back you all the way."

Val tried to get the engine to turn over.

"Listen—they are putting out a warrant for you—"

Val turned on her, still trying to start the car.

"I did not murder Frank."

"Well, maybe not murder, but I saw you kill him."

"I know what you saw but it wasn't me."

The engine kicked over with a blast of evil-looking smoke from the exhaust.

"I told you I was telepathic with this man," Val continued slowly. "Now it's gone much further than telepathy. Now he's . . ."

Maxine watched Val's pretty face twist with confused emotions that had a basic look of fear.

". . . now he's trying to take over my body—" She emphasized "body" in a way that made Maxine cringe slightly. "He's—" Val looked up. She must have seen disbelief etched on the detective's face because she didn't finish the thought.

"I suggest you drop the telepathy bit," Maxine said after a pause, letting a harsher note into her voice, "the police won't buy it."

Val looked utterly beaten down; she didn't respond, so Maxine lightened her voice, "But the warrant isn't for Frank."

Val truly appeared crazy around the eyes as she shot a response to that at Maxine. Maxine felt a guilty twinge at hurting this wounded, frightened human being.

"Some county medic said you attacked him."

The girl chewed on this for a distracted moment. Then resolution pulled her mouth thin and she ap-

286

peared to be drawing on some inner resource as she shifted the car into first, letting it inch out so that Maxine was forced to walk along beside the driver's window.

"Val—*did* you attack him?"

Val's only response was to press down on the accelerator.

The car shot forward slightly, causing Maxine to step back as she called, "He recognized you from your TV commercials. Said you tried to knife him—"

Val slammed her foot on the brake as the flash vision of the paramedic's astonished face assailed her mind. She saw him only for a second, with that startled look in the time it took her to throw the knife. It struck his arm with a thunk. Again she saw her own hands in the body English after such a throw. She knew she had thrown the knife. Her hands had done it, she told herself in some small place where Misha wasn't and where Maxine could never be. Misha used her hands. The difference was all she had left.

Maxine thought Val was cracking up. She had that glazed look of the broken ones.

"You've got to talk to the police," Maxine said. She found a crack at the top of the car window and was forcing her fingers into it, pushing down the old loose glass.

Anger sparked the girl.

"Terrific. What do I tell them? That my boyfriend found me in bed with you and your husband and he came at me in a jealous rage, so I killed him?"

Maxine looked down. "I guess you'll have to tell them the truth," she said. Val could see Maxine felt terrible about what had happened, that she probably wanted to make it up. She looked up at Val through the window glass.

"Actually there's a biblical precedent," she said. "Sarah and Abraham."

"No explanation is necessary."

"Get away from her—" Michael ordered, as insistent as a headache.

287

"Don't drive," Maxine pleaded, hanging on to the window glass. "I feel so responsible."

"Always the Jewish mama, huh, Maxi?"

"I know how you feel."

"No," Val yelled. "You can't know how I feel because you don't believe what's happening."

"I care about you. I want to help."

Val leveled her gaze and said calmly, "By the time you accept what's happening it'll be too late to help me."

"How far can you get before the police catch you?"

"I'm not running from the police or your flaky sex—"

That stung Maxine. She'd never thought of her sex life as flaky, and because the word seemed so apt this morning, she bristled in defense.

"I was just trying to save my marriage—"

"And I'm trying to save my life."

Val leaned forward to see that the coast was clear. She floored the Citroen and it leapt into the right-hand lane. Maxine stepped back and watched only for a moment before she crossed the street again. She ran into the office, mortified that Val was so right, but still wanting to make up for her ill use of the girl. She was determined to help her despite herself. She grabbed her keys and left by the back door, where her car was parked.

She hoped there was little enough traffic that she could see where Val was going up the street and follow her. She just knew if they could talk it out, they could make things right again and rescue Val from the horrible pit into which the poor kid had fallen.

"I can help you with people like her," Misha was saying as Val headed for the nearest on-ramp to the Ventura Freeway.

Val still had it in her mind that she would just drive away from Misha. If she didn't answer him he was bound to lose control over her the farther away she went. She thought she might go to Canada—that was at least a thousand miles away. Surely Misha would fade over that many miles until he could no longer feel her near him. It was the only chance she had and she could hardly wait to get out on the open road.

"I know what you're thinking," he said in her mind. "Thinking that I didn't much help you last night. Okay. I admit, I got greedy. That Maxine is one sexy old broad. She saw me looking at her through your eyes and every hormone in her body started clanging."

Val sighed with relief. So he couldn't read her every thought. She pulled to a stoplight, just barely missing the yellow that would've put her right onto the freeway.

"You know, Val, I can feel your toes and legs now. I can feel your pussy, oh-so-sweet and juicy. Can you feel me inside you, can your hear me and smell me and feel me?"

A car honked behind her when the light turned green.

"I heard that—Val, I can hear through your ears even though you're trying to block me out. It's only a matter of time before I take over completely. I've been learning all along, learning how to drive your body. It's so easy . . ."

Val cried out loud, a little muffled cry of despair as the old engine died again.

"We gotta get rid of this heap. Celebrate with a Mercedes, maybe. I'll buy one for you . . . for us."

The honker behind Val blared again just as the starter caught and she began rolling forward. But by then the light was changing back to yellow, so she backed out of the intersection with the driver behind her glaring holes in her back.

"I'm a much better driver than you. Let me have your eyes—I can feel your hands—"

Val saw her hands grip the steering wheel. She fought to hold on to it, but she could feel Misha's will behind hers, lifting her own hands up in front of her eyes. She moaned a little and through an effort of will lay her hands back on the steering wheel.

"Ah, you're fighting me, baby," he said. "No use to do that. All I want is to help you, to guide you so you can benefit from my experience." She did not like his emphasis on the word *guide*.

She waited tensely for the light to turn green again.

"Val, let me have our eyes."

She whimpered at his use of the *our*.

The light changed and she carefully eased the Citroen out and turned right onto the freeway on-ramp marked with a sign that told her she was headed north on Highway 101. She felt centrifugal force as she rounded the curve of the ramp and merged with light traffic in the right lane. Back at the hospital, Michael had returned to his room.

"They are not our eyes. They're my eyes."

"Ah, so you are there," he said with delight. She realized that he hadn't known for sure. Maybe he wasn't as strong as he pretended to be.

"I knew you'd eventually answer. You always like to get the last word. See how well I know you, Valentine?"

"Get out of my life."

"You're all the life I have left."

A voyeur's life, what kind of life is that?"

"You don't have the right to deny me."

She moved to the left lane, where traffic was moving the fastest and edged the speedometer up to sixty.

"You used by body to kill Frank. That gives me right enough."

"He was going to kill you."

"And that other guy, the paramedic—God, how you've used me."

"He mutilated me—"

"And that mess with Maxine and Hugh—Jesus— things I don't even want to remember."

"I promise, no more kinky stuff. I'll be good." She could hear the calculating child in his voice, appealing to her soft spot for helpless things.

"I don't know for sure, but I suspect you were a user even before all this happened, Michael."

"I like for you to call me Misha."

"You aren't a helpless child anymore. Now you're a parasite . . . like mistletoe that sucks a tree dry." Had it really been only four days since the old church gardener told her that? It seemed like forty years since Tuesday. Val was so weary.

"You'll take over."

"Naw—telepathy anyone can buy, but body snatching? Only in the movies."

There was no use arguing with him. She had been foolish to think he was rational. The only hope she had was to distract him enough to drive away.

"You can't win, Valentine. I'm the sender. The books you brought over say men are more often the sender. You're the receiver. I've learned a lot from the books you brought to me." She was trying to force her fingers to move with her will. Her right hand and arm were tensed with their conflict.

"You think you're going to just drive away, right? Well, according to the books, telepathy doesn't diminish with distance. I think I could pick you out of a crowd in Bombay," he said with genuine pride in his voice.

She forced her hand to move slightly on the wheel.

"It doesn't have to be like this, darlin'," he said in a smooth Barry Fitzgerald Irish accent. "You're my Good Samaritan. Whoever heard of the poor victim attackin' the Good Samaritan?"

"Get out—"

"Come on, darlin' girl. Come back to me." As he spoke, her right hand started turning the steering wheel slowly then with increasing pressure to the right. The Citroen edged over; another car immediately to the right started honking, but it hung back when the driver saw the crazy woman behind the wheel was coming over no matter what.

"Come on," Misha whispered. The Citroen moved over another lane. There was an off-ramp ahead. "Why don't you just give me your eyes and let me drive, darlin'?"

Val was trying to pull the wheel back to the left, but her effort was causing the car to sway. Drivers on either side were getting out of the way.

Misha seemed to own her right side, while she retained more control over her left side, her naturally dominant side.

Val heard tires squeal as the Citroen rounded a long curve and sped off on the Topanga Canyon off-ramp. The wheel seemed miraculously to be hers again as she took the green light and turned left. Through a small commercial area and across Ventura she aimed the car up a tree-lined street, thinking she would pull over to the curb, but her bare foot pressed down on the accelerator.

"No," she cried, fighting to bring her foot up.

The Citroen moved up the twisting Topanga Canyon Road. Tires screamed again, but she held on to the steering wheel, fighting momentum. Suddenly she seemed to be alone as the speedometer edged back down into the small numbers.

She was about to pull the car off the road into a shoulder turnaround when she heard the low hiss of Misha's voice inside her head.

"If it's a fight you want, you got it, sister." She felt her hand turning the wheel away from the shoulder, felt her right foot press down on the accelerator with increasing pressure. She grimaced with the effort she was expending to bring the car to a stop, but she just wasn't strong enough. The steering wheel suddenly jerked hard right and the car sped forward with a burst of speed as her foot pressed the accelerator to the floor.

The edge of the roadway, with the San Fernando Valley spread like a miniature railroad layout just over the edge, moved closer as the car gained speed. Val cried out and just barely managed to regain control and turn the Citroen onto the blacktopped road, missing the precipice by inches.

"I could do much better if you'd let me see," he whispered.

Val's mouth was a set line of determination as she leaned tensely over the wheel, stroking it with her thumb just to see how much power of movement she still had left. All she really had full control of now was her eyes.

"The Blond Butcher is going to be a problem," he said, and Val knew he meant the paramedic. "They'll accept that Frank was self-defense, but the medic said he knew you from the tube."

Val uttered a little cry.

"That's the price of stardom," Misha hissed sarcastically. When it was apparent she wasn't going to respond, he said, "Well, I think Aaron can get to him, buy him off. How much could a guy like that make? Three, four hundred a week? A thousand bucks can buy a lot of plastic glue."

She was concentrating on her right hand. As Misha talked, she was regaining control over her fingers one by one. If she could keep him talking she might be able to catch him off guard.

"Imagine a grown man doing that all night long?" Misha laughed.

"Doing what?" she asked.

"That's right, you weren't there, were you? Model cars. The bastard builds model cars. Hundreds of them."

"I guess in his work he needs a hobby," she replied tentatively, feeling sensation in her entire right hand returning.

"Hey—" Misha said suddenly. "What're you doing, girl? Oh, no you don't—" Her hand was spread out like an unfolding fan, her fingers stiff and minutely trembling. Then, like a rock, the hand dropped to the steering wheel and gripped it.

Val almost cried out, but she bit her lip instead.

She knew she had to at least appear strong. No tears.

"You just keep your eye on the road, sweetheart," he said in his cracked Bogie. "Keep on driving. We'll work this out . . ."

Suddenly he wasn't there. Just like that. Val felt full tingling control of her fingers as she listened with a cocked head. She suspected this was a trick to divert her while he tried to take over her eyes.

"Misha?" she asked out loud and in her mind.

She håd her feet back again. For some reason he had abruptly let her go.

He was no longer here at all.

CHAPTER 28

"What do you mean he's acting funny?" Tanna asked Bunch as they hurried together back to Room 20. She had been afraid last night he might have another seizure, so she had stayed. It seemed like she had been asleep only moments when Bunch shook her awake.

"Like he's having a fit or something," Bunch said as he followed her into the corridor.

Tanna didn't say anything else as she headed for Michael's room. She suspected the trouble last night was from brain damage that had gone undiagnosed since the accident, maybe due to the concussion. When she opened the door and saw the condition of her patient she was even more certain. His hands gripped the headboard and he was tensed and strained as if having a seizure. He was whispering to himself. It sounded like he was saying, "Keep on driving, we'll work this out."

Tanna spoke his name and shook him. His eyes popped open. His face glistened with sweat as he stared at her a second as though looking through her. "You're having a nightmare."

He came awake, saw her and dropped against her arms.

"Just a bad dream," she said.

Michael shook his head, and, as if that movement wound a spring tightly in him, he exploded with a violent scream, slamming her back with his hand. But his effort was weak, and she motioned that Bunch should not interfere, at least not yet.

"I almost had her—"

Tanna struggled not to fall and stay out of the way of his fist.

"You stupid cunt—I almost had her—"

He threw himself back on the pillow, his eyes squeezed shut. Tanna had not expected that—she thought he would continue screaming. But he was whispering, as if trying to call someone.

"You're okay, Michael—I'm here now." She saw Bunch waiting near the door and made a motion that said, Leave but stay by the door.

Michael forced his eyes open and swallowed. His energy seemed to have been spent by the outburst. Slowly he turned his head and looked at Tanna.

"I came so close."

She stepped to him and lay her hand on his.

"Honey . . ."

Like a petulant child he shook off her touch. He was about to cry.

Tanna reached out and hugged him. She sat on the edge of the bed with him in her arms, rocking back and forth.

"You had a nightmare," she said softly.

His face buried in her bosom, he muttered, "No, it's real."

"It's only natural to have bad dreams."

He shook his head, but let her hold him.

"It means you're getting well—"

"There is no getting well," he cried, pushing her away from him. He saw the wheelchair close to his bed and hit at it, shoving it away so that it hit the wall and bounced back.

"This fucker's forever—"

She tried to comfort him, hold him, but he fought

295

her. He finally let her win. She began massaging his shoulders, his chest, his arms.

"God, baby, you're tight as a drum," she said close to his ear.

He moaned, leaning back, letting her have him. She massaged his stomach and thighs, delighted to see his cock stir beneath the sheet.

"These muscles are all tensed up," she whispered. Like a cat his back arched as she kissed his navel. His fists unclenched and touched her head near her ears, guiding her mouth downward.

"Open up, Mama," he said, eyes closed. "I'm—"

"—coming in," Val heard Misha say inside her head. She had relaxed and was looking for a turnaround so she could head back down to the freeway and get away. She had briefly thought about the north coast above San Francisco, the unblemished, uninhabited beaches of Humboldt County. She had been as far north as the California-Oregon line and knew that country for its beauty and isolation. It seemed the perfect place to run to. Now she was sure she could keep driving and eventually lose Misha. He would get tired and leave her alone. It would be over, this horrible nightmare of togetherness.

The feeling that she was not alone in the car was as strong as the smell of burning tar. Without thinking she looked in the rearview mirror.

For a sickening moment she actually saw the luminescent orb of one of his eyes looking back at her. It must have been a trick of the mirror because when she blinked, the awful, lidded third eye was gone. But his voice was strong in her ear as he said, "I'm coming in," with renewed energy.

"Let me be with you, Valentine."

"You don't want to be *with* me—"

"Please—"

"You want to *be* me." She concentrated on the road ahead which was growing more twisted. She saw

Mulholland and took it quickly; it was a better road and wider.

"What's it going to cost you to let me ride your shoulder?"

Tires squealed as the Citroen rounded a curve.

Another car passed from the other direction, swerving to avoid hitting her car as it took up its half from the middle.

"This is my body," she said.

"I can make better use of it."

Val felt her right foot grow heavy. She glanced down as it pressed on the accelerator.

"No—" She willed her foot off the pedal, but only managed to ease up on it. Her naked toes curled with the effort.

"See? I'm already part of you."

Her foot irresistibly pressed the pedal to the floor, causing the Citroen to jump forward.

"God, it's so good to have toes again."

She grimaced with the effort to take her foot off the pedal.

"I've already got your legs."

Gradually her foot lifted.

"I want all of you," he said with a crazy sound in his voice. "Isn't that from an old song? I want your hands, your mouth, the north and south of you."

Her foot floored the accelerator again. Val couldn't repress a scream.

"You can have *my* body," he said as if he had just thought of an exchange. "We'll swap. I'll take your body—though, really girl, I wish there was some way I could have connected with another man. I guess I have to take any old port in a storm."

That infuriated her more than anything he'd said or done so far, that he'd disparage her sex while using her.

"I'll take your body and you can have mine." He laughed bitterly. "You said it yourself, the most important part's still here. That's all you women want anyway, some man's balls."

Val's face was frozen. She knew it was over. She couldn't stop him from taking over her body. She'd just been fooling herself. But she could stop him from using it.

To the left was the edge of a deep canyon. She gripped the steering wheel and aimed for that edge. Just then, coming from the other direction, a gardening truck appeared on the narrow two-lane road. It was in her sights just above her hands on the wheel, close enough now for her to see the startled truck driver—leathery benign face in shock—scramble out.

"Come on, Val—a trade," Misha said inside her head.

He should have been aware of the change in her voice, the compliance that had never been there before, but he wasn't as he heard her answer: "Okay, Misha. You've got a deal."

She closed her eyes because she didn't want to watch the truck and her car collide. Everything was dark, noisy. If Misha were truly in her body, they would both be killed together. The natural order that had been ruptured by their unholy union would be restored. To insure that they were connected, Val reached with her final conscious thought for Misha's body. "If there is a God, forgive me."

She was ready to die like that. She had found a rationale for suicide.

Her eyes blinked open, but Valentine was not behind them. It was Michael who looked out through her unblinking hazel eyes, and he knew in that last instant she had planned this, planned to kill him.

Tanna saw Michael let go of the headboard as though it were suddenly red hot. His back was arched in climax as she looked up in wonder at what she assumed was his response to her wonderful mouth, her practiced "yielding resistance."

She was sitting on the bed beside him, touching his face with her trembling hand. Tears were running down his cheeks. He was making a sound that could be

298

cries or laughter. His eyes opened slowly, almost cautiously.

"My God," he stammered. "It worked." Inside Val could detect no trace of Michael's personality. She was certain now that he had died in her body. He must have, else she would have felt his presence.

Tanna watched as delicious laughter possessed the man.

"Doesn't it always?" she asked, mildly perturbed. To her Michael appeared uncharacteristically hesitant as he looked up at her.

He reached out with exquisite gentleness and touched the flesh beneath her eye.

"Tanna . . ." he said, "you're Tanna."

"What's wrong with you?" she demanded. Instinctively she sensed an altered personality, and her fears that he had slipped into schizophrenia returned like a chill to the room around her. But oh, how she loved this new personality in him; such gentleness along with masculine strength was a rare combination in her world.

She thought he might be going to have another seizure or whatever it was he had had earlier. His eyes looked so strange, all round and white.

"To give like that," he was muttering, "not asking anything for yourself in return." He hugged her; over his shoulder she looked as surprised as if he'd bit her. "How can I thank you?"

She smoothed the dark hair on the curve of his neck. Soon she could feel their heartbeats matching. She could have stayed in his arms like that for the rest of her life. In fact, if she had died at that moment, it would have been all right.

But he presently broke away from her. The light in his green eyes startled her again.

"How can I ever explain what's happened?" he asked hoarsely.

Tanna started to protest that no explanation was necessary, but he went on talking in his softened new voice. "I guess it doesn't matter that I can never explain it to anyone, not even you. All that matters is that I'm alive." Hesitantly he looked down at the ends of his legs just barely covered by the sheet. The inside of his thighs were slick with drying love juices; chillbumps rose on his skin as he pulled the sheet up higher.

"If I can just get used to . . ." He looked up at Tanna, stricken with what she would've sworn was a new acceptance of his injuries.

"Ain't nothin' wrong with you," she murmured.

He pulled back from her as his hand slid down her neck-to-hem zipper. She started to protest.

"Why not?" he asked, his voice cracking. "Why can't I love you the way you loved me?"

She shook her head. Oh, God, she thought, he mustn't see me down there. She knew he would be likely to project his self-revulsion on to her.

"No," she begged, though she desperately wanted him.

His hand stopped. Now, that she would have never expected from him. It was as if he had just slipped into another personality, she thought with an ache. They'll take him away from me for sure. . . .

"Let me love you."

She shook her head again, beginning to cry. His gentleness confused her.

He kissed the tears on her cheeks. "Why not?"

"Because I'm a virgin," she whimpered a reason, any inane reason.

So am I, honey, Val thought silently but didn't speak. She had already decided, somewhere in the dark last few moments, that she was never again going to refer to her other life. She had a new life now.

Tanna was aware of his hand pulling her down to the bed. The tip of his cock entered the thicket of her pubic hair, then she felt him enter her without hesitation; apparently he didn't even realize how smooth and unencumbered his lover was. There was new tenderness in his green eyes as he watched her with a wonderment that was unnatural for this man. Tanna didn't stop to think about the consequences of his change.

Val in Michael's body had no preconception of how this was supposed to feel. There was no room for analysis because it felt so good, this inside out sexuality that was both so different and so much the same as what Valentine experienced in her woman-body.

It confirmed what she'd always suspected but until now could have no proof of: that men and women had many more similarities than differences, and those differences were mainly in emphasis, not in quality.

Oh, she thought as it mounted, there's definitely a build-up here I haven't experienced with such intensity. She supposed women made up for that by having multiple orgasms. But the pleasure was the same. The capacity was in the mind, not the body, as was the capacity for anything in life. The joy was in the celebrant, not the celebration. What better way to celebrate being alive than this?

For a few moments only these two loving bodies existed, and Val was able to shut out all thought of what might have happened to her old car and its new driver.

CHAPTER 29

Maxine's car pulled up with a screech. She flung herself out and ran to the truck driver, an old Oriental man. Stumbling, she glanced back over her shoulder to see the inferno that had been a gray Citroen.

The I BRAKE FOR ANIMALS bumper sticker was written in flame.

"That's her car," Maxine cried.

"I couldn't stop," the old man said, shaking. "She come at me outta nowhere."

"My God, oh, my God, oh, my God."

Maxine took a step or two toward the burning Citroen, but the heat was terrible. Far away she could hear a siren. A flash of red moved on the road below, beyond the greasy black smoke thrown up by the fire.

The fire truck pulled up, but the firemen shook their heads as they unloaded their equipment. They knew now all they could do was put it out. Anybody in that car was dead already.

Maxine stood watching as the flames were smothered, thinking about how the girl's obsession that she was a telepath had finally killed her. Fleetingly Maxine thought, What if it were true?

"No way to know, no way to ever know," Maxine said to herself as she turned away. She didn't want to see them take the body out. She walked back to her car and climbed, sobbing, inside. "Unless . . ." she thought out loud, finding the notebook where she'd written the name of the convalescent hospital Frank mentioned. When she put the notebook back into her purse the broken heart-shaped frame of her little daughter's face fell out. She stared at it a moment before putting the sad thing away, then started her car. She drove quickly down the road without looking at the smoldering wreck behind her.

Tanna was warmed to glowing over the most loving response she'd ever gotten from Michael. He really seemed to care, she thought as she lay in his arms, eyes closed, full for the first time in her life with loving.

He appeared asleep beside her, exhausted from lovemaking. But after a time she heard a low sound from him that was an unmistakable "Om."

"I didn't know you were into yoga," Tanna said.

"Hmmm?" he asked dreamily. He opened his eyes.

"That sound. Ommmmmmm."

"Mmmmmmmmmm," he hummed, matching her pitch. When his breath was gone he enfolded her in his arms, holding on for dear life, rocking gently with her.

"Learned it from a friend," he said.

302

Tanna stroked his chest. "Your body's almost well."

"Thanks to you . . ."

"Are you happy with Mi—me?" he finally asked, his voice loaded with hesitancy she'd never seen in him before.

"Yes," Tanna lied, then added, "and, no."

He coaxed up her chin and asked, Why? with his eyes.

"I wish you loved me as much as I love you."

Michael shook his head with great sadness. "He was just using you."

"Honey, you're talking funny."

"Bastard—"

She started to protest, but something in his tone of voice stopped her.

"Using you like he used everyone." His voice faded, then he appeared struck with a new thought. "Tanna?"

She looked at him expectantly.

"Will you stay with me? No matter what? Even if I seem . . . *different?*" He said the word with an odd intonation.

Tanna was bawling. She nodded, hugging him.

"I've got to get my life started again," he said with new energy. He reached for the wheelchair. "Got to get out of this bed."

Tanna sprang to her feet and found her uniform where he had tossed it. "Hold on a minute," she said, slipping into the white nylon dress and zipping it closed.

He was getting into the chair. He seemed to be using his body with a new grace, finding his adjusted center of gravity.

"You can't now—you have to be sedated."

He backhanded the medicine cup on the bedside table.

"No more dope."

"You just settle down now—I'll get Dr. Raymond," she said as she got into her shoes. "I'll be right back," she added as she walked to the door, forcing her heels into the nurse's shoes as she took a step or two. "You stay put, you hear?"

"Yes, ma'am."

Tanna saw him roll to the closet and begin looking through the selection of shirts, rejecting a red and gold disco number in favor of an old blue kaftan. He slipped it over his head as Tanna left the room.

The arms were so strong, Val marveled as one hand touched the biceps of the other. I could get used to this, she thought, then laughed inside. I'd better get used to this. A little at a time, she told herself, purposefully not looking at the legs.

The hands rolled the chair back toward the bed, passing by the mirror on the way.

Val looked through his eyes at the reflection in the mirror. A tentative finger lifted to the masculine cheekbone. "Not a bad face." The hands ran through the bushy beard. "Beards itch on the inside as well as the outside."

The face smiled at its reflection. She felt the hands on the wheels rolling to the telephone, chinned the receiver and gave a number off Lazlo's script to the operator. There were moments of silence no thought could fill. On the bedside table were roses. Val knew who had sent these roses. Petals dropped. The note card in the foliage read *Get well soon. Love, your secret valentine.*

An officious voice on the other end of the line said that this was Lazlo Stefano's office. This must be the infamous Ms. Peach.

"Mr. Stefano, please."

The officious voice wanted to know who was calling. Of course, Michael's uncle would've given him his private office number.

"It's me, Peachie. Michael."

The voice said he sounded different.

"Well, I guess so."

There was a moment or two of soundtrack from a Stefano sit-com and then a gruff voice instantly recognizable as Michael's uncle. "This really you?"

304

"It's me, yeah. You said I was to call when I was feeling better. Yeah, yeah—much better," Lazlo heard his nephew say, but there was something different with the voice. Lazlo couldn't place it; he figured it was just a bad connection.

Uncle Lazlo said something about how it was all a lousy shame, and Val in Michael looked down, having avoided that view in the past few minutes. Never to dance again. Tears welled. Val had been through this before with Misha and that helped some. But still there would be no more dancing. A flash vision of the old Valentine doing tai chi exercises came to Val's consciousness. Tinny Oriental music accompanied the two Vals—herself and her reflection in the floor-length mirror.

"Good-bye Val . . ." The vision was gone.

"Michael?" the uncle's telephone voice questioned.

"I said that you're right, Uncle Lazlo—it is a lousy stinking shame—thank you, yes. You've taken good care of me." The Band-Aid was coming loose on the slashed wrist. "I'm sorry for the embarrassment I caused you over that."

The Band-Aid came off to reveal the healing suicide scar. "I know our business is sensitive to suicide."

The uncle lectured mildly. A hand toyed with a lock of Michael's dark hair that was not quite long enough to reach the lips. It was a completely unconscious gesture that was totally Val.

"Well, I can swear that I'll never try it again—Yeah, I have it on right now—" The hand reached for the fine watch in its gift box, and slipped it on over the wrist scar.

"Yes, the stopwatch will come in handy if I direct."

Val was feeling more confidant in this body now. It felt more like home. No more dancing, but there were compensations.

"What do you mean, *if* you direct, my boy?" the old man was saying and it came to Val that he was speaking to her. It was suddenly so poignantly funny that

305

now she was finally going to get a chance to direct. What had Brenda said? Grow balls . . .

"Man to man, Michael—what brought you around?"

For a long time there was no response, so that Lazlo thought maybe the phone had cut out, but finally he heard his nephew answer. "When I woke up—"

There was a sound at the half-closed door. Tanna and Dr. Raymond were entering, both smiling.

Tanna's smile was that of the happily laid as she approached Michael. She touched his shoulder as Dr. Raymond joined her beside Michael near the window. There was an expectant, professional grin on the doctor's face that spoke eloquently of his emotions: His problem patient was going to cause fewer problems now.

"When I woke up it was such a beautiful morning—"

Tanna couldn't miss the reference to their lovemaking.

"It started out kinda gray," Lazlo was saying, "but it's getting better all the time." Val took an immediate liking to this man she knew Michael had detested, and wanted to comfort him.

"What happened to me was a shame—"

There was a noise behind Raymond. It was Maxine throwing open the door to Michael's room.

"—but," Michael continued, "it's a hell of a lot better than being dead—" Lazlo laughed agreement and hung up.

Maxine took a step toward the young man in the wheelchair.

"Right, Maxi?" the young man said pointedly at her.

Maxine stopped in her tracks.

Only Val called her Maxi, yet here was this famous stranger calling her Maxi, too, an enigmatic smile on his lips, playing with that lock of hair just the way Val used to play with her hair.

The shock of recognition drew Maxine's mouth open.

*   *   *

There was distinct pleasure in watching Maxine grapple with the fact that she was observing Val in Michael's body.

Never again will you look on life so smugly, Val thought, righteous as the agent of someone else's enlightenment. Val could feel the warmth of Tanna's hand on a shoulder and a general pleasant snugness throughout this body. It had a thrilling vitality to it despite convalescence. Even its scars were pink and healthy. It seemed ready to go, like the Citroen had felt to Val after she had been driving something less powerful. But it would take getting used to. Particularly the face.

The super-sensitive parts—tongue, fingertips and the swift sure match of clit and cock were mere variations on the human theme, maps by different sailors of the same island. But the face held too much personality to give up quickly. Especially the lips. The smile was crooked. This mouth was wider than Val's. In fact, the single impression of difference was that there was one third more room in Michael's body.

"This is my body now," she silently corrected herself.

It was unmistakably Michael's voice that answered, "Oh, no it's not," and Val realized she was trapped in here with him from now on.

Epilogue

Bunch came in agitated while Phyllis was cleaning the last of that crazy guy's stuff out of Room 20. They had moved him out kinda fast, to a special clinic, she heard Dr. Raymond say. The quick move left some odds and ends behind: a telephone file, a notebook and oddly, a pair of shoes. Phyllis thought that was funny but she didn't laugh.

"Where are they?" Bunch demanded vaguely, not necessarily to the maid. She looked up from the cardboard box she'd found to put the patient's things in.

"Where's what?" She set the box on the bare mattress.

"The glasses—ah—" he said in a pleased way when he saw the binoculars hanging on the inside doorknob. Phyllis probably would have missed them.

"You can't take those."

Bunch held the binoculars close to his huge T-shirted chest. "Why not?"

"Come on. They'll think I took 'em. You know that Peach woman's coming to get this junk this afternoon." Phyllis saw Michael's guitar standing against the wall. She put it on the bed beside the box.

Bunch regarded the glasses. They were beautiful, streamlined with metal fittings. The initials M.C.S. were engraved on a silver plate affixed to the mount.

"She'll never know," he replied, looking up at her. "How will she know he had these here?"

His look pleaded with Phyllis, who simpered a little in her awareness of her power in this briefly defined moment.

"Those old guys have been moping around ever since he dropped their glasses. I tried to reach 'em, but I could get myself killed."

Phyllis chewed the inside of her mouth.

"He lost theirs," Bunch concluded. "It's only fair."

Phyllis cocked her head and looked at the cardboard box.

"I guess he won't care, huh?" she asked.

Bunch was gruffly relieved. He carefully wound the leather strap around the twin cylinders of the glasses. These things usually came with a case, so he looked around to see if he could find it.

"You hear that guy when they took him away?" Phyllis asked, cranked with scuttlebutt.

Bunch didn't want to stand here talking with this

dotty old woman, but he also didn't want to offend her so that she'd go blabbing that he'd taken the glasses.

"You hear all kinds of strange things in this work."

"Never heard nothing like that before," she said in a close, confidential way. Bunch could smell the peanut butter sandwich she'd had for lunch, and for some reason that made him sad and he wanted to get away from her, get the glasses up to old man Goldman. He'd asked about them again, not wanting to push, but really desiring those binoculars.

"Screaming in two voices, mind you, one high voice and the other deeper voice, arguing with himself. It was enough to give you the creeps."

Bunch had heard. The memory pulled goosebumps up on his thick arms.

Phyllis glanced at the glasses in his hand.

"For the old guys," Bunch said sweetly, giving up on the case.

Bunch was okay, she decided. She smiled a snaggled grin and waved him out.

She looked around as she snapped off the light to see if she'd missed anything. She saw some library books on a shelf in the bedside table and gave them a quick flip-through in the light from the hallway.

Something about that psychic stuff. She tossed them into the cardboard box.

Those books didn't have any pictures.

A NOVEL OF SENSUAL HORROR BY

R. R. WALTERS

LUDLOW'S MILL

**In a small Florida town by the
deserted ruins of an ancient mill, the evil
spirit of the Lamia lies in wait.
It is here, under the cool shade of the
towering pines, that Karen
Sommers often comes for quiet picnics...
until that gruesome day when she
encounters an unspeakable horror that would
shatter her life—and the lives of those
she loves—forever.**

☐ 48-006-7   LUDLOW'S MILL $2.75